Visit Carolyn Miller at www.carolynmillerauthor.com

Cover design by KT Design

Edited by Katie Donovan

Bible references are from the New International Version.

PRAISE FOR CAROLYN MILLER

"Carolyn Miller keeps on turning out these beautifully written, tender hearted books!... There was humor and brilliant bantering conversations, heart stopping romance, as well as exciting descriptions (and sometimes dangerous passages of play) of hockey games. Well worth the late night/early morning read!" ~ *KAYE'S REVIEWS & NEWS*

"A sweet love story that continues the Original Six Hockey series by Carolyn Miller. The setting of Montreal with the Gardens and all the French woven throughout was delightful!" ~ *GOODREADS review*

"I am emerging out of my book hangover after reading *Checked Impressions* by Carolyn Miller....The romance, humor and themes of identity are so enjoyable and make for a great read!" ~ *BECKY'S BOOKSHELVES*

"A fun sports-themed contemporary romance, this makes for a great, quick read...perfect for those days that you want a story about trust and love and navigating the ups and downs of being with that special someone." ~ *GOODREADS review*

"Adrenaline, chemistry, romance, and lots of wooing!...You do not have to be a fan of sports or even knowledgeable in hockey and short track to appreciate *Love on Ice*." ~ *GOODREADS review*

"Carolyn Miller scores another win with *Love on Ice*, the second book in her Original Six Hockey series. I absolutely loved the faith thread in this story. It's message that success does not lie on what we do, but who we are is powerful." ~ *GOODREADS review*

"*The Breakup Project* is a fun, charming, and faith-filled contemporary romance with adorable characters set in the competitive North American ice hockey world. Highly recommended." ~ *NARELLE ATKINS, Author of Solo Tu & Her Tycoon Hero*

"Displaying a flair for comedy and witty dialog, Miller is clearly an author to watch...with clever, snappy repartee, creating an exciting and fast-paced read." ~ *LIBRARY JOURNAL*

HEARTS AND GOALS

CAROLYN MILLER

ALSO BY CAROLYN MILLER

The Original Six hockey series
The Breakup Project
Love on Ice
Checked Impressions
Hearts and Goals
Big Apple Atonement
Muskoka Blue

The Independence Islands series
Restoring Fairhaven
Regaining Mercy
Reclaiming Hope
Rebuilding Hearts
Refining Josie

Regency Brides and the Regency Wallflowers series

CHAPTER 1

Montreal, Canada
August

Oh, what were men to rocks and mountains—or at least to beautiful gardens? Magdalena Joly's heart was full as she surveyed the gardens of le Jardin botanique de Montréal, stretched beneath her. Was it possible to love a garden too much? To be too thankful for a job that permitted moments such as this? Surely no man could fill her heart with a fraction of the contentment she found here—except for the one she'd left at home.

She moved carefully on her perch high in the old oak tree, leaning back against the strong trunk, carefully lifting the camera to capture the scene below. Summer sunshine lit the Japanese Garden's manicured topiary and trees, creating few shadows and making it the perfect time to capture such beauty. She snapped one picture, then another, before taking a moment to check the shots. Serenity stared back at her, the flashes of gold and orange from the koi in the pond providing contrast to the pinks of the shrub peonies. Everything else, from the pines and maples to the foliage of rhododendron, offered dozens of shades of green.

Damp hair clung to her neck, and she blew out a breath in a vain attempt for coolness. She had been fortunate this morning to avoid too many visitors straying into view. Perhaps today's heat had kept them away. After a careful readjustment from her precarious position, she lifted the camera and focused in on the stone lantern arching across the water. There. A smile filled her heart. Was it truly possible to have a better job? What else managed to incorporate a love of photography as well as a love of horticulture? Maman often said she was blessed indeed.

A crunch of gravel drew her gaze to the path. Two men, one shorter with dark hair, the other very tall with a tawny man bun, walked along the winding path that led to the teahouse. She hoped they didn't think to look up and spot her here. It was enough that some of her colleagues thought her commitment to the job bordered on extreme, but she had no way of communicating exactly why she did this. How exactly did one explain the rebellious wish to step out of the ordinary and safe that confined every other part of her world? Neither had she any wish to concern the public or worry those who might think occupational health and safety should take precedence over capturing the perfect pictures to entice the public to visit. Like this morning's shots taken from her post high up here.

The men paused, the taller one gesturing to a little vantage point where a stone seat was positioned to best capture the view. She'd caught many couples taking advantage of this most romantic scene—even a proposal or two, which elicited feelings both of tenderness and regret.

"It sure is beautiful," the tall man drawled, his voice holding a Southerner's twang.

The other man murmured something she didn't hear, but

she saw his nod and wondered where they were from. Locals? The accent suggested *non*. Perhaps tourists, friends or work colleagues, then.

The men took several photos, then the shorter one pointed to the cultural pavilion, a building with the Peace Bell prominently displayed out front. It was funny how so many tourists just clicked a picture but didn't linger as these gardens had been designed for people to do. Oh well. If they moved on, then there was less chance of her being seen.

The big guy shrugged, then sat down, his legs stretching out as he clasped the back edge of the stone seat. From this position she could see how the T-shirt he wore strained across the breadth of his shoulders, the muscles in his arms and legs not unlike Alain's. She swallowed, pushing emotion down, and dragged her gaze away. She had a job to do.

"Come on," the shorter man called, stealing her focus again, his impatience evident in his shuffling feet and frequent glances at his watch.

The taller man murmured something she couldn't hear, but he obeyed, albeit reluctantly it seemed, as he rose and snapped another photo with his phone. She did not blame him. The Jardin japonais was widely considered to be one of the finest in the world. Her lips lifted as she recognized a fellow appreciator of beauty, and she waited, curving her body along the stretch of solid branch to maintain her discreet location as the men walked away.

It was funny how so few people looked up to see what might exist above them. But then, she had always been the type of person distracted by the shapes of trees, who loved the winter sculptural forms that held poetic beauty in their branches. Trees had another advantage, too. When they died, they often became a thing of beauty rather than leaving a hole in one's heart that could never be filled.

Maggie swallowed, blew out a steadying breath, and grasped

the nearest branch. Now was not the time to think on such things. Now was the time to take the shot and descend before the next visitors came and spoiled the view. She inched higher, stabilizing against the smooth bark of another strong branch, and lifted the camera, this time zooming in on the waterfall that provided soothing background music to this part of the garden. Like the garden below, the water cascading over rocks had been designed to evoke feelings of tranquility and to inspire meditation and, like the nearby stand of pines, helped to shut out the noise and bustle of Canada's second largest city. Another reason she loved to work in this oasis of calm.

It was not surprising that so many people enjoyed coming here, even if it was simply locals wishing to sit under the trees. How many others had found this place had brought healing to their soul? To know she had the privilege of working here, that she was part of the huge team that could use nature to minister to weary hearts, was something she did not take for granted.

The men had disappeared—probably wondering about the meaning behind the placement of rocks in the Stone Garden or marveling at the bonsai trees—and she carefully took the last series of photos before turning off the camera and slipping it into the pocket of her khaki work shorts, then buttoning the pocket carefully. She'd learned the hard way the consequences of not doing so.

A careful grasp of the slender branches, then she slid one booted foot to the deep fork where the branches veered away. High above, a chattering sound drew her attention to a squirrel, who seemed most indignant that she'd dared trespass upon his territory. "I promise I'm leaving," she assured the little creature. The squirrel scampered away, as if it didn't believe her. Ah well.

Another cautious movement and she was ready to descend. A quick glance side to side showed no visitors or—worse— fellow employees within sight, so she grasped the branch and swung her feet down.

But now the ground seemed too far away, the descent much farther than it had seemed when she'd climbed it in a burst of defiant tomboy exuberance not so long ago. A dilemma. What to do? Her arms were getting sore. She could jump, but such an action held an element of risk she was reluctant to invite these days. Oh, she should have thought this through. The garden's "no climbing trees" safety measures had probably been written with this in mind. Too late now.

Gritting her teeth, she calculated the distance. A couple of meters could scarcely cause injury, could it? Nevertheless, what choice did she have? How else was she going to get out of the tree?

"Miss?"

She squeaked and let go, the ground rushing to meet her as she yelped.

Bang.

"Ah!" Shock rippled through her body, followed by a wave of pain. Vaguely aware of the sound of pounding feet, she bit back words her mother would frown upon as she clutched her knee, startling again as someone grasped her upper arms. The hands instantly released.

"Miss? You okay?"

Did she look like she was okay? She winced, ignoring the voice as she checked her pocket with its expensive secret. Trembling fingers undid the button, and she drew out the camera, relief pulsing through her as it appeared unharmed. Until she turned it over and saw the viewing screen had smashed. Non. Oh non.

"Are you hurt?" the voice said again.

She finally glanced up, meeting startling green eyes and concern in the strong-featured face. Monsieur Man Bun from before. Her breath hitched. If his hair was out, with that scruff on his face she'd bet he would look like a modern-day Viking.

"Here, let me help."

He bent, arms reaching down, but Maggie shrugged away and pushed to wobbly feet. Then managed an equally wobbly smile. "*Merci*, monsieur. Now if you will please excuse me."

"Is your camera okay?" he asked softly.

The care in his voice buckled her composure, and she sucked in her bottom lip. Non. Today was a cry-free day. She raised her chin, lifting her gaze to almost touch his. At five-foot-ten, she was tall by most women's standards, but this man must be a good eight inches taller. "It will be fine. I will be fine. Merci."

His face lit with a smile. "I love how everyone speaks French here."

She only just managed to refrain from rolling her eyes, her earlier good opinion of his intelligence at appreciating the gardens dropping several points.

"Can you walk okay?"

Okay, so maybe she'd revise her opinion again. It *was* nice to have such a big man fussing over her. It had been so long—

"You really shouldn't be climbing trees."

Maggie looked away to meet the owner of the new and nasal voice—a wide man with graying hair and a disapproving turn to his lip. Looked about the perfect age and temperament for her mother. She shook away the disloyal thought and winced at the gathering crowd. "You're right," she murmured, easing away. "Excuse me."

"Wait—were you spying on us?"

"Pardon?"

"You were hiding, taking pictures," the fussy man said, gesturing to the camera. "Mildred," he called, beckoning an equally large and joyless woman forward. "This woman was taking pictures of us."

"No, no. I was not taking pictures of you, sir. Now if you'll excuse me—"

"Do you work here?" the woman said, eyeing the logo on her shirt.

Uh oh.

She moved to leave, but her knee buckled, and she would've collapsed on the ground had Monsieur Man Bun not swooped in, wrapping a strong arm around her shoulders. "Gotcha." He grinned.

Her lips lifted in automatic response, and she grew uncomfortably aware of a fluttering in her stomach. Non. *Non.* She was not going to find the man attractive. Even if the tingles evoked by his scent of moss and musk suggested otherwise.

"Beau, have you always gotta be charming the ladies?"

She peered back to see the shorter man from before studying them with his lips pulled to one side.

"I can't help it if women find me charming, Dodge," Beau said.

Dodge? What kind of name was that?

"I expect it has more to do with the accent than anything else. Although my folks did teach me the importance of being a gentleman."

The other man—Dodge—snorted, albeit with a reluctant grin.

"Tell me, do you think I'm charming, ma'am?"

It took her a moment to realize he addressed her. "Ma'am?" she asked.

His lips hitched higher as his friend laughed. "I guess that's a no, then."

"You can let me go," she murmured.

"I don't think I can," Beau Man Bun said, even as his actions proved the contrary. But as she staggered, he clutched her arm again, balancing her upright. "See?"

Hmm. It would seem there was no easy way out of this.

"I'm real sorry I startled you before," he continued.

Maggie blinked. He was apologizing for her stupidity in exiting the tree? "That was my fault."

"What were you doing up the tree anyhow?" he asked.

How to explain, how to explain…

"Miss!"

She exhaled as the voice from before drew her to peer over her shoulder. The gray-haired man now wore a scowl. "What's your name? I'll be reporting you to the authorities."

Maggie knew an insanely hysterical desire to laugh. As far as many employees here were concerned, she *was* the authorities.

"Now, sir, I really don't think things need come to that," Beau said, friendliness in his voice and face. "Not when the little lady is injured and all."

Little lady?

"Come on," Beau continued. "You wouldn't want to be making her day any worse now, would you?"

Challenged like that, the older man hmphed. "But she was spying on people," he complained.

"*Were* you spying on people?" Beau asked her, humor glinting in his eyes.

"But of course," she shocked herself by saying. What was it about today that dared her to act like the teenager she hadn't been for ten years? Climbing trees, engaging in tease… Was it simply a result of the heat of the day, or was it something about the appeal of the man that had melted sense from her brain?

His green eyes rounded. "You were?"

She nodded. "It's our new way to evaluate visitor engagement with the gardens. Some might use surveillance cameras, but we prefer old-school methods."

"Like climbing trees to watch people," he said, chuckling.

The sound tugged at her, reminding her how long it had been since she'd made an attractive man laugh, which further reminded her of the need to put up her walls. Non. She could not fall again.

"What is your name, Miss?" Mr. Grumpy called.

Oh dear. She'd forgotten he was still there.

"Sir, I really think it's inappropriate for you to be asking about an attractive young lady. And to do so in front of your wife just ain't right." Beau tsk-tsked.

Maggie stifled another wild impulse to laugh as the man huffed away, trailed by his wife, who wanted to know what had been said.

"I'm guessing he won't be telling her the truth anytime soon," Beau said with a grin.

Non.

"Dude, we gotta go," Beau's friend said.

"But not before we see this lady safely to first aid." Beau turned to her. "Do you want me to carry you?"

She choked. "Er, I should be okay."

"You sure?" He grinned. "I don't mind showing Dodge a thing or two about how a gentleman ought to treat a lady."

She eyed his muscles. He looked strong enough to carry her. But fortunately, before her stupid emotions weakened her resolve, she spied one of the park's small golf carts being driven in the direction of the Chinese Garden. She pointed to it. "If you could please get Frederic's attention, that would serve well."

Beau glanced across, nodded, and told his friend to wave the employee down. The other man sighed, then jogged over, waving attention, then pointing to where Maggie stood, Beau's arm still wrapped around her. She winced. Eased away.

Beau glanced down at her, and again she was struck by the eloquence of his eyes. Right now she thought she read surprise and confusion, then fresh amusement, something that wrinkled her soul with the strangest sense of disappointment. "Well, it looks like your chariot'll soon be here," he drawled. "I hope you feel better soon," he added kindly.

"Merci," she managed, drawing further away.

"It was nice to almost meet you," he said, eyes twinkling again. "I'm Beau."

"I know."

"You do, huh?" he said, as if forgetting his friend had called him that already. "And you are?"

He might've proved sympathetic, but she didn't need her name getting her into any more trouble. And she definitely didn't need to be feeling any of these feelings being near him had stirred within. How desperate *was* she to be attracted to a stranger? She shook her head.

"You'd prefer to remain a woman of mystery."

"Oui," she said firmly.

Relief filled her as Frederic slowed and stopped. Maybe she could get away with nobody being the wiser—

"Maggie? Are you injured?" Frederic asked.

"Maggie, huh?" Beau said, smirking.

Ignoring him, she hobbled to the golf cart, murmuring thanks to the man called Dodge, who nodded before reassuring Frederic she was fine and only needed to rest.

"Yeah, and maybe get some ice for her knee," Beau called.

She glanced at him once more. "Merci."

"Stay safe, Maggie." His lips curled as his grin pushed to one side.

"You know him?" Frederic asked her in French as he drove her to the employees' section of the main building.

"Non," she said, refusing to give in to the temptation to turn around. Non. *Non.* She needed to tether these recalcitrant feelings, tamp down these emotions and focus on what was real. Like the threat of the chubby gray-haired man. Like the crack in her camera. Like the fact her injured knee meant she'd likely need some time off work.

"He seemed to know you."

She shrugged, bracing herself on the metal frame as the cart bumped over rocky ground. What would she do if she couldn't work? What would that mean for poor Noah?

"He looks familiar." Frederic's brow creased. "What is his name?"

"Beau," she admitted.

"Beau?"

At his gasp, she turned her head. "What?"

He swore in French. "I cannot believe it."

"Believe what?"

He grinned. "I think you just met Montreal's new goalie."

INTRIGUING THOUGHTS of dark eyes and hair and sweet sass were interrupted by Beau's new teammate's snort. "What?"

"Honestly." Jake Dodgewell—one of the NHL's most aptly named players—rolled his eyes as they continued the slow trek back to the main gate. "Could you have been any more obvious?"

"What do you mean?"

"Look, I know we're both new, but is that how you play all the time?"

"Huh?"

"You. You're a flirt, man."

"Moi?" Beau asked. "I think you're mistaking me for someone else."

"I think you're gonna have to work on your French, dude."

"Not the only one," Beau said with a grin. "Good thing they're setting us up with language classes, huh?"

Jake snorted again.

Beau would take that as a no, then.

He, for one, was glad for the chance to learn the main language spoken in Quebec. It was part of the fun of moving to a new team, part of the appeal of transferring from the desert to one of the NHL's Original Six teams. *The* Original Six team. The one with the most championships. The place where it felt like a dream to walk its hallowed halls. *Les Habitants.* This cosmopolitan city tucked beside the St. Lawrence River, a bastion of European tradition, had long held his heart for many reasons. Diving into the culture was just part of that. But Dodge's comment about flirting…

"I was being friendly, not flirting," Beau said firmly, as much to himself as to Dodge. So Maggie was pretty, with those sparkling brown eyes and dark hair. And okay, he'd liked her scent in that all-too-brief encounter when he'd helped her stand. But how could he even think of more when he didn't know where she stood with God?

"Is that what you call it?"

"Listen, I can't help it if you Wisconsin boys don't know the difference."

"Michigan."

"Same difference."

That earned him another snort. "I don't even know why Southerners play hockey."

"Ouch! Tell that to Tampa Bay."

Jake laughed, and conversation turned to teammates they knew who played in some of the warmer climates of the league and the challenges players faced when moving across the continent. But joining Montreal's team, Beau's third club in four years, was living his dream, and his introduction to the organization and city had proved relatively smooth. Of course, it helped to be negotiating this on his own, to not be assisting a wife and family with the ins and outs of language and cultural expectations. Not that learning French was a prerequisite—their head coach spoke English—but Beau wanted to immerse himself in the culture as much as he could, and not simply by eating poutine, smoke meat, and baguettes.

Later that night, he reiterated this on the call to the Bible study guys. The online group started by Jai Mullins and Josiah Abrahams had grown in recent years, with players from the Original Six teams—Mike Vaughan, Brent Karlsson, Jai, Beau, Tim Carruthers, and Dan Walton—now joined by others, like

Chris Thomas from Vancouver, Ryan Guillemette from Edmonton, and Luc Marchand who played for Winnipeg. Given the number of players based several time zones away, maybe one day they'd need a northwestern division of this Bible study group.

"So, are you settling in?" Jai asked. Jai had surprised them all a couple of months ago by announcing his engagement, then shocked them further by saying his upcoming season with newly crowned champions Chicago would be his last before he followed Allie to San Jose. The latest of the guys to find a girl and settle down. "Meeting some new people?"

A face flashed through Beau's mind. He suppressed it. "My new teammates seem cool. The ones I've met, anyway." He'd meet the rest in a few weeks when training camp began. "The apartment is nice."

"I bet," Ryan laughed. "What is it, the penthouse?"

"The sub-penthouse," he clarified.

"Oh, right. My mistake. The *sub*-penthouse. I bet that's really different."

"Yeah. A little smaller, one less bedroom."

"What? Only five?" Tim asked, mouth curled up on one side.

"Four," he corrected meekly. Could he help it if goalies were amongst the highest paid in the league?

"You're so humble with the flex," Jai teased, which earned Beau's good-natured shrug.

"Living in Montreal would be like living here in Toronto," Dan said. "You need privacy and good security, even if it looks ostentatious."

"You calling me conceited?" Beau bantered.

"I'm saying you're wise to be careful. Let's just say you don't want your address getting out to the crazy fans."

Beau nodded. He'd appreciated going under the radar—well, as much as his height allowed. But so far it seemed few people had recognized him, even though he knew his face had been splashed across the media since being traded back in July. He'd wondered if Maggie had recognized him today at the Botanical Gardens, but the fact she'd said little, and then after that little moment of intriguing sassy tease had basically withdrawn, said she didn't care to know him more and had put his vanity firmly in the trash. Dodge was so wrong.

After more catching up, including Mike sharing about his latest trip to the charity he fronted in the Philippines, Josiah joined them and the study began.

Tonight's message was from Proverbs chapter eleven, with a focus on the verses about generosity. "I think the Message version puts it best," Josiah said. "'The world of the generous gets larger and larger; the world of the stingy gets smaller and smaller.' And the next verse continues this theme. 'The one who blesses others is abundantly blessed; those who help others are helped. Curses on those who drive a hard bargain! Blessings on those who play fair and square!'" Josiah smiled. "Now, I know I'm preaching to the choir here, but I wonder how many of us can still take something away from these verses?"

"It's talking about giving," Luc said. "Not being a tightwad."

"And if you give, you get back, a bit like investing," Ryan said.

"But it doesn't have to just mean money though, does it?" Dan mused. "Things like generosity of spirit, forgiveness, or kindness are all things we can work on."

"Or trusting God," Brent added.

"Absolutely," Josiah said. "And as we give in these ways, our hearts expand, and when our hearts are bigger, we have more room to care for others and in turn be cared for."

Beau thought about his life and what areas God might be wanting him to trust Him in. *God?*

"I think it's fair to say we've all seen instances like this, where people try to protect themselves from further hurt. But so often it leads to isolating, to cutting off those very connections that can help promote healing."

"Like what bullies do, putting the walls up and attacking first," Tim said thoughtfully.

"Exactly." Josiah sighed. "I've seen this so many times in ministry, and I'm sure you've seen this with people you know too."

Beau nodded. "My mom has always been outgoing, but it took her some time after my dad died to bounce back and engage with others again. She was in shock for a while."

"Did she bounce back?" Jai asked. "Or was it a longer term thing? I don't know if my mom has ever really recovered from my dad leaving. But then, she's still on the God journey."

"That she is." Josiah nodded. "And getting closer to salvation every day."

"Amen," Jai said.

"I was only young when it happened," Beau said, "but I remember a few bleak years."

"Which is only natural," Dan said quietly.

"She did have Jesus, but it still knocked her around." Beau thought back. "I think it helped to have family and a great church community supporting her. And to know she had my sister and me to focus on."

Olivia. His thoughts shifted to his sister, who had struggled with her own loss. Sorrow panged. His father's death he'd come to terms with, but the loss of little Joey was something he'd really like God to explain. One day. He could only marvel at his sister's composure in the face of great grief. But perhaps that was part of what Josiah was talking about and the legacy of his mother's experience and faith. Liv had always been outward focused, others focused, and that longstanding habit meant that grief had not curled in upon itself, her faith such that she knew with certainty she'd see little Joey in heaven one day. He swallowed, emotion throbbing in his chest, and refocused on the conversation.

Ryan was sharing a prayer request for a teammate who'd

injured himself in a painting accident by falling off a ladder, which brought memories of the woman in the tree today. Or more specifically, the woman out of the tree. Beau's lips flicked up.

"It's not funny," Ryan complained, obviously misinterpreting Beau's smile.

"I wasn't smiling at that," Beau protested. "Just, what you said reminded me of something that happened today."

"Spill," Chris said, which drew another smile.

"Okay, fine." He briefly explained about the woman and the tree-falling incident, which drew a round of stares and smirks instead of smiles. "What?"

"What's her name?" Brent asked.

"Maggie."

"Maggie," Chris said. "Uh huh."

"What? Why do you say it like that?"

"We've just never heard you even mention a girl's name," Brent said, arms folded, grinning in a way Beau didn't trust. "And here you are smiling over a girl."

"I'm not smiling," he scoffed, doing his best to tweak his lips down.

"Is she French?" Ryan asked.

"I think she speaks it," Beau said, shrugging.

"Well, yeah, Einstein. If she lives in Quebec she probably does," said Luc Marchand, a Quebecois-born newer member of the group who was still working on his off-the-charts sarcasm levels. He'd proved helpful with some of the expectations and adjustments Beau had needed to make in moving from Arizona to the city of Luc's birth, even if his tone sometimes had Beau digging deep for patience.

"Ooh la la." Chris waggled his heavy eyebrows.

"Dude, you know we French speakers don't actually say it like that, right?" Luc continued.

"Didn't know, don't care," Chris said. "If it impresses the wife, then I'll say it however I like."

"Christopher," Josiah cautioned. This wasn't the first time exchanges between Chris and Luc had become a little heated.

"Fine, fine." Chris held up his hands, and the time continued with other prayer requests that saw them praying for the health of family and friends, wisdom for the growth of the Philippines charity, and Jai praying over his fiancée's job before adding, "And bless Beau with the woman of his dreams."

"Amen," Brent said with a grin.

"Amen," Mike agreed.

"Amen," Ryan said, not bothering to hide his chuckles.

Beau wasn't sure whether to laugh or agree but figured it was only fair their attention had turned to him. He'd not exactly been shy about encouraging—okay, pushing—some of the guys, like Jai, to try new things. Like a relationship.

"Hey, I'm not opposed to the idea," Beau said. "But I don't think you should count on this Maggie woman being the one."

"Nobody said anything about Maggie, man," Dan said with a slight smile.

Oh. "I, um, ignore me."

"Never," Josiah said with a smile of his own.

"Yeah, ignore Beau Nash after all he's done for me?" Jai said. "Couldn't do that to you, man. Wouldn't do that to you."

Awesome. Looked like tonight's Bible study meeting had descended into studying Beau squirm. "Hey, look at the time," Beau said. "I'd better bounce—"

"You did *not* just say that," Luc scoffed. "You're living in the classiest city in North America, Nash. Live up to it, dude."

Said the man calling him *dude*.

"I'm looking forward to seeing what happens with you," Jai said.

"I just bet you are," Beau drawled.

"Trying new things is the spice of life," Jai said. "Or so I've heard."

Beau winced as his words from months ago came back to bite.

"Remember, friend," Josiah said. "The world of the generous gets larger and larger, so just imagine what trusting God might lead you to."

"The man's right," Jai said, his grin as wide as the St. Lawrence River. "Let's see what God has in store for you."

CHAPTER 2

"*M**aman?*"

Noah snuggled close to Maggie, and she wrapped him in her arms. Only another week and he'd begin school—*maternelle*, as the kindergarten program was called—and the last chance to hold onto his babyhood would be lost forever. She could not regret yesterday's incident at the garden if it meant she could capture a precious day of enjoying his company before school changed him forever.

"Is your knee better yet?" His little hand rubbed her knee gently, and her heart melted a little more. How good was her little boy, how soft-hearted. As if in accord, her chest knew a tug as she wished—fiercely—for the thousandth time that Alain could see his son growing up.

"It will be soon," she said, grasping his hand and pressing his palm with a firm kiss. She held his hand firmly and continued kissing up his arm to nuzzle his neck amidst the shrieks of laughing protests before concluding—as she always did—with blowing a loud and squishy raspberry on his cheek.

"You spoil that child," her own mother said, pursing her lips.

Was it any wonder? Maggie kept her protest behind gritted

19

teeth as she obeyed the silent summons to move to the dining room for dinner. "Come, Noah. Help your poor maman to the table."

"Oui, Maman."

With a series of progressive hops—"I'm a bunny!"—that he said were like her movements, Noah bounded to the small table and took his seat between where Maggie and her mother sat. He was the man of the family now, even if only five years old.

Stephanie LeRoux served the meal—chicken and vegetables—taking care not to attend to Maggie's oft-repeated request to not serve her grandson more than one stalk of broccoli. Maggie refused to meet her mother's gaze, instead silencing Noah's wriggled protest with a swift glance. They were fortunate to live here, in a good neighborhood not too far from Maggie's work. And she did appreciate that this fact meant Noah could be cared for while she was working, even if it came at the price of her mother's sighs and not-so-silent admonitions about what Maggie could be doing better. If only mothering came with a manual.

"You will go to work tomorrow?" Maman asked.

Maggie nodded, heart clenching as Noah protested. She smiled at him. "I know, sweet boy. Today has been good, non?" One of the best days in recent times. Enjoying summer, even if it had been limited to the small house and smaller yard. For a few hours at least, she'd felt as free as those perfect little families that visited the Gardens for their parties. She ruffled Noah's hair and returned her attention to her mother. "The doctor thinks I will be fine, especially if I'm mostly in the office."

"I still don't know how you could get injured taking photos."

Maggie forked in her creamed potatoes to avoid a reply. Her explanation—that she had fallen—was technically true, but may have implied that it had occurred from tripping over rather than falling from a tree. Not that she'd ever admit to climbing trees to her mother. She could imagine the objections to such a thing: climbing trees was unladylike, was not what anyone over the age of twelve should do, people could get hurt that way. Maggie's lips pulled down. People could get hurt in many ways.

The rest of the meal was filled with the usual: Maman's complaints and fears about the new neighbors, the way the neighborhood was changing for the worse, that it was so much louder and busier than before. It was futile to suggest they might move. That would require money they did not have, and Maggie knew her mother would be reluctant to go somewhere new. New meant different, new meant strange, and after all the changes in the past five years, Maggie knew her mother's fragile mental health meant certain things were better left unsaid.

But it didn't mean she did not wonder sometimes about what else could be. Maggie could feel how her mother's worrying seeped into her own heart, made her mistrustful of others and fearful of the future. Of course, she couldn't blame her mother for that entirely. Maggie might not yet be thirty, but life had shown her that one could not trust that things would end up well. Those Disney movies had a lot to answer for.

"Maggie?"

She refocused. What had Maman been saying? Something about the weather? "I understand there may be rain tomorrow."

"Anything to break the heat would be good."

"Will it be this hot next week, Maman?"

Maggie smiled at Noah. "The forecast is for sunny weather, although not this hot." One of the consequences of working in gardens for so many years was a constant awareness of the weather, which proved of benefit with her photography too. Sunny conditions, cloudy days—they all had their benefits in taking certain kinds of pictures. It just helped to be prepared. To predict what could happen, as best one could.

Her mind flicked to what she might expect tomorrow. She was rostered to be on the gardens again, which was always more challenging with damp conditions. But given her injured knee, and with the shield of today's medical excuse, she would probably be indoors working on the marketing aspect of her job.

A little knot of tension made her wonder yet again whether anything had been said about yesterday's incident—more specifically, whether any complaint had been made about her. When she returned to the administration building yesterday to learn her little episode had gone unmentioned, relief had filled her like a hot-air balloon. But was the gray-haired man simply biding his time? The other man, Beau, she was not so concerned about, although she now regretted that she had not expressed her thanks more fully, as she could have. She had likely come across as very rude, which had not been her intention. But despite this, she'd sensed that he was a kind man, as evidenced by his humor and the smile lines around his eyes. His seemed to be a genial disposition, not unlike Alain's had been, and it was therefore not so very surprising that she'd felt a hammer of attraction. She blinked.

"Maggie?"

"Forgive me. I'm a little tired."

"But not too tired to read me a story?" Noah pleaded.

"I'm never too tired for that," Maggie said with a smile. "What is it tonight? Do we continue with Babar's elephant adventures?"

"He's my favorite elephant in the whole world!"

"You love your elephants, non?" She ruffled his hair again, wishing desperately that they could afford to take him to parc safari in Hemmingford or Granby zoo to see the elephants there. But between the time commitments to her work, the cost, and her mother's fears about crowds, such a thing seemed impossible.

The evening passed in the rituals of bath-time and bedtime, including the requisite dog-eared story about the little elephant and his adventures, before she tucked Noah in and kissed him goodnight.

Later, as she sat in the window seat of her old bedroom, her mind trailed back two decades to when she remembered her father reading the same book to her. Back when she had felt safe, had thought the world was one glorious rainbow of possibility, before the darkness had stolen such confidence and his life had been stolen away.

She blinked against the sting, drawing the pale pink throw closer around her shoulders. How could it be that her heart still ached for her father? Was it any wonder her mother had not recovered from his death? Here one minute, gone the next, the heart attack so massive they could do nothing, so the first responders had said. That didn't mean much to her mother, however, and to this day their response fueled her deep mistrust of medical assistance, a fact only compounded when Maggie's world had been further turned upside down and her mother added hospitals to her long list of mistrust and avoidance.

Somewhere outside, a car horn beeped angrily, and Maggie pulled back the curtain to see who dared intrude on their quiet street. Her lips flattened as she recognized the house across the road and two doors down as the new neighbors Maman complained about. Raised voices soon drew her to push the window shut, even though it left the room devoid of fresh air. Better to have quiet, even though it was stuffy, the room too full of memories and wasted dreams.

Wasted dreams? She rolled her eyes at herself. She was starting to sound far too much like her mother, forgetting the things she had to be grateful for. Like the little boy sleeping in the next room, who remained healthy still. Like her amazing job, for which she had been so thankful just yesterday. But even though she could recognize these things, even though she was—deep in her heart—truly glad to know her life was blessed in many ways, still there was this tendency within to slip into despondency, to tip into despair. And to then be surrounded by negativity felt like the abrading of her good intentions, the eroding of hope, which only left her feeling exhausted from the fight to stay positive all the time.

She leaned against the glass, staring up at the sky, the stars obscured by the bright lights so close to the ground. The priests talked about how God could see all people, that He cared for everyone, but He felt so far away she sometimes didn't know why she bothered to pray.

"But if You are there, could You please help me?" she whispered.

"Hey, Mom," Beau said, giving his mom a salute as he answered the phone on FaceTime. "You're looking good."

"Thanks, honey. So are you."

He grinned, taking out the band that secured his shoulder-length wavy hair. "I got a haircut today. Can you tell?"

"Which one?" she teased.

He laughed at their old joke and moved from the kitchen to slump into the oversized suede lounges that overlooked the city. The sheer gray curtains that covered his huge floor-to-ceiling windows could not obscure the last pinks of the sunset as it bled into the river far below.

They shared about the past few days, then she asked, "And what plans have you got for the rest of the week?"

"I'm supposed to visit the local hospital for a charity thing with some of the other new guys tomorrow, then the rest of the week is probably training and stuff." *Stuff* including getting in some golf practice so he didn't embarrass himself in the team's Children's Foundation golf tournament happening before training camp in a few weeks. Why people thought hockey players must love golf, he didn't know. He hated it. Which meant he channeled a lot of frustration into some of those big drives along the golf course in a way he rarely managed on the rink.

His mom's face softened, as it did any time they mentioned hospitals. "I hope that goes well."

"Me too."

"So, did you hang that picture I sent you?"

"Yep." He shifted the phone so she could see the room and where he'd hung the oil painting she'd sent—a picture he'd always liked of his home town near Charlotte, North Carolina. It was a great little reminder of home, even if he was happy to not live there for a long while.

"The place is looking good, honey."

"I had this great interior designer come help me."

"That you did," she said, echoing the grin he wore.

Mom's designer skills were in hot demand, and she'd loved her recent visit to the Paris of North America, marveling over the culture and the history and architecture while he'd reveled in the time spent with the woman he loved best in the world.

"Any time you want me to return to fix some things, you just let me know," she said now.

"You know there's an open invitation, Mom. Just get on the plane and come. There's always room."

"Hmm." Her head tilted. "I'd rather those rooms be filled with grandbabies, son."

And here they were again. "I'm doing my best, Mom. I go out, I meet people."

"By meeting people, do you mean female people?"

"Well, yeah." Sort of…not really. Not unless you counted the older women in church or the married ones or the too-young ones, which made him wonder why there seemed so few in between. Weren't women supposed to outnumber men in church? Regardless, he was pretty sure Mom didn't mean any of those.

"When was the last date you went on?" she asked, as if she didn't believe him either.

"A while ago," he confessed. Months? Years?

"How much of a while?"

"Look, it's not always easy to meet women, especially Christian women."

"I know, honey," she said sympathetically. They'd had this conversation before.

He'd had this conversation with the Bible study guys more than once, too. Trying to find someone who had more than just a Sunday relationship with God, someone who wasn't interested in the cash he could splash and with whom he had enough in common, was harder than it might seem. Most of the Christian guys he knew—people like Mike and Brent and Chris—had known their spouses for years, before NHL spotlights and paychecks. Call him crazy, but here in a new city, especially a hockey-mad, French-speaking city, he knew finding someone who might like him for himself would be more challenging.

"Are you still going to that church you took me to when I was there?"

"When it's Sunday."

"You might need to be a little more intentional than just Sundays if you really want to connect," she said gently. "I know you can't expect to find Miss Right at the first church you go to, but keep trusting God and who knows? Maybe she'll fall out of a tree or something."

He choked.

"Beau? Honey? You okay?"

He cleared his throat. "I'm fine, Mom."

"You sure?"

Explain to her what had happened just yesterday? He didn't think his matchmaking mom would be sensible about it. Especially when she'd always claimed to have a "sense" about these things, just as she had when his sister met Jesse and she'd prophesied they would marry and have sweet babies. If only she'd foreseen the anguish that would come Olivia's way only a few short years later.

Before his heart could wind down those roads, he distracted her with what the guys had said last night.

She sighed. "Oh, I'm so glad you have some good male friends in your life who are praying for you too. It's important to have mentors and people on a similar journey who can encourage you."

"Preaching to the choir here, Mom."

"I know." Her look turned wistful. "I just want you to be happy, honey."

"I am happy," he insisted.

"But maybe sometimes a little lonely too?"

Okay, well, maybe. His condo might be of grand proportions and befit a goalie in one of the NHL's most storied teams, but he would like someone to come home to, to share his days with. He knew once the season started he wouldn't feel this to quite the same extent, but even then, to have someone he could trust to care about him—someone for whom he could do the same— would be awesome. And while he'd joked in the past about dumb things like meeting Brent's sister—before he'd known Mike had her in his sights—that desire to be part of something more than him only seemed to grow a little more each year. So yeah, he could admit it. He wanted a wife. A family. He loved kids.

"I'll be praying for you, honey," Mom said, drawing him back to the present.

"Thanks, Mom." He asked her what things she might need practical and prayer help in, and after he mentally filed those requests away, they said their *goodnights* and *love yous*.

He studied the scene before him. The night had darkened to deep blue, the lights winking on Mount Royal, the giant cross illuminated in white—a modern representation of the founding city's father's original cross erected nearly four hundred years ago. He exhaled. That's right. God *was* on the throne, His light as ever faithful as the cross that remained sure.

Ever present. Ever watchful. Ever loving.

"Lord."

Stillness gathered around him, and he closed his eyes and focused heavenwards.

"I believe You have good plans for me. I believe You love me. You know I want to find someone, so please help me to trust You to bring her along at the right time. I don't want distractions," he added as a face flashed through his mind. "And whoever she is, wherever she is, please help her to trust You too."

"Beau Nash! Thanks for joining us today. You too, Dodge."

Beau joined his fellow newbie teammate in shaking hands with the director of the team's Children's Foundation outside the Montreal Children's Hospital. "Great to be here."

"How's your French coming along?"

"*Très bien?*"

Maurice Bergevin laughed and replied in rapid French that left Beau far in his wake and exchanging wry glances with Jake, who seemed equally overwhelmed.

"Sorry, sir, you're gonna have to go a little slower for me here," Beau apologized. "The jersey fits," he said, plucking at his red-and-blue hem, "but it'll take a little longer to feel comfortable with the language."

"Don't worry. We'll have you speaking French soon."

"Oui."

Maurice grinned. "Now, I wanted to introduce you both to Brigitte St-Arnaud, the community engagement officer here at the Children's Hospital, who will take you to meet some of the children here today."

Beau nodded, joining Jake in greeting the pretty, dark-haired woman who looked to be in her early thirties.

"Welcome to you both," she said before flashing her smile up at Beau. "It certainly is a pleasure to meet you."

Beau nodded and glanced away. He didn't think himself any kind of Casanova, but knowing Jake apparently thought him one, he'd determined to behave in a way that made it extremely certain he could not be accused of flirting. Not that he wanted to be rude—just send the message that he was unavailable. Best to keep the conversation and eye contact to a minimum.

Patrice went on to explain about the role of the team organization with respect to the hospital, the fact that the community engagement component meant players regularly checking in with some of the sick kids here. "I know this can be very confronting, which is why I'm really glad you two have volunteered."

"No problem," Beau offered. Nothing could be more confronting than seeing his own nephew struggling in the hospital, something which had cemented his commitment to doing whatever he could to help kids facing medical challenges.

"Well, I have to tell you," she said, smiling up at him, "some of the kids are very excited to meet you." She turned to Jake. "Both of you."

"Sure," Jake said with another exchange of glances and a roll of the eyes at Beau that suggested he recognized Beau was way more of a big deal. And while Beau didn't want to go tooting his own trumpet, the truth was there was a reason Beau had been traded here and done more interviews than some.

"Yeah, who wouldn't want to meet the missile known as Jake Dodgewell?" Beau said, slapping Jake on the back. "Faster than a speeding bullet, more powerful than a locomotive, able to weave his way through mountain-sized men to shoot the puck and score."

"You got this guy doing your PR, Dodge?" Maurice asked Jake.

"Really cheap rates," Beau offered with a wink.

"How about we get on with things?" Patrice gestured to the elevators. "I don't want to keep these kids waiting."

"Absolutely," Beau said. "Let's go."

Five minutes later they were in one of the wards, meeting children who had been wheeled out to meet them.

"Hey, ladies!" Beau waved at a group of little girls whose wheelchairs were decked out with balloons and sparkly streamers. He crouched down to their level and began asking names while Patrice lamely introduced Jake and Beau.

"Whoops," he murmured to one girl. "I think I started a little early."

She giggled. "You're funny."

"Thank you! And you have a very pretty smile. Are you a princess?"

Delight lit her face as she showed him her gap-toothed grin and nodded proudly.

"I thought so." He shifted on his haunches to the next girl. "Hello. What's your name?"

This continued for a few minutes, his heart melting a little more as he listened to their stories, occasionally needing their parents or nurses standing behind them to translate. But kindness was a language that needed no translation, and a smile and a blown kiss could go a long way.

"You're really good with them," Patrice murmured.

He shrugged. "I've always liked kids."

The boys called for him to draw near, and he spent some time talking hockey with parents and staff alike and signing some jerseys a few enterprising family members had brought from home.

"You're really tall," one little boy called Theo said.

"I know, right?" He tugged his hair loose from the signature bun. "What do you think? Do I look a little shorter now?"

"Put your hair up," one little girl cried.

"You look like a girl," another boy commented, inspiring laughter from around the room.

"Really?" Beau asked, rubbing the scruff on his cheeks and chin. "How many girls do you know who have this growing on their face?"

The boy's nose wrinkled.

"At least, I hope you don't know any girls who are growing whiskers," Beau continued, giving the kid a wink before moving to the far corner, where a boy with glasses sat watching proceedings. "Hey, buddy. Do you mind if I sit here?"

The boy simply stared at him, which Beau decided to take as a yes. He took a seat, shifting the chair closer, and held out his hand. "Put it there, pal."

The boy obliged, and Beau grinned. But even as he smiled his heart ached. He recognized the suffering in the deep shadows underscoring the boy's eyes, the way his face looked way older than any kid had a right to look. "How old are you, buddy?"

Whether it was his accent or his sheer size, the boy still refused to speak, leaving it to a woman Beau presumed to be his mother to murmur, "Jacques is ten years old."

Ten years old. *Lord, heal this boy.* "Do you like hockey?"

Jacques's mother quickly spoke to her son, who nodded, his eyes lighting. He spoke rapidly with his mother, who then translated for Beau. "He says you're his favorite player."

Beau chuckled. "But you haven't seen me play."

"Oh no," she corrected. "Jacques has, many times on TV. He was so happy when you were traded. Said we needed a good goalie."

Beau glanced at Maurice, wondering if he'd heard, then swiveled to face the boy more fully. "*Enchanté*, Jacques."

The boy's face lit, and he began speaking so fast that Beau chuckled and had to hold his hands up to slow him down. "Pardon, Jacques." He said the boy's name as the boy's mother had said it, with a soft *J* and *ahk* sound instead of an *ack* like he might expect it to be.

Between his frail grasp of French and Jacques's mother's considerably more proficient grasp of English, they were able to make enough conversation that Beau realized afresh just how important these kinds of things were. Sure, he might have some challenges in life, but these families, these battles, were so much bigger and more important than anything else. It only spurred him on to want to learn French even more.

They signed more things, including pucks and bears, and he and Jake posed for more pictures, but Beau was determined to not make today's visit to the Children's Hospital his last. He would come as regularly as his schedule—and the hospital—allowed. For who knew how long some of these poor kids might have?

He mentioned something of his desire to return to Maurice and Patrice as they exited.

"You were really good with them," Patrice said, warmth in her eyes and smile.

Uh oh. "Like I said, I like kids."

Her gaze shot to his hands, then trickled back up again. "Do you have children?"

Why did that question leave him feeling slightly uneasy? "Nope." He glanced at Jake, who had done his bit but had ended up spending more time looking at his phone than talking to the kids. "How about you, Dodge? Bet you can't wait to have a few little Dodgers of your own one day, huh?"

Jake side-eyed him. "You know it."

Beau swallowed a chuckle. "Just gotta find the right girl, huh?"

"You and me both, brother."

"One day." Beau clapped him on the shoulder, then turned to Patrice. "Thank you for today. I really had fun, and I hope it brought the kids some joy."

"You are more than welcome to come any time you like, Mr. Nash. I can give you my card if you'd like to set up a time."

Beau slid a look at Maurice, who didn't seem to object. Maybe that was how things were done here and not through the team's PR. "Uh, sure."

He picked the card free from her fire-engine-red nails and shoved it in his back pocket while Jake sent him another of those raised-eyebrow smirks that suggested he thought poorly of Beau's girl awareness radar—something that was confirmed when they made it out to the taxi and Jake eyed him. "Not a flirt, huh?"

"How was I flirting?"

Jake shot him a look.

"I'm serious. I really don't wanna go giving anyone the wrong impression, but by the same token, I'm keen to return there to talk with the kids again. I wasn't joking about that."

"I know they'd love to see you," Maurice said. "That little boy in the bed—Jacques, was it? He was something else, wasn't he?"

"He's really sick," Beau said quietly. "Anything I can do, I mean it. I want to be there for them."

"You made that little guy's day."

Beau looked at Maurice. "My nephew died of a rare blood disorder three years ago. I'll do whatever it takes to help kids and families and make these awful circumstances even a little bit easier."

"I'm sorry, man," Jake said.

Beau nodded. But he meant it. Caring for kids burned soul deep within. And while he might enjoy defending goals, he'd much rather defend kids from the fears and torments of this world.

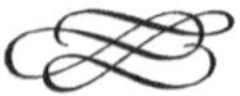

CHAPTER 3

Maggie stood outside the school gates, waiting to glimpse Noah. She exchanged nervous smiles with other parents, none of whom she had exchanged more than a few words with. She could do friendly. Well, once upon a time she'd been okay at it. But her nerves now were all for her son, leaving little capacity for meaningless chitchat in this moment.

Yesterday's first day at school had gone rather less well than she'd hoped, with poor Noah collapsing into her arms in tears. She'd tried to learn from both the teacher and Noah himself just what had proved the problem, but neither could offer anything except that Noah had not seemed to make many—if any—friends.

"Don't make me go again, Maman," he'd pleaded last night, refusing to go to bed until she'd rocked him to sleep in her arms, at which point she'd finally been able to carry him and place him into bed. And while he might have been slightly more positive about attending today, she couldn't forget her mother's comments last night.

"He's too young, Maggie."

"He's five, Maman. He's supposed to begin school now."

Her mother sighed, her lips one flat line. But she hadn't needed to speak for Maggie to understand her. This was what happened when people ventured outside their walls. The world was a dangerous place. Bad things happened. People couldn't be trusted. People could get hurt.

Maggie had fought the negativity, had tried to believe the next day would prove better. Noah wasn't the only child who had been teary. He'd just been the *most* teary and the most vocal in his dismay. So she'd hoped and encouraged and even tried to pray that God would help her little boy.

And now she was here. Hoping Noah's day had proved better than hers.

The bell rang and the doors opened, and streams of small children appeared, trailing behind teachers. This was the parents' cue to enter, and they did, the pretense of exchanging niceties forgotten as all eyes fixed on their sons and daughters.

Maggie saw Noah holding hands with the teacher, and she rushed to them, relief easing through her heart at the small smile her son wore. Thank goodness.

"Hello, sweetheart. How was your day?"

He placed a thumb in his mouth and glanced shyly up at his teacher, who nodded and said softly, "Noah had a much better day today."

"Ah, merci." Maggie hugged him close to her. "Are you ready to go home?"

He nodded, and with another word of thanks to the teacher, Maggie collected Noah's bag and held his hand as they headed out the gates.

"Did you make some new friends?" she asked, hoping against hope that he'd say oui.

He shrugged instead, but she'd take that as a win. At least there were no tears.

"Would you like to get some ice cream?" she asked.

Now he smiled. Ice cream. The love language of all children.

They walked to a nearby famous crèmerie, where she allowed Noah to pick two fruits—bananas and berries—which were blended into the ice cream. This place was popular with tourists—even more so today, given the warm and sunny conditions that made diving into dairy goodness all the more appealing. Maybe she could bribe Noah with ice cream every day until he associated school with good things.

"Is that delicious?" she asked, smiling as she paid and he took a lick, his eyes widening with delight. As they should, considering he'd rarely had such a treat.

"Come, let's go outside."

They moved outside and turned, only to bump into a tall figure. A really tall figure. And for Noah to splat his ice cream straight onto the tall man's bare knee.

"Whoa!"

"Non!"

"Je suis vraiment navrée! Oh my goodness, sir, I'm so sorry."

Ignoring Noah's crying, Maggie grabbed the spare paper napkins from her handbag and bent to wipe at the poor man's knee but was stopped by a large hand that closed over the napkins and finished the job without complaint. Her gaze lifted to green eyes she'd seen before. Green eyes that once more sent a jolt of electricity through her.

"Hi. Again." He smiled, throwing the wadded napkins into a nearby trash can. "We met before, right? At the Gardens. I'm Beau."

"Er, *bonjour*." Did his eyes just crinkle a little more?

"I should've said that, shouldn't I? Let me try again. Bonjour, mademoiselle."

It was technically *madame*, but she wasn't about to call him on that. "I'm so sorry."

His brow pleated. "Is my pronunciation that bad?"

"No! I mean, about your knee."

Beau's mouth ticked up. "Why? Did you tell him to smash me with the ice cream?"

"Pardon? No, of course not."

As he grinned and dropped to a squat, she couldn't help but notice how muscular his legs were. Really muscular. Maggie blinked. Non. *Non.* She would *not* notice things like that.

"Hey, buddy," he said to Noah, who wore fat tears on his cheeks. "I'm real sorry about your ice cream."

Noah's bottom lip quivered. He veered away to seek refuge in Maggie's waist, and she wrapped her arm around him as she wondered what to do. Apologize again? Buy the man an ice cream cone? Hurry Noah away before this turned into something she didn't know how to handle? Oh, who was she kidding? This was already more challenging than she wanted or needed.

"Aww. Can I make it up to him? Get him another treat?"

After being attacked by dairy, Beau now wanted to make it up to them? "Er, I think we owe you an ice cream." That was only polite, non?

"Well, hey, I'm not gonna say no, because that did look really good." He smiled down at Noah, then his gaze met Maggie's again. "Can he have another one?" he whispered.

She swallowed. She wasn't made of money, but it had been an accident, and she had no desire for Noah's day to worsen more than it already had. Stifling a sigh, she nodded and drew out her purse.

Beau—*why was he still watching her?*—shook his head and murmured, "My treat."

"No. We caused—"

"It was an accident, and hey, I came all this way because I was told the ice cream was the best, and it'd be rude to not buy the little man a new cone just because I was dumb enough to get in the way."

"But it was our fault," she protested again.

He opened the door and held it wide for her, leaving her no option but to move under his T-shirted arm—she didn't have to duck—and escort Noah back to the counter.

"What will it be?" the server behind the counter asked.

"Don't look at me," Beau said. "There's so much good stuff here I'm still deciding." His head tilted down. "Maybe the young man here might know?"

The server nodded to Noah. "Hello again." Her face softened, and she glanced at Maggie. "Was there an accident?"

"I'm afraid so."

"Another of the same?"

Maggie bent to Noah's level. "Would you like another of what you had before?"

He nodded, thumb in his mouth, eyes darting to Beau before glancing shyly away.

Maggie straightened. "Yes, please." She glanced at the tall man beside her, who was squinting at the chalkboard on the wall. Awkwardness filled her. Asking a near-stranger what he wanted to eat was not part of her usual routine and certainly not something of which her mother would approve. For some reason, that thought spurred words to her mouth. "What would you like?"

"Man, there are so many nice flavors." He turned to her. "What would you recommend?"

As he smiled at her, his attention fully focused on her, her heart knew a weird tumbling palpitation and words fled from her brain.

"Maggie?"

He remembered her name?

"What's your favorite?"

She swallowed past the dryness in her throat. Managed a shrug she hoped looked non-committal. "I like the peach and mango duet."

"We'll have one of those," Beau said to the server. "And I'll have—"

"Pardon? I was not having an ice cream," Maggie murmured, inching closer to him.

"Why not? It's a beautiful day. A day made for eating ice cream. And I should know, coming from a place where the summers get so hot it's a crime to *not* eat ice cream." He grinned again. "You wouldn't want me being responsible for such a crime, now, would you?"

Her breath suspended, and she had to drag her gaze away to where the server held out a cone of peach-mango goodness to her. When she didn't move, Beau handed it to her and murmured, "Make it two of those."

The server nodded, leaving Maggie to gaze at the dairy treat. Was she supposed to wait for him, like this was a restaurant meal? It had been so long since she'd done something like this. If ever.

"That good, huh? Should I change my order?" Beau teased. "Come on, that cone won't lick itself. I don't want to have to be cleaning you off when it's melted just because you've obviously got more manners than you can poke a stick at."

Good gracious. If she didn't know better, she'd almost think he was flirting with her. Maggie glanced away and obediently took a small mouthful, the flavors bursting onto her tongue in sweet, creamy, fruity goodness. Oh, it had been too long. Way too long since she'd indulged. This was so good, well worth the price—

A shocking thought paused her movements. *Did* she have enough money? Her pay didn't come in until tomorrow, and now she remembered that her purchase before meant she'd barely have enough cash to pay for Noah's second ice cream cone, let alone pay for hers and this man's. Agitation rose, and she scrabbled one-handed through her bag. Should she insist the server cease with Beau's order and Maggie give her cone to

Beau? She winced. That was kind of gross. But accept his help she could not do, not when he'd been too nice already.

"What's wrong?" he asked.

She glanced up from studying the meager amount of change to see him tapping the payment machine with a credit card, holding his own cone.

"Thank you, sir," the server said. "Wait, do I know you?"

"I don't think so," Beau said, taking a swipe of ice cream. "Hey, this is really good."

The server smiled but still wore a furrowed brow.

Maggie sidled closer to Beau. "I thought I was going to pay."

"Guess you out-fumbled me this time," he said easily. "Although I'm pretty sure I said I'd pay. Hey, do you mind if we go now?"

"Er, of course." She was conscious of a stupid pang of disappointment. Of course he'd want to leave. And of course they *should* leave. Noah really should get home soon. They'd taken much longer than she'd anticipated, and no doubt Maman would be getting worried soon.

Beau opened the door for her, and she exited, holding Noah's hand, then waited, unsure what to do as Beau remained there, patiently holding the door and nodding as some other patrons entered. She couldn't just leave. She had to thank him. She bent to Noah's level. "We have to say thank you to the nice man for our ice cream."

He nodded solemnly, his mouth already covered in dark-pink creamy goodness, and she rose as Beau joined them again, conscious of just how large the man was compared to most men. He had a big heart, she realized, and possessed such an easy smile and kindness that it was no wonder people were charmed. Not that she was charmed, she told herself crossly. She didn't even really know the man. But she did appreciate the generous way he'd overlooked the earlier incident and then paid for their ice cream, like doing so simply made his day.

Beau motioned to a nearby tree, and they moved away from the crowds, some of whom were glancing at them like they were wondering what such a fine specimen of a man was doing with a mere ordinary mother and son. They should go, before any of the other mothers from school recognized them and asked awkward questions. Like she could ever explain.

But Beau had slapped a baseball cap on his head and shifted to a position in the shade, his shoulders slumped like he was relaxed and in no hurry to leave.

He glanced up, eyes crinkling again. "Hey, this is really good."

Maggie nodded, and he shifted his focus to Noah. "You enjoying that, buddy?"

Noah nodded, then glanced at her, then back at Beau. "Thank you," he murmured, reminding Maggie of what she needed to do.

"Yes, thank you. You really didn't have to," she felt it necessary to add.

"I really did have to, actually," he said. "This stuff is so good it would be wrong not to try it."

"Is that why you're here?"

"I might've moved here, but it's gonna be a while before I don't think of myself as a tourist," he said before eating some of more of his dessert. "So when someone mentioned how good this place was, I thought it'd be good to check it out, make it a reward for my run. And boy, they were right. It's really good."

"I, er, really do appreciate it," she said.

"Hey, no problem." He glanced at Noah, who had been steadily consuming his sweet treat. "How's that going, buddy?"

Noah's dark eyes lifted. "My name is Noah."

"Hey, Noah." Beau crouched down until he was almost at Noah's eye level. "My name is Beau." He held out a hand. "Nice to meet you."

Noah looked at Beau's hand like he wasn't sure what to do with it.

"Shake his hand, Noah," Maggie encouraged him, miming the action.

"Aw, he doesn't have to," Beau said.

But Noah stretched out his hand, and as Beau grasped it carefully in his long fingers, Maggie knew another heart tug at the sight of the big man and her son. She blinked away a sudden rush of tears. Noah's interaction with men since Maggie's father's death had been negligible.

"I like your name," Beau said to Noah. "Noah was a very brave man."

"Really?"

Beau nodded. "And he loved animals."

Noah smiled shyly as Beau released his hand. "I love elephants."

"Really? Me too," Beau said. "I'd really like to ride on one someday." He shot a look at Maggie. "Not PC, I know, but hey."

Her lips tugged up, like they held an automatic response to his charm. "I think Noah would like to do the same."

"How about you?" Beau said, straightening again, his height and nearness meaning she could see the golden facial fuzz fringing his cheeks and chin. "Ever wondered about traveling someplace where you could do such a thing?"

The same alluring musky scent from last week drew a tug low in her stomach, and she had to think for a moment when he asked the question again. "Me? Ride an elephant?" Maggie dare travel? Do anything risky her mother might not approve of?

"Or do you prefer to keep your climbing adventures to trees?" He grinned, his smile sliding under her defenses and pulling at her heartstrings.

"Maman?" Noah blinked up at her. "Were you climbing trees?"

"Maman?" Beau asked.

"It means mom."

He nodded, and it seemed his smile dimmed a little. "I should've realized."

"What did you think I was?"

"I don't know. Maybe an aunt or a sister."

A sister? She was nearly thirty, for goodness' sake. Pity the poor parents having children twenty-five years apart.

"I guess I wasn't thinking." He finished the last of his cone with a gulp and wiped his hands on the back of his shorts. "Well, hey, I better get going." He bent to Noah again. "Nice to meet you, Noah." Noah nodded shyly as Beau rose to his full height and backed away. "Good to see you, Maggie. Glad your knee is better. Guess I'll see you around."

"Thanks again," she called as he saluted, turned, and jogged away without a backward glance.

Heart strangely sore, she grasped Noah's hand and watched the tall figure disappear around a corner. See her around?

She'd bet a million dollars she'd never see his face again.

Wow. Beau's sneakers slapped the pavement as he made his way through Montreal's streets to home. Talk about a giant misread. Okay, so maybe he might've wondered about this woman and felt a tug of attraction to her, but no way was he ever going to muscle in on someone else's turf. And now he thought about it, everything about Maggie and her son screamed protectiveness and family, right down to the same colored hair and eyes and the dimples in their chin. What kind of doofus was he to not have known?

The fact she didn't wear a ring—yeah, he'd checked—was maybe just another French thing that happened here that he didn't understand. Or maybe she wasn't married, and her partner was elsewhere. Whatever. He wasn't gonna intrude.

And from the blank stare of the kid when he mentioned Noah, he guessed there wasn't a lot of Sunday school action there, so she might not be following God as much as Beau was, if at all. Which was another reason to put distance between them.

And okay, maybe he hadn't exited that situation as gracefully as he could have, but he'd never needed to before. The last time he'd been interested in a woman, it sure hadn't been this confusing. And time and experience had shown that it wasn't worth getting into complicated situations—which meant sometimes avoiding women he found attractive. Especially when they were involved. And when they weren't Christians. So, God bless Maggie and Noah—and gee, the kid *was* cute—but God could take care of 'em. Beau sure as heck didn't need to.

He waited at a traffic light, breathing hard, wondering about the wisdom of this run today. He hadn't calculated on the city being quite this hilly. And breathing in traffic fumes as school buses roared past wasn't really what he'd had in mind when he set out earlier today. Maybe he'd need to limit his runs to Mount Royal Park or the Botanical Gardens—if he could be assured he wouldn't see Maggie at the latter.

By the time he'd taken his sweaty self into his apartment's foyer, he'd decided his next stop would have to be a gym. He'd been recommended a few by the team but had kinda enjoyed the chance to explore the city during what some people said was the nicest time of the year. It sure was different from his small home town.

"Hey, Edouard," Beau said, nodding to the apartment's doorman. Eddie, as Beau privately called him, had proved a little excited about having one of the Canadiens moving in.

"How was your run, Mr. Nash?"

"It's Beau," he corrected, "and yeah, it was good." And surprising. And a little disappointing, if he was really honest with himself.

"Did you try the crèmerie I recommended?"

"It was awesome."

"You may have to go there again."

Beau nodded, but he didn't want to freak out Maggie by showing up in her territory or giving her the wrong idea, so as good as that ice cream place was, he might need to find someplace else. Not that he should be indulging too much in that kind of thing anyway.

A stab at the elevator button, and he waited, feeling a little out of place in his sweat-stained T-shirt and shorts amid the elegance of the foyer. The front door opened, and Edouard admitted two other residents, whose stylish office outfits contrasted with Beau's clothes.

They moved to the elevator, and he nodded. "Bonjour."

The woman, who looked to be in her forties, gave him a slow once-over before her gaze drifted back to his face. The man— her husband, Beau presumed, judging from the way he'd positioned an arm around her waist—simply nodded and turned away. Okay, so maybe friendliness was overrated here. The woman murmured something to the man, which caused him to look back at Beau and begin a volley of French Beau had no hope of understanding.

"Sorry. Excusez-moi." That was the more correct term here, wasn't it? *Parlez-vous anglais?*"

"American," he thought he heard the woman mutter, accompanied by a roll of the eyes that could rival Jake's skills in that department.

Great. He shrugged as the elevator doors finally opened, then waited as they entered.

"Mr. Nash!" Eddie raced over with a small package. "Désolé. This came for you today."

"Merci," he said, accepting the parcel. See? He was trying. Maybe he'd have this French thing down in a hundred years.

He glanced at the parcel and smiled at the team logo. The

organization had been really awesome to him, and it looked like this was yet another little thing to help ease his way in.

He glanced up and, in the mirrored doors, saw his companions glance away. His lips curved wryly as the elevator neared the top floors. Movement suggested they were getting off here, and a little part of him took pleasure in the fact their eyes widened when it became obvious he was not getting off here but at the more expensive floors above.

"*Au revoir*," he called just before the door closed, smiling to himself. Okay, so he didn't want to tick off the neighbors, but neither did he mind letting people know their preconceptions of him might be wrong. And he'd seen that look before, where people thought a scruffy man-bunned guy who looked like him must be either a Norwegian actor or a construction worker—more often the latter. And while he knew not everyone in this city would care about the Habs—judging from her cool reaction, he didn't think Maggie knew or cared—the fact these snooty neighbors might discover he wasn't quite the down-and-outer they thought him made him smile.

The doors opened and he exited onto the nineteenth floor, the doors to the other apartments remaining resolutely shut. Eddie had told him those apartments were occupied by executives who spent a lot of time overseas, which Beau had appreciated, as it meant he wasn't likely to be bothered by loud parties. He smiled. Nor would they be bothered should he be so inclined to get his party on.

Back inside his apartment he ripped open the package, finding a T-shirt in the size he'd requested. He slipped off the sweat-stained one and tugged the new top on. Yep. Much better. He wasn't sure what kinds of "big man" stores existed here, but he'd appreciate finding some soon. Fortunately he was already on a first-name basis with a few US stores that handled people who were tall but not too wide, and shipping wasn't a problem.

His phone buzzed, and he tugged it from his pocket. "Hey, Dodge. Whatcha up to?"

"Not as much as you. You seen the pics?"

"What pics?" Beau pushed the call to speaker and opened his social media. Ah. Notifications. He winced. Lots of them.

"Who's the chick?"

"Huh?" Beau opened Insta and saw he'd been tagged in a bunch of photos that looked like they'd been taken not two hours ago. Someone who looked awfully like Beau, sharing his height and breadth of shoulders, faced away from the camera while eating ice cream. With a woman. And a small boy who was smiling up at him. "Oh no."

"Oh yeah," Jake said. "What's it been? Three weeks and you've found a lady friend? Settling down, huh?"

"It's not what it looks like," Beau protested.

"It's looking mighty cozy if you ask me. Not a flirt, huh?"

Man. "I bumped into her. I didn't know she'd be there."

"She looks a bit like that garden chick from last week."

There was a good reason for that. "Really?" Beau said, flicking through the comments. He winced again. People who didn't know him were making comments about the Habs' new goalie and the secret family this supposedly single Christian guy seemed to have. He could only hope the organization wasn't too bothered by this chatter about their expensive import.

And that Maggie and her son would not be aware of the rumors involving them.

CHAPTER 4

"Maggie."

Maggie nodded to her colleague and stepped outside, thankful her knee was feeling better even as she wondered at the remarks and looks being tossed her way. She managed a weak smile and refocused on her roles for the day. Fortunately, the camera incident of two weeks ago had only cracked the viewfinder and not damaged anything internally, so her photos had turned out well. She'd spent the morning uploading some of those pictures to the website and social media channels and now had the next hour or so to work in the garden alongside Frederic and some of the others. And given it was such a beautiful day, with nary a cloud in the sky, she couldn't think of a better way to spend the afternoon.

She slipped her work gloves on and met Frederic, waiting beside the golf-cart. She'd protested at first, not wanting to seem like she was a diva, but he'd insisted on remaining cautious with her knee. "It is a beautiful day, n'est-ce pas?" she asked him.

"Pas pire," he replied.

She shot him a glance, saw him look away as he started the cart. "What is it?"

"Nothing," he replied, rolling his shoulders.

"I must be imagining things," she said, pushing her hair back into its usual ponytail. "I seem to be thinking everyone is looking at me strangely today."

He gave a non-committal answer that didn't exactly assuage her fears. Tempted as she was to pursue it, she kept silent. It wouldn't do to create a problem if none existed. And if for some reason there was a problem, well, she might prefer not to know.

Frederic drove to the Jardin japonais, and when he stopped, she collected her clippers from the back. Today's task involved trimming the shrubs, especially the rhododendron, which had put on a recent flush of growth given the favorable growing conditions of the past few weeks. Regular pruning was required to keep things neat and visitor-worthy, to shape the garden into what it ought be.

Once more she marveled at the vision of the original garden designers and of botanist Brother Marie-Victorin, whose determination to create a special park was made possible through the work of horticulturalist Henry Teuscher. She smiled, thinking of the passionate plea to Montreal's mayor, that the city's three hundredth birthday be celebrated with a special corsage, the garden for the city that would "fill her arms to overflowing with all the roses and lilies of the field." She sighed. How romantic some men were in the expression of their vision for such things.

Her arms soon grew tired—gardening was better than any workout—and she took a moment to study their work. This truly was her favorite part of the Gardens. Some might prefer the Jardin de Chine, or the Rose Garden, or the Arboretum walks, but the peace found here was second to none.

"You working or non?" Frederic asked.

"I am appreciating our labors," she said, not turning around. "Is it not perfect today?"

"It will be more perfect when I have a beer in my hand," he griped.

"Very well. Let us not hold you back from your beer," she teased.

He grunted.

Half an hour later they had finished disposing of the clippings, and she was once more being transported in the golf cart. Again he slid a look at her that drew unease.

"Frederic? I can't help but think you know something I do not and you are wanting to tell me. Is there something I need to know?"

He sighed, and they drove to the work sheds to put away the equipment.

Her stomach tensed. What was so awful that he could not say? "Frederic? Please. Have I done something to upset people? Have I upset you?"

He shook his head and drew out his phone.

He was not going to answer her now? Oh, men could be so frustrating.

"Two weeks ago, when you had your accident, the man who helped you, what was his name?"

"Beau. But I thought I told you that already."

He inclined his head, scratching at his grizzled cheek. "You know who he is?"

"I thought you said he played hockey."

"Oui." He glanced at her as if wondering what to say, then simply handed her his phone.

"I didn't know you had Instagram," she said before zeroing in on the photo he displayed. A photo from last week. A photo that looked awfully like something that might have been taken by that group of people who'd been standing at the crèmerie, pointing at them. "Oh."

"You left early because you said you were picking up your son."

"And I did. See?" She pointed to the dark-haired figure on the screen. "That's Noah right there."

"Hmm."

Her chest heated. "What do you mean, *hmm*? I went and picked Noah up early, just as I said I would. We stopped to get ice cream because I want him to associate going to school with good things."

"If you say so."

Offence layered her words. "Not if I say so. It *is* so. What does any of this have to do with things? Why do you even have my picture here?"

It was only then that she saw what he was referring to—the hashtags under the picture pointing out someone's name. And judging from the dozens of comments, there was a great deal of speculation about Montreal's new goalkeeper and a certain mystery brunette.

"Oh non."

"Mais oui," he said. "Look, I feel like perhaps you don't know just what others might be thinking, so let me spell it out to you. There were people talking this morning who thought you'd been taking time off work because you're having an affair with that man."

She gasped. "An affair?"

Another shrug. "If you are, that is none of my business. But—"

"I most certainly am not!"

"Like I said, it's none of my business. But there were some jealousies among the women this morning, wondering how much of what you said is true, and I thought you might want to watch your back."

"I cannot believe it! How could people think such a thing?" Of Maggie who, apart from an unfortunate descent from a tree, rarely risked anything. "I didn't know he would be there. And we talked for maybe five minutes."

He shrugged, which only fueled her ire.

"What am I supposed to do? I can't help it if people think I was doing something wrong, especially when I know I wasn't."

"Just be careful, that is all."

"Thanks for the warning," she muttered, collecting her gear and moving back inside the work center.

She went inside to clean up, working as efficiently as she could so no one could accuse her of wasting time. She had never been accused of misusing company time before, and she certainly wasn't about to let anyone accuse her of it now.

A minute later she was powering up her computer, determined to sit here until past her scheduled time of departure. Fortunately, she had arranged that her mother would collect Noah from school, which meant there would be few to accuse her of not working as she ought today. And as tempting as it was to seek out social media for her own purposes, she was equally determined to not give anyone a single chance to comment.

"Ah, Maggie. You are back, hard at work I see," said one of the researchers in the Institut de recherche en biologie végétale.

"Oui," she said firmly, returning her attention to the screen.

He soon moved on, and she exhaled, doing her best to keep her focus on her work, writing up reports and uploading the latest images to social media.

"Are you seeing if you can find him on Facebook?" Maggie's head jerked up to encounter Danielle Dupras's wide smile. "He is very handsome, non?"

"Pardon? I do not know what you refer to."

"Your friend. Frederic said he was here the other day. A hockey player, eh? I didn't think that was your style."

Seeing as Maggie had never thought of herself as having any particular preference when it came to men, let alone any real style, it was not hard to dismiss the communications director's remarks.

"I hope you'll invite us all to the wedding."

"Quoi! What?"

Danielle grinned. "How long has this been going on for?"

"There is nothing going on." Maggie remembered what Frederic had said earlier. "And I assure you, the only reason I left early that day was to pick up my son from school. Nothing else."

"This was not a date, then?"

"Non!"

"Hmm. Well, if there is a date, then know that I would be happy to see him visit the Gardens again. A little more publicity means more people through the door and more tickets sold to the Pumpkin Ball."

Maggie gritted her teeth. Danielle's brainchild, the Pumpkin Ball, was their chief fundraising event in autumn, before winter made it harder to attract visitors to the Gardens—except those fond of snowshoeing. "I wish I could help you, but I barely know the man."

"Well, if that changes, let me know. And if you don't want to pursue it further, then perhaps I should tell my cousin to have a go at seeking out this handsome man, oui?"

"Oui." Maggie offered a gritted teeth smile, her heart a mass of writhing emotion.

Beau, kind as he was, had made it very clear he wanted nothing more to do with her. And really, she couldn't blame him. She was no beauty, and motherhood had softened her body with a few extra curves. Someone who looked like Danielle, with her long blonde waves and carefully made-up face, would probably be far more appropriate for a famous man like him. So why did her chest hurt at the thought?

BLUE FILLED THE SKY as the car swung around the curve. Up ahead, a gate attendant smiled and indicated for Beau to lower the window, to which he complied.

"Good morning, Mr. Nash. Just follow the flags to the main entrance."

"Parfait. Merci," Beau said, trying out his awesome language skills with a smile before powering up the window again.

Ahead, he could see a parade of vehicles making their way along the avenue of trees that signaled the entrance to this prestigious course that would see the team mingle with sponsors, clients, and friends of the organization while raising money for the Children's Foundation. It would also prove one of his first major media moments since the ice cream incident of a week ago.

He followed the signs and pulled his Audi into the designated zone, behind a black Lincoln that was evidently defenseman Johan Tomasson's ride. The Swede was the high-profile signing from two seasons ago and had reached out to Beau a couple of days ago and made him feel welcome. While they would be paired up with club supporters and sponsors—pity the poor person matched up with him—Beau appreciated that there were at least some people here whom he might consider friends.

Along the drive was a huge array of cameras and media. His stomach tensed. This was certainly a much bigger deal than playing in Phoenix. He stepped from his vehicle and gave a quick wave, then grabbed his bag from the backseat with his change of clothes, slapped on his cap, and gave the giant orange bear mascot a high five and a hug.

"Beau! Beau! Over here!"

He glanced at the media personnel before noticing a podium set up on the front lawn with what looked like a dozen microphones. As this year's major signing, he'd be willing to bet his entire salary he'd be one of those called up to speak, so he'd give the media that time then. But for now, he'd give them a quick "hey, great to be here" soundbite, as his priority was getting inside and greeting the management and his teammates.

Black-clothed personnel drove his car away, and he moved past the three-piece jazz band at the base of the clubhouse's white steps. Another pose for a photo, then it was up and onto the front patio, where he was greeted by Johan with a handshake.

"Beau. Good to see you."

"And you. Hey, this is cool," Beau said, gesturing to the crowds.

"They like their hockey here."

That was for sure. "The weather looks pretty solid. Should be a good day for it, huh?"

A woman with a red-lipped smile and a clipboard drew near. "Mr. Nash?"

"It's Beau. Hey. What can I do for you?"

He was taken out the back, where he was greeted by some people from team management, then shown to a room where he could sign merchandise and jerseys that would be auctioned off later. Then he did an interview with the team's TV crew, then went back out the front to face the media.

After a short introduction, he took his place behind the white podium to face a bank of microphones and cameras.

"Beau! Tell us how you feel about coming here. Have you settled well into the city?"

He nodded. "Montreal is an awesome city, and it's a real honor to be here. I've always wanted to play for an Original Six team, so now, to be in this position, well, I feel super blessed."

"And what's it like coming here, especially when Montreal is a much bigger hockey market than your previous teams?"

"It's really exciting. I loved playing in Carolina and Arizona, but coming here is really special. Obviously there's a lot of attention, and a lot of things that come along with that, but I'm looking forward to that, and playing in a hockey-centric environment will be really fun. And to be here today, to support such an important cause, is something I'm really glad to be involved with."

"You have a passion for helping sick kids."

He dipped his chin. "I'm extremely privileged to get to do the kind of work I do, and knowing there are many kids out there without such opportunities means I don't take this for granted." He swallowed. "Some of you may know that my nephew Joey was really sick for a long time, so I know some of the challenges families face, and I'm committed to doing all I can to help other families who are facing similar circumstances. If I can do something that will brighten one sick kid's day, then that's a good day as far as I'm concerned."

More cameras flashed in his face, then his attention was drawn to someone from the Gazette. "Tell us about your off-season preparation."

"Obviously I want to do the team proud and do all I can to prepare for a great season. It's gonna be a big year for the team, and me personally, so I'm putting in as much work as I can to be the best player I can be."

He explained some more about his training, sharing about his particular methods to prepare for the season which—all going well—would see him play over eighty games in the regular season alone.

"And how do you feel about your new teammates?"

"I'm really excited about meeting some of the guys today—which is not to say I'm not excited about meeting some of the others." He paused for their laughter. "I've been lucky enough to play with some of them like Rakoluv and Kaspar on other teams, like World Juniors, so it's gonna be nice to reconnect. And with premier players in the league like Johan and Gabriel, this is definitely a strong place to play. Those guys in particular—everyone actually—have been really welcoming, and I can't wait to get to know some of the others and to see us click as a team. And I'm looking forward to training camp next week."

There were a bunch of other questions, then he was finally released to grab a coffee with some of his teammates.

Johan introduced him around, and he talked with the captain again, Gabriel Lemieux, who invited Beau to join them at the coffee table. Gabe's heavily tattooed forearms crossed as he eyed Beau. "Settling in okay?"

"Okay enough," Beau said, before remembering Gabe was a local. "It's a great city."

"With great ice cream, huh?" Kris Sekkonen, Montreal's first line left wing, smirked.

"Love it," Beau said with a grin, ignoring the edge in his new teammate's voice. Okay, so maybe everyone wasn't being completely welcoming. He'd heard rumors that Kris hadn't been happy about losing his line-mate and friend in the trade that saw Beau arrive. But then, all players knew money ruled this game and sentiment only went so far. It wasn't like he had much say in who team management determined would come and who'd leave. And Beau had learned long ago that the best way to treat people was to behave as if no problem existed. They were all men. If Kris had a problem, then he could say something. As far as things depended on Beau, he'd try to live at peace with others.

The conversation turned to who'd been doing what this summer, and he was able to share a bit about a camp he'd done with Bible study friend Dan Walton over in Muskoka, Ontario.

"He plays for Toronto, right?" Kris frowned.

"Yep."

"You know the Leafs are our traditional enemies, right?" Kris said.

"Yeah, I've heard that." Beau finished his coffee. "But hey, I was still playing for Arizona then, so I don't think it mattered."

As if he'd let it matter anyway. Dan was his friend, and solid through and through.

Fortunately, the team manager was calling them to a presentation, so Beau could leave the tension and go have a team photo. Then it was time to meet some of the kids the foundation was supporting from the hospital, and he crouched down to meet the young boy who had been selected to walk out with him, Emile. "Bonjour."

"You're really tall," the boy said.

"Am I? Or are you just really short?" Beau teased.

The boy's jaw sagged, then he chuckled. Beau grinned and offered him a fist-bump.

They chatted for a moment longer until there was another call for photos, this time with the kids and the sponsors—the kids in their red Montreal shirts, Beau and his teammates in their navy blue ones. Then they walked out, hand in hand, to where the golf carts waited. Each golf bag held a hockey stick, and Beau smiled at this blending of sports.

"*Bonne journée*! Have a nice day!" one of the sponsors called.

"Merci," he said.

There were more announcements, then the Habs players were called out one by one and matched with the people who had paid to play with them.

He'd been matched with a man named Robert Bernier, who looked to be in his mid-forties.

"I'm so excited to meet you!" Robert exclaimed as Beau shook his hand.

"So, what is it that you do, Robert?" Beau asked as they headed to the golf carts.

Apparently Robert headed an IT company that was a minor sponsor for the team, so Beau knew his role today was important. These kinds of opportunities helped to show the team's best face, although Beau knew his golf skills weren't exactly going to do that.

"I gotta admit, I'm better at blocking than teeing off," Beau confessed.

"I think we'll do great."

He said that now. Obviously, Robert rated Beau's golf skills on par with his goalkeeping, which meant way higher than he ought.

They found their golf cart, and Beau insisted Robert drive, so they waited until the rest of the pairs had been matched up, during which time he signed a few more autographs for those nearby. He caught Kris and Jake chatting, their gazes fixed on him, and he shot them a grin and a salute. Okay, so their expressions hardly seemed encouraging for team bonding. He pushed it to one side, though, and kept focused on Robert, learning that the man was married and had two daughters in elementary school and that he didn't see them nearly as much as he wanted due to the long hours demanded by his business.

"It's a tricky thing," Beau said when Robert finally paused for breath. "My dad died when I was ten, but I do remember that when he was there for me at games and things, it meant the world to me."

The cart steered over a small bump. Beau glanced across at Robert, who shot him a wry smile. "I guess you get one chance at this fathering thing, right?"

"If you're lucky enough to have that chance in the first place."

Whew. He'd never expected the conversation to get so deep so fast. He spent a minute praying for the man as they approached the first hole, where a number of other carts and players waited.

The tournament would be played so that groups of four teams would progress around the course together. Judging from the carts waiting, Beau's group included Johan, Kris, and Jake, and their respective playing partners for the day.

"Well, this should be fun," he said.

"I can't believe I get to play with you," Robert said, his manner like Beau's mom's when she'd gushed about meeting Ryan Gosling at a charity event a few years ago.

"Robert, I think it only fair to say that I'm not the world's greatest golfer. To be completely honest, I don't even like golf too much."

Robert mock-gasped. "I can't believe you said that out loud."

"Our secret, okay?" Beau said with a wink.

"Gotcha."

The day progressed pretty much as most of these types of events did for Beau: the golf nuts, like Kris and Robert, doing well, while Beau trailed everyone save Bill, the wide dude who was Kris's partner, who clearly didn't exercise and was now wheezing his way to the green. But even so, the day was proving more fun than Beau had expected.

After lunch they headed back out on the course, by which time Beau's conversation with Robert had basically run dry, prompting his attention to turn to the others a little more. It was funny how with some people there was an instant connection, where you felt like you could never truly plumb the depths of what made them tick, and others…well, nada. Or should that be *non*? Smiling to himself, he selected a club for a segment that was going to be filmed by the club's TV crew, which would see which of the players had the longest shot.

"Got your tee?" Kris asked.

Man. With a hands up gesture for the cameras as the others chuckled, Beau groaned and said to the camera, "You'd think I'd know by now, right?"

Robert handed him one, and then Beau was forced to wait as his teammates moved to the mound for the tee-off. A drone was set up, its whirring noise slightly distracting as, one by one, the guys hit the golf balls to see how far they'd go. All this for bragging rights.

The cameraperson and Juliette, the team media person,

coached them to the best positions to stand and give a little introduction to what they were doing today.

"Bonjour," Johan said. "My name is Johan Tomasson, and I'm here with some of my teammates for the longest shot competition."

Johan went first, the defenseman with one of the most powerful shots in the league hitting the ball halfway down the fairway.

Next was Jake, who spoke to the cameras. "I don't think I'm going to win today. I just keep my eyes on the ball and aim straight down the fairway, hoping to clear those trees."

He swung, and his ball veered straight for the ditch, about half the distance of Johan's shot, to the amusement of the others.

"I've done okay today," Kris said to the camera, the humble words belied by his cocky tone. "I'm hoping for another straight ball today, so let's see how we go."

He smashed the ball, which went arcing up and out several hundred feet, landing the farthest, to the applause of the others.

Last was Beau. "Salut," he said to the camera. "I'm Beau Nash, goaltender for the Canadiens, and to be honest, I don't play golf much, so I have no technique. I might be able to hit it long, but not straight. Then again, I might not be able to hit it long anyway. I never know what I'm gonna get. I just walk up to the ball and hit it."

He placed the tee in the ground, positioned the ball, and did exactly that, watching as the ball sailed in the air, veering slightly to the left.

"Huh." He grinned, laughing as it matched Kris's shot to the applause of the others. "Who woulda thought, huh?"

Not Kris, judging from the sour look on his face as he chugged his water.

"Okay, so we might just get some more footage of you guys

chatting to each other," Juliette said as the other men took their positions to tee off. "Are you enjoying the day, Beau?"

"It's been really fun," he said, adjusting his cap, conscious the camera was still rolling. "The weather's glorious, and I haven't hurt any ducks today with my un-awesome golf skills."

"I'm glad to hear it," she said, smiling up at him.

Oh boy. Time to dim back his own smile. He nodded and glanced to where Bill was openly perspiring. "Hey, Bill, you okay?"

The man shook his head. "I don't feel too great."

"Excuse me," Beau muttered, then strode closer. "Bill? You wanna sit down? Want me to drive you back?"

"I should be okay. Just some indigestion."

Beau knew a hammer of fear. He lowered his voice. "Are you on heart medication at all?"

This earned him a glance up. "How'd you know?"

"My dad had heart issues. I know people have to be careful. Have you got your medication with you?"

Bill nodded, patting his trousers' right pocket. "The wife never lets me leave home without it."

"Good." Beau gently steered him to the golf cart. "Come on, let's get you back to the clubhouse."

"I don't—oh!" Bill clutched his chest and lolled, and Beau swooped in to hold him upright.

"Call nine-one-one!" Beau carefully lowered Bill to the ground, glad for the assistance of Robert and Jake as Kris spoke urgently into a phone. "Bill? Bill, can you hear me?"

Heart attack—what to do?

Loosen tight clothing. He unbuttoned the top few buttons of Bill's polo neck and drew his shirt out from his pants.

Heart medication. "Bill? I'm just going to get your heart medication, okay?"

Not what he'd expected to be doing, feeling about a stranger's pockets, but hey. He found a round container, drew it out, quickly read the instructions. "Someone help me get him up."

Johan helped ease Bill upright, and Beau's shaking fingers retrieved two of the pills. "Okay, Bill, I want you to swallow these. Open your mouth and tip your head back a little, that's right." Beau shoved in the two pills. "Now swallow. Hey, who's got water?"

Kris handed him a bottle, and Beau tipped it gently so Bill could swallow.

"You're gonna be okay, bud," Beau said as Bill's anxious eyes met his. "I'm praying for you, okay?" he said in a lower voice.

A jerk of Bill's head indicated he'd heard, and Beau and Johan continued to work to keep the man calm.

Jake offered to drive Bill back, the consensus of the others being that this would allow them to meet emergency services sooner. Robert offered to drive another golf cart to ensure any help already sent out would not be missed and to assist if needed. This propelled Johan to offer to join him, and with a quick scoop of clubs onto the back of the carts, they departed, leaving the remaining two sponsors talking awkwardly with Kris, Beau, the cameraman, and Juliette.

"Wow. That was unexpected." Beau released a huff of breath.

"You were amazing," Juliette said, sidling up to him. "You really kept your cool."

"That's what they pay me for," Beau said. A big part of a goalie's job was anticipation, brain ticking into high gear to work through the potential scenarios while keeping calm on the outside. A goalie's job was more than stopping pucks. It meant instilling confidence in the team so they'd trust him as a linchpin they could depend on. A goalie who lost his composure and was easily rattled proved an easy target for the opposition.

"So I guess that's that for the day," Kris said, his tone one of disappointment.

"You wouldn't really want to play with all that's happened, would you?" Beau asked.

"Hey, not everyone got the chance to show off their superman skills. Anyway, I was thinking of these two," Kris said, gesturing to the men who had paid big money to golf with them today. "There are still two holes to play."

"Let's ask them, hey?" Beau strode over to them, his question receiving two firm negatives, the joy in the day sucked away by Bill's medical scare. "Yep, that's us done, then."

"That sucks," Kris muttered.

Was he serious? Or simply addicted to golf? "I think I'd like to see how Bill is doing. Anyone else care to return with me?"

Somehow it was Juliette who ended up beside him on the cart, and he had to make polite conversation with her as he steered the cart back to the clubhouse.

"So, you've found a nice place to live?" she asked.

"Yeah." He briefly explained the rough whereabouts of his apartment complex.

"Oh, that sounds like it's close to some of the other guys." She turned to face him more fully. "You know we have a series on the players' cribs, where we go have brief visits to their homes. It's always fun for the fans to get to know the players a little more and especially good for newer team members to be seen to be involved and engaging with the fans by participating in such things. Not that I think we'll need to worry about you being popular with the fanbase," she said, her bare arm touching his. "It's obvious that you're already really popular with the fans, and after today's incident, well, that'll only get better."

"Today's incident?" he asked as he slowed the vehicle to a pause.

"With Bill. You knew we were filming all of that, didn't you?"

Whoa. "No. And I really don't think Bill will appreciate any of that being shown."

"Oh, don't worry. We'll keep it all tasteful, but it is a

wonderful chance to show the caring nature of our team and to highlight that we have some great new members."

"I still think you should check with Bill."

"Oh, we will." She got out, flashed him another smile. "Let me know if you want a tour guide for the city. I'd be really glad to help you out."

Yeah, he needed that like he needed a hole in the head. "Thanks. I'll let you know." Like, never.

He hefted the golf clubs in and deposited them with a club volunteer, and after enquiring about Bill, was pointed in the direction of a small room set up for medical needs. Outside, he found Robert, who gestured inside. "He's doing better, but the ambulance should be here any minute."

Relief flowed through Beau's chest.

"He said if you get here to go inside," Robert continued.

"Thanks."

Inside, he found Bill and a man dressed in a first aid bib. "Hey, Bill. How are you feeling?"

"Better." A grimace crossed his face. "I don't think I should've eaten so much at lunch."

Maybe not. "I'm glad you're feeling a little easier."

"The wife won't be happy," Bill said with a sigh.

"At least you're alive to see it," Beau said. "And I bet that makes her happy."

Bill laughed. "You might be right."

Beau wished him well, assuring him of his prayers, then retreated to where Robert still hovered near the door. "Hey, thanks for all you did. I'm sorry the day didn't work out as smoothly as you might've wanted."

"Are you kidding? Today has been one of the best days of my life. And yeah, sure, I didn't want this kind of thing to happen to anyone, but I appreciate knowing our team is in safe hands."

"Well, uh, good." What was he supposed to say to that?

Just then he noticed Paul Forges, one of the senior team

executives, was standing talking to Juliette. He beckoned to Beau, so Beau excused himself and moved to Mr. Forges. "Hello, sir."

"I've just been hearing some rather wonderful things about you, Beau."

"About what happened with Bill? Honestly, it was all of us," Beau demurred.

"That's not what Juliette was saying." He stretched out a hand, and Beau accepted it. "Bill Blaine is a good friend of mine. Thank you for looking out for him. I knew we were right to hire you."

"No problem."

But as Beau looked over Paul Forges's shoulder and saw Kris's scowl, he wondered if there might be a problem after all.

CHAPTER 5

"Maman, I don't feel too good."

Maggie paused in her washing up, wiping her hands on the towel near the sink as she strove for an appearance of calm she did not feel. "What kind of not good?" she asked carefully. She'd learned over the years not to suggest various forms of illness, as she suspected her son had inherited some of her mother's hypochondriacal tendencies, where each sniffle became the flu and each scratch would lead to infection. Of course, Alain's death had not exactly filled any of them with confidence regarding each other's health. But still, Maggie refused to put words in her son's mouth, even if she instantly knew fear whenever he complained of feeling ill.

"My tummy hurts."

Thank goodness her own mother was out tonight, the rare outing in honor of a friend's birthday. She'd nearly refused to go, seeing it was nighttime, but when Maggie insisted she go and have fun and that Denise would be disappointed if she did not go, her mother had given in. Maggie could just imagine the wailing that would ensue if Maman were here now.

"Is that from eating too much dessert?" Maggie asked him, ruffling his hair.

"I like ice cream," Noah said, putting his head on her waist as she stroked his back. "Do you think we can have ice cream at the crèmerie again?"

"One day," she promised.

He yawned, his little cat-like meow sound tugging out her smile. "I wonder if we'll see Beau again."

"I don't think so," she said. Beau had made it clear that he didn't want to see her. She wasn't stupid and had long ago learned how to discern a man's lack of interest.

"I liked him," Noah said sleepily.

Her heart stuttered. Okay, so while Beau might have made his feelings clear, she could not deny the fact that she, like Noah, had enjoyed the time with Beau. He was such a refreshing change from the men she knew, most of whom were either too old or too stiff in their manner to ever talk easily with her, let alone bother to talk to her son. But the very fact her son was still thinking about him, over two weeks after that encounter, did not bode well. She couldn't afford for Noah to fixate on anyone who was guaranteed to let them down, and she especially did not want him getting ideas about getting a new papa. That way heartbreak lay.

Maggie rubbed Noah's back and felt his body slump into greater ease. "Is your tummy still sore?" she asked.

"It feels better now," he mumbled.

Perhaps tonight he would be better off going without a bath and being put straight into bed. When he was like this, she often felt this was a better solution than trying to wrangle bath time and nightclothes. Her mother might think it poor parenting, but sometimes motherhood was a matter of making do, doing what one could to survive to get through another day.

She settled for a quick wipe of his face, and sure enough, not twenty minutes later he was asleep, a smile on his face after her reading of another of the Babar stories.

Maggie poured herself a wine and sat at the dining table, letting the stillness of the house absorb her. This was rare. Outside, only the occasional beep of the traffic intruded. Inside, she could appreciate the scents from their simple dinner, bringing further ease. She'd heard stories from some of the people she worked with about how they found comfort in a bottle, and she never wanted to be that person, unable to find peace without a drink. But there was something soothing about this, like the worries of the world were easing in this moment.

She was tempted to flick through her phone, but there was something restful about not being bombarded with social media posts that always dared her to compare her sad life to those far more glamorous and more fully lived. Sometimes she wondered if she was ever really living, or whether she was merely existing—whether what she did would ever measure up to the hopes and dreams she'd once indulged in. But then other thoughts would creep in, and she would remember to be thankful for the gift that was her son, to recall that if she'd chosen a different path—if she'd said non to Alain instead of oui—then Noah would not be here and her world would be so much smaller. Sometimes, looking back only meant regrets about her future.

It wasn't long before she finished clearing up and moved upstairs, going in to kiss Noah goodnight before making her weary way to her own bed. She got changed and snuggled in under the sheets, not even bothering to finish the book she'd started last night—a historical novel about a duke, which only fed dreams that would not come true. If she had to live in the real world, then she would at least choose to read things that didn't fuel impossible fantasies. Even if the reason she'd chosen the book was because the hero depicted on the cover looked not unlike a person she'd encountered recently who possessed a certain Viking charm.

Eyelids heavy, she soon dropped off to sleep, only to be woken several hours later by a crying sound. Noah. She pushed back the sheets and ran to his room. "Noah? Sweetheart? What's wrong?"

"My tummy hurts," he said.

She placed a hand on his forehead. He was hot. "Do you feel like you want to be sick?"

"Oui."

She helped him up and took him to the toilet, noticing her mother's bedroom light had now switched on. Maggie gave Noah a bucket and sat him on the toilet, where he intermittently groaned and cried and did unpleasant-smelling things that suggested he was very sick indeed.

"What's wrong with him?" Maman asked from the hall.

"I don't know." Maggie crouched in front of him. "Noah? Can you show me where exactly your tummy hurts?"

He pointed to his navel, and she knew a pulse of dread. He was too young to have appendicitis, wasn't he? "I'll be right back, sweetheart," she promised, quickly washing her hands then racing to find her phone. A quick Google search and she was staring at a page filled with information about childhood diseases. And there, a step-by-step outline on what seemed to be Noah's symptoms. Fear clutched her chest. "Maman?" She hurried back to the bathroom. "I think I need to take him to the hospital."

Her mother's eyes widened. "No. He can't be that sick."

"It might be appendicitis."

"It might not be, too."

"But surely it's better to know for sure. I'm going to pack a bag and take him there now."

"But it's two in the morning."

"And he's sick now." She moved back and changed, then quickly packed some essentials for both Noah and herself and returned to the bathroom. "Noah, I think we're going to have a little adventure."

"I don't want adventure. I wanna feel better."

"I know." She managed some quick wipes of various body parts, then drew him up in her arms. "We're going to go to see someone who can make you feel better."

"Don't wanna go," he said, sniffling against her neck.

"Come, darling. You'll feel better soon."

She took him downstairs and placed him inside her old car, thanking God it was summer and her car could easily start. Twenty minutes later, she was clutching him as she walked into emergency, her car a vomit-laden mess, Noah's tears drawing her own perilously close.

"He has a stomach pain," she said as the nurse rushed to check him over.

The next few hours were a blur of medical staff, questions, and testing procedures before further examinations revealed her worst fears: Noah would need an appendectomy.

"It is unusual in such a young child, but not unheard of," said the doctor, whose pressing on Noah's abdomen had drawn her son's screams. "He can have antibiotics until it's time for the operation."

They were fortunate to be admitted and given a room where Noah could rest under the watchful eye of the nursing staff, which meant Maggie could finally relax, slumped in a chair beside the bed. Fortunately, she'd packed Noah's favorite elephant toy, so she placed that beside him, and he instantly drew it into his arms and cuddled.

But try as she might to relax, worry still trod elephant-sized holes in Maggie's heart. How could she have missed the signs of his illness? Was she such a bad mother that she didn't know how to care for her child? Failure, an ever-present companion, taunted her as she tried to sleep.

She must've managed some rest, for when she next woke it

was to see daylight seeping past the blinds and a nurse checking her son's signs.

"Bonjour," the nurse said.

"Bonjour," Maggie echoed.

She learned that a doctor would be in soon and that the surgery would likely be scheduled this morning and usually took an hour. She was advised to go home and rest but refused. "He will worry if I'm not here when he wakes up."

"At least visit the bathroom now while he sleeps, d'accord?"

This advice she took, returning to find Noah as solidly asleep as he'd been before.

She glanced at her phone, realizing that in her rush last night she'd forgotten to pack the charger, and it was now very close to flat. But she needed to let her mother know and let work know she wouldn't be in today. There was enough battery to send two messages, then the screen blacked. The loss of her phone meant the loss of distraction, the loss of other ways of connecting with the world beyond the hospital room. It meant, too, that she had more time to think, to worry about what all this would mean.

How long did it take for a child to recover? Today was Friday, so at least she'd have the weekend to hopefully bring him home and then see what might happen. Her mother might be able to look after him, at least until he was well enough to return to school. But Maggie would need to go to work, to earn money. Thank heavens for Medicare, but there were still bills to pay. For a moment, she allowed herself to wonder what it would be like if Alain had lived, if she were not the sole parent and facing this constant struggle on her own, before dismissing the thought as pointless. Alain was gone, she was alone, and she *would* have to face this on her own. There was no point in wondering. She needed to get on with it.

The doctor made his appearance at nine, by which stage Noah was well and truly awake and complaining about being hungry. The doctor assured her that Noah's operation should be routine, to which she wanted to say "this isn't routine for us!"

It was another hour or so, then another nurse appeared and things were finally underway. Maggie accompanied Noah downstairs to the operating theater, where she was requested to stay outside and encouraged to perhaps go eat something in the cafeteria. This reminded her she'd need to negotiate the elevators and correct floors to retrieve her purse and suddenly weighted her with the sensation that this whole experience was too much.

Tears filled her eyes, and she stumbled outside to the waiting area. No phone. No wallet. No support. And all the while, insidious fear slithered around the facts the doctor had shared moments earlier. What if Noah was one of those poor unfortunate few whose appendix burst during surgery? What if he ended up with severe ongoing health issues because she hadn't realized his symptoms were as critical as they were? What if he needed ongoing treatment and she had to give up work to take care of him full-time? She breathed in unsteadily and scraped her fingers down her face.

High above, a TV screen flickered, and she glanced up at this box of normality. Normality for some, at least, as people in blue shirts played golf and laughed. She looked away, resentment rising within. Why was it some people got to live a carefree existence, while others had to struggle and stress without ever seeming to make headway?

She glanced back at the screen, her anger dissipating as her sleep-deprived mind struggled to make sense of the clues in the news story's images. A fat man. An ambulance. People talking. A shot of navy-shirted players. Beau being interviewed.

She watched for a moment longer, but the very remoteness of him, his happy, secure life so removed from hers, weighed upon her heart. He didn't want anything more to do with her, he'd made that clear.

She clenched her fingers. Why was she still thinking about that? Was it because of the emotions stirred by what Noah had said last night? Oh, she didn't care. She couldn't care. She needed to stay focused on what was, not on what would never be. Plunging her head in her arms and slumping onto her knees, she glanced out the window to the sunny skies above. *Could you give me a break, please, God?*

She might've dozed a little, because next she knew, a voice stole into her consciousness. A nice warm voice, one she'd heard before, which drew open her eyes.

"Uh, Maggie?"

She looked up, and with bleary, stress-fogged eyes, saw the man who had been on the TV just minutes ago standing before her. She straightened in her seat. Was this real life? Or was it some kind of fantasy?

Beau studied her, concern in his eyes, and her skin prickled with consciousness that she must look like such a mess. And that she hadn't brushed her teeth this morning. And that she hadn't brushed her hair since yesterday.

"Are you okay?" he asked.

The kindness in his question filled her eyes with tears, and she hunched away, emotion clogging her throat as she placed her hands over her eyes.

"Hey." She was vaguely aware that he sat near her and his hand was on her back, moving in soothing circles. "What's happened? It's Noah, isn't it?"

She nodded, wanting desperately to ask why he was here, like some visiting angel. Her attempt to speak was cut short by an urgent need for a tissue, which he seemed to recognize, as he handed her a square of folded cloth. She stared at it through blurred eyes. What kind of guy had a handkerchief these days?

"It's clean," he assured her. He'd angled his broad shoulders in such a way that she was shielded from curious eyes. Or maybe it was so he wasn't recognized. "And hey, I know it must seem weird, but Mom always insisted a gentleman be prepared, and I'm such a momma's boy I always do what she says."

The words *momma's boy* dug deep into her heart, spilling more emotion, and she turned and leaned into him. After a moment of emotional release, where she couldn't help but notice the way his soothing strokes on her back had become more of a hug, she realized that instead of snotting into his handkerchief, she'd managed to snot onto his shirt.

Dear heavens. Embarrassment ignited in a raging inferno, blazing across her skin, and she pulled back, trying to wipe vainly at the signs of emotion on her face, wondering if she should try to clean his shirt too. Poor man. Watch the Good Samaritan flee from the crazy lady. "I'm so sorry."

"It's okay."

Maggie shook her head. No, it wasn't okay. Noah was sick, she'd failed him as a mother, she was alone, and the only person who was offering to help she'd likely managed to chase away. How could she cope? Panic wound through her shame, clamping her chest, making it hard to breathe.

"Maggie? Tell me what's happened. Where's Noah?"

She drew in several unsteady breaths, then finally found enough calm to admit what had happened.

"He's in surgery now?"

She nodded, freezing as he grabbed her hand.

"Do you mind if I pray for him?"

"Please?"

He nodded, gentleness lighting his eyes, then he closed them, leaving her unable to avoid noticing the length and thickness of his eyelashes. "Dear God—"

Wait. He was praying aloud? She closed her eyes.

"—please send your healing mercies to Noah right now, and fill him and Maggie with your peace. Amen."

She blinked and glanced up, then felt another heart tremor

as his gaze pierced hers. She swallowed. "Merci." He smiled, and she had to swallow again. "What are you doing here?"

"I was due to visit some of the kids here when I saw you."

"What kids?" He didn't have family here, did he?

"The team has some connections with the hospital, and I like kids, so I volunteered. When I was last here I promised to visit one of the kids for his birthday, which is today."

Oh, he was such a good man. She inched back. "Then I shouldn't keep you."

A faint line furrowed his brow. "Are you okay? How long until you know how Noah's operation has gone?"

"They said it would be an hour or so." She glanced at her non-existent watch. She couldn't even pull out her phone to check. "Er, what's the time?"

He glanced at his watch. "Eleven thirty."

She knew a wave of dizziness, as if by finding out the time she had permission to be tired and hungry.

"Maggie?" he frowned. "When did you last eat?"

"Last night," she murmured.

"And your husband? Where is he? Have you got someone here with you?"

She shook her head, suddenly unable to speak. How to explain her husband lay in Montreal's largest cemetery, and her mother—oh non. She winced. Her mother.

"What is it?" he asked.

"I need to call Maman, but my phone died."

"Here." He pulled out a sleek black one. "Use mine."

"Are you sure?"

At his nod, she pressed the buttons and held it to her ear. "Maman?"

Her mother answered in French, forcing her to answer in kind and explain in far greater detail what had happened before.

"You had me so worried!" Maman continued in French.

"Poor little Noah. I almost didn't answer when I saw this number, so you're lucky I did."

"My phone died, which is why I'm calling you on this one."

"Who is with you?"

Maggie glanced at Beau. "My friend."

MON AMI.

Beau listened to the volley of French, his brain sluggishly slow to identify the phrases. But that one he understood, and the way Maggie looked at him, all uncertainty and doubt, as if she wondered if that was true, made his heart warm a little more.

She thought they were friends? He'd take it. He could do with more friends, and okay, there was something about this woman he hadn't been able to get out of his mind. Even with the open invitation he could see in the eyes of people like Juliette.

Maggie finished the conversation and handed the phone back to him. "Merci beaucoup."

"Everything's okay at home?" he asked. He didn't want to pry, but he couldn't help wondering about the husband or partner or whatever he was and why he wasn't here.

"That was my mother," Maggie said. "She's inclined to worry, so I'm sorry it took so long."

"Gonna send me broke, the length of that phone call," he teased.

"Well, er, thank you," she murmured, her gaze flitting away as she finger-combed her dark hair. She sighed. "I must look like such a mess."

"You look like you've had a big day, and it's not even lunchtime."

Her stomach growled, and her cheeks flushed again. "I'm sorry."

"For being hungry?"

He wondered whether it was acceptable to ask a woman in a relationship to eat with him—given food was an essential part of life—or whether it would be misconstrued. Likely misconstrued, given the flame-throwing gossip bombs he'd already witnessed in this city. And he'd only been here a month or so. But given he'd been holding hands with her—innocently, to pray, like he had with his sister in a similar situation back in North Carolina—and there was no way of knowing if the people on their phones here had snapped a pic of that already, maybe it was time to really clear the air.

"I can get you some food if you like, but are you waiting for, um, someone?"

"I'm waiting for the doctor to tell me Noah is okay, that's all."

"So no…husband, or boyfriend or anything?"

Her lips flatlined. "There's nobody like that."

Why did that big gush of emotion feel a lot like hot relief? He pushed it down and rose. "Want to get something to eat, then? We could go downstairs. You need to eat. Noah will be fine for the moment, and when he wakes up, he's going to need a mother who's alert and well. Let's get you fed, then we'll come back and it'll be time for Noah."

"But what about your little birthday boy?"

"Jacques isn't going anywhere." Poor kid. "And I didn't specify a time I'd visit. So if we go now, then I can catch him soon."

She nodded, then stood, chewing her lip.

"What?"

"I should get my purse."

"My treat. I'm all about finding out whether French-Canadian hospitals serve better food than what I've seen in hospitals before. You don't want to deprive me of that, now, do you?"

Her lips lifted.

"I'm taking that as a yes. Or should I say, a oui?"

A few minutes later they'd descended in the elevator, and he'd only had to sign two autographs. Sure wasn't the way he'd anticipated spending his day. After the news had broken last night about Bill's misadventure on the golf course, with an unnecessary spotlight thrown on Beau's involvement, he'd been determined to keep a low profile today, to visit Jacques and some of the other kids, then scoot home. But something about Maggie tugged at him to stay, and if the price was a few photos, well, he could live with that.

A scan of the food options saw him lean toward the Copper Branch. "Do you care what you eat?"

She shook her head. "I need caffeine."

"Or at least a power smoothie, huh?"

She rubbed her hands over her eyes. "Anything to recharge would be good right now."

"Sounds like you need the Edison Electric, huh? And an avocado toast?" When she hesitated, he added, "You picked a nice ice cream flavor the other day, so I hope you'll return the favor and trust me to pick for you this time. That a deal?"

"Okay."

He ordered those for her and a power bowl and smoothie for himself, paid, then they found a table. He'd seen some of these places around, and it was good to have healthy organic options to counter the delicious-but-carb-laden poutine and ice cream he'd tried.

And when the food arrived, he knew he'd found a winner. "This is good, huh?"

She nodded. "I didn't think you'd be the type to eat at a place like this."

"Let me guess. You thought I'd be all steak, catfish, and grits, right?"

"No." But her pink cheeks suggested otherwise.

"Don't get me wrong, I love my meat, but with training camp and medicals next week, I'm doing what I can to be careful."

He glanced up, saw the female staff member behind the counter give him a smile. He smiled back automatically, then wondered if that would be misread. Man, so many things he'd never needed to worry about before coming here.

"Mr. Nash?"

He glanced up. "Hey."

"Sorry to interrupt," the middle-aged man said, "but I wanted to say welcome to Montreal. We're glad you're here and part of the team."

"Thanks," Beau said. "It's great to be here. The city is beautiful and the people are really nice."

Somehow his gaze tangled with Maggie's at that last statement, which led to her ducking her head as awkwardness filled the space.

"Er, can I get a photo?" the man said. "For my son. He'll never believe I saw you here today."

"He's not in the hospital, is he?" Beau asked.

"No. I work here." The man flashed a laminated card identifying him as a medical aide. They took a selfie and the man shook his hand. "Pleasure to meet you. Looking forward to seeing you play, sir."

"Thanks. Have a good day," Beau said politely, waiting until the fan had moved from earshot before saying in a lower voice to Maggie, "Sorry about that."

"For being kind?"

"Yeah, okay. I'm not that sorry."

Her smile peeked out, and he felt like he'd scored a win.

"Thank you," she said, gesturing to the food. "I feel a little better now."

"You're welcome." Helping her out, sharing a meal, well, it was what Jesus would do, right?

"You're really nice to come here and visit sick kids like Jacques."

"I know." He glanced across and caught amusement curling her lips higher. Good. She needed to do that more often. And hey, he didn't mind knowing they had a similar sense of humor. "And you're really nice to consider another little boy's feelings when your own son is unwell."

As soon as he said that he wondered if she'd plunge back down into despair, but after a beat, she glanced up at him, her smile shy. "Jacques's feelings or your own?"

He blinked. Whoa. Wasn't expecting sassy tease from her. "Did you just call me little? I gotta tell you, I haven't been considered little for nearly twenty years."

"You're the one who called yourself a momma's boy."

"Wow." He slumped back in his seat and grinned. "Banter. I like it."

She shook her head. "I didn't mean it. I just felt sorry for you—"

"Whoa." He held up a hand. "You wound me, woman. I think it must be time to go, right?"

Her lips pulled up on one side, and he suddenly found himself wondering about her. She mightn't be married—did that mean she was divorced?—but that was no excuse to start thinking about what her lips would feel like. He barely knew her. Although, the more time he spent with her, the more he wanted to know.

Maggie pushed back her chair, and he could see she was looking a little brighter. And not just because of the little smudge of avocado on her chin. "Maggie? You may want to..." He mimed wiping his chin.

She copied, and her cheeks flamed brighter as she mumbled something he couldn't quite catch, which twisted compassion for her inside.

"Hey, I bet Noah will be excited to see you."

Her eyes widened. "You don't think he'll be out of surgery already?"

"If by that you're asking whether he'll be waiting impatiently for his momma, then no, I don't think so. It takes a while for these things to happen." He pressed the elevator. "That was my sister's experience, anyway. She said hospitals were one long waiting game."

Maggie nodded, the light in her face fading, making him wonder what experiences she'd had in hospitals before. Was Noah someone who'd experienced medical issues before? He hadn't struck Beau like that. Beau had been more struck by the kid's enormous brown eyes—much like his mother's, which seemed to offer a glimpse into her soul as they gazed into his.

The doors opened, they entered, and once again he was conscious of people staring, nudging each other, as he realized afresh just what a big deal hockey was in this city. He hoped his interactions with Maggie had been able to fly under the radar, or at least that people would have enough respect to acknowledge that perhaps there was a reason he was here in a hospital and that people might want privacy. It made him wonder whether, if he ever met someone he'd like to know more, there was any chance of keeping a relationship on the down-low, like Brent Karlsson had managed. But there was likely a world of difference between a long distance relationship between Detroit-based Brent and Australia-based Holly compared to two people trying to live under the radar in a big hockey town. Not that he and Maggie were a thing. But he couldn't help wondering where she stood with God so he could wonder if maybe one day they *could* be a thing...

The doors whooshed open, and they exited onto the children's surgery floor, where Maggie immediately made her way to the nurse's station. "Hello. I'm Maggie Joly, Noah Joly's mother."

"Ah, Mrs. Joly, we've been trying to reach you."

Maggie gasped. "Is he okay? My phone died, and I needed to eat, and—"

"He's fine, Mrs. Joly," the nurse said, glancing at Beau as he stood next to Maggie. "He's out of surgery and will be back in the room he was in before really soon."

"Oh, thank you," Maggie said, sagging.

Beau slid an arm around her back. "You okay?" he asked.

"I'm so relieved," she said.

And he was relieved that she was relieved. "Are you happy if I leave you to go visit Jacques?"

"I never expected you to be here. Of course."

He still lingered. "Would you mind if I came and saw Noah after my visit to Jacques?"

"Of course not. I think he'd be happy for the distraction."

He found out what room they'd be in and made his farewell, then walked down the hall to the oncology unit. And wondered at his reluctance to leave and what this might mean for his future.

CHAPTER 6

"Noah!"

The bed was wheeled in, and it took all of Maggie's control not to rush over to her boy and give him a huge hug. Noah was pale, his brown hair mussed, his eyes closed. From the lines on his face, it was obvious he was still in pain, so she didn't want her need for reassurance to trump his own need for rest.

"Everything went fine," the nurse said. "He's a little trooper."

"I know," Maggie said, reaching to hold his hand, to warm his little fingers in hers.

The nurse shared a little about what to expect, and Maggie nodded, but she would likely need things to be explained several times over for the instructions to have any way of sinking in. Thank goodness Noah was doing better. Thank goodness he was going to be fine. She didn't know how she would have managed if that were not the case. But thank goodness that Beau had been here too, waiting with her, distracting her from thinking the worst. Beau had proved to be an unexpected blessing, a man of patience and warmth and charm, whose kindness had helped her through this past hour. How unexpected. How surprising. But how unnecessary for her imagination to stir up things that simply could not be. It would be best to avoid thinking on this at all.

She stroked Noah's fingers, willing him to rest some more until he'd recovered, and glanced around the room. With no phone, there was little in the way of distraction from further worry save for the TV. She picked up the remote control from the side table and clicked it on.

The picture wobbled for a moment, then firmed and cleared. It looked like a soap opera, the kind of mindless TV that toyed with one's intelligence and the kind of thing she rarely watched, seeing as she was rarely at home at this time of day.

Whatever the storyline was—it seemed to consist mostly of long, earnest gazing—the drama cut to news headlines followed by an advertisement. An advertisement for Montreal's hockey team and next week's training camp festivities. She'd never been a big hockey fan and was likely the only one in the city—apart from her mother—who didn't know much about Montreal's hockey team, but she hadn't figured that Beau would be such a big deal that he'd score his own promo photo as part of the advertising. "Is he that famous?" she said aloud.

She chewed her lip. Was that why he'd received all those requests for autographs and photos? Was that what all Montreal players had to put up with every time they ventured outside their houses, or was Beau a special case? How difficult that must make it to have any kind of normal life.

The drama series returned, and she watched for a minute longer, but the endless repetition of what was obviously already known bored her, and she flicked it off. Just in time for the door to open and the doctor to appear.

"Ah, Mrs. Joly. I'm pleased to say that Noah did very well. You have a strong child there." He moved to the foot of Noah's bed, checked his charts, and signed something. "I think you can expect to see him wake shortly, but we always find it best to leave children to rest as much as possible." He motioned to the drip attached to Noah's arm. "This IV will be used for his pain medication and for fluids."

"When will he be able to eat?" she asked.

"I'd expect him to feel fine tonight, then tomorrow he should be almost back to normal. But he may need to stay a couple of nights until we're sure."

"Merci, doctor."

He nodded and exited, and she wished hard—again—that she'd thought to bring her phone charger. Her mother would need to know this, and now Maggie had spent so long here she was in dire need of a shower and change of clothes. She winced, once again wondering just how disheveled she must have appeared to Beau before. But he hadn't seemed to notice the poor state of her clothes or her makeup-free face and lack of brushed hair. He'd been too busy offering comfort, which said a lot in itself and drew new respect for the man.

A stirring from the bed drew her attention. "Noah! *Mon chéri.*"

Slow blinks, and then he focused on her. "Maman."

She grabbed his hand and carefully kissed it, taking care to avoid the IV line as she kissed up his arm to his neck, where she gently blew a raspberry. "How are you, baby boy?"

"I'm not a baby," he protested, but much more feebly than usual.

"Non, you are my big brave boy," she said. "The doctor said you did very well."

"My tummy doesn't hurt so bad now."

"I'm glad."

His blinks grew long, but his clutch on her hand firmed. "You'll stay, won't you, Maman?"

"Of course, darling. I'll always be here for you."

She watched him for a moment longer, but his eyes

remained closed, his grasp slacked, and her stroke on his face soon proved he was asleep. Poor love.

A snatch of sound at the door stole her attention, and she saw Beau standing there, awkwardness on his face. "Am I interrupting?" he murmured.

The sight of the big bear he held, which looked a little like the team mascot she'd seen on the news report earlier, drew softness to her heart. "He woke for a few minutes," she said, gesturing him to come in. "How did your visit to Jacques go?"

A smile curved the corners of his lips. "He was a little bit excited, let's say that."

If the little boy's reaction was anything like those of the far older fans she'd witnessed earlier, then that was an understatement. Another point in this man's favor. She nodded to the bear. "Is that a gift from a fan?"

"I guess you could say that." He brought it in to sit on the seat on the other side of the bed. "I gotta admit, I thought Noah was pretty cute the first time I met him, so I suppose it's fair to say that I'm a fan."

His words curled warmth around her heart. "That's very sweet of you."

"You know it." His lips quirked. "I don't do this for just anyone."

Sure he didn't. But something about the sincerity in his eyes dissolved her doubts and stifled the thought he did this just because he was a nice guy. For all Beau's jokes, she sensed a deep, authentic kindness to the man. She motioned to a spare seat, which he lowered his big body into.

"What have the doctors said?" he asked quietly.

"That he should be eating tonight and going home tomorrow or the next day."

"Well, hallelujah! That's a real answer to prayer, isn't it?"

"Yes." Oui. It was. Merci, *Dieu*.

"I'm so glad. Poor little guy." Beau's gaze rested on Noah for a moment longer before lifting to hers. "Hey, I was wondering if you'd mind me asking some others to pray," he continued.

Protectiveness drew her in on herself. "Like who?"

"My family. Some friends. My church."

Really? "I, er…" She didn't know what to say.

"Hey, no problem if you don't. I just thought—"

"No, it's okay. I'd appreciate it. It's just that I'm not used to people asking about praying for us."

"Do you have a church family who care about you?"

Non. She had a church she attended occasionally, but people barely spoke to her, let alone knew her name. "Not really."

"You should come with me sometime. I found this great church not too far from where I live. There are some families, so there are other kids for Noah to play with. The music is cool, and the sermons are applicable to life."

She couldn't imagine a sermon that might be applicable for life. Weren't all church sermons supposed to be dry and irrelevant and about ancient, dusty things?

"Look, I'll give you the address, so if you can make it sometime, I hope you do so."

"Thank you."

Somehow she found herself giving him her phone number so he could send her the address with a map link.

"And if it's all okay with you, I thought I could include Noah's name in the church prayers on Sunday. Don't worry, it's only his first name, and he gets included in a long list of other people, but it's a great chance to feel connected with others who care."

She thought about what he was offering, the friendship in his offer, and was touched. "Merci beaucoup."

"That means *thank you very much*, doesn't it?"

"You'll be a French expert in no time," she surprised herself by teasing.

He relaxed in his seat, stretching out his long legs. "The team is organizing for me and Jake, the other new guy, to get some French lessons, so I'm doing what I can to get a head start."

"You are competitive."

"Maybe. Just a little. Or a lot. But don't tell anyone."

His grin made her stomach curl. Non. She could talk with a handsome man without it meaning she was attracted. She glanced at Noah, who remained blissfully asleep. Glanced around for inspiration for further conversation. The television reminded her of the news she'd seen earlier and provided a chance to put the attention back on him, which might remove his unnerving focus on her. It had been so long since a man had paid attention to her. "I saw you made the TV news."

His brow creased then cleared. "Yesterday, that's right." His lips pulled to one side. "That wasn't exactly the way I expected the day to go."

"What happened?"

He explained about a guy in a golf tournament who'd had a suspected heart attack. "I didn't do much, but they're making it out to be bigger than it was."

"Because you're the new guy?"

His eyebrows rose, as if in surprise. "I hadn't thought about it like that, but I guess so." His lips twisted wryly. "They probably want to be seen as the team getting good value for money."

She wondered how much he'd been paid to come here, then reminded herself it wasn't any of her business. She glanced at Noah, shame filling her as she realized her attention had been focused on Beau and not her son.

Noah stirred again, his dark lashes lifting. "Maman?"

"Hello, darling." She shifted so he could see her better. "How are you feeling?"

"You're here."

As if that was enough, Noah closed his eyes again and succumbed to sleep.

How long would he rest for this time? Would she have time

to return home and change from these awful clothes? But what if he woke while she wasn't here? Could she trust the nurses to notice?

"What is it?"

That's right. Beau was still here. Her skin prickled in awareness that his gaze lay heavy on her. Why he bothered to remain was still a mystery, but it was nice to have someone to talk to so she need not bear the burden of her whirling thoughts alone. "I'm wondering if I should go home."

He nodded slowly. "That's probably a good idea. If you can get some rest—"

"Not to rest," she said. "Just to change. Let Maman know."

"Do you have a car?"

"Downstairs." She glanced at Noah lying blissfully still. "I'm just not sure if I should. What if Noah wakes up and I'm not here? I don't want him to be worried."

"The nurses here will pay attention."

"But it's not the same as seeing your mother." She bit her lip. "I just don't know what to do."

Beau's heart twisted as memories of his sister's plight melded with compassion for this child now. Before he could think much more, he said, "Would you like me to stay?"

He realized as soon as the words escaped just how awkward he'd made things. He barely knew the kid and wouldn't blame her for saying no. But something about this situation tugged at him, reminding him of his sister's trials, when all she'd wanted to do was sit by Joey's side—at the expense of her own health. Olivia had ignored the nursing staff's advice and Beau's and their mom's pleas to rest, his sister's stubborn devotion nearly costing Olivia her marriage. And while Beau could never fully understand the pain, he'd witnessed firsthand how necessary it was to step away, even if only for an hour or two. Knowing this, he wanted to help, clumsy as that offer to help might be.

Maggie was shaking her head. "Thank you, but no. You've done so much already, and I could never presume to ask for your help."

"You didn't ask," he countered. "I offered." He eyed her. Should he share about his sister? "I understand that you want to be here, and I know how hard this must be, but I really think, for your sanity's sake, that taking a break for a few hours will be good."

"But what if he wakes up and I'm not here?"

"Then the nurse or someone else will be here."

"But he doesn't know the nurses."

"He kind of knows me," Beau said, then put up his hands. "But hey, I get it. You don't trust me, you think I'm weird—and that's kinda true, because I am a little weird, or at least a bit unusual, according to some of my friends. But then, they don't understand that it sometimes goes with the territory of being a goalie. Goalies *are* a special breed, after all."

She eyed him uncertainly. "But why would you want to spend more of your day here?"

"I told you. I like kids. And, well, my sister had a sick son, and I saw the strain that caring for him placed on her, and I don't want you—or anyone else," he quickly added, "to feel like you have to do it on your own."

She still looked undecided, so he grabbed his phone and pressed his favorite contacts, then held it to his ear as he kept his gaze trained on hers. "I'm gonna get a reference."

"A reference?" Maggie murmured, clearly puzzled.

His call was answered. "Beau?"

"Liv. Hey, how're you doing?"

"I'm fine," his sister answered. "How are things with you?"

"Good," he answered, smiling as Maggie studied him. "I'm

here with someone who's questioning my ability to babysit a little boy called Noah."

"What?" Maggie's jaw dropped. "I'm not—"

"Put them on," Olivia commanded. "I'll let them know you're the best uncle ever."

"Here she is. Olivia, this is Maggie. Maggie"—he handed the phone to her—"this is my sister."

Maggie stared at the phone, then at him, before holding it to her ear. "Er, hello?"

Beau had to gauge what was said by the answers Maggie gave, and even then, the embarrassment blooming on her cheeks made him wonder if he'd pushed too hard. But his impulsive nature seemed to have a gift for such things today, and the way Maggie eyed him shyly before angling partly away made him wonder what else his sister had to say.

He didn't have to wonder for too long, as Maggie said goodbye and handed him the phone again. "She wants to speak to you."

He nodded. "Liv?"

"Who is she?" his sister hissed. "Have you found yourself a girlfriend?"

Man, he was glad this phone was not on speaker. "Maggie is a friend." And all woman. Not a girl. "So you put in a recommendation for me?"

"Of course I did," she said impatiently. "But you know I'm going to be telling Mom about this."

"I'd expect nothing less," he said with a grin. "Okay, thanks for putting in a good word. Talk soon. Love you."

"Wha—?"

He ended the call before he could hear any more of his sister's protest. Then was unsurprised to see her call back immediately. He flicked the phone to mute and glanced up. "So, you chatted with my sister. Did she convince you that Noah would be in safe hands?"

Maggie nodded, her eyes shining with what he suspected were unshed tears. "You're a really kind man."

"I know."

Just as he'd hoped, her quivering lips flicked into a smile. "You'd really stay? It'd only be for an hour. I'd rush there and come straight back, I promise."

"I've got nothing else to do, I promise." Apart from maybe arranging another online chat with Dan and some of the other Bible study guys tonight. And she wouldn't be that long.

Before anything else could be said, the door opened and a nurse came in. "Mrs. Joly. Oh, and…" She peered at Beau. "Do I know you?"

"Beau Nash. Family friend."

Her eyes widened. "You're not… Wait. *The* Beau Nash?"

"I'm sure there are others," Beau said easily.

"Of course. Well!" As if remembering the purpose of her visit, the nurse turned back to Maggie. "Oh, forgive me. I didn't know. I didn't realize."

"It's no matter." She slid Beau a glance, her eyebrows raised as if begging a question.

Beau nodded, and her shoulders relaxed as she returned her attention to the nurse. "I was wondering about taking a quick break back home. Noah has stirred a few times, but I didn't want to leave him alone." She gestured to Beau. "Mr. Nash has promised to remain here while I go, if that's okay."

"Well, of course, we would usually prefer it to be family members only, but given the circumstances, if Mr. Nash is happy to remain, then I can't object." The nurse shifted closer to the bed, studying the sleeping form. "He's a sweetie," she murmured before glancing at Beau. "I'll be sure to let them know a family friend is staying." She grinned. "I just might not mention who that family friend is."

"I'd appreciate it."

She dimpled, and Beau once more rued his too-quick smile that seemed to be an invitation for flirtation. Oh well.

Maggie turned to him, worry pleated in her brow. "You're sure you don't mind staying?"

As if he could say no to those big eyes. "We'll be fine. As long as you don't think Noah will mind." He shoved his hands in his shorts pockets. "I don't want him to be startled by a stranger. I mean, I'd hate to be considered forgettable, but then, he is pretty young."

"He remembers you as the nice ice cream man," she said shyly.

"In that case, we'll have plenty to talk about. Favorite ice cream flavors. Elephants." He gestured to the bear sitting beside him. "Other amazing creatures. Don't worry, we'll be fine." He leaned back in his seat, stretching his arms before clasping the back of his head. "Go."

With a quick press of her lips to Noah's brow and a quicker smile and mouthed *merci* for Beau, she exited, and he was left there, wondering at himself. Really? How had this happened? His sister was right.

He glanced at his phone. Three missed calls. All from Liv. Ah well. Might as well deal with the inevitable. He pressed the green button as she rang again.

"Finally!" Olivia exclaimed. "What the heck is going on?"

"I told you. She's a friend. She has a son who's sick here in the hospital, and from what I've gathered, she doesn't have much family. She needed to go home, so I offered to look after the kid for an hour or two."

"Are you serious? Are you sure she's not someone pulling the cute kid card, trying to trap you into a relationship?"

He laughed. "If she was anything like that, do you think I would've needed someone like you to back me up? If anything, I was the one needing to convince her to let me stay."

"But isn't he in the hospital? Aren't there nurses who can do that?"

"I remembered what it was like for you," he said quietly.

"Oh." She was silent for a moment, then, "Is she pretty?"

"Her name is Maggie," he said.

"Oh, forgive me," she said sarcastically. "Is Maggie pretty?"

"Pretty enough." Which was an understatement. "But not why I helped out today."

"Is this the same woman you had ice cream with the other day?"

The other week, but whatever. "I didn't know she'd be here. I was at the hospital anyway for a kid's birthday and saw her crying."

"Oh." A beat. "My soft-hearted baby brother."

"Two years younger than you doesn't make me a baby."

"Always has, always will. So go on. Tell me more."

"So you can tell Mom?" he asked cynically.

"Of course!"

"There's nothing to tell. Except I did say we'd pray for her son."

"Oh, you did, did you? Who is this *we*?"

"You. Mom. Me."

"Wow."

When she didn't say anything more, he knew a desperate temptation to ask. But then figured it might be best not to. He had no desire for his sister's surgical skills to be put to work on his motives. "Okay, well, I'd better go—"

"No! You can't just hang up. I need to know more."

"There's nothing more to tell," he protested.

"Come on. There always is. Like when are you going to see her next?"

"When she returns."

She blew out a noisy breath. "I don't mean that. I mean are you dating?"

"No."

"Is she dateable?"

His easy conversation with Maggie said yes, but he still didn't really know where she stood on the whole God relationship thing, so until he did, it was best to deflect. "Liv, have I ever mentioned that I don't really appreciate you intruding into my personal life?"

"You may have. Once or twice."

Times a million.

"But coming from the man who calls me to recommend his babysitting prowess, I think that's kind of rich. What did you expect, making such a call?"

Yeah. "That was a miscalculation on my part," he admitted.

"It's just that I haven't heard you go on about a girl in the longest time. I'm glad if you like her."

He liked her, sure, but, "It's not like that."

"Are you sure?"

Nope. But he sure as heck wasn't going to admit that to his sister. Who knew what she was going to say to Mom anyway? "I'm simply helping her out," he said firmly.

"Well, I don't know if I believe you, but I suppose I have to take your word. Is everything else going okay?"

The conversation moved to more mundane things, and he enjoyed the chat with his sister before her youngest child's cries could be heard in the background. "I'd better go."

"Say hi to Bailey and Bronson for me," he said.

"Hey, Bronson," he heard her call. "Come say hi to Uncle Beau."

Beau smiled as he heard the heavy breathing of five-year-old Bronson through the phone. "Hey there, Care Bear."

"Uncle Bobo," he thought his nephew said.

Beau was pretty sure his sister had been referencing Bobo the clown when she first suggested the name, but he didn't mind. If it made her happy, he'd put up with it.

There came more mumblings that made Beau wonder exactly why Olivia thought he could engage in any kind of conversation with his youngest nephew, but he played along as best he could, asking questions of Bronson and responding as best he could to what he could understand of the somewhat garbled conversation. He'd witnessed Liv's actions when unwanted telemarketers called and she would put her children on the line, and he hoped she wasn't doing that now as some kind of punishment for Beau not divulging every secret she clearly wanted to know. But then, there were no secrets. Only this strange tug of the heart that bade him to care, bade him to stay, and made him wonder—and okay, hope—that maybe Maggie might one day be someone he could date.

CHAPTER 7

"Hey, Maggie." Frederic stopped by her desk. "How is your son?"

She exhaled. How wonderful to be able to say, "He's fine." Gratitude ballooned in her chest as the events from the past three days paraded across her mind. After a second night in hospital, Noah had come home, and they'd spent the day yesterday snuggling, reading, and resting while she tried not to think about the enormous kindness of Beau.

Maggie had known her mother would peck her with a hundred questions should she admit to the identity of her mystery friend, so she'd glossed over it with "a friend I bumped into," which was pretty much true. Except calling Beau Nash her friend still seemed such a ridiculous exaggeration of the facts that she'd felt as much guilt as when Noah had sleepily responded to her mother with "ice cream man" when questioned about his time in hospital. As the previous encounter concerning this particular ice cream man had not been mentioned, Maggie felt some remorse at the secrets she kept. But some secrets were worth keeping, for they added peace, not stress.

"Maggie? Have you got the acceptances for the invitations?" Danielle asked.

Maggie nodded and shifted aside as Danielle came to look.

The Pumpkin Ball was in less than a month, timed to be the week after Canadian Thanksgiving on the second Monday in October. The response so far had been much as could be expected, and she knew from experience with organizing other events that not everyone replied with their acceptances in good time.

"Ah." Danielle's sigh held frustration. "When will people learn that it is only polite to RSVP? Don't they know we have to organize the catering?" She peered closer at the screen. "Good to see we'll have some celebrities appearing."

The Gardens' Pumpkin Ball might not pull the younger crowd of TV, film, and music, but there were enough people who attended who liked to be seen as supporting worthy causes. And if it helped provide the sheen of environmental credentials for some companies, then c'est la vie. People's motivations weren't Maggie's concern. Apart from boosting the guestlist, her main objective was to work on the display that would help set the mood for the night.

"We do what we can with promotions, but it is hard to see our efforts not meeting with the response they deserve."

True.

"I don't suppose you know anyone famous, eh?" Danielle asked Maggie, a little smile on her painted lips.

Maggie shook her head, ignoring the inner voice that begged to leap up and say *Si tu savais! I have Beau Nash's number in my phone.* Admittedly, it was because he'd sent her the information about the church as he'd promised, along with a short message that said he hoped Noah was doing okay. Even though they had been unable to go to the church service—Noah needing to spend the day quietly at home—she'd known an obligation to reply and had responded with a simple *Yes, thank you.* She'd thanked him so much on Friday that she now felt embarrassed. How much gratitude could one show before it became excessive and embarrassed the recipient as much as the giver?

She still could scarcely believe someone as popular and famous as Montreal's new goalie had bothered to stop, let alone help as much as he had. Upon returning to the hospital the other day, after fending off her mother's concern and having the world's fastest shower, she'd discovered Beau learning some French words from her son. Apparently he'd mastered *éléphant*, *hôpital*, and *glace* and was entertaining Noah and the nurse with his awkward expressions of introduction. She'd stood in the doorway, wondering if she should've taken an extra few minutes to style her hair instead of shoving it into a ponytail. Especially when the nurse looked way too young and carefree as she smiled at him. Not that she should've been thinking on that.

"Maggie?" Danielle's voice intruded into her memories.

"Pardon?" Oh, she *really* needed to stay focused.

"After his visit here, I will admit to following your goalie. Did you know there was a picture of him at the hospital last weekend?"

Maggie's mouth dried and she shook her head.

"Apparently he's quite the saint, visiting those poor children. I saw a picture of him with a woman who looked a little like you." Her gaze sharpened, not unkindly. "What hospital did you say you took your son to?"

She swallowed. "The Children's Hospital."

"Mmm. That is where he was. Curious, is it not?"

Maggie managed a shrug, sure it wouldn't be wise to answer honestly. How could she admit all that had occurred without it seeming more than it was? Who would believe that the man on TV ads and billboards was the one who'd told her son stories about a man with the same name as Noah and a boatload of animals? Would anyone believe that? Non. She scarcely believed it herself.

"I fear I've lost you again," Danielle chided. "Distracted, are we?"

"Forgive me. I have been a little distracted with thinking about my son."

"That is very understandable," Danielle said sympathetically.

Maggie released a silent breath.

"But if you were to see your hockey friend again, it could perhaps be a good chance to help promote the ball, would you not agree?" Her eyebrows lifted. "By inviting him to come?" she explained, like she thought Maggie a slow child.

"If I *were* to see him, but I do not think I will," Maggie said, shaking her head.

"But that is twice now, non?"

Three times. But she was not about to admit to that. "Shall I send the list to you?" Maggie asked, desperate to divert the subject.

"Hmm, perhaps we will wait until we have a few more names. But of course"—her eyes twinkled—"if anyone particularly famous decides to come, you'll let me know straight away, n'est-ce pas?"

Maggie nodded, smiling weakly. As if she'd ever see Beau again. And even if she did, as if he'd agree to help her in this thing. He might be good-natured, but no way was she going to press this tentative friendship a fraction deeper than it needed to go. She was already neck-deep in obligation and had no desire to fall into more. Really, she'd be better off escaping the whispers of speculation and getting some fresh air.

After retrieving her tape measure and phone, Maggie went outside to the glasshouse where the pumpkin display would be held. In addition to the ball, the yearly pumpkin display would see people from all over Quebec decorating pumpkins and gourds in an array of shapes and sizes for the chance to win certificates and awards. The prizes were more for glory, consisting mostly of annual passes to Espace pour la vie, the sites that included the Botanical Gardens, the former Olympic site, and the Biosphere closer to downtown Montreal. But that seemed enough incentive for children and adults of all ages to decorate pumpkins as everything from Cinderella's carriage to oyster shells containing pearls. It was a highlight and something she enjoyed doing with Noah. She'd brought him here last year, and they'd had great fun making an elephant from a grayish gourd. And while she couldn't help him this year, she wondered if Maman would consider helping him. The more displays the better, especially with the ball approaching soon.

Fresh air and renewed focus helped invigorate her enthusiasm for the event, and she chatted with Renaldo, the glasshouse manager, as she took measurements.

"Provided the little children don't try and touch all the exhibits and run into the gardens, it should go well," she said.

He nodded, but his expression was tight. "As long as we do not see a repeat of earlier today."

"Why? What happened?"

"A little boy, he could not be much older than eight, had the insolence to stomp on a frog."

"What?" Horror and disgust heated within. "How awful!"

"I know. I remonstrated with the parents, but the father seemed to think it a fine joke."

Her fingers clenched. "I hope you kicked them out."

"I tried, but I was so shocked and angry that my English was not good, and his French was non-existent, so I couldn't make myself understood."

"That's terrible. When was this? Are they still here? Should I call security?"

"It was a little while ago now. I think I heard them say something about going to the Terrace Café."

Tightness in her stomach rose to her chest, and she knew a

furious desire to go and find them and give them a piece of her mind.

"You would not let your son be so cruel," Renaldo continued.

"Of course not. I cannot understand any parent permitting their child to get away with such a thing!"

"Some people have hard hearts," Renaldo said. "They do not appreciate nature for what it is."

"It's so sad some people are so self-centered." She exhaled. She needed to calm down. Getting angry was not going to help. She forced her fingers to straighten.

Renaldo shook his head. "I do not understand the tourists who come here and think we're obliged to speak their language. Not when they're here in our part of the world. Who do they think they are?"

She knew renewed appreciation for those who tried to learn the language, even if their accent might render words a little peculiar. At least they—okay, Beau—tried.

"As for those who have no care for what we do here—pah!"

Maggie nodded, asking for a brief description of the culprits. "I shall keep an eye out, then."

"You speak English much better than I do," he said. "But I suspect theirs is a culture that disregards women," he warned.

"And I suspect they need to learn that cruelty to animals is not something we overlook here." She retrieved her walkie-talkie and put a call out to security, describing the incident and alerting workers to be on the lookout for the family.

It wasn't long before someone reported that the family was indeed at the Terrace Café. Maggie repeated the clothing descriptions to Renaldo, who nodded, confirming it was them.

"I'll get security to attend, and we'll make sure they're never admitted again."

He nodded and saluted.

She drew in a steadying breath, hurrying across the grass to where the café overlooked the landscaped gardens. Here were all manner of lovely plants and trees to create a sense of peace and tranquility, emotions that felt far from those writhing through her chest. How dare people treat the creatures of this garden so abominably? Did they not know that every creature had a special purpose, a role to fill? From the insects that helped pollinate to the birds, amphibians, and small mammals that eliminated pests and weeds, every small creature had a God-given function and role. And while the loss of a frog might seem negligible to some, its loss would impact the frog's habitat. But more importantly, the callous cruelty of the incident, the lack of remonstration from his parents about such things, meant the little boy would likely progress to other incidents of torment. A squashed frog that was laughed about could become a tortured cat which could become a bullied child.

She glanced up, and sure enough, there was the little boy—not so little, judging from his wide girth—on the terrace, oblivious to other diners as he rushed and yelled at swooping birds while two adults she presumed must be his parents ate their food unconcernedly. She watched as a waitress spoke to the family, who seemed to ignore her. The waitress then moved to speak to the boy, who made a rude gesture and laughed as the young woman backed away.

Enough was enough. *"Excusez-moi!"*

Just as before, the family ignored Maggie, and she felt the frustration mount. She moved across to the terrace steps and strode over to where the family ate. "Parlez-vous français?"

The woman glanced up but said nothing. The man kept eating.

Maggie tried again. "Do you speak English?"

The man's black eyes flicked to her. Apparently he understood English, then.

"You need to tell your son to stop teasing the birds."

The man lifted his paper napkin and smeared his face before

throwing it on the table. She just knew he would not be one to put his rubbish in the trash.

Very well, then. She moved to the boy, frustration building up inside. "Stop!" she screamed.

He jumped.

"You need to stop doing that," she said in a still-loud but slightly calmer voice. She willed herself to be pleasant. "No more. Leave the birds alone."

The boy glanced at his parents. His father rose, his black eyes seething, before yelling at her in a volley of such heavily-accented English she could barely understand.

Chest heaving, she moved closer to the trio. "In this country, we do not treat animals or birds or frogs cruelly. You must leave," she said, pointing to the door.

The man said something to the boy, who sidled up to his mother. Sure enough, the remains of their lunch stayed on the table as they stood.

The man repeated his volley of invective, this time concluding by spitting near her feet.

She flinched before fresh disgust at his actions drew new rage. Her chin rose. "How dare you? Who do you think you are?"

He muttered something, but the raging pulse in her ears blocked all other sound.

"I don't care who you are or where you're from. It's unacceptable. You must leave."

"You say this because I'm foreign," he said, his English suddenly improving.

"I would say this to anyone who came here." She straightened. "In this country, at these gardens, we do not tolerate such behavior."

"Do you know who I am?"

"I don't care who you are," she said again. "You are not welcome here."

She knew she was sailing close to dangerous territory and dropped her voice to explain. "Such behavior is not welcome here," she clarified. "Here at the Gardens, we do not tolerate people who are bullies. Here at the Gardens, we seek to provide people with a tranquil, peaceful place to escape to. Your actions and disregard for the wildlife here and your contempt for the staff who work here are intolerable. You must leave."

"No."

"If you do not leave, I will call the police."

That last word galvanized the man's wife into speech, which seemed to frighten the boy, too. "Papa, papa!"

Her pulse slowed at the boy's cry—perhaps he wasn't a little monster in the making but simply someone who had not been taught appropriate boundaries—only to ratchet up again as the man stepped closer to her. She forced her feet to not retreat, even as his breath smelled of the beer he'd consumed and his eyes flashed as his gaze traveled down and up her body. Bullies fed off fear, she'd always told Noah. She needed to hold her ground.

"You will be sorry," he said, eyes glittering.

"I already am," she said. Sorry the man had thought to come here today. Sorry for his lack of parenting skills. "Sorry for your lack of personal boundaries that make you think cruelty is entertainment and intimidation is the way to get ahead in this world."

He sneered before spitting again. Only this time he didn't miss. This time it landed on her shirt.

THE RESTAURANT WAS FILLED with wood paneling and soft chatter. Beau glanced around the room before looking back at his dining companion. He'd been surprised to meet Brigitte on his exit from the hospital last Friday, although now he thought about it, it shouldn't have surprised him at all. But what had surprised him even more was her invitation to dinner that night.

"Are you free for dinner?" she'd asked.

He had been, but the day's events had also left him tired, and all he'd wanted to do was go home and puzzle out the events that seemed to have burrowed deep inside his heart.

"I'm sorry, what was I thinking? Of course you'd be busy," Brigitte had said with a laugh. "How about tomorrow night?"

That one he'd more easily refused, having plans already to eat with Gabriel and his wife as part of a "welcome to the club" kind of meal.

But when Brigitte had asked him for Monday night, adding, "Come on. It's just dinner. Don't worry, I won't be putting any moves on you," he'd found himself unable to manufacture an excuse, even though her persistent invitations felt a lot like a move. So he'd said yes. Which was why he was here today. Eating. Pretending to have a good time, even though he knew he wouldn't do this again as, apart from an interest in the welfare of the children in the hospital, they had zero in common.

"It's good, no?"

Whether Brigitte referred to the meal or the restaurant or the night, he had no clue, but he nodded anyway. The food was good, as was the restaurant, and after the tension he'd witnessed at his last meal out—Gabe and Claudine were having issues, it seemed—it was nice to eat and not feel the undercurrent of tension.

Brigitte placed her napkin on the table and excused herself. "I'll be back in a little moment."

He nodded and sipped his mineral water, eyeing the door. He hoped she didn't want dessert and he could get an early night. Which made him sound like a grandpa, liking to be tucked in by ten. At least he had the excuse of training camp later this week as a reason to exit early.

Around him, whispers and smiles and nods in his direction made him uncomfortably aware that he was likely the subject of many conversations, so he slid his phone from his back pocket, scrolling through until he found his latest trick to fitting in to the city and team.

Insider's Montreal was a YouTube channel he'd recently subscribed to, which explained in two-minute clips some of the lesser-known news items, places, and events that helped him understand this city a little more. Gabe's wife had recommended it, saying the fact it was in English and French had helped others when they first moved here. Beau hoped it might help him feel like he'd have more to say to the guys as he worked hard to fit in.

He found the English version and pressed play, and even though it was on mute, the headlines summarized what each twenty second clip was about. His heart pricked at the mention of Jardin botanique, then prickled more when he recognized the woman in the footage.

He watched as the video from a phone camera showed Maggie confronting some guy who looked like he wanted to hit her. Protectiveness surged. What had happened? He wished he could play this aloud. The clip moved on, but he paused, looked up, and seeing no sign yet of Brigitte, rewound it to watch again. This time he put the volume on and held it to his ear like he might be listening to a call.

"A confrontation today at the Botanical Gardens has gone viral after a visiting family accused a staff member of racial discrimination and bullying. Park management refused to answer questions, despite reports the police were called in, no doubt concerned with how this will impact next month's popular Pumpkin Ball, one of the Gardens' biggest fundraising events of the year."

His heart tightened. What had happened? From what he'd seen of Maggie, she would never harm a flea, let alone racially vilify a family.

Should he call her? His heart thumped yes. But calling up one woman while on a date with another wasn't exactly cool. He settled for sending a text instead. ARE YOU OKAY?

He drummed his fingers on the table, waiting for her answer. He hadn't been invested in tonight's date with Brigitte before; now he was agitated and just wanted to leave.

He checked his phone but had to slide it away when Brigitte reappeared.

"Sorry about that," she said with a smile before glancing at the phone. "Phone call?"

"Just checking some things."

She nodded. "Would you like dessert?"

"I can't," he said as apologetically as he could. "Training camp won't let me. Which reminds me, I probably should go soon."

"Oh." Her face fell. "Of course."

"But tonight has been fun," he said.

"We should do it again sometime," she said eagerly as he signaled the waiter for the check.

How to answer, knowing that he'd disappoint her but also knowing he needed to speak the truth like the gentleman his mom had raised him to be? "I think I'll be rather busy once the season starts," he said as kindly as he could. "Although, I've enjoyed getting to know you. It's always good to meet people you can call friends, don't you agree?"

Her mouth fell, then clamped shut as she nodded.

Phew. The waiter delivered the check, and Beau signed it, adding a tip, then said to Brigitte, "Can I walk you to your car?"

She jerked her head no, and Beau's chest kneaded with regret. But how else was he to let a woman down gently? He wouldn't lead her on. Although, he suspected that the number of phones out in his general vicinity meant he'd be featuring in a few more gossip columns. Maybe he'd better chat to his Bible study friend Jai Mullins and find out how he'd managed featuring in last year's online fan forums.

Beau helped Brigitte with her coat and thanked her again, aware that such things and paying for the meal certainly made it look like a date. But the lack of God relationship in common meant there could never be any future there, and the lack of connection or spark meant he'd never chase a more personal relationship with Brigitte, even if she believed as he did.

And as he drove home, his car filled with prayers, he wondered about the woman God had for him and where she was—and how long it would be until he could send Maggie a text message again.

CHAPTER 8

"**You're** a meme, Maggie."

A meme?

"Do you even know what a meme is?" Danielle continued.

Maggie shook her head.

"There was a picture of you shaking your finger at the man, like some old schoolmarm dealing with a naughty schoolboy."

"I never meant for it to get like this," Maggie said quietly.

"And yet it has," Danielle said with a sigh. "Do you know how much media I've had to turn away?"

"I don't understand how this has turned around on us so quickly," Maggie said. "That man was the one in the wrong. He was virtually encouraging his son to stomp on our frogs. And then he spat at me!"

"I know. But unfortunately—or perhaps fortunately—we don't have footage of that. Only of you speaking to them." Danielle's mouth tipped up. "I'll admit I did like what you said. It was both true and sounded very girl-power. But of course, I'll deny it if anyone asks."

"Of course." Maggie's spirits lifted a little. Perhaps others might see it like that too.

"I really don't think we can expect others to see it like that, however."

Maggie's heart sank.

"It's not like we can explain things easily. And especially now..." Danielle slumped behind her desk.

"Especially now what?" Maggie shook her head. "You know that what they were doing was wrong. I said nothing that wasn't true."

"It might've been true, but it turns out that Mr. Lee is the new vice-chairperson of one of Montreal's most important tech companies—one which we had been in negotiations with as a chief sponsor for the Gardens."

Oh non.

"He and his family had apparently just flown in and are getting acclimatized to the city. This was not exactly the welcome they were expecting."

"I wouldn't have thought that behavior to be considered acceptable in any country," Maggie said, bristling. "How could they expect to behave that way in a country that is new to them?"

"I'm sorry, Maggie. I think it's best that you don't venture out into the gardens for the rest of this week. You should probably stay inside, where you're less likely to be accosted by members of the public."

"I haven't been accosted—"

"I'm afraid the comments on social media mean it's likely you will be."

"Are you serious?"

Danielle flicked a long strand of hair behind one ear. "Unfortunately the recording didn't show all of the encounter, so I'm afraid it came across as favorable to Mr. Lee, which is why there are so many comments from people on social media making things very difficult." She exhaled heavily. "Keyboard warriors without a clue."

"I'm sorry this has become so difficult."

"I know. But I'm afraid the Gardens needs good PR, especially with the ball coming up. I've sent an email to all staff detailing some of the situation, so everybody knows not to speak to the media and especially not to mention your name, but I'm afraid with your picture on the website, it'll only be a matter of time before people piece it together."

"Can we change my picture on the website?"

Danielle brightened. "Of course. Why didn't I think of that? Do it now."

It felt wrong to be hiding her identity when she wasn't in the wrong, but Maggie obeyed, accessing the program whereby they could easily update the website and deleting her picture from the communications page. She hated how this made her feel, like her hard work was for nothing simply because somebody had the nerve to complain.

"I wish we could find someone who had filmed the entire exchange," Maggie muttered. "Or release a statement explaining more of what really happened."

"We could release something, but the Board of Trustees may think they need to be involved, and I'm reluctant to give this any more air. Let's just hope there'll be something new that will draw people's attention so they forget this."

Maggie nodded. So would she.

But deleting her picture seemed to have come too late, as her work inbox flooded with requests from media accompanied by some not-so-pleasant emails from sponsors and people who belonged to the Friends of the Gardens. Soon her phone began buzzing with dozens of calls, and her message box filled with messages from random numbers she didn't know. And while she was tempted to reply to some of the requests, as they offered to tell her side of the story, others were filled with such vitriol her heart trembled.

She flicked over to Facebook, which held a bunch of other messages and comments, most of which had to do with her being racist. She switched her settings to private, thankful she rarely used the platform save to keep up with some old school friends, then clicked over to where the Gardens' social media accounts lay. She winced, as again the keyboard warriors had come out to play. While most were full of righteous anger at the denigrating of visitors, some were applauding her bravery for being a female willing to stand up to someone they recognized as intimidating. She appreciated their comments, but deleted those along with many others, including some that had linked to the video, which she was sorely tempted to watch again.

She glanced at Danielle, who had resumed her seat and was wearing headphones as she spoke with another Friend of the Gardens, who seemed decidedly *un*friendly, from the side of the phone call Maggie could hear. So, taking a leaf from Danielle's book, Maggie grabbed her own headphones and watched the footage again.

Her teeth clenched as she remembered the fear she'd felt, the words he'd spewed, and the hate he'd shown. Why the person filming hadn't shifted to include the man's spitting she did not know. She thought back, calculating where this person had been standing. How had the footage been leaked anyway? Had Mr. Lee paid them? What did any of this gain for him? She didn't think it would reflect on his business in any positive light, and it would certainly not draw sympathy from females.

Her phone buzzed again, and she grabbed it to turn it off. Maybe she should delete her number. As she moved to power it off, she glanced at the message. But this message was from a number she'd seen before. And this message was the same as yesterday's. Now, as then, she had no idea how to answer. The enormity of the three simple words had ricocheted through her heart, sparking so many questions. Beau knew? Or had he accidentally sent this message to her? What must he be thinking of her? Why was he asking about her wellbeing like he was her friend? She'd ignored it yesterday. But now she stared at the message again.

Are you okay?

Her vision blurred as she considered what to do. Reply and possibly draw Beau into this mess? Continue to ignore him and ensure she would not hear from him again? She didn't know what to do. She didn't know what to do about so many things.

But when her phone buzzed with a reminder of his message, her fingers replied without her permission.

No.

She dropped the phone on her desk and stared at it, wondering if he'd reply. Which was stupid. He had training camp starting tomorrow, and he'd be so busy that he'd never have time to—

Her phone started ringing. Breath suspended. It was him. She swallowed. Glanced at where Danielle remained oblivious on her call, then picked her phone up and pressed Answer.

"Hello?"

"Maggie?"

"Beau?" she said tentatively, although she didn't know anyone who said her name in quite the same way, with that endearing bounce to the second syllable that made her smile.

"Hey, I saw that video posted online. I'm so sorry. How are you doing?"

"Not too great, actually." Her voice was raspy.

A beat. "I'm really sorry. Is there anything I can do?"

Apart from stop the noise and haters? "You're very kind, but no."

"You sure?" he said softly.

The sincerity and care in his voice slid under her defenses, filling her eyes with unwanted tears. "I don't know," she managed to whisper.

"Do you need a friendly face?" he said.

"My boss is really understanding."

"You're at work, then?"

"Barely," she admitted. "I mean, I'm here, but I've been advised to stay indoors. Apparently there are some people out there who don't like me very much."

"Have you got time to talk?" he asked.

"Don't you have things you should be doing?" she asked. Then, conscious it sounded rude, added quickly, "Not that I don't appreciate your call. I do. I really do. But I don't want to hold you up, as I know you must be busy, especially with training camp coming up so soon."

He chuckled. "Here's the thing. I've done my training for the day, and I don't really know too many people in the city, apart from my teammates. And I'm gonna be spending a lot of time with them anyway, especially later this week, so I really am at your disposal, if you want me to be."

She nearly choked. Would anyone ever believe she had the great and famous Montreal goalkeeper saying such things? She barely believed it herself. She slid a look at Danielle. Still busy. "That's really sweet of you," she murmured, "but I don't want to impose."

"Impose away," he said. "I'm really happy for the distraction."

Emotions that had risen at his earlier words dropped. She was a distraction?

"Not that I mean it to sound quite like that," he said quickly. "I mean, I think you are distracting, and— Hey, ever feel like your mouth is bigger than your brain?"

Oh, mets-en! But somehow his honesty endeared him to her all the more. He thought about her? What were the chances? A smile released, the first one all day. "I think everyone has moments like that. Especially everyone who has seen that video," she added wryly.

"Some people are dumb," he said. "Others of us believe there was way more to that story than what was shown."

"Thank you," she whispered, her voice wobbly.

"Look, you get a lunch break at some point, don't you? Want to meet somewhere?"

She rose, peering out the office windows. Looked like the media that had been there before had been called to something more pressing. Maybe she could get away.

"Or is it easier for you if I come there?"

She gulped. And have him seen by Danielle? Possibly questioned and dragged into an invitation to the Pumpkin Ball? She'd hate for him to think she'd used this friendship—it was a friendship, right?—in that way. Oh, this was hard. Too hard.

"I'd love to know how Noah is doing," he pleaded.

"You play dirty," she said, even as her heart lifted at the words.

"I'd like to see you," he said. "And hey, I'm prepared to do whatever it takes. But I do want to know how Noah is doing."

God bless the man. "If you come to the main entrance at twelve, I can meet you there."

"Great!" His voice sounded like sunshine. "See you then."

"See you then," she murmured before ending the call.

Maggie glanced across to where Danielle was looking at her.

"Who was that? Anyone to be concerned about? Do I need to prepare a statement or something?" She frowned. "You're not going to be talking to any media people, are you?"

Maggie shook her head. "It was, er, just a friend." Her cheeks grew hot.

"A friend?" Danielle raised a plucked eyebrow. "Does this friend have a name?"

"It was Beau," she admitted in a small voice.

"Beau? As in Beau Nash?" Danielle's eyes widened. "*Franchement?*"

Maggie nodded.

"He's your friend?"

Another nod.

"Wow!"

Maggie wasn't sure if that was shock or admiration in Danielle's eyes.

"That's amazing."

Sure was.

"And he's coming here? At twelve?"

How much of her phone conversation had Danielle heard? "Oui."

"Très bien." Danielle nodded decisively. "You can meet him and then introduce him to me, and we'll see what we can do to get this situation sorted. I'm not going to let a little frog-stomping spitter of a man spoil all the hard work we've been doing here." She smiled. "Especially when we have a much bigger man on our side."

"Danielle," Maggie protested. "I don't want Beau to feel obliged—"

"Maggie, if the man insists on seeing you, you're going to do your best to be honest and tell the truth about your side of the story. And if that leads to things improving here, then that's just a happy benefit, isn't it?"

Maggie offered a weak smile. "Si tu le dis, oui." If you say so.

But she couldn't help wondering just what Beau would say.

OKAY, SO BEAU may have stretched the truth a little. He did have other things he could be doing. He could be writing emails to his MPFG sponsor children in the Philippines, part of the charity organization that his friend Mike had fronted for the past few years. He could be sending an email to his sister or his mom or his agent. He *could* be. But he'd much prefer to visit the Gardens and speak with Maggie again.

Had it really only been four days since he'd seen her? He swapped his smelly workout gear for something nicer. It'd felt much longer. And he hadn't lied. He did want to know how Noah was doing after his hospitalization. And apart from a simple response saying he was fine, she hadn't replied again. And now he *really* wanted to know how she—and Noah—were doing.

He locked the door, got into the elevator, and descended to the parking garage, even as he questioned his reasons for going. Sure, it was one thing to call, but it was quite another to visit in person, and he really didn't want to be sending the wrong message. But something about Maggie and her son had buried deep in his heart, much deeper than any woman in recent years had managed to. And while he'd prayed about God's direction, he didn't really feel any sense to *not* go...

He negotiated Montreal's busy morning traffic and soon was pulling up in the front parking lot of the Gardens. A glance at the clock revealed he was still a few minutes early. No problem. He tugged out his phone and flicked through his social media feed, liking and sending emojis as necessary. He wasn't on Facebook much, keeping it to only family and those friends he really wanted to stay connected with, but his agent had always encouraged him to post more of his funny, relatable stories on Instagram, so he tried to do this on a semi-regular basis. But he didn't feel like being funny now, so he left it, only to wonder if the woman he was here to meet was on social media. But after several frustrating minutes, it seemed no amount of combinations of Maggie, Margaret, Marguerite, or any other name he could think of combined with Joly could be found. Which was probably not a bad thing, he realized, considering the backlash the video had caused.

Poor thing.

It always amazed him how quick people were to jump to the wrong conclusions. But in this instant world, where everyone could have an opinion about anything and shout about it from the safety of their screens, it seemed people were less interested in hearing two sides of any story and focused instead on pulling down the side that went against their personal convictions. Not that he suspected many people of holding convictions these days. Those he'd come across didn't like feeling convicted about anything really.

Was that judgmental, when he didn't like his sins being pointed out either? "Sorry, God."

A flick through the social media of the Jardin botanique and he realized more of what Maggie had had to face. Yep. Plenty of accusations of bigotry and the like. Poor thing. He couldn't wait to hear her side of the story.

Another glance at the clock and he knew it was time to go inside. He shoved on sunglasses, beeped the Audi locked and moved inside.

"One ticket, please," he requested of the attendant who collected admission money.

"Beau?" a soft voice murmured.

He glanced across, his smile growing. "Hey, Maggie."

She was dressed in what he assumed was her usual work attire: a polo shirt, cream jacket, and khaki shorts. "Aren't you cold?" he said, gesturing to her shorts. There was a nip in the breeze.

"This is still considered beautiful weather up here," she admonished.

"Hey, I'm from the South where we feel the cold."

"Do you want to come inside?" She eyed him uncertainly. "I

know you were here the other week, but if you want to eat, there are some places you could go."

"I always need to eat," he said firmly.

"Something healthy?" she said, her half smile holding a hint of tease.

"Exactly. If there's something here, then that's fine, as long as it's no trouble for you."

She nodded. "It might be easier, especially as people seem to recognize you no matter where you go."

True. "Lead on, then."

He nodded to the attendant, who quickly asked if he'd sign a park guide. Beau obliged, then it was a scoot through the gates and off on a path he'd not gone down on his previous visit. Around him, he could see the top of the pagoda from the Chinese Garden and that the leaves had begun to turn. It being a cooler day, there seemed less people around, and he was glad, for it gave him the chance to concentrate on the woman walking beside him.

Maggie seemed tense, which was not surprising, considering the comments he'd read only minutes ago. "How are you doing?"

She glanced up at him. "Today has not been great," she admitted.

"Want to tell me what happened?"

She paused, hesitating, her gaze shifting to a small building nearby. "I could show you what happened."

"Sure."

Over the next ten minutes he met a man named Renaldo, whose shock at being visited by Montreal's new goalie was outweighed by Beau's own when he learned about the frog-stomping incident. Guilt rose at not-dissimilar incidents in his past, which he suspected might be something many young boys did before they grew a conscience and a brain. But admit that he would not do. Not when confronted by an environmentally-aware woman with big brown eyes he was fast feeling like he'd struggle to say no to.

"It's one thing for a kid to do that—it's another for a parent to basically egg him on," Beau said, looking for honesty amid his memories.

"*Exactement*," agreed Renaldo before continuing in a volley of French that left Beau floundering.

Maggie appeared to recognize this and explained something of what her colleague was saying. "So I knew about this, and when I found the boy at the restaurant doing virtually the same thing, except this time to birds, well, I couldn't help myself." Her head drooped. "I know I didn't express myself the best way, but I just wanted him to stop."

"And that's when the dad got in your face," Beau said.

She nodded. "I'm glad you could see that."

That was more from what he'd surmised than from any actual footage he'd seen, but okay.

"I don't know who was filming, and I wasn't aware of it at the time, obviously." She shot him a wry look. "But they only caught my response and didn't seem to catch what the man said."

Beau's chest heated with anger. Oh, he'd caught enough of what the man said.

"And then he spat at me."

"What?"

She shrugged. "I ignored it the first time—"

"He did it twice?" Beau asked.

"Once near my feet, the second—" She pointed to her chest.

Beau's gaze lifted, not wanting to linger on her curves. "That's disgusting."

"And everyone is blaming me, when really, I was only trying to do my job."

His heart twisted with compassion.

"And yes, I could've explained things differently, but I didn't. And now I can't defend myself, and everyone is blaming me, and I blame myself, and I really don't think you wanted to hear all of this, did you?"

He shrugged, glancing at her workmate, who had offered various kinds of sympathetic understanding but probably didn't need to be privy to everything Beau thought. "How long is your break for?"

"I have another thirty minutes."

"Okay. Point me in the direction of lunch."

Ten minutes later they were walking down another path, this time holding food as Maggie led them to a location she said would enable a more private talk. "I really didn't know it would be that busy inside," she apologized again.

"Hey, it's no problem. It's a beautiful garden, and we've got food, and to be honest, I can do without the attention. For a few minutes at least," he teased.

"You sure?" she said, lips curving to one side.

"Well, only for a few minutes. After that, well, who knows what'll happen? I might self-combust from not having my photo taken."

"You'd better eat your food before that happens, then," she suggested, eyeing his salad roll.

He chuckled and once more felt that ease, something he hadn't experienced with many women before. He could be himself, and he got the impression that Maggie didn't care about his celebrity or his money; she just liked him anyway.

He ate his salad roll while she ate hers, and in the silence knew something else. His mom had always said that if you could be comfortable in silence with someone, then that person was a true friend. He didn't know any other women he'd been able to be comfortably silent with, apart from his mom and sister. But Maggie's presence was soothing, and even though he'd come to try and bring her a little peace, he'd found that exact quality in her. Or maybe it was the effect of the Gardens. Whatever, it was nice to escape the rush and stress and tension of before.

When they'd both finished their picnic lunch meals, he leaned back on his hands and stared at the sky. He knew she'd need to return to work soon, but he still wanted to see what he could do to help her. *Lord, what do I say?*

"Thanks for coming," she said softly, giving him an inroad.

"I don't know if I did anything, but I hope you feel a little better."

"I do, thank you." She fiddled with a blade of grass. "It's been a little tough reading all those comments online, about all these people judging me when they don't know all of the story, let alone know me."

"Well, I think anyone who knows you would realize what was shown was not the whole picture. I think your friends would, anyway." He paused. "I did."

He glanced across, saw she was regarding him uncertainly. "Do you consider us friends?"

"Well, I hope so. I mean, you're scarcely a stranger, especially now we've had two meals together. Or is it three, if you count ice cream?"

"I don't know if I do count ice cream," she said.

"Maybe we'll have to have another meal to make it three, then," he said before hearing how his words sounded, like he was asking her out on a date.

He waited, heart thudding a little harder as he wondered what she'd say. Some women in his past had been easy to read, their eagerness to spend time with him screaming of a desperation that was a little off-putting, to say the least. Maggie was just the opposite, her careful consideration and arm's length interactions inspiring him to work a little harder.

Fortunately—or unfortunately, he didn't know—she

changed the subject, which reminded him he'd meant to ask about her son. "How is Noah?"

"The doctor said he should be able to go back to school next week provided he takes it easy, which he likely will while he's at home with Maman." Her gaze lifted to his again. "Thanks for asking."

"Of course. He's a nice kid."

"I think so," she said before her ever-mobile lips twisted to one side. "But then, I might be a little biased."

"As any parent should be," he assured her. He hiked an eyebrow. "So I guess a visit to the training camp open day is out of the question?"

She nodded, seemingly missing the fact he'd posed the question as an invitation. Maybe it was another cultural difference. Or maybe he was just bad at reading women.

"I don't suppose you'd want to come? It could be a fun day out, get your mind off other things," he added so it wouldn't sound too date-like.

She shot him a shy smile. "Thank you, but I don't know who I could go with."

"Well, let me know if you change your mind."

"Thank you. But I wouldn't want to be a distraction."

He smiled, recalling his earlier comment about finding her distracting—which was true, especially her eyes and her lips— before realizing she was referring to the negative publicity concerning her.

He wondered what else he could do—having lunch together was hardly going to stop her worries—so he asked her outright.

"Anything you can do?" She shook her head. "You've done so much, Beau. I'm so grateful already. And I could never presume to ask you for more."

"Presume away. That's what friends do."

She glanced at him as if she couldn't quite believe he thought them friends, then bit her lip.

"There is something, isn't there?" he asked in an effort to avoid focusing on her mouth.

"No. Not really."

"'Not really' means there is. Go on. Tell me."

She shrugged. "We have a function coming up, the Pumpkin Ball, and—"

"The what?" he asked, intrigued.

"Nothing. Forget I said anything."

"Yeah, not gonna happen. Spill, Ms. Joly."

She shook her head. Not even when he begged.

"Okay then, will you tell me something else?" he asked.

"Depends on what it is." She collected their trash and compacted it into a small ball.

"So, okay, confession time: I tried to look you up on Facebook. Hey, it's only fair if we're going to be friends," he added as she looked at him in surprise. "But I couldn't find you, so I want to know, what's your first name? Is it Margaret? Marguerite? Or Margarita, like the drink?"

"It's Magdalena," she said in that shy manner of hers, as those big brown eyes studied him cautiously.

"Like Mary Magdalene," he said, to her nod.

"But you wouldn't find me on Facebook under that. Not Mary Magdalene or Magdalena Joly," she added, her mouth curving into that small smile.

"What would I find you under?" he said, enjoying the banter.

"You might find me under Maggie Rose."

"Like the singer?"

"I don't know about a singer, but I have a pink rose in my profile picture. In case you look me up," she said, her expression shy.

He'd definitely be doing that. "So, a pink rose because…?"

Her cheeks reddened. "Because it's my favorite flower."

"A classic, huh? Like my mom." Wait. Had he just compared Maggie to his mother? "I mean, it's her favorite flower also."

"That's what I thought you meant." She scrambled to her feet. "I'd better get back to work." She tossed their garbage in the trash can and led the way through the trees, occasionally pausing to point out various trees she obviously considered beautiful.

Beau had never really stopped to look at trees—he was often too busy keeping his eye on the puck to bother looking up—but there was something majestic and yet peaceful about the trees here. Enough to inspire him to snap a few photos and consider posting this online. He liked this woman, with her big eyes, shy smiles, and the way she could surprise him with everything from jumping from trees to standing up to bullies to her tease. She might hold him at arm's length, but it only made him keen to want to draw close and know her more.

They returned to the main complex, where she was accosted by another woman, who eyed Beau like a hungry Southerner might eye a pile of ribs. "Are you Beau Nash?"

He nodded, and Maggie completed the introductions.

"Hmm. A friend of Maggie's."

"Yes, ma'am." He grinned internally as her nose wrinkled at the *ma'am*.

"I wonder, has Maggie spoken to you about the ball?"

What ball? Oh. "The Pumpkin Ball?"

"She did?" She flashed Maggie an approving look. "Then you'll come?"

"Remind me when it is?" he asked Maggie as if they'd had this conversation.

"The third Friday in October."

"I'll need to check the schedule, but if I'm free, I'll be here for sure."

"You will?" Danielle clapped her hands before patting Maggie on the back. "Oh, this will make up for all the bad press of the past twenty-four hours."

It would? Then, "Good. Happy to help."

"Oh, you've got a good one there, Maggie. Well done."

The startled look Maggie shot him held as much surprise as he must be wearing.

But he'd take it. He'd take anything Maggie offered. Except her cold shoulder.

CHAPTER 9

By week's end, Maggie was fairly sure she knew far more about Montreal's new goalkeeper than almost anyone else in the city. After accepting a Facebook friend request from him, she'd trawled through all of his posts and now knew something about his family and whom he considered his closest friends. To be added to such a list felt like an immense honor and privilege, especially as she'd only recognized a few names as his new teammates. And while she hadn't commented on his posts, she had liked one he'd recently posted about Montreal's beautiful trees—a post she dared believe might have been inspired by her—and the fact he'd willingly shared such a thing suggested he really did consider them to be friends.

That thought helped alleviate some of the drama surrounding work. While the rest of Montreal seemed happy to concentrate on their hockey team's training camp, there were a few among the Trustees and Friends who still wanted Maggie to be brought to task. Whether this was at the instigation of Mr. Lee she neither knew nor wished to find out. But it seemed a stain had been cast upon her name, and she'd need to do all she could to see it wiped clean.

Perhaps the attendance of Beau Nash at the Pumpkin Ball would help. Danielle was so excited. Maggie had been surprised when he said yes even though he obviously didn't know what he was getting into, but when he texted Maggie later that night to confirm he was free, her heart had leapt before she'd needed to settle it down again.

He'd said yes to attending. It didn't mean he was going to dance with her or anything. As if she'd get a chance anyway. As if she should. Like Mr. Withers, the president of the Friends, had said, the Gardens could not afford any more bad publicity, so it would be best for Maggie to avoid doing anything that would draw her into the limelight again.

"Maman?" Noah reached up and stroked her cheek. "Are you sad?"

"Non, darling boy," she said, affixing a smile on her lips. "I was just thinking."

"What were you thinking about?" he asked sleepily.

"Oh, just something about work. I'm sorry. You want me to read another elephant story, don't you?"

"Oui," he said on the edge of a giant yawn.

She snuggled him closer, wrapping an arm around him as she read the next Babar story. Part of it, anyway, before the fact that Noah was asleep drew her to close the book and tuck him in with a press of her lips to his brow.

Downstairs, she found her mother wiping down the kitchen sink. "Maman, you should have left that for me," she protested.

"It's done now," her mother said. "You've had a big week, and you should relax."

"But you've been the one caring for Noah."

"He's a good boy, an easy boy. He's no trouble."

"Well, he should be back at school next week, so you can enjoy your days again."

"I enjoy my days with him," her mother said. "I miss him when he's at school. It gets lonely here."

Perhaps now was her chance to ask if her mother might be willing to consider a small house companion. "Have you given any more thought to having a pet? We could afford to look after a little cat."

"Too much mess," her mother protested.

"Not if Noah and I care for it," Maggie countered. "It might do Noah good to have a little pet to love, and we could look after it with no trouble to you."

"And yet you're the one at work all day, and Noah will be at school. Who will take care of it then?" her mother asked, her gaze growing suspicious. "Is it Noah or you who wants a pet?"

Surely her mother remembered Maggie's many requests for a pet when she was growing up. A puppy, a kitten, a hamster, she didn't care. Just something to love, something to hold, something that connected her with outside and made her live a little bigger than her life felt right now. She wanted the same for Noah, too, but her mother's response made it seem unlikely.

Maggie motioned to the television, sitting in the corner of the yellow-painted room. "Do you wish to watch your show tonight?"

"I don't know why you want to stay in," her mother said. "Don't you have some friends you could go out with instead?"

Maggie thought guiltily about Beau's invitation, issued earlier this week. She could have been sitting in a stadium watching a hockey game tonight, but non. She was here, with her mother. As she was most Friday nights. "It's fine," she said.

"Is it?" Her mother studied her and sighed. "I know I've not been especially encouraging, but I know you're a young woman and might want to live your life. I really don't mind looking after Noah if you have things to do."

Such an offer was so unexpected Maggie had to sink on the seat in order to hide her surprise. When was the last time her mother had wanted her to go out? Even when Maggie had been going out with Alain, her mother had tended to prefer her to keep near home. And once Noah arrived, well, that was the end of that. But perhaps people could change.

"I'm happy here," Maggie assured her now, turning on the TV.

The screen showed the hockey game being broadcast live, and her eyes glued to the screen. Her heart skipped a beat when she saw the large frame of a certain Southern somebody filling up the goal net.

"Turn that off," her mother said.

"Just a moment longer."

Her mother sighed and went to make a cup of tea, and Maggie turned up the volume.

"...he's had a great first few days and really seems settled between the pipes," a man with a raspy voice said.

"The good thing is that, at twenty-eight, Nash has a few more years before he can expect to see some of the things that plague goalies, such as injuries to hips and knees."

Maggie didn't hear anything else, her mind flicking back to what had just been said. Beau was only twenty-eight? Her heart sank, then creased with agitation. Why should it matter that he was a year younger than she? He was her friend. That was all. That was enough, she told herself fiercely. She didn't—wouldn't—hope for more.

But she couldn't help wondering what it would've been like to be there tonight. To be there in the crowd, cheering him on, letting him know he had a friend in the stands. The world could be cheering from the sidelines, but she suspected it meant more to know there was someone who was there for him and not the score line.

Maggie swallowed as the roar from the boiling water drowned out what the commentators were saying. She chewed her lip. Would he have appreciated her going? It still surprised her that he seemed to care, that he paid attention. She was nothing special. Definitely not like one of those girls in tight tops with painted faces and perfect hair, whom the cameras seemed to linger on. She was way more ordinary than that. Was it because of her very ordinariness that he noticed her? Maybe he'd felt sorry for her or felt a twisted sense of high-minded obligation to help out the poor little widow. It wasn't like she could ask him why he continued texting or why he issued invitations for meals that almost sounded like he was asking for a date. As if he would. Rolling her eyes at the depths of her self-delusion, she changed the channel and settled in to watch one of her mother's favorite shows, about antiques in places Maggie would never visit but which made her wish she had attics of old stuff worth millions.

"Here you go."

"Merci, Maman." She accepted the cup of tea and pulled the blanket over her legs, wondering not for the first time why she so meekly agreed to this life. She might not be yet thirty, but she'd subscribed to a great-grandmotherly kind of life.

She eyed the TV controller, wondering if she could pretend to adjust the volume and "accidentally" adjust the channel. No. That wouldn't be fair to her mother. Maybe she could just keep up with Beau's progress on her phone instead. A sigh bubbled up, and she suppressed it. She really should've just said oui.

WHEW. Talk about close. Adrenaline surged as the puck collided with the post with a ping, then shot back to where Kaspar scooped it up and passed to Rakoluv, who raced back to where the backup goalie waited at the other end of the ice. A shot, a rebound, then score.

The rink lit in a blaze of red and blue as the spectators for this exhibition game roared their approval. Beau had sensed quite a bit of approval in the past few days, with everyone from team management to reporters keen to talk with him and find out how he was gelling with the team. Team medicals had gone well, with only the slightest question about his heart rate. He'd explained about his dad, and previous medical reports showed there was nothing to worry about. His reflex and weight training via the dead lifts and such had garnered him praise from the team's fitness crew, who Gabe said were notoriously picky. But that was only to be expected from one of the NHL's most talked-about teams. Everyone hoped that this would be the year to lift the Stanley Cup, and Beau's goal was to do whatever it took for him to be proved a worthy asset.

The siren blared at the end of the period, just like it would do in a normal game, the team exiting the ice while entertainment begged the crowds to stay. In the team room he found his locker—the nearest to the door, given he had the most equipment to cope with—and he unstrapped the pads, listening to the coach's instructions.

Today's result meant nothing—it was basically a test to check which lines worked well and which would need to be adjusted—but he, like every man here, was keen to prove himself. He'd noticed Jake struggling with a few passes on the line he'd been assigned to, and it wouldn't surprise him if Jake was demoted to the third line. And while Beau had no intention of letting any pucks by him, he was keen to prove that the hefty price tag that had brought him north was justified.

Another bark of instructions, then equipment was readjusted and they trooped back onto the ice. He knew his other Bible study friends were participating in similar events this weekend as all of the teams prepared for the preseason games next week. So this was really the last chance for the team to play together before Montreal took on their traditional rivals, Toronto, next week. He was glad that game would be played here so he could experience the hometown roar of a traditional hockey market, and he was glad that he'd get the chance to see Dan again. Dan "Dizzy" Walton might be a quiet guy, but he played hard, with a toughness that saw his hip-checks add to the fun of a game. As goalie, Beau was protected from such things, although that didn't stop the slash of sticks or skates from entering his domain. But he'd suffered no real injuries in his career, and he trusted God that this would be another year where he could do what he'd felt born to do: use his awesome reflexes and defensive skills to protect the cage and win.

The next period followed with yet another goal up the other end, and even if there had been any question about who the starting goalie should be, he knew there wasn't now. The period ended, and the team came up to pat him on the helmet since he'd shared that was his preferred method of acknowledgement. Goalies had a strange honor of rarely being captain but often receiving more on-ice acknowledgement, leading the team onto the ice and being the one the other players would seek out to thank at the end of play. Some might argue the rates of pay, but considering his was the last line of defense, he supposed it was worth it. And considering it was his paycheck they were considering, it was definitely worth it.

He joined the others in lifting a stick as they skated around the rink, his gaze lifting to where the team's families and girlfriends sat. He recognized some of them, but he couldn't help the sense of disappointment that Maggie wasn't here. Yeah, it was probably way too early to have asked Maggie to come tonight, but it would've been nice to have had someone he knew sitting there cheering him on. Mom and Olivia were coming for his first game next week, and he'd already started thinking about how he was going to fit his sister's two kids in his apartment and what they'd need. He probably should've been doing that instead of looking at trees, but hey, no one was perfect.

He shook off thoughts of a certain tree climber and showered and changed. After the game there were the usual questions from the media, and as the new goalkeeper, it was no surprise to see he was really popular. After finally escaping, he joined the others in a room set aside for the team's families. Part of tonight involved getting to know some of the other players' wives, girlfriends, and children. It would be a good chance for him to connect a little deeper.

Beau nodded as Gabe gestured him to draw near.

Claudine, Gabe's wife, smiled. "How are you doing?"

"Great. I was happy with how we played. How about you, boss?" Beau asked Gabe.

"Don't call me boss," Gabe warned as the team owner, Tony Francois, drew near. "Someone gets a little touchy."

"Noted."

Beau nodded to Tony—the man worthy of boss status, considering he paid the salaries. Hockey was like any business, filled with politics and personalities, which meant the on-ice hits weren't the only moves being made. People could be hired and fired with little warning, and he'd played on teams where guys had been traded and coaches fired with no notice.

"Nice game, Beau," Tony said, grabbing a drink from the table.

"Thank you, sir. I'm starting to feel like I'm settling in."

"Between the pipes, in the team, or in the city?"

"All of the above, sir."

"Good to hear, good to hear." He shifted to talk to Gabe, leaving Beau to smile awkwardly at Claudine, then wonder if that might be misconstrued, so he turned to get a drink himself.

He grabbed a bottle of Powerade, the drink sliding down his throat, replenishing the electrolytes he'd used. He'd used to play with a forward who had diabetes, and he remembered how the poor guy had needed to leave the game to monitor his blood sugar levels on a regular basis and watch his consumption of drinks like the one Beau held, to ensure his blood sugar didn't spike. He shot up a quick prayer for poor Max.

Claudine sidled closer as her husband and the team boss

continued talking. "They'll go on for hours," she murmured in an undertone. "Gabe is always focused on hockey."

"I guess that comes with the territory of being a captain," Beau said easily.

"Perhaps." Her gaze traveled around the room before returning to Beau, eyeing him with a look that sent prickles down his spine.

Okay, he didn't want to do unfriendly, but the woman seemed to be wanting something he was pretty sure only Gabe was supposed to give. He needed to distract her. "So, who do you think I need to meet?" This kind of stuff was usually more the woman's domain, which might sound sexist, but he'd already met all the guys.

"Now, you didn't bring anyone, did you? You're officially single?"

"Officially and unofficially," he agreed easily, even as the image of a certain brunette with big brown eyes stubbornly refused to go away.

"That's good to know." Her gaze traveled the length of him, her lips hooking to one side. "You're really tall, aren't you?"

Story of his life. He bit back a sigh and nodded to Gabe, who drew close to Claudine and wrapped an arm around her, bending to press a kiss to her cheek.

Claudine giggled and leaned into Gabe. "You have a nice talk?"

"Nice enough." Gabe said. "What are you two talking about?"

She pivoted on her heel to smile at Beau. "I'm wondering which of our friends would be good to hook up with Beau. I guess you need someone who is tall too, yes?"

"Actually, I'm not really looking," he tried to explain.

"Oh! You have your eye on someone, do you?"

Gabe smirked at this, which forced Beau to denial. But how to explain that he wasn't in the market for hook-ups and that he wanted a Christian girl with similar values to him? Again, the image of a certain brunette crossed his mind, and he batted it away. She might be pleasant company, but the lack of any interest on her part made it plain she'd never consider them as more than friends. And that was fair enough. He'd never considered marrying someone who was a widow and a mom. He coughed. Not that he was thinking marriage at all.

Gabe lifted a brow, which forced Beau to reassure him, "All good here."

"I think I saw something on social media about you, didn't I?" Claudine continued. "You were having dinner with someone?"

Brigitte. Not that he'd advertise that here. "It's weird, but I tend to eat most days."

She blinked, then laughed.

"Come on, baby, don't pick on the man. A guy's gotta eat," Gabe said before excusing himself to talk to some older men Beau didn't recognize over in the corner.

"Hmm." She eyed Beau with a flirtatious look that made his neck itchy.

"Well, maybe next weekend you and Gabe should join me for a meal when my mom and sister are in town." As soon as he said it he regretted it. "They're bringing my niece and nephew, so it should be a hoot."

"Sounds fun." Her voice said what her eyes did not. "Oh, look, I'd better go."

A hand slapped him on the back. Team executive, Paul Forges. "Good game out there, Beau."

"I'd sure hope so, considering it was hardly a game."

"It was game enough," Paul said. "Hey, I talked to Bill Blaine a few days ago. Remember him? Well, you must, because Bill mentioned you messaged him a few times asking about his health. He was really impressed."

"It's good to hear he's on the mend."

Paul nodded, his expression lightening. "Hey, did I mention

we've got some of our new sponsors joining us here tonight?" He pointed to a few men who were over near the food table. "Come on and I'll introduce you."

"Sure." Beau followed and was soon shaking hands. "Robert, good to see you again."

"You played awesome out there! I loved that old-school save you did with a bit of a roundhouse."

A knees together move with a kick save. "I tried."

Robert continued in a similar vein for some time, and Beau did the small talk thing for a while, his gaze wandering around the room as Robert's verbal deluge didn't require much more than a *hmm* or a *yeah* in response.

Johan was talking to Jake, and over near the drinks table, Beau could see Rakoluv and Kaspar chatting with their Nordic-looking wives. Maybe he should join them soon, and they could be the European-looking crew. In another corner, he saw Gabe talking with a few other sponsors. Claudine had moved from a bunch of blonde lookalikes to chat with Kris, who smiled at her. It was nice to see the team seemed to get on with each other, like they really were the family Paul and Gabe and others promoted.

"And how are your kids?" Beau asked, conscious Robert had paused to sip his drink.

"They're good." His smile grew wry. "I think seeing Bill's episode helped me to realize that life isn't guaranteed."

"Nothing is. But hey, a bit of perspective like that can be a beautiful thing."

"That's very true."

A cleared throat made Beau turn to see Paul gesture him to draw near. "So, I've been reading up on you, seen a few of your posts. I see you've been to the Botanical Gardens a few times. You like gardens, huh?"

"Sure. I think the Jardin botanique is a real jewel in the city. I've really enjoyed my visits there, and the staff are really knowledgeable and caring." Well, his interactions with Maggie had proved that to be the case.

"Hmm." Paul frowned.

"I can't wait to show my mom and sister around next weekend on our day off," Beau continued, feeling a surge to protect Maggie.

"They're coming up from Georgia, huh?"

"From North Carolina," he explained. He supposed some Canadians might consider the southern US states to be pretty much the same, just as he knew some Southerners didn't know much about the different Canadian provinces.

"Well, that should be nice for you," Paul said a trifle absently before his gaze sharpened again. "But about the Gardens. You may be aware there was an issue there recently."

"I heard, and actually—"

"We need to be careful with how the club is perceived," Paul interrupted. "You know we consider ourselves a family here. Any whiff of racism or such things is not tolerated."

"Of course not," Beau said, his chest tight as he remembered how maligned poor Maggie had been with the accusations made against her. "You'll have to excuse me, but I'm not sure where you're going with this."

Paul's brow lowered, as did his voice. "We don't want there to be any trouble, you see."

"Trouble? With what?"

Paul tapped another man on the back, who turned around. A man whose face Beau recognized but whom he'd never met before. A man who filled Beau with loathing.

"Beau Nash, let me introduce you to one of our newest sponsors."

The man stuck his hand out as his black eyes glittered.

"Beau," Paul continued, "this is Mr. Andrew Lee."

CHAPTER 10

*A*ll through her Saturday and Sunday, Maggie vacillated between oui and non. Oui, she wanted to go and watch the hockey. Non, she didn't want to leave her son to watch the hockey. Oui, she was really touched that Beau had sent her another message about attending church. Non, the thought of attending a different church filled her with trepidation.

Why the man kept persisting, she didn't know. She appreciated it but couldn't think of the last time a man had been so keen to spend time with her. The thought that Beau might be keen scared her.

She wasn't anyone special. She wasn't a model or an actress or a Swedish television personality. Yes, she'd looked up who the Montreal players had dated or married. She was ordinary. A single mother. A woman whom no man apart from Alain had ever really noticed. So why was Beau so keen?

After replying *Thank you, but no. I really need to make sure Noah is well rested for his return to school the next day,* she instantly regretted having sent the message. How long would Beau persist in his invitations? She found his offer of friendship—because it truly couldn't be anything more than that, could it?—

tantalizing, something she desperately wanted but feared where it might lead. Because it could only lead to a broken heart when he realized she wasn't special.

And now that she'd said non—yet again—she wondered if this keep-him-at-arm's-length policy would eventually discourage him from bothering to reach out at all. She wouldn't blame him if he thought it all too hard.

"Are you going to be looking at your phone all day?" her mother asked in French.

"Non," Maggie said, pocketing her phone. Her mother was right. She really needed to focus and get something done today.

She smiled at Noah, who had spent the morning watching cartoons on TV in a perfect weekend morning like she remembered from her childhood. Noah was feeling a lot better, his good sleeps at nighttime refreshing his body and mind for the coming week of school. She could perhaps have taken him to church, either with Maman or to the one Beau had recommended. But she had enjoyed this morning of relaxing, of feeling cocooned in a bubble of rare ease. Deleting the Facebook app off her phone had helped, as had directing a lot of her personal email to junk folders. Now the only people who could contact her were those she actually knew and people she could trust to not send her unkind messages.

"It's a lovely day," Maggie said, mussing up Noah's hair. "Do you want to go outside?"

He glanced at her and nodded. Poor pet. Between her mother's anxious cossetting and the inclement weather, he'd spent a lot of time indoors this past week. She sent him upstairs to put on shoes and a jacket. The sun might be out, but he could do with protection against the cool breeze.

"Are you going for a walk?" her mother asked with a frown after he'd gone upstairs.

"Just a short one," Maggie assured her. "Around the block to the park, but no further."

"Noah needs to be careful he doesn't overestimate his strength," her mother warned.

"And he needs to make sure he has enough energy that he can cope with school tomorrow," Maggie countered. "A little walk won't hurt."

"I hope not."

Maggie found a tight smile—why did Maman's worry always make Maggie feel as though her decisions were being questioned?—and retreated to retrieve her own jacket and shoes and to help her son with his laces. "Two bows, then here comes Mister Dinosaur," she said, threading one loop under the other. "And now hold him tight."

He giggled as he always did, then stood and held her hand.

"Now, you must let me know if you feel too tired. You want to be able to go back to school tomorrow, don't you?"

"Oui, Maman," he said with a sigh.

She chewed her lip, wondering if her mother's overprotectiveness and his constant TV watching had drawn this new reluctance. "Remember your friends?" she asked as they headed down the stairs, hoping he'd say oui and prompt her with their names.

The teacher had mentioned some of the other children Noah had been friendly with when Maggie called the school last week, but she couldn't remember their names now. There had been so much else going on that her brain felt like a sieve.

But instead of reassuring her, he shook his head, and she wondered what to say. "Perhaps after school we could see about another ice cream."

This at least brought a smile from him, even if it brought a sigh from her mother with a look that said *You spoil that child, Maggie.*

"Bye, Mamie," Noah called to his grandmother with a wave.

"Be careful," she warned.

"Of course."

But that same stubborn impulse that had seen Maggie climb a tree flared. And as she and Noah walked hand in hand across the street and along the pavement, she knew that same desire to rebel. Maman was always so careful, so protective, so safe. But Maggie realized now that such a way of living had shrunk her world, had narrowed her existence to the parameters of her son, her mother, and work, and she didn't want to live that way anymore.

"Bonjour," a woman called. One of the new neighbors Maggie's mother had complained about as being too loud and not fitting in.

Maggie's steps slowed and she found a smile. "Hello."

The headscarf-wearing woman smiled wider. "You speak English?"

"Yes."

"I am very glad," the woman said, her accent clearly indicating she was not from this country originally. "We move here, but people not talk English much."

Maggie's heart constricted. People did not talk much because of fear. "I am sorry." She drew Noah to her side. "I am Maggie, and this is my son Noah. We live in the pink house there." She pointed to her mother's house.

"I am Fatima," the woman said, gesturing to herself before bending down to Noah's height. "Hello, Noah."

Noah still had not said anything, so Maggie prompted him with a gentle nudge.

"Hello," Noah finally said.

"You are very sweet," the woman said, reaching out as if to touch him, but Noah flinched away. She straightened. "How old?"

"Five."

"My boys were sweet too, once. Now, so loud." She shook her head, pointing to the older-make vehicles littering the front yard. "Drive their cars, too noisy."

Exactly what the other neighbors believed. "Children grow up," Maggie offered.

"So sad." Fatima glanced at Noah. "You wait here. I have something for you."

"Oh, you don't—"

But the woman ignored Maggie's protest, hurrying away saying something in a language Maggie couldn't understand. Never mind. They'd wait here, enjoying the kiss of sunshine on their skin, something they should make the most of before the long, dark days of winter set in.

Maggie gazed around at the other houses in their street. How long had it been since she'd really talked to any of their neighbors? Between work, caring for her son, and doing what she could to help her mother, it had been far too long since she'd made an effort to connect beyond her immediate world.

An old verse she had once learned in Sunday school floated through her mind: Love your neighbors. She knew it meant more than just literal neighbors, but in all honesty, she couldn't even claim to have done that. How could she, when she didn't even know their names? Remorse washed through her as she realized just how small and self-centered her life had become in recent years. And she couldn't blame her mother, not when Maggie herself had chosen to live this way.

Fatima returned and held out what looked to be a bag of candies. "For you," she said, handing the bag to Noah, who seemed reluctant to accept it.

"Oh, thank you," Maggie said, "but we really don't—"

"Go on," Fatima said to Noah.

"You may have one," Maggie said, recognizing both Noah's reluctance and Fatima's persistence.

"Take it," Fatima encouraged Noah, handing the whole bag over. "For you."

Oh dear. But refusing would not help the tentative relationship that was forming. "Say thank you, Noah," Maggie said.

"Merci," he murmured as the older lady placed the bag in his hands.

Fatima beamed. "You like, huh?"

"You are very kind," Maggie said.

"*You* are kind." Fatima motioned to the houses around them. "No one stops to talk anymore. Very lonely."

Again Maggie felt regret. She knew that Fatima was not the only person in this street who would claim loneliness. It would do Maman good to get to know some other ladies in the neighborhood.

The thought whirled in its intensity. Maman would never agree to going out to meet Fatima. But perhaps Maggie could...

"You go to the park, yes?"

Maggie nodded, words spilling out. "Would you like to come?"

Instant regret at her impulsive offer filled her. Today was supposed to be about reacclimatizing Noah to the wider world, not making friends with strangers. But something about the wistful way the older woman looked at both of them had propelled words from Maggie's mouth.

"Thank you, but no. I should stay."

Relief mixed with a strange desire to make her come. "Are you sure you cannot come? It's a lovely day."

"No, no." Fatima glanced at Noah. "You enjoy."

"Perhaps you could come to tea," Maggie said, still gripped with the desire to connect with this woman and make amends for her lack of kindness.

Fatima's face brightened. "When? Today?" she asked eagerly.

Oh no. Today felt far too soon. She would need to check with her mother, somehow convince her this was a good idea.

But if not today, then when? It would be a whole week before Maggie had the time free again.

"I will make cake," Fatima said with a pleading quality to her voice that softened Maggie's refusal to a oui.

"I will need to speak to my mother first," she said, conscious it made her sound like a child. "And I first need to take Noah to the park."

"Of course you must." Fatima smiled down at him. "Sweet boy."

"We'd better go, then," Maggie said. "See you this afternoon?"

Fatima nodded, and Maggie frantically wondered what she would say to her mother to convince her to allow a near stranger to cross the threshold.

She and Noah continued on their walk, and the question continued to peck through Maggie's attempt to provide a fun little outing for her son. But just as she now recognized that maybe living in an isolated manner wasn't good for her, Noah's reaction suggested that it wasn't good for him either.

Noah ran to the swing and climbed in, shouting for her to push him. She obliged with gentle pushes at first, glad to see he possessed a fearlessness she wished she owned too.

She didn't want her son to grow up fearing people who were different from him. She wanted him to appreciate the world and all its many variations, to not be hardened to it but neither be afraid. He would encounter new experiences in school, but he also needed to see her living that way. And if ever he was to learn of what had happened at the Gardens, he needed to know that his mother was someone who was not racist but treated others as equals, in the way she hoped he would live too.

She pushed the swing again, letting Noah know it would be the last time. She needed to return and let her mother know what joy awaited her this afternoon. Perhaps she should call her now. Her mother's usual inclination tended to the negative, but sometimes, given enough warning, she could be brought around.

Before she could talk herself out of it, she called, and sure enough, her mother was horrified. "You mean the loud ones from three doors down? What were you thinking?"

"I'm thinking that the woman is lonely and needs a friend," Maggie replied evenly.

"Well, *I* don't need friends," her mother replied adamantly.

Oui, she did. "We all do. And I thought it would be neighborly."

"You thought wrong," her mother said. "I do not want that woman in my house."

Great. What to do now?

"When are you coming back home?" Maman demanded.

"We will be back soon," Maggie soothed. After she'd figured out what to say to Fatima. Poor Fatima, who was probably baking now in glorious anticipation of finally meeting some neighbors. How could she let her down?

She ended the call, realizing that Noah had moved to the slide, and watched him, hoping he'd be careful. Then realized that, mere minutes ago, she'd been silently applauding his willingness to be brave.

Oh, how ridiculously cautious *was* she? This tentative friendship with Fatima only reinforced how much she wanted to move beyond her safe little world. And that she did want her son to be brave, which meant she would need to be brave too. In all parts of her world.

Her phone buzzed with a message.

HEY, HOPE YOU'RE HAVING A GOOD DAY AND NOAH IS FEELING BETTER. NOT SURE IF YOU'RE FREE AT ALL NEXT WEEKEND, BUT THOUGHT I'D ASK.

She stared at Beau's message. Was this another part of her life that she needed to be courageous about? Before she could think for too long she tapped out YES. Then studied the three letters, wondering what this would mean for her life, for her future.

Then pressed Send.

~

Beau had wondered whether he should bother sending one more message. He didn't want to harass Maggie or make her think he was a stalker. And given the way the club felt about her, he didn't exactly want to get into trouble there. But neither did he want to let bullies get away with treating an innocent woman badly or be forced to behave in a way that was contrary to what he believed, especially by a man he'd be real happy not to see again.

"I still can't believe the nerve of the guy," Beau had complained to Dan last night on FaceTime, knowing Dan would also still be in that same weird space Beau was, when adrenaline refused to fade after a game. He'd thought he would've been better by now, having played for so many years, but some nights took him a real long time to sleep. And nights when he was in no great hurry to sleep, because it might mean unwanted dreams tangling his brain with helplessness, he was happy to put it off a little longer.

"Why do you care so much?" Dan had asked him.

Beau hadn't known how to reply. He'd asked himself the same question many times. "I guess it's just that I hate to see injustice," he'd hedged.

"It's just that?" Dan had asked with a knowing smile.

How to admit a woman had gotten under his skin? "Okay, maybe I like her," he'd finally admitted. "Maybe I feel like she could do with a friend."

He'd tried to emphasize the *friend* part, which had been met with raised eyebrows and a smirk. "Sure you do."

But it was true, he'd told himself stubbornly after Dan had needed to hang up. Even if the hope hammering his heart as he watched those three dots indicating she was about to reply said something else.

Yes.

He fist-pumped. Then he paused. Okay, it was one thing to put a nebulous question out there and see if she was free. It was quite another to intentionally ask this next thing. He chewed his lip, wondering how best to say this.

But before he could compose his message, his phone rang. Mom. He'd need to take this.

"Hi, honey," his mom said. "How are you? What are you up to today?"

Telling his mother he was wondering how best to ask out a single mom certainly hadn't featured in his Sunday afternoon plans. "Um, had church this morning. It was good. Just taking it easy before tomorrow's preseason game. How about you?" He'd always found deflection to be a good form of defense.

"That's great! Oh, church was good here, too. I had to tell the gals I'd miss them next weekend, and they all wanted me to pass on their good wishes."

"That's real sweet of 'em." There were times he was glad he lived alone and didn't share an apartment like some of his teammates, who'd no doubt mock him for using terms like sweet. "It should be a good night. I've been told Montreal usually plays Toronto in the preseason opener, but it's rare to have a home game, so it should be fun."

"I can't wait."

He smiled, knowing her comment came more from her love for him rather than any great love for the game. "You got your bags all packed?"

"Just about. Of course, travelling to Montreal isn't exactly like flyin' to Timbuktu."

"Although it may feel like it with Liv's youngsters with you too."

"Oh, stop it. You know they're so excited about seeing their Uncle Beau."

"It'll be great to see them too. And Liv, too."

"It's a shame Jesse can't come, but work won't let him get away."

"What? Didn't Liv tell them who I am?" he teased.

"I think she might've mentioned it a time or two." He could hear the smile in her voice. "Now, tell me, what are the chances of meeting this gal I've been hearing about?"

He coughed. "Which gal?"

"Why, the one who spoke to your sister, of course. Olivia was pressing me for details, and I was ashamed to admit I knew nothing. Which felt really unfair considering I'd been there just a few weeks ago. What was her name again?"

"Um, who?"

"Why, how many girls are there, son?"

His neck grew hot. "There's no one, Mom."

"Are you sure now? Who was this woman who spoke to your sister, then?"

"Maggie?"

"That's the one! I just can't wait to meet her. Is she a sweetheart? Well, she'd have to be a sweetheart if she's won your heart."

"Mom, you know you get a little carried away sometimes. I don't even know if she's a Christian."

"Oh. Well, that's important to find out. But even if she's not a believer just yet, it's not to say she won't become one. Especially if she spends time with a certain someone we know who isn't exactly shy about sharing his faith."

"Come on, Mom. We're just friends." Although, that message his trigger-ready finger longed to send said they were more.

"Well, whatever you want to call her is fine with me. I just want to meet her."

Beau released a long, slow breath.

"Did you just sigh on me?"

"Mama..."

"I declare, Beau Samuel Nash, sometimes I get the feelin' you really don't like me meddling in your affairs."

It wasn't meddling. He knew that. But he also knew his mother just thought—

"I wouldn't ask if I didn't care," she insisted, echoing his very thought. "And you know I just want to see you happy, son."

"I'm happy, Mom," he maintained.

"You're not lonely?"

Maybe if he had someone he could unwind with, someone he could download and share the stresses of the day with, he'd sleep better. His gut tensed. Not that he was thinking of sleeping arrangements. There was a lot to consider—like a wedding—before that ever happened. "Look, I don't mind admitting that it's taking a little while to connect with the team. They might've said the language doesn't need to be a barrier, but it kinda feels like it is."

There was a beat, two, then, "I'm sorry, son."

He could hear the sympathy in her voice, which drew emotion he hadn't anticipated. Another reason he was glad he lived alone. He swallowed and hastened to hide his reaction to her compassion with a joke. "It's not that bad, Mom. It's not bad at all. I'm loving living here."

"Which is why I've been glad to see your posts about enjoying the city sights."

Like the Botanical Gardens. His thoughts strayed to Maggie again, and he wondered what she was doing. Was she still waiting for his answer, wondering what he wanted to say?

"Beau?"

"Sorry, Mom. I was just thinking."

"About this Maggie girl?"

"Mom!"

She laughed. "Oh, I do like how easy you are to tease."

"Don't go giving anyone else those kinds of ideas," he warned.

"Like your sister?"

Especially his sister. Mom might joke, but he could always trust her to have his heart in mind. Liv, well, she seemed to think his pay packet just gave her license to mock.

"You might want to give her a heads-up that if she doesn't behave, I'll make sure not to take her kids to the best ice cream place in town."

"Ooh, but I heard you'd promised."

"Promises can be broken," he threatened, but with a smile. As if he'd ever let little Bailey and Bronson down.

"You're such a tough guy," Mom said with teasing affection.

"You know it."

"You'll be amazing tomorrow night. You know that, don't you?"

"Thanks, Mom." Nothing fueled his confidence the same way as his mom's encouragement.

He finally ended the call only to stare at his phone, wondering whether he should text or just bite the bullet and call Maggie. His mother's words goaded him. But first, he really needed to know something else. Something that would affect everything he did from here on in.

Hey Maggie, he slowly typed. Can we talk?

CHAPTER 11

Maggie's phone pinged with an incoming message. Her pulse—already rapid, thanks to Maman's exclamations and dismay about Fatima's unwanted visit when Maggie returned from the walk—increased some more, until she wondered whether she might need to see a cardiac surgeon. She wondered—hoped—the message might be from Beau. She'd waited for what seemed an age, sure he'd had second thoughts, that maybe a better offer had come around, like maybe a supermodel had knocked on his door. To think that Beau Nash, Montreal's superstar hockey goalie, might actually be hinting at taking her out was almost too much to bear, making her fingers twitchy as she fought to not look at the phone.

She glanced up and caught her mother's frown and knew that if she dared answer it now, all the forbearance created by their neighbor's visit would quickly fade, so she pushed the phone away.

"And how many children do you have?" Maman asked Fatima stiffly.

"Two sons." She raised her hands. "They be such good boys, but wild."

"We have heard their cars," Maman said with a lowered brow.

"I tell them all the time to stop being so loud, but they don't listen. Think they tough."

At Fatima's obvious distress, Maggie's mother's frown eased a fraction. "Boys can be hard to manage," she allowed.

"Since my husband died, they do not listen to me. It is so hard."

The consternation lifted another degree. "I am sorry," Maman said. "It is not easy being a widow, is it?"

Widow. Maggie glanced around the table and realized it was true of the three of them. She didn't know anyone else her own age who had been widowed. It was yet another thing that made her feel like she didn't fit in, neither single nor married anymore but without the anger that fueled so many divorces of people she knew. She had loved Alain, had many good memories of him, and while he hadn't been perfect, she knew the same could be said of her. But he'd been her first love, even though he'd been gone these past five years.

She studied her gold ring, which she wore on weekends. She didn't wear it at work anymore, not wanting it to become tarnished from the physical labor she did or accidentally get lost in a garden somewhere. But on weekends it provided some comfort.

"You are married, Maggie?" Fatima asked. "Where is your husband?"

In Notre Dame des Neiges Cemetery, she could say, but that sounded too blasé. Better to say, "He is with God."

She thought he was, anyway. Alain had not believed in the way that Maggie's parents had taught her, but he hadn't ever mocked their quaint beliefs. In fact, in his last days he had seemed more interested than ever in learning what the priest thought happened after death. She knew Maman still prayed for his soul, although Maggie was sure that God would have made a decision by now, and there was little use praying for something that must surely be done.

Fatima nodded. "So young to be alone."

"I am not alone," Maggie protested with a smile. "I have Noah."

"A sweet boy," Fatima crooned.

"A good boy," Maman said with a nod.

Perhaps approval of Noah might prove the olive branch that brought them together.

Her lips tipped up as a random memory of Beau's comments about Noah flickered. Wasn't an olive branch involved in Noah's story somewhere, something that was supposed to bring peace? She might have to ask Beau if he remembered that part of the story or whether that was something the nuns had just made up.

The hour passed with a general thawing from Maggie's mother, who seemed determined to display her gracious side, something she had protested against until the second Fatima came through the front door. Maggie had been so relieved that she'd done all she could to promote conversation between the two women, both of whom had more in common than either had initially realized. Not that she'd pointed that out. But it was true, as their lives, although starting in very different parts of the world, had tracked in not dissimilar ways. She'd sensed her mother thawing, something which Fatima's delicious, dense raisin cake might have gone some way to assisting.

Finally Fatima rose. "I must go. I know you have things to do, but I am so grateful you invited me." She held Maggie's hands. "Thank you." She turned to Maggie's mother. "Bless you."

"Bless you," Maggie's mother replied, as if startled into saying something Maggie had never heard her say before.

After a long argument about who should keep the remains of the delicious cake, which Fatima won by declaring her too-loud sons were not worthy of it, the door closed, and Maggie's mother turned to her with a frown. "Do not ever put me into such a position again."

"I thought you liked her."

"I spoke with her. That was enough, non?"

So much for thinking her mother was being gracious. "You heard her, Maman. She's lonely. She's been living here for weeks now and doesn't know the neighbors."

"I've been living here for years and I don't know the neighbors."

Maggie sensed that pointing out her mother's choice to not interact with others would not be appreciated right now. Perhaps appealing to her well-developed love of Noah might be a better bet. "I thought it would prove a good example to Noah, to see us interacting with neighbors who are not like us. He's going to encounter different kinds of people at school anyway, and I don't want him getting upset or thinking people are strange just because they don't look or talk or act like he does."

"Noah is a good boy," Maman insisted.

"He is. And I want him to have a big heart that cares about others."

Like Beau did, she realized. He was filled with such kindness and compassion for others she was almost jealous of those he cared about, which reminded her—

"I need to check on some things."

"Like your phone?"

What would her mother say if she knew Beau had messaged her? Today was not the day to push that either. "Thank you for letting Fatima come," she said, going to give her mother a small hug. "I know it was unexpected, but I appreciated your graciousness."

"Hmph," was her mother's gracious response.

Maggie bit back a smile and moved upstairs to finally read her message.

Oh my gosh.

Her nerves—already worn from the encounter downstairs—found renewed energy and pattered faster. Beau wanted to talk to her? Like, on the phone? Or in person?

Just the thought that he might want to talk to her in person made her feel a little dizzy. So far she'd only met him by accident or at work, and on none of those occasions could it be said that she had dressed to make a favorable impression. What did one even wear to meet a member of Montreal's famous hockey team? She wasn't exactly a heels and short skirt girl. She'd always felt more comfortable in jeans. She glanced at her fingernails. Should she paint them? Maybe she could clean out all the dirt, at least. But wait. *Did* he want her to meet him? Maybe he just meant talk on the phone, after all.

So…should she call him? Call her old-fashioned, but it seemed way too bold to just call a man. Especially when she wasn't even sure what he wanted. Maybe he simply wanted to know how Noah was doing and was tired of texting all the time, and all this worrying was for nothing. Of course. That *had* to be it. And his earlier comments about this coming week were just to see…what?

Oh, this to-ing and fro-ing of sifting through his motivations was just too hard.

She typed back Yes.

An instant later, her phone rang. Her mouth dried as she wondered what to say. Well, she could always start with the basics and answer it. She wiped clammy hands on her jeans and did just that. "Hello?"

"Maggie?"

She smiled, his voice like sunshine in her chest. "Beau?"

"Hey, I'm glad to finally talk with you."

"And you." She felt her heart sink a little. So, a phone call was all he'd meant. Good thing she hadn't bothered changing. Or painting her nails.

"Should that be *et tu*?" he asked.

"*Et toi aussi* is more precise," she explained, correcting his pronunciation.

"Right. Man, so many things to learn."

She said nothing, shame at her stupid fantasies wrinkling over her soul. He'd called her up for a French lesson?

"So, I know this is weird, but I wondered if you were free later today for a coffee."

"Why is that weird?"

He coughed. "I didn't mean it was weird to ask you out for a coffee—"

Wait. He *was* asking her out after all?

"—just that I know you're probably busy or doing family things or something. And I guess it's last minute, and you might not want to now."

"You sound like you're trying to talk yourself out of it," she said.

"I'm not!" he assured her. "Which is why I'm calling. But hey, if you are busy—"

"I'm not."

"You sure?"

"Really sure."

"Great!" Happiness lit his voice. "So, are you happy to meet me for a coffee?"

"Certainement."

"What's awesome in French?" he said, tease in his tone.

She thought for a moment. "*C'est génial* might work."

"C'est génial. Well, that's how I feel about you. I mean, meeting you. Today, I mean. Man, this was so much easier in my head."

She smiled.

"I've been told there's a good place not too far from where I live, if you'd like to meet there," he continued. "Or I can come pick you up if you like."

As much as her heart scampered at the thought of Beau

collecting her for a date—*non*, a *talk*, she told herself sternly—there would be way too many questions she'd have to answer. "I can meet you there."

"I don't know what parking is like."

"It should be okay."

"So I'll see you soon? Like, at five?"

"Okay."

"C'est génial," he said carefully.

"*C'est tiguidou*," she replied.

"What's that mean?" he asked.

"That's great."

And the thought she would have coffee with this man? It was *incroyable* as well.

THE LAST TIME he'd been out with a woman sure hadn't felt like this. Beau wiped damp palms down his dark jeans as he waited for Maggie to appear. He still had some things to say, but the fact he'd been so clumsy on the phone made him amazed she'd agreed to meet him at all. But then, he'd always found it hard to be smooth when it came to women he actually liked. Not that he could afford to like her, he thought, watching the door. At least, not until he knew exactly where she stood on certain matters of the heart.

The café was housed in a heritage building, dark paneled with wooden trims and curved leather booths. Gabe had mentioned it as a good place to eat or grab a drink, and while Beau had no need for alcohol, he appreciated the privacy this place seemed to offer, with all its interesting nooks designed around the former bank building's offices. He lifted a hand as Claudine moved along the other side of the space, but she didn't see him. Oh well, he'd catch up with her and Gabe soon.

The doors opened again, this time admitting Maggie. His

heart thudded. She looked pretty, like she'd made an effort just as he had, dressed as she was in a purple top, fitted jacket, jeans, and boots with heels. She also looked nervous, and he stood to wave her over.

"Hi."

"Bonjour."

Should he kiss her cheek, like he might do for his sister or his female friends? Not that he had too many female friends. After an awkward moment he did just that, leaning down and pressing his lips to the left cheek and then her right as people did around here. He was sorely tempted to linger and explore the softness of her skin and scent but figured that might weird her out, so he straightened. "Good to see you."

"You too." She pinked and slipped into the curved seat.

"Are you hungry?" he asked, showing her the menu.

"Not really. But you mentioned coffee, so here I am."

"What would you like?"

Her eyes met his, then glanced down again, and for a second he could've sworn she was going to make a smart comment. He waited, then when she'd made her selection, lifted a brow. "Lavender matcha?"

"I've never tried one before," she responded.

"That makes two of us."

"Are you going to get one as well?" she asked, smiling.

"Why not? You only live once, right? Although, maybe I'll get an ordinary cappuccino as well, just in case."

"Just in case you don't survive the lavender matcha?"

"What even is a matcha, anyway?"

"I'm not exactly sure. I think it's like an Asian green tea."

His nose wrinkled. "Yum."

She laughed, and he moved to order, making sure he got an extra coffee and some pastries as well. He was all about trying new things, but it might help both of them to have something to soothe any taste buds that mightn't appreciate weird flavors.

While waiting to pay, he noticed Kris's blond head several booths away. Huh. This was a popular place to be.

Tempted though he was to go say hi, he instead moved back to where Maggie waited, her gaze shy. "They'll bring it over soon."

She nodded, her fingers playing with the cuff of her shirt. "So, er, how was training camp?"

She kept tabs on him? "It went well. We have our first preseason game tomorrow against Toronto, so I'll be playing against my friend Dan Walton. He's a defenseman, so it should be fun."

She nodded. He was tempted to ask if she wanted to come but didn't want her to feel obliged. Likely she was busy with other things anyway.

Silence stretched, then she said. "So, what did you want to talk about?"

Wow. Nothing like getting straight to the point. *Hey, God, please lead this conversation.* "Well, first of all, why don't you tell me how Noah's doing?"

Her face lit, and he realized how much her world revolved around her son as she shared about his health improvements and that he was looking forward to going back to school.

"Well, *looking forward to* might be a slight exaggeration," she admitted. "But I think he's getting a little bored with staying at home."

"I'm glad he's better."

"So am I." She offered him a shy smile. "I'm still so grateful for what you did at the hospital."

"It was nothing. I was glad I could be of help."

The server brought over a tray with their coffees and food. Maggie raised her eyebrows at the pastries, forcing him to hold up his hands. "The croissant and those eclairs looked good enough to eat."

"Imagine that."

He chuckled. "Ready to try this *delicieux* concoction?" he said, motioning to the purple-hued hot drink before them.

She tried hers as he sipped his matcha. "Whoa." He blinked, tried not to choke. "Wow." Gross. Thank goodness he had a real coffee waiting for him.

She placed her cup down. "You don't like it?"

"You do?"

"I thought you liked to try new things. You only live once, you said."

"And you might not live long if you drink that," he said, pushing his cup away.

"I thought you were tough."

"You thought wrong. But hey, I'm impressed you seem to like it. That obviously shows you're the tougher of us two."

"Apparently." She sipped, a smile playing around her mouth.

"So, tell me about your day."

She blinked. "Okay."

She shared about taking Noah for a walk to the park and how on the way she met this lady that some of the other neighbors had complained about. "Well, not her, exactly, but her sons. They're new to the neighborhood and don't seem to understand that most of the other residents are older and don't share the same taste in loud music or appreciate slammed doors at ten at night."

"Weird."

"Je sais, I know." She smiled. "So I felt this strange compulsion to invite her to visit, which my mother was not too pleased about, but she seemed a little more reconciled to it by the end."

See? He knew she had a kind heart. "The minister at church this morning was talking about how some people have a gift of hospitality. That sounds like you."

"Me? Oh no." Her gaze fell to the table. "I wish I did, but I'm afraid my circumstances, living with my mother, don't make that an easy thing."

He was tempted to ask why she lived with her mother but figured that need not be a conversation for today. "My mom was always pretty generous and loved having people over. I think that rubbed off on my sister and me, but I know that's not the case for everyone."

"Non." The light had faded from her face, pushing him to want to encourage her again.

"But it sounds like what you did was just what that lady needed."

She nodded. "That's what I thought, too. And I hope to do it again."

He smiled, and she offered a small smile in return before sipping her matcha again. He lifted his arm and placed it behind her on top of the booth. She glanced up at him, as if startled, and he smiled. Yeah, it was a defensive play, something that might've looked a little possessive to those walking past. But the space between them felt warm, like she belonged with him, a concept he could feel more than articulate. He hoped she wouldn't ask him to articulate.

"Something today got me thinking," she said, after a moment. "You mentioned previously about Noah and the ark, and today I was thinking about olive branches. Is that in that story?"

Thanks, God. Pleased at how this conversation seemed to have veered around to what he wanted to say, he shared a little about the story of the flood. "So, when the dove returned after the flood had receded, it had an olive leaf in its beak, which showed there were some trees out there. The olive branch has been a symbol in Greek mythology, but Noah's story predates that, so Christians see it as a symbol of God wanting to be friends with us, which I think is pretty cool."

"Friends?"

His heart sank. He guessed she wasn't a God follower, then. "You don't think God wants to be friends with us?"

"It feels presumptuous to be friends with God."

So she believed in God at least. "What do you think the point of Jesus coming was, then?"

"To forgive us of our sins," she said softly.

"Exactly. Which happened because of God's love for us, because God longs for us to be friends with Him."

She sat back a little. "I never really thought of it like that."

"What did you think of it like?" he asked.

"I don't know."

He waited, breaking off a bit of croissant, enjoying the burst of buttery goodness on his tongue, even as he prayed for her.

She sipped her coffee, her brow pleated, and placed the cup back on the table. "I think growing up I was often told I was a sinner, and I knew that because, try as I might, I was never perfect. But I never really thought of Jesus dying on the cross because God wants to be my friend. I just thought it balanced out our sins."

Gently prompted, she went on to share some more about her background, and just as he'd suspected, she had a traditional church background that emphasized sin and repentance over grace and love. "I think it really makes a difference what gets emphasized and talked about in the sermons. That's what I'm enjoying about this church I mentioned to you. They're always really practical and relevant messages you can apply to your life. At least, I can," he added with a grin.

"Perhaps I'll come next weekend," she said tentatively.

His heart leapt. "That'd be awesome." Then he remembered that weekend was the first he'd be playing away. "Except I'll be flying to a game in Buffalo."

She nodded, her look one of disappointment, which propelled him to say, "But maybe the following weekend?"

Her gaze lifted to his. "Okay."

He felt a heart press. "Or you could go this coming weekend with my mom and sister."

Her eyes widened. "Quoi?"

Okay. He probably should mention this to Mom and Liv. They were due to leave earlier that day, but he'd pay for new airline tickets if they could stay. He'd do nearly anything to help Maggie feel like she could be comfortable in a church service. "My mom and sister are visiting this week."

"Not your father?" she asked.

"He died when I was ten."

"I'm so sorry."

"Hey, it's okay. I miss him, but I've had nearly twenty years to come to terms with it."

She waited a moment, then said, "My father died three years ago."

"I'm sorry."

Her gaze met his, and he was once again drawn into the honey-sweet depths. A moment passed, then another as this connection between them seemed to grow stronger.

He had to glance away, quietly exhale. He couldn't afford to get caught up in emotions if there was no place for those emotions to go. And while she might be on the journey to relationship with God, he didn't want to push his agenda onto her so she felt like faith had strings attached. He needed to play it cool, play it calm. Which meant he should probably change the subject.

"How have things been at the Gardens since last week?" He regretted the question as her face clouded again.

"I turned off all my social media, so now things seem almost normal. I've been told I can get back into working in the gardens this week, so I'm looking forward to that."

"Will you be there on Friday?"

She nodded. "I should be. Why?"

How to explain that his mom was interested in meeting her and that his sister wouldn't leave Montreal until she had? "I just wondered if maybe you'd be up for a visitor at the Gardens."

"You should know by now that the Jardin botanique welcomes visitors from all around the world." Her lips curved wryly.

"So, if I happened to swing by, I might find you?"

"Aren't you going to be busy with games?"

"I have a game on Thursday and Saturday nights, which means Friday is only a half day. I'll have practice that morning but should be free in the afternoon. It'd be good to have a little bit of fun." *And see you*, he almost added.

"But what about your family? Aren't they coming to visit?"

"I might have to be a bit of a tourist guide," he admitted. "So if you happen to know anyone who might be a local and might be willing to show them around…" He raised a brow.

She arched one of hers. "That's why you asked to see me? You want me to be a tourist guide for your family?"

"No, no." He couldn't quite decipher the tone of her voice, but it sounded a little like disappointment or offence. "I'm sorry if it sounded like that. Like I said before, I wanted to know how Noah is doing, and I wanted to see you."

"Why?"

Were all women here so direct? Olivia would like this girl too.

Too? He nearly groaned, then realized how that would come across so just settled for the truth. "I like you. I think we're friends. And I like to spend time with my friends. Don't you?"

She nodded, her eyes shaded with something he couldn't quite discern. "So, you're my friend?"

"I hope so," he said honestly. "And I hope you think we're friends too."

CHAPTER 12

Maggie huddled in her jacket. The rainy weather of the past three days had cleared, but while the sun might be out, it was still cool. At least she'd been able to walk to pick Noah up from school and finally give him the promised ice cream for his attendance. She watched the children depart, chatting with their friends in the way she hoped Noah would be able to do one day soon.

Friends.

The word sat souring in her stomach, just as it had since Sunday evening when Beau had first said it to her.

She'd been so wrong, so foolish to have thought he meant something else. Call her clueless, but when he'd looked at her the way he had, their gazes bound as if by more than the loss of their fathers, she'd really thought it had meant more, that perhaps the trembling hopes she scarcely dared admit to might finally be given oxygen to breathe. Clearly, she'd been wrong.

Then he'd veered the conversation to something that sounded awfully like her looking after his family, and she'd realized the depths of her delusions, his comment about being friends drawing hers about a need to return home and twining the tingly feeling of moments before into a tangled mess. Yes, she liked the man. But she was so out of practice with all this that she wasn't sure she knew how to simply be friends with a man. And just because he was one of the nicest men she'd ever met didn't mean she should be looking for things he clearly did not mean to suggest.

Her humiliation had been complete when a look she had dared imagine might be disappointment at her attempt at an abrupt departure turned out to be due to him sighting a teammate. And while she'd suffered through awkward hellos and the knowledge she didn't belong, she'd wondered why Beau's demeanor had turned cold. Propelled from her seat, she'd thanked him and left only to find a parking ticket on her windscreen. All in all, a complete winner of an evening.

How did someone simply de-escalate their feelings to mere friendship? She was usually so careful about who she let inside her heart, and she hadn't realized just how careless she had been. Never mind. It was a good thing she'd never spoken to her mother about Beau Nash and therefore never had to explain just what had happened. Or not happened.

"Noah!"

His round face lit in a broad grin as he rushed to her. She crouched to meet him with open arms.

"Hello, Maman."

"Hello, my darling boy," she said, kissing his cheek. "You look happier than yesterday. Was school good?"

He nodded. "And we get ice cream?"

"Oui."

His beam of delight could power a small planet. "I'm getting ice cream, Xavier."

Xavier, a little boy of South Asian heritage, looked up at his mother. "Can we get ice cream too?"

She shook her head, glancing at Maggie with an *are you serious?* expression. "It's too cold today."

"But Noah is," the boy complained.

"Come, Noah," Maggie said, steering him away from what was sure to be an awkward encounter. Maybe she should make more of an effort to chat with some of the other parents, but she couldn't right now. She still felt a little raw, like her emotional capacity was too thin. Maybe she and Noah could work on their friendship-making ability tomorrow. Right now she had time and energy enough for ice cream and little more.

"So, what flavor will it be this time?" she asked him as he carefully walked along the pavement, avoiding the cracks.

"Same," Noah said.

She smiled. Oh, how like her was he?

They reached the crèmerie and went inside. There were less people here today, the cooler weather no doubt keeping customers away. It meant they had more time to ponder the choices, even though Noah and Maggie herself knew that they would both get exactly the same.

The door tinkled open, and two children around Noah's age walked in, accompanied by two women, one Maggie's age, one older. They hushed the excited children, who spoke in an accent not unlike one she knew, one she'd been trying to get out of her head since Sunday. See how ridiculous she'd become, imagining his voice everywhere?

"Here you go." The girl behind the counter handed Noah his cone before handing Maggie her usual. "And one peach and mango for you."

"Thank you," Maggie said before gently nudging her son. "What do you say, Noah?"

"Merci beaucoup," Noah called before taking a huge bite of his ice cream.

"What did he say, Mommy?" the little girl said.

The younger woman—she was about Maggie's height, with dark-blonde hair—smiled at Maggie. "That was thank you, wasn't it?"

"Oui." Maggie nodded. "Yes."

"That looks delicious," the older woman said, smiling down at Noah. "What flavor is it, may I ask?"

Noah turned shy, leaving Maggie to answer. "Bananas and berries. They blend the fruits into the ice cream."

"Now I know why my son recommended this place," she said. "We've just flown in this morning, and he was supposed to bring us here, but work got in the way."

Maggie nodded politely. It always amazed her how some people were prepared to share such details with perfect strangers.

"What's your name?" the little boy asked Noah.

Noah didn't answer, his shyness coiling him around Maggie's legs.

"His name is Noah," Maggie said, noticing the younger woman's gaze snap back to her from her perusal of the board.

"Doesn't he understand me?" the little boy asked Maggie, pulling at her jacket.

"Bronson, leave the poor lady alone," the younger woman, obviously his mother, said. "I'm so sorry."

"It is no matter."

The woman eyed her until Maggie knew a prickle of concern, then her attention was stolen by her daughter's plea for the raspberry and watermelon flavor.

"Come, Noah, let's eat these on our way home," Maggie said.

"See you next time," the girl behind the counter called.

Maggie nodded, smiling politely at the other customers. "Enjoy your stay."

"Oh, we will," the older woman said. "It's a beautiful city."

"It is," Maggie agreed.

"My son certainly thinks so," the older woman said.

The younger woman snorted. "He's so good-natured he thinks anywhere is beautiful. Not that this place isn't," she hastened to assure Maggie.

Defensiveness rose, and Maggie's smile was less warm than a few moments earlier. She guided Noah from the store, then they moved automatically to the tree where they'd eaten ice cream only weeks before, and Maggie worked to sort out her silly feelings. She waited as Noah reached the halfway mark on his ice cream, the point where it would be safe to walk home without having to worry that he would be wearing most of it by the time they reached the front door.

The store's door tinkled, and the other ice cream enthusiasts exited, each of them holding an ice cream cone.

"Pardon me," the younger woman said as she moved toward them. "I really didn't mean to offend you before with that silly comment."

"It is no matter."

"You sure? I know some people find us Americans a little abrasive, and I really didn't mean to upset anyone. From what I've seen, this city is really beautiful, and I can't wait to explore. It's just that we got up so early this morning to get to the airport, and then four hours on a plane with two small children is no fun, and now my brother has basically left us on our own…well, it's just not easy, you know?"

"I can understand."

The woman smiled. "I'm Liv."

"Maggie."

Her eyes widened. "And this is your little boy Noah."

"Oui."

"And you're from here in Montreal?"

Maggie nodded. What was with the inquisition?

Liv smiled. Glanced at Maggie's ice cream. "May I ask what flavor you have?"

"Peach and mango."

"Aha. Excuse me." She went and spoke to the other woman in an undertone.

Maggie glanced at Noah, who was practicing his English

with the other children. She didn't want to interrupt, but they should probably get home. "Come, Noah. We should go."

"Before you go"—Liv rushed back over—"would you mind helping some tourists out?"

"Certainly."

"See, my brother is new in town. He recommended a few places we should go, but I'm wondering what a local would suggest."

"Are you staying downtown?" Maggie asked. "Many people feel the cobblestoned streets and stores are not unlike those you may find in Europe."

"We'll be sure to check them out. Anywhere else you recommend?"

"Mont Royal is always a popular place to get a sense of the city. There are many paths to walk along, and it has a big cross that lights at night and can be seen for miles."

"That sounds like a good adventure to wear out some kids."

"If you're looking for some other good activities for children, you might want to visit the museums."

"I've heard the Botanical Gardens are worth a look," the woman said.

Maggie stilled. Did the woman know she worked there? How could she? "They are definitely worth visiting," she said, relaxing. "There are a number of themed gardens including a First Nations garden, and the children may enjoy visiting the butterfly house," she added, warming to her theme.

"I love butterflies, Mommy," the little girl said.

"We'll have to make sure we visit, then," the younger woman said, smiling at her daughter as she ruffled her hair.

Should Maggie admit she worked there? She swallowed, the confession on her lips—

"I wish Uncle Beau was here," the little girl complained.

Beau? Maggie's gaze snapped to Liv's. Non, she must have misheard. What were the chances—?

She glanced at the older woman, whom she supposed could be his mother, given the similar coloring. Which would make Liv his sister. Breath sucked in. Not the sister she'd spoken to on Beau's phone in the hospital? She could've sworn the woman had a different name, although now she couldn't quite recall it.

"Have we met before?" Liv asked. "I'm sure I recognize your voice from somewhere."

"Stop teasing the poor girl, Liv," the older woman said, smiling at Maggie. "Hello, Maggie. My name is Andrea. I believe you know my son."

Maggie's heart hammered. Non. It couldn't be. Non non. *Non.*

"My son, Beau Nash."

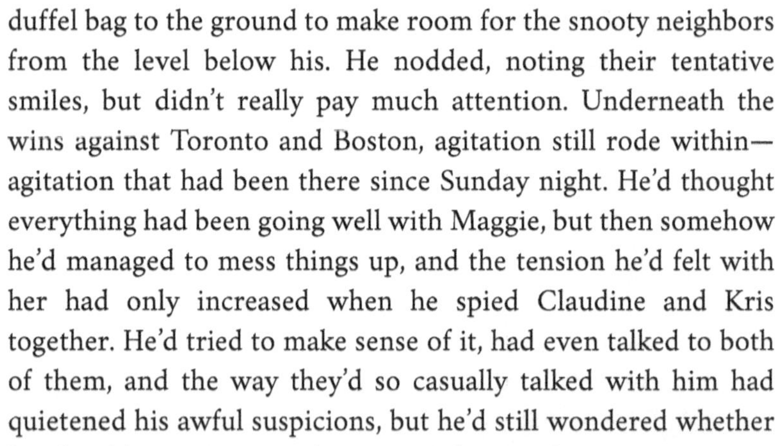

THE ELEVATOR DOORS OPENED, and Beau was forced to drop his duffel bag to the ground to make room for the snooty neighbors from the level below his. He nodded, noting their tentative smiles, but didn't really pay much attention. Underneath the wins against Toronto and Boston, agitation still rode within— agitation that had been there since Sunday night. He'd thought everything had been going well with Maggie, but then somehow he'd managed to mess things up, and the tension he'd felt with her had only increased when he spied Claudine and Kris together. He'd tried to make sense of it, had even talked to both of them, and the way they'd so casually talked with him had quietened his awful suspicions, but he'd still wondered whether he should mention anything to Gabe on the trip to Boston yesterday. He hadn't, and now he felt guilty, even though he'd done nothing wrong.

And now, with his mom and sister in town, he didn't feel like he was in the right headspace to really be the host he should be. A call from the club had meant he'd needed to miss being their tour guide today, so instead of the promised ice cream treat, he'd gone to work for an extra on-ice training session and left them to themselves. He could only hope they'd managed to find some way to entertain themselves and that Bailey and Bronson didn't hate their uncle for standing them up today.

The elevator stopped to release his snooty neighbors—really, he'd have to come up with a more Christian name for them— then progressed to his floor. He exited, taking a moment to draw in the tranquility evoked by the cream walls and tiles, then unlocked the door and went inside.

"Uncle Bobo!" screamed Bronson, hurling his little body at Beau's legs.

"Whoa, dude. You need to calm the farm right on down." He dumped his duffel bag, then scooped his nephew up and chucked him over his shoulder. Poor kid. Imagine being cooped up here all day. No wonder he was going a little crazy.

"Uncle Beau! Can we go see the butterflies?" Bailey asked.

"Um, sure?" He glanced at his sister as she entered the room. "Hey, sis."

"Hi, Beau." She grinned, eyeing him in that annoying way she'd had since they were kids.

"What?"

"Have you had a good day?"

"Yeah. Well, apart from finding out at the last minute that I had extra practice today." He put Bronson down on the couch and began tickling him, ignoring the squeals and giggles from the boy. "Sorry I had to leave you. I hope you got out and managed something fun."

"We did." His sister still held that Cheshire cat grin.

"What?" When she didn't answer, he shrugged. "Where's Mom?"

"She's having a rest. Our little walk tired her out, I think."

"Where'd you walk to?" He turned to Bronson. "What did you get up to today?"

"We had ice cream," his nephew said.

"Nice!" He turned to Liv. "Did you go to that place I recommended?"

"Sure did. It was great."

"What flavor did you have, buddy?" Beau said, tickling Bronson's stomach.

"I had banana and berries. It was good. Yum yum in my tum tum."

"I knew you'd enjoy it," Beau said.

"I'll let Mom know you're here." Olivia pivoted on her heel and walked down the hall.

"Did you like your ice cream, Bailey?" Beau asked his niece.

"It was good. I didn't like all the walking though."

"Think of the ice cream as a reward for all that hard work."

Her nose wrinkled, unconvinced. "Can we go to the butterfly house while we're here?"

"Where's the butterfly house?" he asked.

"I made a new friend," Bronson interrupted.

"Did you?" Beau's gaze shifted from Bronson to Bailey, his eyebrows rising.

"At a park," Bailey continued, unfazed by her brother's interruption.

"We'll have to go there, then."

"Really?" Her face lit in a way that looked so much like Maggie's that he was forced to swallow. He needed to put thoughts of her aside.

"My friend," Bronson said, tugging on Beau's shirt hem as Liv returned, followed by their mother.

"What about him, bud?" he asked.

"Yeah, tell him about your new friend," Liv said again.

"He's nice," Bronson said lamely.

"Well, that's good," Beau said, ruffling his hair before standing. "Hey, Mom." He bent to give her a kiss on the cheek. "Had a little too much fun today, huh?"

"You could say that."

"You like the ice cream place?"

"It was most enjoyable." She smiled, glancing at Liv, who was back to her Cheshire cat ways.

"I thought it was some of the best I've tasted." Or maybe that was because of the company he'd had. "Speaking of food—"

"When do you not?" Liv teased.

"I thought for dinner we could try a restaurant down the street. They have a kid-friendly menu, but they serve beverages that might appeal to a certain someone I know."

"Might that mean something involving teeny apples?" his sister asked with a cocked eyebrow.

"It might. And something mosa-like for Ma."

"I don't drink cocktails anymore."

"Mom, after the day we've had, you've earned a few," Liv said.

"A few?" His mom looked aghast. "I couldn't manage one."

"Okay, well I've certainly earned a few appletinis. Where is this place?" Liv asked.

"I thought your day went well," Beau said.

"It did, apart from the early start and the kids poking each other the whole time on the plane. The walk to the ice cream place was good. It kept them quiet for a while."

"And you liked your ice cream."

She grinned again. "We sure did."

"Uncle Beau." Bronson tugged on Beau's sleeve. "I made a new friend today."

"That's great, man. Was that on the plane?"

Bronson shook his blond head. "No."

"Was that here in the building? Eddie's pretty nice, isn't he?"

"Who's Eddie?"

Okay, so maybe it wasn't Eddie. "He did well to make a new friend, then," Beau said, glancing at Liv.

"He sure did."

Beau squatted, ruing the earlier workout that made this move a little painful. "Take after your uncle, do you?"

"He sure does," his sister said.

"So, what's your new friend's name, buddy?"

Bronson's face wrinkled in deep concentration. "Mommy, what's my new friend's name?"

"You remember," she said, her eyes shifting to Beau. "We read about a man with this boy's name in the Bible last week."

"A Bible name, huh?" Beau said. "You remember this kid's name?"

Bronson grinned. "I remember!"

Man, to be a parent you'd need the patience of a saint. "What's his name?"

"Noah," he said triumphantly.

Beau blinked. "What did you say?"

"Noah," Bronson repeated.

No. There had to be other kids with that name in Montreal. "Where did you meet him?" he asked, heart ticking faster.

"At the ice cream store," Bailey said impatiently. "Can we *please* go see the butterflies?"

Beau nodded, sliding a look at his mom and sister. "The ice cream store I mentioned?"

His mother nodded as his sister smirked.

No. It had to be a different kid. Had to be.

He pushed to his feet. He had to change this subject, if only for his own sanity. "So, who's ready to go out for dinner?"

"Changing the topic, are we?" his sister said with a smirk.

She knew him too well. "Conscious time's a-tickin'."

"You're not going to go like that, are you?" Olivia said, eyeing his work-out attire with a frown.

"I was planning to shower and change, but now I'm not so sure." He moved to her and wrapped her in a sweaty hug.

"Ugh, let me go," she said, laughing as she squirmed to get away. "You smell gross."

"You're welcome."

"You're funny, Uncle Bobo," Bronson said, clapping his hands.

"That I am." He glanced at his mom. "I'll be a few minutes, but make yourself at home."

"We already have," she said.

Yeah. From the way his apartment didn't look like it had this morning, it seemed they certainly had. He pulled his hair free from the hair tie.

"Noah," Bronson said again.

Beau's movements stilled as his pulse picked up pace. Nope. He couldn't do this. He moved down the hall to his room.

"Hey, Beau," his sister called. "Guess what Noah's mom's name is."

He turned to face her, his gut tensing.

Olivia lifted her chin, her look every bit as triumphant as Bronson's earlier. "Maggie."

The season was changing, summer about to give way to autumn. Maggie eyed the oak tree that had proved so fateful all those weeks ago, surprise still rippling at yesterday's events. Of all the people to encounter, it had to be Beau's family. His delightful, lovely family. Granted, Liv would take some getting used to, and the kids were pretty loud, but his mother was so sweet and kind that it was obvious where Beau had gained his good heart.

Maggie blinked, trying to stuff stupid emotions back into professional demeanor. She didn't need to get carried away simply because she'd met his family and they'd met half of hers.

"Maggie? You're needed in the Fern Greenhouse," her walkie-talkie crackled.

"Sure." She moved to the collection of greenhouses that welcomed visitors near the front entrance. The Exhibition Greenhouse was where the pumpkin show would be held, its two tiers and babbling waterfall filled with beautiful plants from around the world. The next room held the miniature trees, the bonsai-type potted plants surrounded by ponds and bridges that drew the eyes. Beyond that lay the Sunlight Conservatory, which displayed perennial plants from arid regions, such as succulents and cacti, all in a hacienda-style setting. This room flowed into the Arid Regions Greenhouse, beyond which lay the humid space where begonias and varieties of African violet delighted visitors. Next were the tropical glasshouses, which included turtles and frogs, then it was the beautiful orchids.

She paused here, ever aware of the delicate flowers ripe for photo opportunities. The pretty blooms of mauve and lilac would photograph well, so she'd be sure to return here as soon as she'd sorted whatever needed to be done in the fern hothouse next door. This bigger space contained many rare specimens from around the world. Montreal's extreme winter climate meant some plants had to receive special care indoors from late autumn, including some of the Japanese maples that couldn't cope with the harsh conditions. These greenhouses had been built to supplement the learning and educational facilities of the Jardin botanique.

The fernery held a collections of mosses and dinosaur-era ferns, with large tree ferns and waterfalls centering the exhibition space. She rounded the cave-like structure at the end and saw Frederic.

"Ah, here she is." Frederic gestured her near.

She fixed on a smile and moved forward, her steps slowing on the faux-stone path as she caught sight of the people standing with him. Two women, two children, and one very tall man. She stilled. Then forced her feet to move forward.

"Bonjour," the man said, his smile as strained-looking as hers felt.

"Bonjour." She turned away, unable to face Beau. Had he set this up? From the awkwardness in his face, she didn't think so. Was this his sister's doing? "Hello, Olivia. Good morning, Mrs. Nash. Hello, Bailey and Bronson." Her smile felt stiff as she glanced at Frederic.

"I was told they wished to speak to you," he said in French.

"I didn't arrange this," she said, knowing she sounded defensive but not willing to let anyone think more of this than it was.

"You need not worry. Danielle will be more than happy for some photos, I'm sure."

"Oui, je n'en route pas." She didn't doubt it at all. She turned to the family, who seemed to be wondering about their exchange. "Pardon."

"Were you speaking French?" the little girl asked.

"Oui," Maggie said. "That means yes."

"I know."

"Bailey," Olivia hissed. "Don't be rude, otherwise we won't see the butterflies."

"You wished to see the butterflies?" Relief filled Maggie's chest. Perhaps she could get away from having to show them anything else. "I'm afraid they're in the Insectarium, which is a little walk away."

"Oh." Bailey groaned. "Not more walking."

"Bailey, honey," Beau said, caressing the girl's hair with his huge hand. "You're starting to sound a little rude."

Maggie lowered her gaze to the girl. "Do you like butterflies, Bailey?"

The little girl nodded.

"You'll love it there," Maggie promised. "You can walk among the butterflies and have them land on you and give you a kiss."

The girl's eyes lit. "Really?"

"Really."

"We can all do with more kisses in our lives, can't we, Beau?" Olivia said.

Maggie's cheeks flamed, and from his pinking features, he felt embarrassed too.

"It's not too late to call Jesse and see if he can come for the weekend," he drawled, brow lowered as he nailed his sister with his gaze.

Looked like it was time to leave. "Well, I hope you enjoy your visit there."

"Oh, can't you come?" Olivia said, her attention flicking back to Maggie. "We hoped—"

"She's working, Liv," Beau muttered, his gaze avoiding Maggie's.

Maggie's chest grew tight. He didn't want to see her? She swallowed. "That's right. It was nice to see you all, but I really should get back to work."

"It's good to see you, Maggie," Mrs. Nash said softly.

"You too," she murmured. "I hope you enjoy your stay in Montreal."

She managed a smile but still did not meet Beau's eyes. The awkwardness of seeing him after the last time, when he'd friend-zoned her—and this in front of his mother and sister—felt like walking across shards of glass.

With a nod to Frederic, she hurried back through to the other greenhouses, her throat and chest tight as she blinked rapidly to keep the moisture away. By the time she'd made it to the arid regions, she thought herself more composed, able to find a semblance of a smile for some of the visitors looking at the cacti.

She'd long thought she could describe herself as such—able to survive in a dry wasteland, complete with prickles that kept people venturing too close. But she also now knew there were vast reserves of emotion locked inside that only the most brave or foolhardy could discern. And that Beau's attention had nurtured her confidence so close to blooming, like those cacti that took years to flower. Talk about foolhardy.

Maggie willed her expression to pleasantness as she returned to her office, nodding to colleagues before she settled back at her desk.

"Are you okay?" Danielle asked.

She nodded, words trapped in her tight throat.

"You are sure?" Danielle moved closer to Maggie's desk. "Your eyes look a little red."

"I must be coming down with something," she muttered, fixing her attention on the computer as she powered it up.

She sensed Danielle's gaze resting on her until she was distracted by a message. Danielle whistled. "Is it true that Beau Nash is visiting the gardens again?"

Maggie's head snapped up, his name like her personal puppet string. She swallowed, conscious that Danielle was studying her with a small smile. What to say? *I didn't invite him. I didn't know. I don't know if I can face him or his family again.* She swallowed. "Oui."

"Have you just seen him?"

Maggie glanced at Danielle's phone. "Was that Frederic?"

"I'm going to take that as oui." Danielle eyed her seriously. "So what are you doing in here instead of out there with him?"

When I'm with him I feel awkward and confused certainly did not sound very professional. "I have work to do."

"*Exactement*, you do. Out there with him."

"Pardon?"

"Maggie, you know part of your job is to be involved with the communications and social engagement of the Gardens, non?"

Maggie nodded.

"Then go out there and communicate and socially engage. Don't you think his attendance here will only help boost the Gardens' visitor attendance? Especially if you can take some nice photos."

But how could she go back out there, having virtually run away?

Maggie's phone buzzed. She glanced at the screen. Bit her lip.

"Is that him?" Danielle asked.

She nodded.

"Does he want to see you?"

"Oui."

"Then go. Don't let whatever is intimidating you stop you from something that could be one of the best things of your life."

"Guiding his family around the Gardens?"

"His family is here?" Danielle's eyes rounded. "Maggie! I didn't know things had grown so serious."

"They're not," she insisted. "It's just the opposite. He only wants to be my friend."

At Danielle's command to share, Maggie did just that, and Danielle's mouth fell open. "He friend-zoned you?"

She nodded.

"Wow." Danielle tapped her long fingernails on the desk. "Then all the more reason for you to go out there, prove it means nothing. And maybe you—or he—will discover it means something after all."

"But—"

"No buts. Whatever other work you thought you had to do, cancel it. This is your priority for the rest of the day." She smiled. "And if you find this means you have to leave a little early in order to maintain good public relations, then do so. And if that means maintaining good private relations as well, then I'm okay with that too."

Maggie's mouth fell open. "Maybe you should go out there, then."

"I can't believe you just said that. Don't you know I'm a happily married woman?"

Still, the comment about private relations bothered Maggie. "You know we're barely even friends."

"Says the woman who keeps getting messages from the man. Go. Have fun. See you next week."

"But—"

"Go!"

So Maggie went.

~

BEAU FIXED a smile on his dial as he returned to where his mom and sister waited.

"You couldn't find her?" his mom asked sympathetically.

"She's working. She probably has her phone switched off or something."

"I'm sorry," Mom said. "I like her."

"Me too." Olivia looked remorseful. "I'm sorry if I said anything that chased her away."

"Sure you are."

"I am." The penitent twist to her lips said it was true. "I can't remember the last time you went chasing after a girl, so I guess she's important to you."

"She is, but it's complicated."

"Complicated how?"

He shrugged, shoved his hands in his pockets. "We have this weird dynamic where she seems to push me away or I push her away."

"She's a single mom, Beau. She's no doubt being careful after being hurt by some guy who left her."

"She's a widow, Liv. Her husband died five years ago."

"Oh. Poor sweetheart." Liv's eyes glistened. "Poor Noah. He must have been so young to lose his father."

Beau nodded, glancing to where the kids reached across to the waterfall. He should have realized Maggie's history probably explained a lot of her standoffish, wary ways. "And I don't think she's a Christian, so that's that."

"How do you know?" Mom asked. "Have you asked her?"

"That would require time to talk, and with everything that's been going on—"

"Would you like to talk with her?" Liv interrupted.

"Well, sure, but I—"

"Then you might need to turn around," she said quietly.

He obeyed, stunned to see Maggie standing there. His heart dropped. How much of that had she heard? "Um, hi."

Her weak smile echoed his. "It turns out that I'm not needed elsewhere, so if there is any interest in a tour of the Gardens, well, I'm available if you would like."

"I would like," his mom said. "Beau? What do you say?"

He studied Maggie. "For real?" he asked softly.

She nodded. "My boss learned that you were here, and she thought that we at the Gardens should make the most of that. But only if you don't mind, and only if you're interested."

"I don't mind," he said, then softer still, added, "and I'm definitely interested."

Her lips flickered to a half smile, then she turned her attention to the children.

"Maggie!" Bailey ran over to her. "Can we please see the butterflies now?"

Bronson tugged at the hem of her shirt. "Where's Noah?"

"He's at school, sweetheart."

Beau's heart grew soft. She was so tender with children.

"Can I see him again?" Bronson pleaded.

"Er, I'm not sure." She flicked Liv an apologetic-looking smile. "I think you'll be very busy this weekend, and—"

"Are you busy tonight?" Beau asked. "We're having dinner at my place. I thought it would be a good chance to introduce the family to my friends, and you could bring Noah. But only if you're not busy. And only if you like."

Her smile at him was shy. "I'm not busy. And I'd like."

He grinned, the world feeling like it had color again.

"Noah?" Bronson asked.

"He'll come visit you tonight," Beau said, swinging him up with a tickle. "Isn't that great?"

"Really great!" Bronson said, giggling.

"Really great," Liv said, her grin matched by Mom's own.

"Really great," Beau said, gaze tangling with Maggie's for a long moment.

Then she blinked. Blushed. And turned. "So, shall we start that tour now?"

BEAU HAD NEVER REALLY KNOWN JUST how fascinating gardens could be until he'd been led through ten exhibition greenhouses by a cute horticultural expert with a sexy French accent. Somehow she managed to bring things to life that would normally bore him to tears, to educate in a way that felt far from the schoolroom. She had the kids transfixed, especially Bailey, who loved the butterflies in the Main Exhibition Greenhouse, even though it wasn't the Insectarium Maggie had mentioned earlier. Maggie had promised they would get there, but Bailey had been distracted by Maggie's talk about the pumpkin festival that would happen soon.

"We have all kinds of pumpkins that get decorated by children from all across the city. We've had pumpkins decorated to look like mermaids, to look like pearls. We've even had one that looked like Cinderella's carriage."

"Really?"

Maggie nodded, retrieving her phone. "Look." She showed her a photo.

"Oh, that's beautiful!" Bailey breathed.

"I think everyone has a lot of fun decorating."

"Mommy, can we please come back here and do pumpkin decorating too?" Bailey pleaded.

"Sorry," Maggie mouthed.

"We'll have to see," Liv promised.

"You always say that, and it always means no." Bailey sighed loudly.

"Perhaps you'll have a pumpkin festival near where you live,"

Maggie said. "Ours happens next month because it connects with our Thanksgiving."

"But it's October next month," Bailey said, frowning.

"That's right. And Canadians celebrate our Thanksgiving in October. So we have our pumpkin festival, which finishes with the Pumpkin Ball."

"A ball?" Bailey's face glowed. "Like in Cinderella?"

Maggie smiled. "Sort of." She glanced at Liv and Mom. "It's a fundraiser for the Gardens, and one of our biggest events all year."

"Are you going to the Pumpkin Ball, Uncle Beau?" Bailey asked, stars in her eyes.

"I think so," he said, his gaze drifting to Maggie. "It sure sounds fun."

"You should go," Bailey said. "You could take Maggie."

Beau grew conscious of Liv's snickering in the background. "We'll have to see."

Bailey blew out an exasperated sigh. "I hope you don't mean no too."

He hoped it wouldn't mean no as well. He had a feeling he'd already agreed, but given the strain between Maggie and himself, he wasn't sure if that was still the case. But that required a conversation with Maggie that wasn't front and center of his family's attention.

"Come on, Bailey. Leave poor Uncle Beau alone." Liv collected Bronson's hand. "Now, Maggie, can you tell me about these flowers here?"

Beau released his own sigh as the trio moved away. God bless his sister for her distraction.

"I like her," his mother said softly. "I'm glad you invited her tonight. It will be a good chance to see if there is anything deeper there."

"I don't know how much chance there'll be," he admitted. "I asked Gabe and Claudine too, so that'll be interesting."

"Well, you'd best make the most of today, then," she advised.

"I still need to find out where she stands with God. I've invited her to church, but she hasn't come yet."

His mother was silent for a few moments, and he glanced at her. He'd always valued his mother's advice. Her expertise may be in prettying up homes, but over the years, she'd proved to have some pretty solid advice for his life, too.

"What is it?"

"You need to be careful, son."

"I know. She's a little wary of dating, because of what happened to her husband."

"Not just because of that." She glanced at him. "You need to make sure you're not just dealing with relationship evangelism, where you want her saved for your own purposes."

"I want her relating with God for her sake," he insisted.

Mom didn't seem to be buying. "You need to be certain that she doesn't confuse the two."

"What do you mean?"

"That her relationship with God isn't based on her relationship with you, and if the relationship with you ends, then her relationship with God ends, too."

Huh. He'd never really thought about it like that before. In the online Bible study with his NHL friends, they'd talked about relationships quite a few times, especially in recent years as a number of the guys had found women they'd formed serious relationships with and even married. And sure, the topic of relationship evangelism had come up, but he'd never really paid attention before. He'd never really needed to. The only girls in his past had been church girls he'd known for years. But now that he'd found a woman who intrigued him, he wanted to know more.

"What happens if it takes years for her to accept God? What then?" his mother asked softly.

Years? His gut clenched. But still a stubborn hope persisted.

"I can't help it," he said. "I feel like there's a bigger purpose with all of this. And I can't help but look at all the coincidences and wonder whether God is using this to guide my steps. You know I'm trusting Him to open the right doors and close the wrong ones, and that I pray that every day."

"I do."

"So I'm trusting Him, Mom."

"That's all we can do," his mother said. "Just remember that you can talk to Maggie about spiritual things, you can invite her to church, but it's the Holy Spirit who really has to do the work in her heart. And until that happens, well, don't let your emotions get too caught up."

He nodded. He'd seen too many other relationships combust because emotions had run far ahead of wisdom.

"And know that I'll be praying."

"Thanks, Mom," he said, pressing a kiss to her head.

His gaze traveled back to Maggie, who was talking about medicinal plants and the poison garden. Her gaze found his and she smiled.

His heart kicked. *Lord, soften her heart so she knows You.* He swallowed. *And untangle my motives so they're pure and good.*

CHAPTER 14

Maggie's mouth dried as she stood at the door. So perhaps this was taking public relations a little further than Danielle could ever have expected. But while she knew Beau's invitation to dinner tonight was because of Noah and Bronson's cute fixation with him, her heart dared to wonder again if Beau was interested in her. That was why she'd spent so much time fixing her hair and changing her mind about the two outfits that could possibly, maybe, be considered appropriate for dinner with Montreal's beloved goaltender.

The dress she'd selected brought back bittersweet memories, being the dress she had worn when Alain proposed. It might be out of fashion, but she loved the way the color and fit made her feel stronger and sexier than her usual work attire allowed. Not that it was inappropriate—she'd never owned anything that showed too much skin. And besides, dinner with her son would scarcely allow for anything like that. But the skirt *was* shorter than Maman liked, even if Noah had declared she looked beautiful and she'd seen a few admiring glances on her way from the parking lot and downstairs to up here.

She swallowed, hand poised to knock. She still had to pinch

herself that this was real. This apartment complex had a doorman—a very nice man who'd told her, when she introduced herself, that Mr. Nash was waiting for her upstairs. She'd thanked him, wondering if she was supposed to tip, this world so far removed from hers she barely knew what to do. How could Beau be so down-to-earth when he lived here? The downstairs lobby was elegant, the residents she'd seen owning a tilt to their noses like they breathed purified air. If the marbled interior of the elevator was anything to go by, then Beau's apartment would be glamorous to the extreme.

"Maman?"

She blinked, refocused, and smiled at her son. Tonight was for his sake, after all. "Ready?"

Lights sparked in his dark eyes as he grinned. Her heart melted. Really, she needed to keep her mind on him. She might feel a little nervous, but at least she'd met all the people who would be here tonight, and she sensed that even if she hadn't quite figured out the dynamics of this relationship with Beau, at least she could manage enough conversation with the others for one night.

Before she could talk herself out of it, she knocked firmly.

The door immediately swung open, like Beau had been waiting for her. "You're here!"

"Bonsoir," she said.

"Bonsoir," he echoed, his gaze traveling down her attire, his face softening when he met her eyes again. "You look beautiful."

And he looked casual. T-shirt and jeans. Hair flowing loose, cheek scruff. Her chest grew tight. She'd overdressed. From behind him she could see Olivia was dressed much the same—casually. Her mouth sagged. Non.

"Come on in."

She gently pushed Noah inside, wondering for a fleeting futile minute if she could turn and run downstairs and somehow go change. But Beau had opened the door wider and gestured her inside, and she had no option but to take her overly dressed-up self inside and fix a smile to her overly made-up face.

"Maggie!" Beau's mother smiled. "Don't you look lovely!"

Non. She looked like she'd tried way too hard. She really shouldn't have worn these heels. "Hello." At least Andrea was dressed nicely.

Her gaze shifted to Olivia, who shot a look at her brother, then snapped back to Maggie.

"Maggie! Good to see you again. You look great. I feel so bad that Beau and I haven't had time to change yet. Can you give me a moment?"

"Uh, certainly." She wasn't early, was she? She glanced at Beau as Olivia disappeared down the hall. "Is there anything I can do?"

"Nope." His smile seemed forced. "Give me a sec, and I'll be back too."

She nodded and moved to look at the view. Sheer gray curtains veiled the city lights, but it was a stunning view. She swiped slick hands down her skirt, wishing *hard* she'd gone with tonight's other option of a maxi-dress. Or at least had not gone the whole pancake makeup deal. Any thicker and it could double as a mask and hide her extreme mortification.

"Hi, Maggie," Bailey said. "You look pretty. Are you going to a ball?"

"No." Her smile felt garish. "Just having dinner."

"Thanks for showing us the butterflies today. That was really fun."

Maggie's shoulders relaxed. That had been really fun, and she'd found herself oohing and ahhing and giggling just like any other tourist. "It's pretty special, isn't it?"

"I can see why you love working there," Andrea said, drawing to Maggie's other side. "It's wonderful to see how versatile the different gardens are."

"The man who first created them had great vision."

"You can see that," Andrea continued.

She smiled at Maggie, and Maggie felt her defenses drop a little more. There was something quite serene about this woman, something unlike the nervous edge her own mother possessed. "Thank you for helping me today."

"In what way?" she asked.

"Helping convince Beau to be in the photos." Maggie had tried to not push, had tried to make it fun, to showcase some of the different gardens like Danielle seemed to want her to do. She'd sensed Beau's reluctance, which she put down to his protests of not wanting to behave like a model. And she couldn't deny it. He did look a little Adonis-like in some of the shots. But his mother's comment that he should help out poor Maggie had soon stopped the objections. "You need to make the most of today, son," she'd added.

Maggie wasn't too sure what she'd meant by that but had been happy to get the requisite pictures, although she wasn't sure she'd need to show all of them to Danielle.

"Sometimes a little nudge is necessary with boys, don't you think?" Andrea continued.

So true. Maggie nodded. She wasn't sure whether it was simply his age or also his gender that made Noah so forgetful sometimes.

"Anyway, as far as I could see, you were the one doing all the helping. I never knew so much about plants before."

"I hope I didn't bore anyone."

"On the contrary, my dear. I think we all found it fascinating."

That was generous. She'd seen the way the kids had grown tired, so she'd done a highlights of the highlights tour until they reached the Insectarium.

"What's fascinating?" a deeper voice asked.

Maggie's ease fled, and she kept her gaze fixed outside.

"More like who," his mother replied with a tinkle of laughter in her voice that made Maggie blush some more. Okay, so she liked Beau's family, but she didn't really appreciate the constant hints they seemed to feel necessary.

"Beau, you look far better now," his mother said, approval in her voice.

Maggie peeked across and saw he'd smoothed his hair and tied it back, replaced the T-shirt with a collared shirt, and changed the jeans to darker pants. He'd shaved too and put on some cologne that tugged at her senses. For a moment she wondered what it would be like to go out on a proper date with him instead of a casual coffee moment where he insisted they were only friends. To be in a relationship with him where she could stroke his cheek and find out if it was as smooth as it appeared. To know what his lips felt like against hers. Her stomach clenched. She glanced away.

"I'm back!"

Maggie turned to see Olivia, now wearing a dress and with her hair and makeup done. For a moment Maggie wondered if Olivia had done this for Maggie's sake, but before she could wonder much longer, a knock came at the door. Her gaze swung to Beau, who bit his lip.

"I'm sorry, Maggie. I should have mentioned I'm expecting Gabe and Claudine as well."

He was? All the insecurities about being dressed this way rushed back. She glanced uncertainly at Olivia, who simply smiled.

"I haven't met any of Beau's teammates, so this should be fun."

Maggie got the impression Beau's family found a lot of things fun. But maybe that was part of who they were. Outward looking, interested in others, expecting positive things, just like Beau was. Maybe she could do that too.

A couple walked in. The woman was the one Maggie had met last Sunday, but she was with a different man. Who—?

"Gabe, Claudine, please meet my mom Andrea, my sister Olivia, my niece and nephew Bailey and Bronson, and this is Maggie and her son Noah."

She'd wondered how he'd introduce her. Not as his friend, it seemed. And it seemed to have confused Gabe and Claudine too, even as they nodded.

"Maggie?" Gabe asked. He was shorter and stockier than Beau, which wasn't hard.

"Hello." She managed the small talk thing for a while, explaining she worked at the Botanical Gardens, where she'd met Beau last month. There was no frown at the mention of the Gardens, so apparently the incident of the rude visitor had not spread too far, which helped the knot in her chest ease. But even as she managed small talk, she wondered who the other man had been with Claudine.

"Hi, Claudine," Maggie said. "We met before, on Sunday. At the coffee place when I was with Beau?"

This scored raised eyebrows from Gabe as well as Beau's mother and sister.

"You didn't tell me, babe," Gabe said.

"I must have forgotten." Claudine's glance switched between Maggie and Olivia. "I didn't realize tonight was formal."

There was a beat.

"Oh!" Olivia laughed. "You mean this isn't how you always dress at night? I figured that Montreal was far more sophisticated than where I was from, so I wanted to make sure I made an effort to blend in."

"We look really underdressed." Claudine winced. "Should I go home and change?"

"You look good," Andrea said, drawing closer. "And dinner's almost ready, so how about Olivia and Maggie get the kids cleaned up, and Beau and I will serve the meal."

Maggie joined Olivia in the bathroom as they supervised Bronson, Bailey and Noah wash their hands. She found Beau's sister eyeing her in the large mirror, a small smile on her mouth, and instantly knew what had happened.

"Thank you."

"For what?"

"Getting changed." Maggie motioned to her outfit. "I didn't know—" Emotion welled, and she blinked it away.

"Hey, it's okay. I love an excuse to dress up, and when you turned up looking so fabulous, well, I knew I should've upped my game. And hey, I don't mind an excuse to help Beau look less like a hockey player and more like a Swedish model."

Maggie choked.

"Come on. Admit it. You like him."

Maggie met the hazel eyes, then dropped her gaze to the children. Olivia seemed to take the hint, as she nodded and shooed them away.

"He likes you, you know," Olivia said.

Maggie's heart rippled, but she shook her head. "He's nice," she whispered, "but we're just friends."

"Uh huh." Olivia smirked.

The fact Beau hadn't left a seat beside him at the table suggested he thought that too, which again prompted her questions about what she was doing here at all. Still, seated next to Gabe, whom she learned was Montreal's captain, kept her on her toes.

"I can't remember the last time I met someone who didn't know much about hockey."

The way he said it made her wonder if it was a bad thing. "It was just me at home growing up," she explained, "and my father was always more interested in his plants than sports. Then when he died, well, it wasn't exactly something my mother was interested in."

"How old were you when that happened?"

She glanced around the table and saw the adults all were listening. "It was only a few years ago."

"That must've been very challenging for you and your mother," Andrea said.

Maggie remembered in that moment that Beau's father had died when Beau was young. "I don't think it's easy at any stage."

"Of course not," she murmured. "But when you had lost a husband as well."

Her sympathy welled emotion within, and Maggie had to look at her plate of veal.

Claudine chuckled. "You make it sound like Maggie is very careless and always misplacing people."

Someone inhaled sharply, and Maggie recognized that her reaction to the callous remark could either tip the evening into strain or smooth it into ease. She swallowed and, from somewhere deep within, found a smile. "Perhaps I can be careless about those I care about," she said mildly. "But I assure you, it is not always. Only sometimes."

She cut a piece of meat and chewed it, glad it gave her something to do. Gladder, too, that she had chosen to overlook what could be considered an offensive remark. Perhaps this was what being generous felt like—letting people make mistakes and not holding it against them. She realized now just how good she was at holding onto the past.

A glance up saw her gaze collide with Beau's and then hold on. His lips curved into warmth, and she knew a wobbly feeling in her chest where her heart must be.

Finally, his gaze switched back to Claudine. "I guess we can all be careless sometimes with those we care about, don't you think?" His eyes held a meaning Maggie didn't understand, but Claudine seemed to as she flushed and drank her wine in one gulp.

Interesting. A quick glance at Gabe showed he didn't really

notice anything, or maybe he was just oblivious to subtleties. His conversation seemed to consist of hockey and little else.

"So, are you going to the game tomorrow night?" Gabe asked Maggie.

A cry from the children's table—the coffee table, with cushions for seats—saved her from answering as she jumped to her feet. Noah had knocked over the water bottle, which even now was dripping onto the expensive carpet. "Oh no."

"Hey." Beau was beside her. "It's okay. It's only water. Grab the roll of paper towel from next to the sink and we'll get it sorted."

She obeyed, and two minutes later, she and Beau had mopped up the excess water while a saturated Noah was crying. "I should take him home. I'm so sorry."

"I can see if Bronson has some clothes that will fit him," Olivia suggested.

But Maggie knew that Noah's tears held embarrassment as well as tiredness, and nothing would appease them apart from sleep. "I'm afraid it's been a big day. He had school this morning, and he's not used to late nights."

"I'm sorry you can't stay," Beau said.

No protest? That was all? She made her apologies and farewells to the others still seated at the table, then moved to collect her bag and her and Noah's coats.

She forced a smile. "Thank you for a nice night." She helped Noah into his coat.

Beau hovered nearby. "We could throw his stuff into the dryer, and I could see if I've got something he could fit into."

"Like what? A sock?"

He chuckled. "Don't be mean, now."

"You're hardly the same size. I don't think he comes up to your knee."

"I'm not that tall," he protested.

He shifted behind her, helping her to shrug into her coat.

She grew aware of his scent, of his size, of the way his fingers brushed her neck as he helped her put the coat on. Her breath suspended, tendrils of wistfulness wisping within.

"I need to go," she whispered. She had to leave. There were too many nice things here she knew she could never have.

"Will we see you again?" Olivia said, drawing near. "What about tomorrow night's game?"

"I don't think so."

"I'm sure Beau can get some extra tickets. We're going. It's against Ottawa, so I'm sure it will be fun."

"I, er, no. I don't think so," she said more firmly. She was obliged enough already, and had no need for any more.

"What about coming to church with us on Sunday?" Andrea asked.

Oh, she was drowning in the warm kindness here. "I can't impose—"

"You're not imposing," Beau said. "It'd be great to have you there." He swallowed, as if he was biting off saying something else.

"I don't know. One day." Maybe.

"Think about it and let me know?" His eyes held a plea. "You know you're always welcome."

She'd said she'd go one day, hadn't she? "I'll let you know."

"Mommy? Why does Noah have to go?" Bronson asked.

"Because it's late, which means it's almost your bed time too."

"Awww." His protest held the universal ascending whine, which drew Maggie's smile.

"You should say goodbye to Bronson," she murmured to Noah.

"Does it have to be goodbye?" Olivia said. "What are you both up to tomorrow?"

"I couldn't—"

"I bet you could." Olivia's face held a wicked grin. "I'll call you, okay?"

"Er, okay?"

"Don't worry," Olivia said. "My big little brother has your number, I believe."

Why did that thought sparkle anticipation through her skin?

She glanced up at Beau, breath hitching at the warmth in his eyes.

He blinked and it was gone. "Thanks for coming."

She nodded, said her goodbyes, and drew Noah to her side. It was time to get this little man to bed. And put to rest her stupid hopes, too.

~

"A SINGLE MOM, HUH?"

"You talking about my sister? Because I can assure you, neither she nor Jesse, her husband, consider her single."

Gabe rolled his eyes as he shrugged off his jersey, the morning's training session done. "Your Maggie chick last night."

Beau swallowed his Powerade and eyed Gabe. Why the man kept going on about this when he should be focused on his own relationship, Beau didn't know. Maybe Gabe didn't want to focus on Claudine. Guilt squeezed his stomach. He really needed to talk to the dude about Claudine and Kris.

But somehow, every time he thought he'd finally found the right words to say, something interrupted or distracted or Gabe needed to be elsewhere. And while Beau had prayed about it, he had no sense of peace, and it was eating into his sleep.

His gaze shifted across the room to where Kris laughed with Johan and Jake. Maybe he'd be better off confronting Kris about last week. Surely it'd be better to ask him than ask the captain, who should be focusing on getting his team into the right headspace for the season.

Lord?

The noise and chatter continued, that same anxious dread stealing his concentration. Enough was enough. He'd talk to Kris now.

"Beau?"

"Oh, hey." He straightened. Phillippe, the strength and conditioning coach, usually checked in with him after each session. Probably the legacy of their previous goaltender, who had apparently hidden his aches and pains until a severe hip labral tear had required major surgery, and something which might normally see him return to play in a few months had instead seen him return to the minors. Beau knew this because Phillippe had been adamant Beau share every little niggle. He probably didn't need to know about this niggling suspicion about Gabe's wife though.

"You're playing well. Hips feeling good?"

"Yeah."

"No trouble with your knees?"

"Not a peep."

"Good to hear."

Beau nodded, the coach moved on, and so, it appeared, had both Kris and Gabe. He huffed out a breath. Maybe he should speak to Claudine instead.

If she was doing the dirty on her husband, then she'd hidden it well last night. No embarrassment, no averted eyes. But then, even when she'd made that tactless comment about Maggie she'd not apologized. Maybe she was just unaware of how her comments came across. Maggie on the other hand... He couldn't be prouder. Not that he had any right to be proud, but the fact that she'd so graciously overlooked Claudine's comment showed the kind of classy woman she was. Mom had said so too before warning him he needed to tread carefully.

He'd thought he had. He hadn't begged for her to watch tonight's game or walked her downstairs as he'd wanted.

Keeping those wishes locked inside might have contributed to his lack of sleep last night. Or maybe that had been brought on by the other thing Mom had said when Olivia—thank goodness —wasn't in the room.

"Beau, from all I know of you, you don't do casual relationships."

That was true. Mr. Monogamy was his game. Not that he'd done any kind of relationship in recent years.

"And I sense from Maggie that she takes her relationships seriously too." His mom had eyed him. "And as much as we like her, and little Noah for that matter, you need to consider what pursuing a relationship with her might mean. Do you really want to be a father to another man's child?"

Whoa.

Okay, so yeah, he liked her, and yes, he liked sweet, shy Noah too. But he hadn't thought about it in quite those terms. Not yet. Not really.

"You need to consider what it is you really want and make sure you're not sending messages that she might misconstrue. And while it's nice for Bronson to have a friend, it's not like he'll miss Noah when he returns home. We all know that child's memory isn't long."

Gnat-like was a term Beau had heard his sister use to describe Bronson's memory.

"So we'll be praying, but you need to figure out what it is that's most important. Obviously you—we all—want to see her fall in love with Jesus, so we're praying for that, but if you're not serious about pursuing a relationship with her, then now is probably an important time to gracefully withdraw."

Withdraw? Did he really want to do that? Could he see a future with her, should she find a love for God? His mom was right. The situation needed more prayer.

CHAPTER 15

This was unlike any place she'd been before. Maggie looked around the auditorium at the jeans-clad people waving their hands in the air, loudly cheering. She might expect to see this at a hockey game, but never in a church. Wasn't church supposed to be a quiet, somber, reflective place? Wasn't it supposed to be a place where she focused on her sins? Here there seemed to be none of that. It might hold a similar dimness, but there was no smell of incense, and the darkness was simply so that the spotlights could shine brighter on the stage.

A man—Olivia called him a pastor—got up and addressed the congregation. He'd already greeted them warmly, in a way that suggested they were friends and not just people who put money in the offering bags. She'd stood, shocked at the music, which seemed to consist of drums and keyboard and guitar and singers who closed their eyes like this was a concert. She didn't know what to make of it. Where were the hymns? Where was the organ? This felt so strange, even slightly wrong, and she knew that if her mother were here, she would think it evil.

"You enjoying the music?" Olivia murmured. "The songs are by one of my favorite groups, Heartsong Collective. Ever heard of them? They're awesome."

Maggie nodded, even though she'd never heard of them and wasn't sure if awesome was quite the word she'd choose.

But amid the confusion, there was something else here—a soft and subtle something that seemed to call to her heart. She'd sensed it in Beau's family as well. That deep kindness and generous nature that let them smile at the world and enjoy life. That life she was jealous of and wanted herself, that for so long had felt impossible to find. She felt life here. In the people's smiles. In the words of the music. Beating beneath the drums. Life that drew her, beckoned to her, like a distant lighthouse offering something that seemed a lot like peace.

"Friends, as we move into a time of communion, let's take a moment to reflect on where we feel like God is today. Close your eyes. Be still. Allow the distractions of this world to fade away."

Maggie peeked at Olivia and Andrea. They both had bowed their heads and closed their eyes, so she did the same. Still, her mind was whirling, whirling, whirling with the tensions of this week. So much to consider. Noah. Beau. Work. Maman. Fatima. Beau. Money. Noah—

"Now think on God. Do you feel like He is near or is He far?"

God? She'd always pictured God as an old man, high in heaven upon a throne, holding a scepter that He pointed at those who died and said oui or non to who could come through the Pearly Gates. She'd never sensed Him to hold much love or compassion, merely that He was distant and uninterested. But was that who He really was?

"If He feels far away, then ask yourself why."

Why? Her chest grew tight. Because He was impersonal. He was so big and far away and had so many more important things to do than to pay attention to Maggie and her little troubles. If He was the God who created the world, then surely there were more important situations for Him to be focused on. She didn't want to bother Him. Too much.

"God loves you."

Sure. That's what people in places like churches always said. A thousand bumper stickers said the same, just like they said unicorns were real.

"God *loves* you."

Non. The backs of her eyes burned. He didn't. Not really. If He did, well, He would've saved her father. He would've saved Alain. But He hadn't, so He didn't. She shook her head, willing the tears to stay away.

"God loves *you*."

Non. God might love Beau and Olivia, and she sensed He definitely loved Beau's mother, but He couldn't love Maggie. She was a giant mess of many failures. There was little to love about her.

"I'm not talking about the person next to you," the pastor continued. "I'm talking about you. You, listening to this today. I'm going say it again, because I think there are people here who need to hear it. God loves you."

Maggie's eyes flew open, goosebumps prickling her skin. Was the man a mind reader? She glanced around. Everyone else had their heads still bowed. She closed her eyes again.

"You might think that you're not worthy, but the very message of the cross, of what Jesus did when He was crucified, was exactly that. We aren't worthy. But because of what Jesus did, offering His life for ours, we have been made worthy. Our lives have significance. Our lives are important to God. God has created you because He wants to have relationship with you. God wants to be your friend. And it's a gift that so many people ignore, but this gift, the offer of friendship with God, is always there. All you have to do is unwrap it."

But how did she unwrap it? What did he even mean?

"For many of you, this is not a new concept," the man continued. "But in case we have people here today who don't know what this is, I will explain it again. God so loved the world that He gave His only son, that whosoever believes in Him need not perish but can have eternal life. John chapter three verse sixteen makes it clear. Whosoever, whoever, anyone, everyone, that's you."

Maggie's heart tingled. That was her.

"You need only believe in Him. Believe that Jesus died for your sins. So think about it. Mull over it. Recall that the Old Testament required sacrifices to make people right with God. Jesus is the ultimate sacrifice that makes us right with God. His existence cannot be disputed. It's there in historical records that Jesus lived, Jesus died, and He rose again. Jesus did it for you."

He had?

"Because God loves you."

A rush of emotion roared through her chest and up her throat.

"Believe this and the Bible says you will not perish. You need have no fear of death. You need not worry about hell. This promise is not based on how good you are; it's about how good God is. And that is what we celebrate when we have communion. We connect with God again and remember all that He has done for us." A beat. "All that He has done for you."

For her.

Her breath caught in a silent gasp as a wave of emotion clamped her chest. God loved her? Despite her inadequacies?

"Why don't you join with me now as we pray this prayer together. Our Father, You are in heaven, but You are also here with us today. Thank You for what Jesus did. Thank You for allowing Jesus to die on that cross in place of us, and that You see Jesus instead of our sins."

She felt shaky. This was all so very different to what she had always thought. She'd always thought that God only saw her sins and faults, but this man seemed convinced that God saw Jesus instead.

"Thank You for loving us," the man's prayer continued. "Thank You that we can trust this is true. Wherever we're at with our relationship with You, help us to draw nearer. Thank You that Your word says if we draw near, You draw near to us. So Lord, this morning we draw near to You." A beat passed. "Help us to know Your love."

That same wretched feeling of emotion swelled, and she exhaled noisily. Tears spilled, and she tried to rein them in but couldn't. Oh, how embarrassing. She felt hands on her back—Olivia and Andrea. But even the reassurance of their touch did not calm the storm within.

"Thank You, God, for Your forgiveness. Thank You, God, for Your great love."

Music played softly in the background as people passed around platters containing tiny cups and bowls of what might be bread. But she couldn't see clearly because her eyes were blurred with tears. It seemed she hadn't seen clearly for years.

"Friends, can you say that with me? Thank You, God, I am forgiven."

"Thank You, God, I am forgiven," Maggie whispered, wiping at her cheek.

"Thank You, God," the man continued, "that because of what Jesus did, I can be friends with You."

She swallowed and repeated this too.

"I *am* Your friend."

"I *am* Your friend," she echoed.

"Amen."

"Amen."

A rushing feeling, like the wind ripping over long grass, seemed to swoop from her belly through her chest, permeating every pore of her body. Heat, like the warmth of a crackling fire after being outside in the snow, seemed to sparkle and electrify her heart. She had never felt like this before. She'd never known this wondrous giddy feeling. Like true joy.

She felt it now. Core-deep joy. A soul-deep peace. A knowledge that, no matter what happened, this God, who only an hour ago had felt too far away, was actually quite near and actually loved her. Loved *her*. Magdalena Joly. God, the creator of the universe, loved Magdalena Joly. She *knew* it now like she knew she breathed.

"Maggie?" Liv whispered. "Are you okay?"

She nodded. She was now.

Beau's mother passed her a packet of tissues, and Maggie pulled out two. The emotion on her face probably looked rather scary, but another part of her just didn't care. What did it matter what she look like when she'd just found the greatest love of all?

Love. She *was* loved. She was loved by *God*.

She wiped her face and felt Andrea's hand on her back. She tried to breathe in but couldn't. A blow of her nose was her only option. But unlike in Maman's church, it didn't seem to matter if people made noise here, and she could hear other people who had been touched blowing their noses too.

What had just happened?

The service continued, but she barely heard the sermon. Her mind could barely grasp hold of the words he said. All she knew was a great sense of love within. Glorious, radiant love. She was loved. *Loved.* Loved by God.

The pastor prayed some more, there was another song, and then they were told to go and be like Jesus in the world. If she'd heard that two hours ago, she would've thought the man crazy. Now she knew what he meant. To be like Jesus in the world meant to love others, to notice, to care. Just like Beau did. Just like Andrea did. Just like Maggie now would.

The congregation started to leave, but Maggie couldn't move from her seat.

"Did you enjoy that?" Olivia asked with a small smile on her face.

Enjoy wasn't exactly the word she'd choose to use. More like had an epiphany. Felt like she gone through the deep clean washing cycle on the washing machine. But that was the thing. She felt cleaner now. She felt like she didn't need to impress God. She knew she couldn't. But then, she didn't have to. Because Jesus had already gone through that process for her.

"How are you feeling, sweetheart?" Andrea asked.

"I don't exactly know what just happened, but I feel amazing."

"Have you ever prayed that kind of prayer before?"

"No."

Andrea's smile could light a hundred candles. "Then I think that might be called getting saved."

"Saved?"

"Finding salvation—realizing what Jesus has done and that He has saved us from an eternity separated from God."

"You mean hell."

"Yes."

"Wow." Maggie took another deep breath. "I didn't know it would feel like this."

"What does it feel like?"

Maggie thought. "Like the most wonderful feeling ever. That I'm loved not because of what I do but because I exist. And that means I can just be."

"How wonderful." Andrea's eyes seemed to glisten with tears. "You don't know how happy I am to hear this."

"Were you praying for me?" Maggie asked.

Andrea nodded. "I know that there is no greater joy we can find than when we have peace with God. And that peace with God means we can have peace within ourselves and we can have peace with others. You'll find your life won't necessarily be easy, but I think you'll find that peace and joy make all the difference in the world."

Maggie nodded. "I…I can't believe that I've attended so many church services in my life and never really realized this before."

"Sometimes we just have to wait for the right moment, when our hearts are really ready to receive. It looks like that day was today for you."

Maggie exhaled and wiped away a few more tears before noticing that the man who'd led so much of the service had drawn near. She straightened in her seat and wished her nose weren't bright red. Oh well. Her nose would match her eyes.

"Good morning, ladies," he said. "I thought I should come over and introduce myself, especially as I believe you're all new today."

Andrea completed the introductions, which was just as well, as Maggie suddenly felt shy.

"And what brings you here today?"

"My son lives here," Andrea continued, "and suggested we come to this church. And we're very glad we did, aren't we, Maggie?"

She nodded shyly. "Thank you for what you prayed."

"It helped?" he asked, a twinkle in his eye.

Had he seen her cry? Oh well. She didn't care. "So much."

"I'm glad." He eyed her kindly. "I hope we'll see you back here again."

"I plan on it." She smiled.

He mentioned something about women's groups, but she could scarcely take it in, the wonder of the previous moment still glowing within. She nodded anyway and listened as he shared something about a new believers class, which sounded funny, because she'd always believed in God and known that

Jesus was real. It was just she'd never really connected the two as being personally relevant to her.

"Oh, I should go and check on the kids," Olivia said. "Do you want me to collect Noah as well? I signed him in under my name, so it shouldn't be a problem."

Maggie nodded. She could quite happily bask in the feelings of this moment for the next five hours.

By the time she returned home, after lunch with Olivia and her mother, Maggie still had that feeling of walking on air. Why had nobody ever shared about this before? It was like a treasure kept for only the initiated to know. She couldn't wait to tell her mother about what she'd learned.

But when she tried to express something of what had happened that morning at church, her mother looked at her like she was insane. "Are you sure you haven't just come across a cult? It sounds very much like that to me."

"Maman." Maggie laughed. "This is nothing but a church. We read the Bible. You should be glad that I'm finally understanding what it is the priests have talked about for so long."

Her mother still looked suspicious. "I would be glad if I could be sure that it is something genuine and not just a passing emotion."

The exhilaration of earlier dimmed a few notches. But Beau's mother had warned her that not everyone would understand, especially people whose idea of God was steeped in tradition. But it didn't matter what others thought, she told herself. What mattered was that she had found life in the Bible. And after living so long in the confines of the past, she was excited to see what might lie in her future.

~

"Are you for real?"

Beau's mom nodded on the FaceTime call, and his heart pattered with excitement.

"You better not be messing with me, Momma." Excitement burst out with a grin. "I know you like to mess with me."

"I promise I'm not messing with you," she said with a smile. "It was beautiful to see. She was sitting between your sister and me, and as the pastor spoke, she just seemed to soak it in. I don't know if she's ever been any place like that for church before. And then he basically prayed the sinner's prayer and she prayed it. It was a privilege to witness, actually."

"Wow." He could barely wrap his head around it. "Wow."

"So yes, you could say church went very well this morning."

He burned to ask what she thought this might mean. Did it mean that he had God's blessing to finally see a future with Maggie? *Lord?*

"I should call her." He would. As soon as he found a moment of privacy on this road trip. Who knew when Johan might return?

"Son." His mom hesitated.

"What?"

"I know you're excited about what this could mean going forward, but I would caution you to leave it to Maggie to share. It probably wouldn't be helpful for her to think that your goal was to see her come to faith in this way. And like we talked before, you don't want to confuse the issues of her faith with her relationship with you."

"But I'm excited for her."

"Of course you are, and you should be. Just let her tell you."

"Are you telling me that I shouldn't contact her?"

"You're a grown man. I'm not about to start telling you what you should or shouldn't do."

Wasn't that what she'd just done?

"Just pray about things," she advised. "Trust God's leading. Pray for her. I can't imagine it's going to be too easy. I imagine there's still a lot of dismantling of religious ideas before she'll be at a place where you both can agree."

"But the main thing is there now."

"That's right." She paused. "You do care about her, don't you?"

"I haven't felt like this about anyone before," he admitted honestly. "And yeah, I'm so excited for her, regardless of what happens in our future. But I also can't help hoping that this is God's yes for a future together. One day."

After renewing his thanks for his mom and Olivia remaining a few extra hours and his regrets he'd not returned in time to say goodbye, the call soon ended, and he stared at his phone, his heart full.

His mom was right. He would have to hold back and leash his desire to talk with Maggie. He'd do anything to make sure he didn't mess this up.

"OKAY, PRAISE POINTS TIME." Pastor Josiah grinned over the online Bible study Zoom call. "Who wants to go first?"

"I will," Mike Vaughan volunteered. "I heard the other day from John Ramirez that the charity in the Philippines now has over four hundred sponsors. They're so thrilled by everyone's generosity that they've been able to expand the children's feeding program. And the sponsorship for the education program now includes those studying tertiary education. Not bad for kids who grew up in a slum, eh?"

There came murmurs of *that's awesome* from the various guys online.

"I got word that one of the boys who attended the camp this past June is now in church," Dan offered. "It's been really cool to see the value of this extending more than just a few days in June."

"Who was that?" Beau asked.

"Do you remember Connor? The little redheaded kid?"

Beau nodded.

"Yeah, he made a commitment on the last night, which was really good, but to see him committing to walking out his faith a few months later is where it's really at."

Beau nodded again. This was something of what his mom had been trying to say. It was one thing to get caught up in the emotions of a spiritual awakening—which was not to say it wasn't real—but it was another thing to still be living and relating with God each day after that initial buzz had settled.

"How about you, Beau? What's going on with you?" Josiah asked.

He swallowed. Should he admit what he'd learned just yesterday?

"He looks like he's got something on his mind," Brent teased.

"Uh, my mom and sister were up this past weekend—"

"I thought you were in Buffalo," Chris said.

"Been there, won that, now we're back."

"So you're aiming for winningest goalie, huh?"

After winning against Ottawa on Saturday night, yeah, "Something like that," Beau said. "Anyway, it was good to have my family here, and even better that they took this girl to church today and she got saved."

"Cool."

"Which girl?" Dan asked with a slight grin.

"Oh, what do you know, Dan my man?" Chris asked. "Beau, come on, spill. What's her name?"

"Maggie," he admitted.

"Mag-gie," Luc crooned, like he was in elementary school.

"Dude." Beau rolled his eyes.

"That's awesome," Brent said. "Both about your girl and that you've got a girl."

"She's not my girl," Beau protested.

"Anyone else think the man is protesting too much?" Mike asked.

"Sure sounds like it to me," Chris said.

"Can we change the subject?" Beau pleaded. "Somebody else must have something they want to share."

"Nope. Nothing as good as this," Chris said to a chorus of laughter and jeers.

Later, after the Zoom call had ended, Beau got a message from Dan to FaceTime. It was far easier, just the two of them, without the heckling of the others.

"I sure didn't mean for that to escalate as it did," Dan apologized.

"Chris can't help himself. I think he thinks it's his personal mission to get all the guys happily married."

"You're thinking marriage?" Dan asked.

Beau's mouth dropped, then he recognized the glint in Dan's eye. "Don't. I can't take it anymore. Besides, I talked to my mom, and she thinks I should back off from anything to give Maggie time to get her relationship with God sorted."

"I know you don't want to hear this, man, but it's sounding pretty serious if you're talking to your mom about it. Let's just say I couldn't see me telling my mom about anything unless there was really something to tell."

His words distracted Beau to wondering about Dan again. He knew Dan had had girlfriends in the past, but like the rest of them, Dan wasn't exactly in the market for leading a girl on. Beau was curious to see the kind of girl that would finally turn Dan's head.

"My mom and I have always been really close," Beau explained. "And she was there at church when Maggie got saved. And now she's wanting me to take things slow so Maggie isn't confused about things."

"Sounds wise," said Dan. He paused a moment. "Is this the

same chick that you had the warning about from some team executive?"

Man. "I'd kinda forgotten about that."

"Maybe you'd be wise for all sorts of reasons to not rush into things," Dan said.

Maybe he would.

The talk turned to observations about their upcoming games as the preseason schedule drew to its conclusion, then Dan said goodnight and the call ended. But even though Beau agreed in his head that taking things slowly was wise, his heart couldn't help but pump with the desire to contact Maggie and see how she was. What could it hurt to ask how church had gone this morning? It would only be polite, wouldn't it? Especially considering he'd invited her to go with him before. Maybe he could just hope she'd take it upon herself to let him know how things had gone.

His phone buzzed with another text. His heart thumped. Was it—?

Hey man. Free tomorrow after practice?

Beau sighed and tapped out an affirmative to Johan. He probably needed to make more of an effort to connect with the guys.

His phone buzzed again.

Hi Beau. Thank you for telling me to go visit your church. I had the best time. I hope you had a good day. Maggie.

He stared at the message, yet another answer to prayer. What should he reply?

Hey Maggie, I'm glad you enjoyed your time at church.

There. That was innocuous enough, wasn't it? Even Mom couldn't take issue with that. He pressed Send.

He watched as the little swirlies showed she was composing another message. His heart thudded, as it always seemed to do when Maggie was involved.

Your mother was really sweet and has offered to send me some stuff. You're really lucky.

He smiled. Yes, he was blessed.

God bless moms, he texted back.

Then he remembered Noah and realized how his message might be received. And hoped she'd know he wanted God to bless her too.

CHAPTER 16

"Maman, how do you feel about inviting some of the neighbors to spend Thanksgiving with us?"

As soon as the words escaped, Maggie knew this had not been the right way to broach the topic. But the inspiration from last Sunday had lit her heart in a completely new way all week. No longer did she feel a sense of doubt and oppression. Instead, she seemed to notice all the little ways in which God actually cared for her. A parking space near the entrance on a rainy day. The visitors from Australia who had thanked her and made her smile with their accents and *g'days*. The baked goods that Fatima had insisted Maggie and Noah have, saying he needed to grow up big and strong. The parcel of books that Andrea Nash had sent her, and the links to more Heartsong Collective songs that Olivia had forwarded. All of it showed that she was loved, that her life was richer when she connected with others. And this renewed awareness made her long to pass that love on to others. Even if her mother would take more convincing.

"I cannot like it," her mother said. "It would be so different for us."

"Surely a change would be good for this holiday. Just think

of how much fun we could have," Maggie pleaded. "Don't you think Fatima would enjoy learning what a Canadian Thanksgiving can really be like?"

Love your neighbors had been the message at church yesterday. "We love because He, that is God, first loved us," the minister had said. "So why not look for ways in which you can love and be a blessing to your neighbors?" Maggie wasn't sure if this was exactly what he'd meant, but the idea had sprung in her heart and wouldn't leave.

"We could still do the usual foods," Maggie said. "And if we ask people to bring a little something, then that can help make the food go further."

"But I do not want Fatima's loud and noisy sons here," Maman complained.

"You can't ask Fatima without asking her boys," Maggie said.

"I'm not asking Fatima or her boys," her mother said dryly.

Maggie smiled. "And what about poor Mrs. Chang next door?" she persisted. "How long has she lived there and we've never invited her in?"

"I don't see why we need to suddenly be inviting people," her mother said crossly. "It's not like they ever do anything for us."

"But isn't that the point, Maman?" she asked. "We are blessed with our family and circumstances that mean we're safe and happy and have enough to eat. I think God has blessed us so that we can bless others who might need a reminder that He cares for them too."

"I cannot like how you keep talking about blessings and feeling like God uses you." Her mother eyed her askance. "You sound like you've joined a cult."

"I'm sorry you feel that way. But I feel like, before, I only used to believe in God. Now I feel like I love Him."

Her mother shook her head. "I cannot like this. You've changed too much."

"But is this not what Jesus has asked us to do? To care for the widows and the poor?"

"But *we* are the widows," her mother insisted, tapping her chest. "*We* are the ones who are poor."

Maggie's heart twisted with the realization that this had long been how her mother had viewed herself. She saw from the perspective of what was missing, not what they had. And it was amazing that Maggie, after so long resisting the sermons she had heard all her life, now heard similar things mentioned from the Bible and it suddenly made sense. God was a God of love. He *loved* her. Maggie knew this now and wanted everyone in the world to know His love. And the only way she could do that was by demonstrating it in whatever capacity she could.

"We're not poor," she said softly. "We have a roof over our heads, we have food, I have a job. I will buy whatever we might need for Thanksgiving, but Maman, I really would like us to do this this year, please."

"If you do this, I will not lift a finger to help," her mother warned.

"I'm happy to do it all myself," Maggie said. "I think it would be good for Noah to see us taking an interest in others. Perhaps we could even invite some of his friends from school, or I could invite Frederic from work." She said this more as a tease, but sure enough, her mother reacted.

"Frederic? Who is this Frederic man?"

"You know, my work colleague? He's on his own, and I'm sure he would appreciate a nice family meal."

"I'm sure he would, but I cannot like the fact you would be inviting a man to join us here. Why have you never mentioned this Frederic man before?"

Because she had spent far too many years caught in her own lost little world. "I don't know why," she said. "But I feel like it's time I paid more attention to those around me."

"Is there something I need to know about this man?" her mother asked suspiciously.

"Of course not. He's a work colleague, that is all."

But the way her mother looked at her made her wonder what Maman would say if Maggie confessed to having dined with Montreal's favourite goaltender on more than one occasion.

"I do not like this," Maman continued anxiously. "You seem so different."

Because she was. God had changed her.

"Next you'll be saying we should invite Denise."

"Why not?"

Her mother's jaw sank. "How big do you want this to be? We don't live in a palace."

"Then perhaps we could invite people to drop in—have some visit at lunch, some at dinner," Maggie suggested, mind whirling with how this could work. "But when I think that there are some people, like Mrs. Chang, who never have family visit them, don't you think they would be lonely and have that loneliness reinforced on days when others are visited by many?"

"Don't you I think I get lonely too?" her mother demanded.

Oui, Maggie thought, which was exactly why she thought this would be a good idea. But say this she could not, so she instead moved to give her mother a hug. "Thank you, Maman," she said. "I promise you will not need to lift a finger, and I promise that you'll have far more fun than you realize."

THE REMAINDER of the week passed in work, Noah, and preparations for the pumpkin festival and Thanksgiving. Maggie might have watched a televised hockey game or two, which did little for her peace of mind, as she couldn't help but wonder why Beau hadn't contacted her for nearly two weeks. The rush of excitement and gratitude that had filled her on that Sunday had been enough for her to want to express such things, but now she looked back on it, it probably had been too forward of her. He might've been all gladness for her, as his text suggested, but he probably didn't appreciate her intruding on his personal space.

Still, she couldn't help but wonder what he might be doing for Thanksgiving. He'd probably received a dozen invitations from his teammates to spend the day with them, but a secret part of her wondered what it would be like to invite him to their place. Would he come? Would he think she thought more of this friendship than he did? She didn't want to overstep, but by the same token, she would like to know what she'd done that had made him back off. And Maman's reaction to Maggie's mention of Frederic made her wonder just how her mother might accept a new man in Maggie's life one day.

She issued the invitation to Frederic and was pleased to see his eyes light up, just in the way that Fatima's and Mrs. Chang's had. It seemed there were a great many people simply waiting for an invitation. And even though each person had initially refused, with varying excuses from "I don't want to trouble you" to "I can't leave my sons," she had managed to talk them around and get them to agree to come. Denise had plans already, which only reinforced Maman's concerns, but Maggie hoped and prayed that even her mother might be persuaded to enjoy the day.

"Maggie? How are the preparations for the Pumpkin Ball?" Danielle called from across the room.

"We still have a score of tickets remaining unsold," Maggie said with a sigh.

"It's such a shame there was that bad publicity earlier on. Normally we're sold out by now," Danielle said with a sigh.

Maggie nodded as a whisper of memory surfaced. Had Beau said he was coming to the ball? She had the vaguest notion that at some point he had said oui. If he did say oui, could that not be a selling point for others to come? But if the ball was promoted as such, would he feel like he'd been used?

"What is it?" Danielle asked.

"I'm just trying to remember something."

"Something about?"

"Whether someone said he was coming or not."

"Would that someone happen to play hockey?"

Her skin grew hot. "Probably. Especially if he's Canadian," she admitted.

"Ah, but what if he's from South Carolina?"

"North Carolina," Maggie muttered.

Danielle grinned. "I thought you said he was coming."

"Well, I haven't heard any confirmation," Maggie said weakly.

"So get confirming! Honestly, what do you think this is? If we have him coming, don't you think we could sell the remaining tickets in a snap?"

Oui.

"Do I have to spell it out to you? Get on the phone now and call him. You do have his number, non?"

Maggie nodded, and retrieved her phone. Perhaps she could just message him instead of calling. She scrolled to where his last message remained.

God bless moms.

Her eyes pricked as they had when she'd first read it. A sliver of hope had wondered if he'd included her in his blessing on mothers. Not that it mattered. She believed it too and was extremely grateful for his mother and hers for all they had done.

"I hope you're not thinking of just texting him," Danielle said. "You need to call him."

Maggie hesitated. "He's probably at work. Leaving a message might be easier."

"You can leave a voice message as easily as you can a text. Go on. He might pick up. Then we'll know straight away and can get marketing it sooner."

Maggie swallowed. It was funny how her sense of peace seemed to be greater everywhere except where Beau was concerned. Still, she would trust God, as the pastor had said on Sunday when it came to inviting their neighbors. Trust God to open the right doors at the right time and close the wrong ones as well.

She dialed, waiting as the phone rang. Sure enough, she had to leave a voice message.

With a glance and grimace at Danielle she said, "Hello, Beau. This is Maggie Joly from the Jardin botanique, just wondering if you are able to confirm your attendance at the Pumpkin Ball on Saturday next week. If so, could you please let us know as soon as possible. Thank you." She ended the call, heart racing.

"There. That wasn't so bad now, was it?" Danielle said.

Said the one who hadn't made the call.

"Now we wait and hopefully find out soon—"

Maggie's phone started ringing. Her pulse increased.

"Is that him?" Danielle murmured.

Heart tensing, she glanced at the caller ID and nodded.

"Then answer it!" Danielle hissed.

So Maggie drew in a deep breath and pressed Answer. "Hello?"

"Maggie."

Just the sound of his voice made her want to shut her eyes and savor it. "Oui."

"Of course I'm coming."

She smiled and shot Danielle a thumbs-up.

"You need to tell me what's involved. Is it black tie? Are there tickets left? Should I be telling some of the guys to see if they can come?"

"Would you?" she asked.

"Sure. I bet some of them could make it."

"That would be amazing." She picked up a pen and started doodling. "I, er, didn't want to ask in case you thought we might be trying to cash in on your celebrity," she said in a lower voice.

"Cash away," he said. "I don't see the point in having a profile if I can't use it for good."

Her chest rippled with warmth. He was such a good man.

"So, is this something you take a date to?" he asked.

Oh. Her heart tipped to disappointment. "Er, of course you can bring someone if you wish." Her mind started spinning, wondering whom he might possibly bring. Why hadn't she known? She'd never thought of herself as a cyber stalker, but in the past few weeks she might have checked out his social profiles a time or ten, and she'd never seen mention of a girl.

"So, are you going with anyone?" he asked tentatively.

"Me?" She glanced up and caught Danielle's enthusiastic nodding. "Er, I usually only go to support the event. Not as a guest."

"You're going as a guest this year," Danielle whispered loudly.

"Er, but apparently this year I am," Maggie said meekly.

"Going with someone?" Beau asked.

Did that downward inflection suggest disappointment? "No! I mean, no one has asked me," she concluded lamely.

"I'm asking you," he said softly.

Her chest filled with a thousand butterflies. Beau Nash was asking her out?

"Please?"

Oh my goodness. Her mouth had dried to the consistency of the arid lands' sands. "Okay."

"Great!"

"Oui! Je capote!" Danielle screamed, clapping her hands.

"Is there someone there with you?" he asked.

"I'm at work," Maggie said. "It's Danielle, my colleague."

"I met her before, didn't I?" he asked.

"Yes."

"Hey, I know you're at work, but I wanted you to know that I've been thinking about you."

"You have?" she asked, lowering her voice and shifting in her seat so Danielle couldn't see her.

"I…" He paused. "Would it be okay to see you sometime?"

Was this the time to invite him to Thanksgiving? "Er, oui."

"I have a couple more games this week, then we have the Thanksgiving break, and I wondered about seeing my family—"

"You're not staying here?" she asked, disappointment lacing her heart.

"Well, I've had a few invitations, and I wondered about maybe visiting the kids in the hospital again, but I didn't really know…"

This was her moment. "You could have Thanksgiving with us," she offered.

A beat. "Really?"

"Only if you want to. If it doesn't clash with your visit to the hospital."

"I'd love to. Thank you. Yes."

Happiness bloomed. "I feel I should warn you that there will be a number of neighbors there as well. We're trying to do things a little differently this year. At least, I am. Maman is not convinced it's a good idea, but ever since church last week, I haven't been able to stop thinking about how I should be living my life. And I'm noticing now that there are people who just need to know they are loved."

A noise behind her drew her attention to Danielle again. "Can I come too?" she whispered, to which Maggie smiled and shooed her away.

"That's so awesome," Beau said softly. "I can't wait to hear what else has been happening."

She couldn't wait to tell him either.

"Maybe we could get together before then." He cleared his

throat. "My schedule makes it a little complicated, but if you could manage a late night, we could catch up after a game."

"What night?"

"Friday? I could get you seats to watch the game, then we could catch a late dinner. It'd be nice to eat with someone who has more conversation than the latest hockey statistics," he said.

Her heart skipped. "I could make that work," she said. "Thank you."

"Excellent! I'll make sure there's a ticket waiting with your name on it at Will Call next to the box office. Then we'll have dinner, okay?"

"Sounds good," she murmured.

"I'll text you the details, as I need to go. My trainer's waiting. But hey, I can't wait."

"Neither can I. Thanks, Beau."

She hung up and turned to face her colleague, whose face was a picture of glee. "I can't believe it."

"He's taking you to the ball?"

"And to dinner this Friday night."

"Oh my goodness!" Danielle screamed. "I'm so excited." She clapped her hands. "And Thanksgiving too, did I hear?"

Maggie nodded. Was this some kind of wonderful dream?

"What are you going to wear for the ball?"

Something that would be totally unsuitable now. "I'm going to have to find something new."

"Shopping expedition?" Danielle said hopefully. "I know a place that has gowns that would look absolutely divine on you."

"But not expensive?"

"Consider it an investment. It sounds like this might not be the only fancy party Beau Nash will take you to."

Oui. Maggie's smile threatened to split her face in two. Call her naïve, but it sounded like Beau was keen. Which only made her wonder why he'd held back before and what might have caused this change of heart. She sighed happily, then paused. It looked like she'd need to have another conversation with her mother about an extra person attending their Thanksgiving.

THE PUCK SCREAMED TOWARD BEAU, and he blocked it with his chest armor. It fell to the ice, and he kicked it to where Johan waited, then the action moved away from his crease and farther down the ice. He breathed out, trying to slow the spike of adrenaline that always came in tense moments. The goal of the goalie: preserve energy to stay focused to protect the goal. The referee's whistle signaled a stop in play as the puck went over the glass and both teams had a line change. Beau took the moment to lift up his helmet and grab his drink, stored on top of the net. He sucked the energy drink down, his gaze quickly traveling to the seats reserved for the team's families. A bunch of wives and girlfriends sat there, and among them, for the first time, sat Maggie. Not that he'd classify her in the girlfriend category. Yet.

He saw her chat to Claudine before her gaze found his and she smiled.

He grinned back, her smile energizing him as much as any electrolyte-laden liquid, then snapped the face-shield of his helmet down as he shifted to refocus on the ice. She was the first woman he'd invited to watch his game in years, and he couldn't afford to be too distracted. But when she'd called yesterday, what could he do? It would've been rude to ignore her. And somehow, that initial yes to a ball had turned into two more invitations. After leashing the desire to call her so many times, he now felt a sense of peace, that this reconnection was right. But he couldn't afford to think on that now, especially not when Brent's team was playing as fiercely as they were.

Play resumed, and Detroit got the puck. Brent barreled toward him, weaving and dodging Montreal's defense as the puck passed tic-tac-toe between him and his winger. Brent was one of the NHL's elite players—had won gold for Canada in Vancouver last year—but while they might be friends, Brent would show Beau no mercy. And neither would Beau.

He moved to block, unsurprised when Brent deked him and shot again, which required a twisting leap to the opposite side as he prevented the aim at top shelf. He grabbed the puck and held tight as one of Detroit's sticks moved close to his face, and he was thankful, not for the first time, for the shield that protected his face. He had no intention of being a poster boy for roughhouse hockey, not like some old-school thugs like TJ Woletsky with their broken noses and missing teeth.

"Nice save," Brent said with a small smile and spray of ice before he skated back down the ice.

"Here!"

Beau scrambled upright, looking for Jake, who had called, before propelling the puck his way. Jake skated behind the net, then passed to Johan, who slid to Rakoluv, who shot and scored.

The Bell Centre erupted in a roar of cheers as the red and white lights flashed in rhythm with the thumping music. His heart eased as he grabbed another drink. Brent had scored on him in the first period, and while Gabe had leveled things the next, this goal gave a little breathing room as they counted down the minutes in this last period. Detroit would get desperate now and might move to an empty net, where they'd replace the goaltender with an extra forward in an attempt to score again. Or maybe they wouldn't, those tactics more common later in the season or in playoffs, when the score line really mattered. It was less common in the first few games of the regular season, when everyone was still hitting their stride.

Two minutes left. The centers made their way to the middle to scrimmage as the puck dropped. Brent got the puck and shot to a teammate as the Detroit players moved from the neutral zone and into Montreal territory toward Beau. Beau lowered to his haunches, watching, his vision zeroing in on where the black disk slid between sticks. Rakoluv appeared, the defenseman knocking Detroit player Doug Lehtonen off into the boards, which earned another roar of approval from the crowds. But a hit did only so much. Beau had to remain steady, stay composed and anticipate where the puck might go.

He crouched as the play moved closer, Johan and Kaspar doing their best to block and steer the traffic away from in front of the net. The puck shot Beau's way, and he bent into the butterfly save. The puck struck him dead in the chest, and he caught it, using his blocker to forcefully push Brent's teammate away before clearing the puck to Jake.

One minute to go. Having played as many games as he had, he didn't need the Jumbotron's countdown to tell him how much time remained. It didn't matter anyway. He had a job to do, which required intense focus until the siren declared the end of the period.

The play grew scrappy, and a trip on a Montreal player saw shoving descend into a brawl. He exhaled, knowing it would take some time to sort the mess out, as Kris swung wildly while Gabe and Brent held their respective teammates back from joining in.

Beau risked a glance at the stands and saw Maggie had covered her mouth before her gaze once again shifted to him, like she felt the connection between them. He nodded, and she lowered her hand and smiled, which he took as a good sign. Maybe the intense physicality of the sport wouldn't prove too off-putting. Way to go, catching a fight in her first game. At least his position meant she'd never see him involved, which would result in an automatic penalty to the other team. His attention moved back to the ice, where the refs broke apart the fighting and sent both players to the penalty box, meaning both teams would play short-handed for the few remaining seconds.

The game resumed, with Brent once more collecting the

puck as he moved toward Beau. He shot, but the puck clanged against the posts. Before Beau could reach it, Brent tried again. Adrenaline soaring, Beau bent into an old-school save with a bit of a roundhouse, kicking the puck free as the crowd's cheering soared. He breathed out, chest thudding, as the siren signaled the end of the game.

Brent skated closer, mouthguard hanging loose. "That save will make the highlights reel."

"Hope so. Your goal might make it too."

"That was sweet, huh?"

"Sweeter because you scored off me," Beau ribbed.

Brent laughed and skated off the ice as Beau's teammates each raised their sticks to acknowledge the crowd before skating over to Beau to pat his helmet.

"Awesome save," Gabe said.

Yeah, Beau kinda felt it had been.

He joined the others in acknowledging the crowd and moving off the ice, only to be told to hang around with Brent and Gabe.

"And the third star of the night goes to Brent Karlsson of Detroit for his goal in the first period."

Brent smirked and skated onto the ice to a chorus of boos. Beau chuckled. Yep. This crowd was as partisan as any arena he'd played in.

"The second star goes to our captain, Gabriel Lemieux." Gabe's reappearance in the spotlight on ice met with cheers.

"And our first star of the night, for his spectacular net minding, goes to Montreal's own Beau Nash!"

Beau grinned and saluted the crowd, whose cheering intensified even more. It was nice to feel his adopted city had embraced him as much as they had. He hoped Maggie was impressed and could appreciate the technique and skill involved, not just see the violent side of things.

He moved back to the locker room, high-fiving attendants

and team trainers, then made his way to his stall. He'd have a few minutes to regroup before the media showed up, and he suspected there'd be a few who would want to talk to him. While he didn't mind media, he didn't want to have to stay too long tonight. Not when he had another important engagement to consider.

"I knew you'd prove the final piece of the puzzle," Tony Francois, the team owner, said, rubbing his hands together.

Beau shrugged modestly. "The guys played really well tonight."

"Stop being modest. You had some tremendous saves tonight. That last one…" Tony shook his head and whistled.

"Thanks." Beau nodded, running two hands through his hair before tying it back up again as the man kept talking. He'd worked pretty hard and would need to have a shower before seeing Maggie, and the longer it took now, the longer the wait would be.

Tony shifted to congratulate Gabe, leaving Beau free to grab his phone. He saw Maggie's message of GREAT GAME! and smiled.

"You got a fan?" Tony asked, pivoting back to him again.

"I hope I've got more than one," he joked.

"From the sound of that crowd, I'd say you do." Tony nodded to the phone. "Someone special?"

"I think so."

"You'll have to invite her to the Halloween night. Gabe has told you about that, right?"

A team function with sponsors and the like, all to support the Children's Hospital. "Looking forward to it, sir."

"Good to hear." He clapped Beau on the back. "And it's Tony, Beau. Call me Tony."

"Thank you, Tony," he said as the owner shifted back to talk to Gabe.

"Been here two minutes and you're on first name basis," Kris muttered from beside him.

Beau shrugged. He wasn't the one responsible for hiring or firing, and he was still learning the ins and outs of the team dynamics here. Anyway, he had more important things to concentrate on tonight.

He took off his pads as another team official announced that the media would be invited inside in two minutes. He reeled off a list of players they'd want to talk to, including Beau, who was also requested, along with Gabe, to the media room to front questions.

He bit back a sigh. While he was glad he'd played well enough to impress, it would now be at least an hour before he'd be able to see Maggie. He didn't want to cancel. The team had a quick road trip tomorrow, and he really wanted to get things off to a good start with her by not cancelling their first date. What could he do?

He grabbed his phone and replied. I'LL BE A LITTLE LONGER, SO IT MIGHT GET LATE.

His phone pinged back a moment later. I DON'T MIND.

God bless her. WANT TO MEET AT MY PLACE? He chewed his lip. Then added, NO FUNNY BUSINESS. JUST MORE PRIVACY TO TALK. And not be hounded by fans or media.

Would she agree?

The incoming message dots swirled round and round.

OKAY.

"All right!"

Jake and Kaspar eyed him, but he had another phone call to make. Then media, then a shower. Then finally, his date.

CHAPTER 17

Maggie hovered at the door. She never did this. Ever. But judging from the crowds tonight, she could understand why Beau had made this suggestion. And it wasn't like they would do anything more than eat and talk. They were both adults after all. Although, it had been sweet to think he'd needed to reassure her with that no funny business comment. She lifted her chin and pressed the buzzer. It took a moment, then the voice asked for her name. "Maggie Joly. To see Mr. Nash," she added.

The door buzzed and she moved to clasp it to go inside, but the doorman beat her to it, ushering her inside the fancy lobby. "Miss Joly. Mr. Nash called to say you were coming by tonight."

Why did she suddenly feel like she was in a scene from *Pretty Woman*? "He wanted to have dinner, and after he played so well tonight, thought this might be better than going out and being surrounded by all his fans."

He nodded. "That's exactly what he told me. He requested that I send up some food when it arrives."

"Oh."

He smiled and led her to the elevators. "He also requested I let you into his apartment, so here is his spare key."

Heat rose in her cheeks. "I'm only staying for dinner," she felt the need to say.

"Mr. Nash made that very clear," he said kindly, handing her the key. "You can return that on your exit, if you like."

She nodded, feeling the embarrassment fade a little as she entered the elevator and pressed the button for the sub-penthouse level. She hoped no one would see her. It was hard enough to feel she needed to justify her visit to the doorman, but she would hate for anyone to get the wrong idea. Coupled with this was the feeling of inadequacy, dressed as she was in her jeans, boots, and fluffy jumper, all of which had proved comfortable and warm at the hockey arena but hardly suited the opulent atmosphere of this building and its glamorous residents.

Fortunately, the late hour meant no one else got on and she could travel to Beau's floor and unlock his door. It still felt so intensely personal to be walking into his space, especially when he wasn't even here. She was glad she'd had that visit two weeks ago, but still, his mossy-musky scent hanging on the air and the fact he'd left some shoes near the sofa and a container of protein powder out near the sink offered tantalizing glimpses of the private side of his life. And now she was here. Wondering what to do.

She pulled out her phone and saw that Beau had left another message. SIT DOWN. RELAX. MAKE A CUP OF TEA, PUT ON THE TV. MAKE YOURSELF AT HOME.

So she did just that, turning on the TV, which instantly showed highlights of tonight's game. She sank into the sofa and watched intently as Beau appeared numerous times and the commentators talked about him.

"He's all business on the ice, all friendliness off it. It's really as team owner Tony Francois says—"

The shot cut to an older man she presumed was the team owner. "Beau Nash will be here for years, playing like that. A true Canadien, even if he's from the South."

She watched as the coverage shifted to what she presumed was a media conference after the game, possibly where he still was now. "Yeah, it was a good game," Beau said, seated at a table that held a bank of microphones. The captain was there too—she recognized him from the dinner last week. "I feel good. I feel like I'm ready to contribute and do all I can to help the team."

"He's already contributing," Gabe said, to which Beau's reply of "Aw, shucks" earned a round of laughter.

How could such a strong, confident guy be interested in her? Why was she sitting here waiting for him to come home, like she was the wife? She should leave. She didn't belong. She glanced at her phone. Should she make up an excuse and just leave?

A knock came at the door. She wondered if she should answer it, then realized there was a peephole. She moved to look through it when she heard the doorman's voice.

"Miss Joly, your dinner has arrived," he called.

Oh. She opened the door. His hands were laden with white paper bags. "Oh, let me help you."

"Thank you. But if you don't mind, I'm carefully balanced and don't want to drop anything, so it might be easier if I take this over there."

She made room for the food on the table, shifting a newspaper underneath the heated boxes. Was she supposed to tip him? She moved to her handbag. "How much do I owe you?"

The doorman shook his head. "Please don't worry about that. Mr. Nash said he would take care of it."

"Merci."

He nodded and moved to exit, and she remembered to hand

him the key. He took it with a smile and a nod. "Thank you. Enjoy your meal."

"Bonsoir."

She eyed the heated boxes, then peeled back the cardboard lid to peer inside. Pasta. Another box—non-heated—held a salad that looked delicious. She wondered how long it would take for Beau to return and decided she could put the pasta in the oven and the salad in the fridge, then set the table. A glance at her phone ten minutes later revealed his message that he was just parking his car, so she removed the food from the oven, retrieved the salad, and found a bottle of water. How domesticated this seemed. It brought back memories of her time as a newlywed with Alain, when every meal together felt like a gift and she'd strived to be the domestic goddess she'd later come to realize she could never really be. She wondered if Beau would notice her efforts, then thought he probably would. His apartment was decorated so beautifully after all.

She'd just set out the glasses when a key sounded in the door, and he appeared and smiled.

She moved out from behind the kitchen island, feeling suddenly shy. "Hi."

He dropped his duffel bag near the door and kept walking, his eyes intent on her. "Maggie."

"Beau," she squeaked as he drew her into his arms. She stiffened, then relaxed into the embrace as his warmth engulfed her and her senses sparked to life. How long had it been since she'd been held? How long since she'd felt so secure and protected? She allowed herself to sink against him, aware of the hard planes of his chest, the gentle power of his frame as she dared to wrap her arms around his middle and her pulse scampered in wonder at it all.

His head lowered so his cheek rested against her hair, and for a long moment they just held each other and breathed. Whatever happened tonight, whatever happened in the future, she'd never forget this moment for its peace and sense of utter rightness.

His hand slid up to stroke her hair, sparking sensation down her skin, then he eased away. "Well, that's the nicest welcome home I've ever had."

Her breath hitched. Did he mean that to sound like it did, like he thought she belonged here? She smiled to cover her uncertainty. "Are you hungry?"

His gaze darkened and dropped to her lips for a long moment, then he stepped back, exhaled, and threw a hand through his hair. "Give me a second to wash up and I'll be at the table."

His absence allowed for several steadying breaths. Sometimes it seemed that his presence was overwhelming, his size and strength as powerful as the big emotions and questions here. She hadn't mistaken that look of desire in his eyes, had she? She shivered, silencing the questions by busying herself with serving the food so that when he returned, she had two plates filled.

"Hey, someone seems to know how much a hockey player likes to eat," he said, seating himself at the end of the table next to where she'd positioned her plate. Opposite each other at the table felt too far away, side by side and she couldn't see him. In this position, she could absorb his presence far more easily.

She glanced at his plate, which held twice as much food as her own. "I remember how much my husband liked to eat after a big day. I imagined it might be similar for you."

He nodded. "We have energy bars and eat something light before the game, but I'm always starving at the end."

Which must explain why he'd ordered enough food for five people.

He held out his hand. "Can we pray?"

She nodded, automatically slipping her hand into his as he

prayed a blessing on their food. At the amen, he said, "Will you tell me about him?"

"Alain?"

He nodded, eyeing her as he forked in the tortellini.

Well. This wasn't exactly how she'd imagined the start of tonight's conversation. But given the lack of time together, maybe it was best to get the tough stuff dealt with. So she told him about her husband, how they had met at college, how she'd fallen in love with the engineer and they'd married. Beau's gaze weighed heavy on her as she shared about learning she was pregnant, then the sudden shock of Alain's heart condition, which had led to the massive stroke when Noah was two months old.

"Oh, Maggie." Beau's face was soft as he reached to hold her hand. "I'm so sorry."

"It was nearly five years ago now. And I only have good memories of my time with him. I didn't have regrets, so I suppose that helped me heal."

"It still would've been so hard though, especially with a little one to care for."

"It wasn't easy," she acknowledged. "And it was why I had to move back in with Maman. It was good for a couple of years there—my papa was alive too, but then he had a heart attack when Noah was two, which meant I had to leave work again to help my mother." She studied her plate. "That was a hard time."

"I'm sorry."

The sincerity in his voice drew her gaze back to meet his. "But we're better now. Well, Maman took it pretty hard, but lately I've noticed she's been less inclined to isolate herself. Of course, it helps to have a daughter who insists on inviting the neighbors in for Thanksgiving." She smiled at herself and scooped up another mouthful of the delicious pasta.

"Are Alain's parents not in the picture?"

"They died years ago. I never knew them."

Beau nodded, his gaze soft with sympathy. "You're amazing."

"Pardon?"

He played with his salad. "The way you've managed to cope and raise that gorgeous little boy while taking care of your mother. I think you're amazing."

"You clearly don't know me very well," she countered.

"I clearly hope to change that."

His smile caught her heart, permeating it with renewed warmth and lightness, daring her to believe that dreams could come true. "So, you know about me. What about you?"

He nodded and ate another couple of mouthfuls before placing his knife and fork on the plate. "I think I told you about my father dying when I was ten. That obviously affected us for quite some time. Mom was in shock, because Dad's heart attack came out of nowhere. He'd always been one of the fittest guys we knew, then one day he had a heart attack while out cycling. Nobody knew where he was for ages. The doctors told us later that he'd likely died immediately, but both Olivia and I think my mom felt guilty about that for some time."

"She couldn't have known," Maggie said. "These things happen. You never know how much time you have left."

"That's what the doctors said, but it's one thing to know it, it's another to live like you believe it."

Maggie nodded. Just like her relationship with God. "Your mother seems so happy now."

He slid a look at her. "She had—has," he corrected himself, "faith that she'll see him again one day."

She bit her lip. Had her father made that commitment? She still wasn't sure if Alain had.

"What is it?"

She shook her head. She'd talk about her faith commitment soon, but right now she wanted to hear more of his family's story. "I guess all of that forced you and Olivia to grow up fast."

"I was the man of the house," he said simply, taking a moment to eat again.

She could just imagine him as a small boy with the same compassion and earnestness he displayed now. "You and your mother seem really close."

"I guess it's to be expected. It might sound weird, but I think she's one of my best friends. I tell her everything. Well"—he eyed her with a sly smile—"almost everything."

Her cheeks grew hot. So he hadn't told his mother about Maggie's visit tonight. "I like her. And your sister and niece and nephew too, of course."

"And they like you. And Noah too, of course," he gently teased.

They continued eating as she pieced together what she'd learned tonight with what she already knew. "I would never have realized Bronson had been so ill."

"Ill?" Beau glanced at her, puzzled.

"You mentioned when we were at the hospital that your nephew had been sick."

A shadow crossed his features. "That was Joey. He was older than Bailey and died of a rare blood disorder when he was two."

"Really? I'm so sorry."

He nodded, and her insides twisted with compassion. He was a good uncle, and it was clear he loved his family. He carried kindness and care that had been wrought in pain.

"Your sister seems so good about it. If you hadn't told me, I would never have known."

"She struggled, but God helped her. And I think Bailey's arrival, then Bronson's not much later, helped too." He ate an olive, his eyes forest-green in the dimness. "I think it helped for her to have seen how my mom coped with things, so she decided not to wear grief like a badge of honor." He shrugged. "Anyway, that's why I'll do almost anything to help sick kids."

"You're a kind man."

"You know it."

She smiled at his attempt to lighten the mood. "And Olivia's husband?"

"Yeah, he's a kind man too." His lips lifted as she snickered. "Jesse works at a law firm in Charleston, so he can't always get away. He's a nice guy, but he's gotta be nice to put up with Olivia."

"Don't say that," she protested. "Your sister is lovely."

"My sister likes to get in my business and in my face. I love her, but sometimes I love it when she's elsewhere."

"You're so mean," she said, trying—and failing—to hide her amusement.

"Me? Man. So all this trying hard to impress you isn't working?"

"Not at all."

He sighed heavily, his own smile peeking out. "I hope the food, at least, is impressing you."

"It's really delicious," she owned.

"Right? Gabe mentioned this Italian place not too far away that delivers, and it's proving to be a life saver."

"For all the late night visitors you have?" she ventured.

His green gaze slammed into hers. "You don't mean that, do you?"

She knew a quick pulse of shame and shook her head.

"I've been in the NHL for nearly ten years, Maggie, and I've never done the girls up in the room thing. Dating has been hard enough with all the challenges of spending half a year away with games and stuff demanding time. I've rarely dated—actually, full disclosure: you may see that I had a meal a few weeks ago with someone from the hospital, but it was a meal, that was all."

She nodded. He'd had a meal with her. That's what he referred to, wasn't it?

"To be honest, I can't even really remember her name," he confessed.

What?

"So it didn't mean anything. But hey, that doesn't matter. Not when we're here now."

She blinked, trying to process this. He meant he'd dined with another woman from the hospital? Oh, what did it matter? Like he said, they were here now.

The atmosphere that had only minutes ago felt intimate and real now felt strained. She studied her plate, chiding her insecurities and loose tongue that had stolen ease away.

"Hey, Maggie." She glanced up. His gaze was intent. "There's something I really want to know."

Her heart tensed.

"Tell me more about your time at church when you went with Mom and Liv."

Heartstrings loosed as she explained about the service and the sermon and her prayer, and he held her hand and smiled and encouraged and said that was the best thing he'd heard all day.

"Better than a first star of the night?"

"Better than a Stanley Cup," he assured, lifting her hand to kiss it.

Her skin tingled even as her heart glowed. "Thank you for encouraging me to go."

"I'm so glad you did. It just makes everything better."

It did. Hope now hummed through her veins, a sense that she was loved. Regardless of what happened with Beau.

He got up to replenish his plate, asking if she'd like more food. When she shook her head, he served himself, then resumed his seat.

"You played well tonight."

He sipped his drink. "It's nice to see us win a few."

"Your boss seems impressed."

"You saw the interview?"

She nodded.

"Yeah, well, it's good to keep him impressed, seeing he's the one who pays my wages."

"It's always good to keep the boss on-side," she acknowledged.

"Speaking of, he wanted to know if you were interested in joining us for the team's Halloween party."

"Are you serious?"

He nodded. "Apparently it's something of a big deal, and while I don't love all things Halloween, the fact that it's a charity event that supports the kids' hospital made me think it would be good to go. And to have you come, too."

"Do we need to dress up?"

"Costumes and stuff? I don't know. I'll find out. But regardless, I'd love for you to be my date."

She studied him seriously. They'd talked about all kinds of things, but with events such as the Pumpkin Ball and the Halloween function, the fact she'd be seen publicly with him put this relationship in a different space.

"What is it?" he asked. "Don't you want to come?"

"I do," she admitted. "It's just...I'm not sure I'm really ready for all of this."

His look turned sober. "You mean you and me? Going out? Being seen to be a couple?"

Her heart skipped a couple of beats. "Is that what we are?" she dared ask.

"Is that what you want to be?" His gaze grew intense.

The moment seemed to expand into weighty importance. She licked her lip nervously, saw his gaze drop to her mouth then lift again. "I...I never do casual relationships with a man. I *can't* do casual relationships with a man. I always have to think of Noah."

He placed his hand on hers. "Don't you think I thought about that? I don't do casual relationships either, Maggie. For a long time, hockey has been my life as I've waited for God to bring along the right girl. And now, since meeting you, I feel like there's more in my life. I want to see if we can develop this friendship into something firm and secure for the future."

Her chest grew tight. Was he hinting at what she thought he was? She glanced down at his hand covering hers, solid, strong, sure. "I just don't want to see Noah hurt."

"I don't want to see him hurt either."

The air seemed to tremble like that time when she'd stood at the cliff edge of the fairytale-like grotto at Mulgrave-et-Derry. Alain had tried to persuade her to jump into the water, to risk and let go. One step farther and she would fall into the unknown. But that was faith, wasn't it? Trusting God, taking one step at a time into what she couldn't see or know but believed held exciting possibilities. And unlike her hesitation at the cliff edge, she'd now decided not to live bound by fear. Living, loving, meant letting go of those self-imposed limitations of the past.

"Maggie." His voice was husky, his eyes sincere. "You can trust me."

Oui. She knew she could. Time and again he'd shown his kindness and consideration for others. The thought that he'd continue to demonstrate that to her and Noah made her heart curl. She nodded.

"So that's a yes?"

Another nod.

"Thank you." He squeezed her hand, then lifted it to kiss her knuckles, rippling her senses to tingling flight.

The conversation veered to what he might expect at both Thanksgiving and the Pumpkin Ball, where she apologized that he might need to expect lots of attention. "I didn't realize just what a big deal you are," she admitted.

"Hey, I didn't realize just what a big deal I am either," his said, his eyes full of tease. "I mean, I'm used to fans who like hockey, but man, the fans here *really* love hockey."

She nodded. She'd heard just some of that love tonight, with the girls she'd been seated with talking a language she barely understood. "I was thankful for Claudine explaining some of it to me," she admitted.

"She knows her stuff." His face shadowed.

"What is it?" she asked.

"I like her, but I just can't get over that time I saw her and Kris at that restaurant, remember?"

She nodded. "I was so confused when I saw her come here that night with Gabe. I thought Kris was her husband."

"I don't know what to do about that," he said. "I feel like something isn't right, but every time I try and say something, I don't get the chance."

"We'll have to pray about it."

His gaze warmed. "Amen."

They talked a little more, then he yawned, and Maggie realized how late it was. "I should go," she said, getting up to clear the plates.

"Hey, leave those."

She shook her head. "The last thing you need to do is clean up after your big day."

"My big day? Didn't you have work today?"

"Yes, but it didn't involve trying to scare off big men hurtling toward me like a train."

"I'm glad." He reached behind her, his arm tingling awareness along hers. "If ever big men hurtle toward you, give me a call, okay?" he teased.

"Okay."

Dishwasher loaded, the leftovers of their meal put away, he drew her to the window where Montreal's lights glowed. He wrapped her close, her back to his front, her surprise at his easy affection tensing her muscles before the peace and stillness of the moment eased such tightness away. They studied the view, and she felt his breath in her hair, contentment competing with the heart-pattering nearness of him. Would he kiss her? Part of her hoped he'd wait. It felt like tonight had cemented their friendship and anything beyond a hug would rush things. But another part, the part that had tingled when he'd pressed his lips to her hand, tugged low, insistent, recalling how Alain's hugs had fueled desire—need—for more. Beau's hug might be innocent, but she'd soon long for more. She eased away. "It's a great view."

"It's a great apartment."

"Just needs some plants," she said, relieved the moment was tipping back to amiable rapport.

"It's funny you should say that, being a plant-connoisseur and all."

"Isn't it?" She moved to collect her bag, and he helped her into her coat.

"I wish you could stay longer, but we have a quick road trip tomorrow, so I'll need to get to sleep soon."

"Will you be at church on Sunday?"

He shook his head. "I thought I'd be, but it turns out we get back late Sunday night. But I'll watch the live-stream of the service and pretend I'm there sitting next to you, okay?"

"Okay." She moved to the door, and he came with her, insisting on travelling downstairs with her, where they encountered a very fancily dressed couple who were entering the lobby. Their eyebrows rose as they glanced at Beau and Maggie.

Beau's grasp on her hand tightened. "Evening." He moved her on, then said in a louder voice to the doorman, "Hey, Eddie, thanks for sending up that dinner. It was delicious."

"No problem, Mr. Nash."

"I'm just going to see Ms. Joly to her car, then hit the hay. She might be able to afford to miss her beauty sleep, but I sure can't."

"Sure thing, Mr. Nash."

Beau opened the door for her and walked her outside, his large hand holding hers firmly.

"You don't have to walk me to the car," she protested.

"I want to," he said.

Okay. She'd object no more. Especially when the feel of his thumb brushing against her skin created such delightful heated sensations.

Two minutes later, he was bending down, arm propped on the car frame as she put on her seatbelt. "Are you sure you're okay to drive? It's late. I could call a taxi."

Her chest warmed. How wonderful to have someone fuss over her in this way. "I'll be fine."

"And I'll see you Monday for Thanksgiving?"

"I'll send you the address and time."

"I'll be there as soon as I've visited Jacques and the others at the hospital," he promised.

She nodded. He leaned closer and stroked her cheek, then pulled back and closed her door.

And she drove away, anticipation filling her at what the next few days might hold.

CHAPTER 18

It was one thing to somehow convince her mother that it was a good idea to invite the neighbors to enjoy Thanksgiving with them. It was quite another to somehow explain that a very famous man who just so happened to be her not-quite-boyfriend was also on his way. In the years since Alain's death, Maggie had never shown interest in another man, so the fact that Beau was coming felt both enormously important and too hard to explain. Maybe he'd be able to hide among the others who were here already.

"Maggie?" Fatima asked. "Where do you want the feteer?"

Maggie glanced at the dish of small pastries covered in powdered sugar. "It is a dessert?"

Fatima nodded. "Food of the gods, they say. My boys love it, and I'm sure your boy will too. Noah," she called. "Come try this."

Noah glanced at Maggie, who subtly shook her head before facing Fatima. "If it's dessert, then I'd rather he wait until he's had some meat and vegetables. I can't wait to try it. You can set it down there." She pointed to the counter.

The house was filled with noise and people, so unlike the

usual quietude. And unlike what might otherwise be expected, her mother was seemingly coping with it all, her resolve to not lift a finger having well and truly ended when she realized just what was involved. The past two days had seen a flurry of cleaning, rearranging furniture, and baking, as Maggie worked to ensure their guests would feel welcomed and that, even if no one brought anything, there would be enough food for all.

So far, Mrs. Chang, Frederic, and Fatima had arrived and were at ease in the living room. Noah's friend's mother had sent her apologies last week, and Fatima was unsure if her sons would still come. Danielle and her husband Denis were due to drop in later, and Beau had texted to say he was on his way. And while she'd sent invitations to the other neighbors, the lack of response made her wonder if they thought she was a crazy lady or if they'd turn up anyway. Regardless, it didn't matter. If they came, there'd be enough. If they didn't, Maggie's household would have dinner sorted for the rest of the week.

The doorbell rang, and her mother wiped her brow. "How many more are you expecting, Maggie?"

"I don't know." She smiled. "Isn't this fun?"

"But how will I know how many more place settings to set?" her mother complained.

"We have the plates ready. We'll squeeze people in. Now, I'd better answer the door."

She shot a quick look at the mirror and quickly smoothed her hair. Was Beau here already? She affixed a smile and swung the door open. And encountered two swarthy men she'd never met before. "Er, hello?"

"My boys!" Fatima exclaimed from behind her, rushing forward to draw them inside and introduce them to Maggie and her mother. "This is Akeem and Kahlil."

The men murmured appreciation for their hospitality, and Fatima took them inside to meet the other neighbors as Maggie wondered how that would go with those neighbors who objected to their loud cars and music. She moved outside, saw the normally quiet street had several extra cars, including—

"Danielle!" Maggie lifted a hand as Danielle walked up the path. "Welcome."

"You remember my husband Denis?"

Maggie nodded. "Welcome."

"Thanks for having us today," he said. "My parents insisted on going on a cruise, which says it all, doesn't it?"

"Maybe it's the year for change." She guided them inside. "This is a first for my mother and me, so if it's a little disorganized, I hope you'll forgive us."

"Something smells amazing," Danielle said. "Look, we brought wine." She handed her the bottles.

"Thank you." Maggie wasn't sure whether Fatima's sons drank, but Frederic did. "Now, let me introduce you to everyone."

After another round of introductions, she moved to the kitchen, where her mother was studying the large roast. "I don't know what to do," she confessed. "I've never been good at carving, and I'd hate for it to be messed up today."

"Can I help?" a deeper voice asked.

Maggie jumped, her mother cried out, and they turned to see a new visitor. Maggie's heart sang. Beau looked so good, wearing an outfit similar to what he'd worn for that dinner with his family two weeks ago, his hair pulled back neatly and, judging from the cologne he wore, his cheeks freshly shaved.

"Who are you?" her mother demanded. "What are you doing in my kitchen?"

"I knocked, but no one came, and the front door was unlocked."

Beau looked uncertainly at Maggie, so she drew near and touched his arm. "Maman, I'd like you to meet a friend of mine. Maman, this is Beau Nash. Beau, this is my mother, Stephanie LeRoux."

He put out his hand and gently clasped her mother's hand within his. "I'm really pleased to meet you."

Maman's head tilted as she stared at him. "You're really tall."

His lips tweaked. "Oui. Oh, and these are for you." He retreated to the hall and retrieved two bouquets of roses from the side table, one of yellows and whites, which he handed to Maggie's mother, the other of pinks, which he handed to Maggie.

Her heart thudded, then thumped some more at the look in his eyes. "You remembered I love pink roses?"

"Of course." His smile held an ocean of promise.

Her mother thanked him, then looked at her suspiciously. "Maggie, how many more of your friends are coming?"

"Beau is probably the last."

"Probably?"

At Maman's sigh, Maggie quickly redirected her mother's attention to their guests, then asked Beau to slice the meat. She wrapped an arm around his back and leaned against him briefly. "Thank you for coming."

"I couldn't miss it."

"How did the hospital visit go?"

"It was worth doing. Jacques, that sick boy I've mentioned before, he's not doing too well."

"I'm sorry." She squeezed his waist gently. He pressed a kiss to the top of her head, the moment of tenderness leading to a poignant pause, the peace from the busyness providing space in which she felt like she could breathe.

"Beau!" Noah's shriek of happiness muffled as he slammed into Beau's legs.

Beau dropped to meet him, opening his arms in a hug. "Hey, buddy. How you doing?"

"You know my grandson?" Maman asked.

"We've met a few times since the ice cream incident."

"Ice cream man!" Noah said again.

"What ice cream incident?" Maman demanded.

Beau's look of amusement faded as he pushed to his feet, his gaze toward Maggie questioning.

That's right. Maggie had never really explained to her mother how they had met Beau several times. "Oh, they met at the crèmerie a few weeks ago, Maman. Noah, could you please go find your seat? We'll be out there in a minute."

He nodded, then she gestured for Beau to keep cutting the meat and took out the trays of roasted vegetables. "We'll put all of this on the table, then people can help themselves."

"Yes, boss," Beau murmured.

"Thank you for helping," she murmured back.

"Of course." He looked surprised at her comment. "This is how we do family meals."

"Can I help with anything?" Danielle asked, trailed by Denis, whose mouth fell open as he saw Beau. "Hello."

Maggie conducted quick introductions as Beau wiped his hands on a towel and shook Denis's hand.

"It's an honor," Denis said.

"Will you be at the Pumpkin Ball too?" Beau asked him.

"You didn't think Danielle would let me get out of it?" Denis said, squeezing his wife around the shoulders.

"Come on," Danielle said. "You're excited, just like Maggie is." She turned to Beau. "Just you wait until you see what she's wearing."

"What Pumpkin Ball?" Maman demanded.

Another secret she'd have to explain. "Maman, you know I mentioned about the fundraising event this Saturday. That's the Pumpkin Ball."

"And he's going?" She gestured to Beau.

Maggie's cheeks heated at her mother's air of disdain. "Beau will be one of the guests."

"One of the most important guests," Danielle said firmly.

"Why?"

She so should've told her mother about Beau. "He plays for Montreal's hockey team, Maman. He's famous."

"But he wears his hair up like a girl."

Beau's snort of amusement drew Maggie's giggle, which she struggled to push down as she said, "Come, we don't want the food to get cold. Let's get the others out here."

Maggie placed the remaining platters on the kitchen table, then invited the others to join them. She noticed Beau hanging back as if not wanting to draw attention and mouthed a *thank you* for his understanding. Maggie encouraged people to fill their plates, then she helped Noah with selecting his food. Finally, Maman helped herself and sat down, then Maggie and Beau served themselves.

They entered the formal dining room, where the long table that was normally covered with Maman's craft and laundry now looked pretty and beautifully set with the long-unused lace tablecloth Maggie had found in the linen closet. The chairs around the table might be mismatched, and the only spaces available at the end would prove a tight fit, but that didn't matter. It felt like family was here at last. And if the squishiness meant she had to sit close to Beau, well, that wasn't exactly a problem.

Maggie encouraged Beau to claim the seat with slightly more room next to her mother, while she took the seat next to Noah. Conversation, which had dropped at their entrance, resumed again, but people still seemed to hesitate about eating, so she took the moment to tap her wineglass.

"I'd like to thank you all for coming today. It means a lot, and I'm very thankful to God for the friendships we have with all of you, whether they be old friendships or new." Her gaze shifted to Beau, and she knew another heart thump at the warm look he offered.

"Here's to family and friendship," she said.

The toast echoed around the room as they gently bumped

glasses, and she tapped Noah's plastic cup before clinking her glass with Beau's.

"To family and friendships," he echoed, his eyes crinkling. "And futures," he added for her ears alone.

THE SUSPICION with which Mrs. LeRoux had regarded Beau on Monday seemed to have faded when she opened the door on Saturday night. Maybe it was the way he got on with Noah. Maybe it was because Beau had spent hours after the meal helping Maggie clean up. He'd never known that washing up could be so much fun when he had someone he could talk to about anything. They'd talked like they couldn't during dinner —about the Sunday sermon, his game, and their impressions of the people who had gathered together. They'd managed to take a photo, a lasting proof of this event that had endeared Maggie to his heart even more. He'd even called his mom, and she'd chatted to Maggie before insisting on speaking to Maggie's mom. Maybe it was his mother's charm that had assuaged some of Stephanie LeRoux's fears. Whatever it was, he was happy to see the smile she offered now.

"Maggie is nearly ready. Come inside," she said.

He obeyed, moving to the family room, which looked different with its furniture rearranged from what he remembered the other day. Monday had been fun.

"Hi, Beau!" Noah offered him a gap-toothed smile.

"Hey, little man. How was school this week?"

"It was good."

"Have you had a tooth fall out since Monday?"

Noah nodded proudly. "The tooth fairy visited."

"Did she now?"

Another nod. "But the tooth fairy is a man. He plays hockey too."

Beau swallowed a chuckle, remembering the old Dwayne Johnson movie. "Of course. My mistake. What's the going rate for a tooth these days?"

But he didn't hear the answer as Maggie moved into view. Breath escaped. His mouth dried. He swallowed. Stared. Stared some more. "Bonsoir."

He struggled to remember the right phrase he'd been practicing for this moment. "*Tu es magnifique.*"

She grinned. "*Tu es très beau aussi.*"

Her one-shouldered, rust-colored satin gown seemed to bring out reddish glints in her dark hair. And the way she'd styled her hair and done her makeup made him very glad he'd bought a new suit and dressed up as fancy as he knew how.

"Wow. You look great. Like a glamorous movie star," he said honestly. English was too weak for the depth of his appreciation.

"Merci beaucoup," she said shyly. "Danielle, my work colleague—her mother owns a bridal boutique downtown and insisted I go with her today." She touched her hair, in some fancy arrangement he thought Olivia called an updo. "They had someone there who did our hair and makeup too."

"Tu es très belle, Maman," Noah said admiringly.

"Tu es très belle," Beau repeated.

Maggie blushed and murmured thanks to her mother for caring for Noah again tonight, then gave her son a kiss that tugged Beau to long for her affection in a similar way.

Her gown begged him to touch her, and he was glad for the company of her mother and son that made that impossible now. He helped Maggie with her coat, not above taking a moment to caress the silky skin of her arms, then managed to school his features as he wished her mom a good night and gave Noah a high five.

Outside, the night air was cold, hurrying them to his car, where he opened the door for her and helped her inside. Then he hurried around to his side, lifting a hand as Mrs. Chang peered past her curtains. She hurriedly closed the curtains, the sight prompting his smile.

"What is it?"

"I still don't think your neighbor knows what to make of me."

"That's not surprising," she said. "I barely know what to make of you."

"Wow. And here I was, about to say you are the most beautiful person I've ever seen, and then you come out with a comment like that."

She shifted to face him, her gaze soft. "I simply meant that you keep amazing me with the things you do."

"So you meant it in a good way?" At her nod and shy smile, he was desperately close to kissing her, but refrained. He sure didn't plan to have their first kiss in front of all her neighbors. "In that case, I suppose I'll just have to tell you that I think you're the most beautiful woman I've ever seen."

Her breath caught. "Careful now," she murmured. "Between tonight's pumpkins and comments like that, you'll make me believe I'm Cinderella."

"Bailey would approve. In fact, I'll be sure to get some pictures tonight and send them to her. She'll be so jealous."

"Spoken like a loving uncle."

"Hey, I can't help it if I'm glad I don't have to share you with others tonight."

"I'm afraid you'll have to, for a little bit anyway. I'll be busy—"

"Stopping traffic," he interrupted.

She laughed. "With some of the sponsors and Friends of the Gardens, and you'll be busy being a celebrity."

"Please. Do you really think your garden friends will be interested in someone like me?"

But it turned out they were, and Maggie's comments about

the evening and his popularity were well-founded. No sooner had he entered the pumpkin-strewn room, with its candles and artful creations carved from pumpkins and gourds, than he was surrounded by people wishing to speak with him and have their photos taken. Maggie introduced him to various people, like Mr. Withers, the president of the Friends of the Gardens, but even her colleagues seemed hockey mad. Gabe and Claudine's arrival later, followed by the arrival of Johan and Jake, only saw the level of noisy chatter increase. For much of the evening, Beau and his teammates were buttonholed by people who seemed more interested in Montreal's prospects for this year's Stanley Cup than they did gardens.

"Whew," Beau said as he and Johan posed for another photo. "I didn't think tonight would be quite so hectic."

"This is Montreal," Johan said. "Everywhere we go is going to be demanding."

Beau nodded, his eyes searching the crowd for Maggie. He found her talking to two silver-haired men who seemed to be paying more attention to her gown than her words. He muttered an excuse and plowed through the crowd to place a hand on her back. "Hey, Maggie."

"Beau!"

He pressed a kiss to her cheek and stood there, knowing he looked possessive, hoping the men would get that impression and back off. "Introduce me?"

The two men were arts sponsors, and after some conversation, they moved away, the taller one touching the shorter one's hand. Oh. He glanced down to see her amused gaze. "I thought they were checking you out."

"They were," she said pertly. "Checking out my gown. Pierre is in fashion and was admiring the cut."

"He was?" Any red-blooded man would be admiring way more than the cut, but he figured that might not be appropriate to say.

She shot him a look of amusement. "Have you seen the items on display for the auction?"

"Not yet. Lead the way."

They went into another room, where Maggie gravitated to the corner to admire several paintings including a large one that looked to be of the Japanese Garden's water lily pond. "Isn't that beautiful?"

"Very beautiful," he agreed, checking out the price tag. Hmm. Maybe it would work in the dining room.

He studied the other auction items on display, many with a link to the Gardens. A jewelry display held some items of interest and included a silent auction option. He waited until Maggie had moved on to put in his bid. Who knew with this crowd whether it would be successful or not, but the money would go to a good cause anyway. And if he did win, well, it would go to a very good cause indeed.

"May I take your photo?"

He paused. "Hey, Maggie, someone wants to take our photo."

She looked at him, then at the photographer. "I think they just want you," she said gently.

"Of course they want to talk to you," he insisted, drawing her near and snaking an arm around her waist. "Maggie is one of the organizers for tonight's event, so you definitely need to take her photo."

"Of course."

He reveled in the moment to hold her as she explained a little bit more about the event. He loved watching the passion on her face, the way her face lit up as she talked about the importance of making time for nature and the God-given beauty to be found in plants and trees.

"It's such a privilege to be able to work here," she said. "And I think every person who visits the Gardens understands what a blessing this place is, which is why it's so wonderful to see so many supporters here tonight."

"And you, Mr. Nash? What brings you here tonight?"

"Apart from Maggie, you mean?" He smiled at her. "I was lucky enough to visit the Gardens on one of my first weekends here, and I found it such a relaxing place to be. The staff here are obviously wonderful"—he gave Maggie's hand a squeeze —"and the gardens have been designed to help people find that moment of relaxation in their busy lives. It's definitely worth supporting, and I encourage people who haven't visited lately to make sure they do so soon, as there's so much to see."

Someone moved to talk to Maggie, and Beau took the moment to talk to Danielle and make an outrageous bid to secure the painting, which he asked her to keep quiet.

She nodded, wide-eyed, and promised to keep it a secret. There were more photos and meetings and greetings and food and wine, and he took a moment to thank his teammates for coming.

"It's good to have a night out that's not hockey related," Claudine said, an edge to her voice that made Beau wonder about her and Gabe's relationship again. Gabe just shrugged, and Beau found himself wondering what was best to do. This was hardly the place to mention seeing her with Kris all those weeks ago. Maybe things had been resolved. Maybe it was none of his business. But the thought that Gabe might be hurt still niggled at him as he prayed for wisdom about what to do.

The auction began, and he egged on Johan to buy one of the paintings for his wife, which soon became a contest between Johan and the silver-haired man from before. The bidding crept higher and higher and made Beau smile, as he strongly suspected Johan didn't really like the painting. But the competitor in him would not stop, especially when Gabe was goaded to join in and the bidding crept higher still. Eventually Gabe was the victim, which led to Claudine's clapping, big hug, and loud exclamation of "I knew you would win!"

Her public display of affection seemed a little over the top, and he caught Gabe's rolled eyes, like he thought that too. It was funny seeing how different situations brought out different qualities in people. He'd always wondered if Maggie was shy or simply unsure in certain situations. Seeing her in this environment, Beau realized just how strong and confident she could be. She was able to talk to people from all kinds of backgrounds, and the knowledge that she was like this, that she was following in God's way, brought him to realize something else.

He loved her. She was everything he'd prayed about for years. A kind-hearted, family-oriented Christian woman who saw past the shiny gloss and saw him. He might not have known her forever, but they seemed to click and fit together in a way that felt God-ordained. Mom seemed to recognize it too. And what he'd said to Maggie only days ago was true. He would do anything to protect her. He would do anything to seek her best, and he would do his best to help Noah as well.

But while he longed to tell her his feelings, a niggling thought wondered what this might mean for his career. He hadn't wanted to think too much on what Paul had said about Maggie, that he should stay away in order to appease the team's sponsor. That was wrong, dumb, so no way. And given the media here tonight would likely tip Beau and Maggie's relationship into the open, it was only a matter of time before someone said something. But that was okay. If he cared for her, he wouldn't hide her away but instead do all he could to show the team the treasure he'd found in this woman.

Apprehension still wormed under his enjoyment, so he was glad for the distraction of the music when the band started to play. The room had twinkling lights overhead, which combined with the candles to create a romantic atmosphere. And as they were summoned to join the dancefloor, he forgot the tension, and non-dancing him soon found he didn't mind dancing after all.

Maggie was light on her feet, which was just as well, as he

was pretty sure he'd trodden on hers. "I'm really sorry. You'd think a guy who needs to be careful where he moves would be better at this."

"To be dancing at this is a dream. To be dancing with you—"

"Is a nightmare?"

She smiled. "I like that you're confident enough to be insecure with me."

"I like you enough to be confident that way," he admitted honestly.

He could only count a few people with whom he could be so honest. Mom. Pastor Josiah. Jai. Dan. And now Maggie. "I really like you," he murmured close to her ear, where a tendril of her hair had escaped. "Ma belle Maggie."

She shifted, her sleek gown slippery beneath his touch. "*Je t'aime bien aussi, mon bel Beau*," she murmured, her eyes dark as she gazed up at him.

Okay, so he was still learning this French stuff, but that sounded awfully close to the *I love you*s he'd heard sung in many a café. "What did you just say?" he whispered, his feet stumbling to a pause.

She gazed up at him, her lips curved in a smile. "Is it just me, or is it hot in here?"

"I'm hot," he admitted, realizing how that sounded as she laughed. "I meant—"

"No, no. That is true," she said, her gaze flicking to his chest then up to roam his face.

Now he really was hot. Or at least his cheeks were. "If it makes any difference, I think you're hot too."

Her amusement rippled again, and he took the moment to draw her to a corner, behind a curtain. "You keep laughing at me when I'm trying to be serious," he complained.

She sobered, although her eyes still held a mischievous twinkle. "You want to know the difference between *je t'aime bien* and *je t'aime*?"

"Oui."

"Some may disagree, but I've always understood *je t'aime bien* to mean *I like you well enough.*"

"Well enough?" His chest panged.

"Whereas *je t'aime,*" she said, inching closer, her heels meaning her face was in perfect kissing range of his, "means something more."

"Really?" He wrapped his arms around her, reveling in the feel of her body nestling close to his.

She nodded, her throat white in the light from outside. "The meaning can depend on the intonation, what gestures accompany the words."

"Is that so?" he asked, bending down to press his cheek next to hers.

"Mm-hmm," she murmured.

He closed his eyes. He didn't need to be dancing for this moment. His heart was dancing enough. "So, if I was to do this"—he pressed his lips to her cheek—"that might imply *je t'aime?*"

"Mm." She drew back, her eyes sparkling. "You may have noticed we often kiss on the cheek, so that could still be considered *je t'aime bien.*"

"I see." His heart beat faster as he completed the action, pressing his lips softly to one silken cheek then the other, as he drew in her perfume. "Je t'aime."

"Bien."

"Bien?" He sighed. "Maybe you'll just have to show me what you mean."

"Très bien."

Maggie curved one arm around his neck and pushed to her toes. She stroked his cheek, her touch like silken fire, her eyes alive with promise, her mouth hovering enticingly near. So he closed his eyes and took up the silent invitation, lowering his lips to graze hers.

For a second she froze, and he broke the connection before her murmur of "non" saw her push into his space. Her breath whispered a promise over his skin, then her lips met his in a tentative, feather-soft touch.

Magic lay there—delicate, heart-clenching magic. Wonderful, sense-tingling magic.

He waited, letting her lead, leashing his desire for more.

She tugged his head down, and her kiss firmed into certainty, her hands sliding to press into the back of his shoulders. He pulled her closer, heart thrilling as she snuggled in until there was no room between them and he could feel her softness heating his senses. One hand cradled her waist as the other slid up her back to cup her head as he poured himself into the kiss. Je t'aime. *I love you*, his heart seemed to roar.

Her neck tipped back, and he nudged her lips apart, deepening the kiss until everything was a whirl of heat, light, love, as his senses roared into need. He wanted more. He needed more. He pulled back in retreat. Exhaled unsteadily.

"Maggie." Her expression looked as dazed as his must be. "How do you say that was the best kiss of my life and that I'm falling in love with you?"

"Just like that," she whispered, then pressed her lips to his again.

CHAPTER 19

The Bell Centre held the same roar, but this, Maggie's second game, felt a little more comfortable than her first. At Saturday's Pumpkin Ball, Claudine had invited Maggie to sit with her during today's game against L.A. Maggie had accepted, knowing that it helped to have someone she hoped she might one day call a friend.

Relieved that Beau had again arranged the ticket as he said he would, she made her way to the private suite where the wives and girlfriends sat, then smiled at the women she'd met at the previous game.

"Maggie! Come sit here," Claudine commanded, holding a half-empty glass of wine.

Claudine introduced Maggie to some of the women who hadn't been there last week, and Maggie soon found herself talking a little about herself, where she worked, and her son.

"That was at the Pumpkin Ball I was telling you about," Claudine said, whipping out her phone and showing some photos to the women, including Johan's wife. "Don't we look amazing?"

"You look like Rita Hayworth," Bryn Tomasson, Johan's Swedish television hostess wife, said to Maggie.

At the sharp look Claudine shot Maggie, embarrassment washed over her. "I think we all looked very fine."

"Beau looks fine," one of the blondes said. "Not as fine as Kaspar, though," she added, laughing.

"But he does have that Viking model thing going on, doesn't he?" someone else said.

"How long have you two been going out for?" another woman asked.

Admit it was less than two weeks? "Not too long," she murmured.

"He's a good guy," someone else said.

"Are we here to watch a hockey game or not?" Claudine demanded. "Maggie, get yourself a drink, then let's get ready. They'll be out for the warm-ups any minute."

Maggie found a small bottle of cider and resumed her seat next to Claudine. The woman vacillated between ease and edge-filled agitation, something perhaps linked to the amount of alcohol consumption, and that drew Maggie's compassion and hope that she'd find the peace Maggie had found so recently. *Help me to be her friend.*

"Thank you for helping me with all this," Maggie said.

"With what?" Claudine asked.

"Getting to know the others, making me feel welcome. I appreciate it."

Claudine nodded, took another sip from her glass. "It's not always easy, trying to fit in. And I say that as the wife of the captain of the team."

"How long have you and Gabe been together?"

"We knew each other in high school."

The stadium's noise increased as the players came onto the ice. Beau was among the first, going to his net, where he conducted a bunch of stretches that showed how supple he was.

"He's really fit, isn't he?" Claudine said, her eyes on Beau. A smile slid onto her bright red lips. "I bet he's really flexible, too."

Was that innuendo lurking in Claudine's eyes and words? Maggie returned her gaze to the ice, waves of embarrassment shimmering from her skin. "I wouldn't know."

"You haven't—? Oh, don't mind me. Gabe is always telling me my mouth is too big."

Perhaps with good reason. Maggie kept her mouth closed, even as pity threaded through her. It sounded as though Claudine and Gabe's relationship wasn't as shiny as the photos might suggest.

Maggie kept her eyes on Beau, wondering if he'd look up to see her here. Not that she wanted to be needy, but it would help to reassure her that this was where she was meant to be. As if knowing her thoughts, he glanced up, lifted up the face shield of his helmet, and smiled in her direction. She smiled back and lifted a hand, then pressed her hands together in a praying motion, then pointed to him. *Praying for you*, she mouthed.

He nodded, smiled, and returned to focus on the ice as the players completed their passing and shooting, then departed again. Claudine went to find another drink, and after some attempts at talking to another of the players' girlfriends, Maggie settled back into her seat. It was okay. Just because she didn't have anyone here that she felt truly comfortable with didn't mean she wouldn't one day. Since God had transformed her, she'd grown aware that she needed to keep her heart open, be aware of others, and see what she could do to bless them.

Claudine resumed her seat beside her. "So, what are you wearing to the Halloween party? Beau told you about it, right?"

"He didn't tell me much," she admitted.

"It's a fun night," Claudine said, her features lighting. She really did seem to like a party. "We all dress up, have food, hang out with some of the sponsors, and it's all for a good cause."

"It supports the kids' hospital?" She thought that was what Beau had said.

Claudine nodded. "They make it a family night, so you can bring your son."

"As long as it doesn't go too late."

"Such a good mother," Claudine said, an edge to her voice.

Maggie bit her lip. Was she mocking her?

"How is your little boy? Noah, isn't it?"

Pique faded, replaced by gratitude that Claudine had remembered his name. "Noah is well. He had appendicitis a month or so ago but is better now and back in school."

"What happened to the father?"

"Alain died," Maggie reminded her quietly. Hadn't she explained during that meal at Beau's?

"Oh! I didn't know. I'm so sorry."

"It was a few years ago now. Noah has proved to be the joy of my life. I don't know what I would have done if I hadn't had him to focus on," she admitted honestly. Thank God He had given her the gift of Noah. Thank God that He had been there with her through all that time and more.

"You must have had Noah when you were very young."

"I'm nearly thirty," Maggie said with a smile.

"Really? You don't look it."

"Maybe Noah just keeps me young," she said.

She glanced across. Claudine's jaw had hardened.

Should she ask? She barely knew the woman. But something, that very something that had unfurled in her heart a few weeks ago, towed compassion from her heart to her mouth. "Do you want children?" she asked softly.

Claudine's lips tightened, her gaze remaining forward, her busy fingers twisting her wedding ring. "Gabe wants to start a family. I'm not so sure. He's always so focused on hockey that he barely notices me. And I think I'll be stuck with raising the kids while he's off doing his thing yet again."

What should Maggie say? She barely knew this couple or their relationship. *Lord, give me wisdom.* "I'm sure if he wants kids, he wants to be involved in their care."

Claudine's gaze swung to her. "He's not like Beau," she said. "He only thinks about hockey."

"I'm sure that's not true," she protested. "Didn't he buy that lovely painting for you at the auction the other night?"

"The only reason he kept bidding was because of the guys."

"I've seen the way he looks at you. He cares for you, Claudine."

Her features tightened, then she shook her head. "I need another drink."

Maggie's heart wrung with compassion. Was this why Claudine had spent time with Kris? What could she say to encourage her to focus on her husband?

Claudine soon returned, drink in hand, and Maggie offered a smile. "I was thinking about what you said before," she ventured. "No relationship is perfect. Alain and I, well, we married straight after college, and it wasn't always easy. Money was a challenge, and he could be sarcastic. He wasn't perfect—"

"What husband is?" Claudine muttered.

"—but then neither was I. I know I never will be."

Claudine lifted her drink and sipped, her gaze on the ice below.

"But looking back," Maggie continued, "I know that our relationship was good, even though it felt hard at times. I've also realized that whatever I focus on grows stronger, so if I focused on his faults, then they seemed worse in my mind. But when I focused on his good qualities and appreciated him, then our relationship improved."

Claudine said nothing but hadn't turned away, so perhaps she'd be open for Maggie to say more.

"Lately, I've realized I can focus on my fears and the things that aren't right, or I can focus on what's good and the fact that

I'm loved. I want to focus on what I know is good and the fact that I know I'm loved."

"Loved by Beau?"

She nodded. He'd said as much, hadn't he? *Falling in love* had been his exact words, something that made every part of her tingle, as did the memory of his kisses, which certainly suggested the same. But that wasn't quite what she'd meant. "And God."

Claudine's face tightened, and she drained her drink and set the glass down. "Oh look!" She pointed to the Jumbotron. "The game is about to start."

Heart sore, Maggie silently prayed and refocused on the ice. The music and light show intensified as Montreal's team, led by Beau, entered to cheers. Beau skated to the net, then did some more of those limbering up exercises, which included stretches that looked like he was doing the splits. No wonder his leg muscles were huge. Her skin heated at the memory of seeing him all those weeks ago wearing shorts. She didn't want to be someone who focused on those kinds of things, but she couldn't deny that the man was very…fit.

"Here we go," Claudine said as the skaters moved into position for the national anthems.

Gabe lined up with Kris, Kaspar, Jake, and Johan, while Beau stayed in his crease. The Los Angeles team lined up on the opposite side. She joined in singing the Canadian anthem, appreciating the switch to French for the second verse, which echoed off the rafters. Then the referee dropped the puck and the game commenced.

Maggie's heartbeat increased. Within the first minute, even she could see that L.A. was a strong, physical team, and it was obvious they had come to play hard. The action moved down to the L.A. goal, then one of their forwards slammed one of the Montreal players into the boards, which filled the arena with loud booing.

"Ouch!" Krystle, Kaspar's girlfriend, cried. "Poor baby."

"That's TJ Woletsky," Claudine said. "He's a goon. Likes to think he's an enforcer."

"What's an enforcer?" Maggie asked.

"They're players who get used to stop or respond to dirty play."

"But the game has barely started."

"Exactly," Claudine said. "He's a law unto himself."

Maggie bit her lip. Thank goodness Beau's position meant he was not in a position to get hurt. At least, that's what he'd told her, anyway. *Lord, keep him safe.*

As the game progressed, Claudine continued to explain a few things here and there, and Maggie could appreciate the skills involved. It would take enormous energy to continue to move so quickly, yet stop at great speed, pivot, muscle past opponents, and resume speed. It was no wonder Beau spent so much time training.

Her attention shifted to him, waiting in the net, eyes on the play. She marveled at the contrast between the jokey, super-kind guy she knew and the one crouched ready with laser focus. He was amazing. His kindness was amazing. His kisses were amazing.

She hunched forward, hands on her cheeks, elbows on knees as she pretended to watch the play. But her thoughts drifted back to their kisses at the ball. Had that been the most romantic moment of her life? She was ashamed to think that it might just have beaten Alain's proposal. But there had been enchantment in that corner of the room, allurement in those eyes, and definitely wonder in his lips, which had drawn her to say and do the most extraordinary things. Her initial hesitation had been snuffed as her body responded in powerful fascination, mesmerized by this powerful man with his gentle touch. She could've kissed him forever. Maybe her mother was right. Maggie barely recognized herself these days either.

The period ended scoreless and allowed time for bathroom and refreshment breaks. Maggie didn't move from her seat, her heart going to the man who had left the ice. This was exciting, but there was definitely an element of danger, something which she had grown more aware of as she overheard some of the wives talk about the injuries their husbands had sustained. How did they manage to cope with such things? How did they not have so much fear when their husbands returned to the ice? Maggie still felt too new to ask these questions and thanked God that Beau had never suffered much. *Lord, keep him safe.*

The Jumbotron showed an interview for the Children's Foundation, with a woman talking about the difference the team made in their visits to hospitalized children. There was a video of Beau talking and laughing with some of the kids in hospital beds, giving them high fives. So caring, so compassionate. Her heart thudded. She loved him.

"Look, it's your man!" Claudine said, slipping into the seat beside her. "He's such a nice guy."

Maggie nodded. He was. He'd told her about his Thanksgiving hospital visit, and this footage seemed to be from then, judging from the pumpkins decorating the room. What kind of man gave so much of himself to others? Someone she could give her heart to.

She smiled at herself. She pretty much had already given him her heart, what with her kisses the other night as they danced around saying *I love you.* There wasn't much else left to give, except that which Claudine had alluded to before. Something which Maggie knew she wouldn't do until Beau had slipped two rings on her ring finger. And while this all seemed shockingly fast, life had taught her what to seek and value and to make the most of it while she could.

"We're starting." Claudine pointed as the skaters moved to the ice. Once again, Beau skated on first for the Canadian team, and Maggie knew a sense of pride in him.

"He's been playing well," Claudine observed.

"Gabe?"

"Beau. To have won all his games so far has put us on top of the league. Gabe says that everyone's really impressed with him."

"He is impressive, but they have only played six games," Maggie felt the need to say.

"Plus the preseason," Claudine said. "If you count that, then it makes him the winningest goalie this year."

That sounded a little biased, but "Okay."

The play this time seemed to be focused more on Beau's end, and there were a number of shots that forced Beau to leap, dive, and save. Maggie clasped her hands together, her knuckles turning white, as a shot rebounded off the goal post to the crowd's undulating sighs and cheers. This was nerve-wracking. *Lord, keep him safe.*

The action moved back down the zone into L.A.'s territory as skaters moved off and onto the ice. Yet another reason why Beau was so amazing. He had to stay on the ice the entire game, his focus sharp and sure that whole time. It amazed her that he had any energy at all after games to talk to her. She'd be exhausted, for sure.

The momentum shifted back to Montreal's end, and she felt her pulse increase again. She was sure people must have heart attacks watching these games, with the stress and anxiety of it all. For a moment she wondered whether this was something she really wanted to do—deal with the stress several nights every week for half the year.

"It's exciting, non?" Claudine said, clapping as Johan intercepted a pass.

Maggie sipped her drink, then made a face and moved to the water bottle. She needed a clear head and still had work tomorrow, so she couldn't face a headache then.

The bruiser skated back on the ice for L.A., and she clenched her hands. The way he played seemed just like a bully—agitating, stirring up trouble, yelling at others, just like that horrible man at the Gardens weeks ago. Why couldn't bullies be outlawed instead of lauded?

There was some pushing and shoving, which soon escalated into a fight. The whistle blew to break it up, and the bruiser guy was sent off.

"Woletsky gets a penalty for two minutes," Claudine said.

"He should get kicked out of the game," Maggie muttered.

"You don't like the violence?"

"Non," she admitted.

"Perhaps you should reconsider being with Beau."

Maggie cut her a sharp look.

Claudine's look held amusement. "Just joking."

Maggie wasn't sure if she believed her, and kept her eyes on the ice, following Beau's every move. He was like a wall, blocking shots, bending and twisting to save a goal, and she wondered just what strain that put on his body. Did hockey teams appreciate the sacrifices they demanded of their players? She'd heard of some players with concussions, some who had retired from the game because of their injuries. Oui, they worked hard to stay fit and healthy, but accidents happened. She clasped her hands. *Lord, keep Beau safe.*

BEAU SCANNED THE PLAY, watching as Woletsky skated back onto the ice. The guy was a thug. He'd hit Mike Vaughan a few years ago and cracked his ribs, and since then had been bounced around the league on one-year contracts because he couldn't keep his temper. A week ago he'd taken out Buffalo defenseman Nick Grenier in a huge hit that had seen the poor guy end up in a coma, and rumors were that he'd never walk again. Beau had encountered Woletsky and his mouth a few times in the past, but the guy rarely made it past Beau's defensemen.

Beau bent his knees, trying to keep his limbs loose and soft and ready to spring at any moment. Usually the puck was kept in motion, but sometimes a player, usually a defenseman, might try to shoot from point, hoping that the traffic in front of the net would confuse the goaltender.

The play shifted closer, and Beau leaned on his haunches, shifting from left to right. He trusted Johan and Jake to do all they could to keep the puck from getting past them, but they trusted him to be alert should it slip by. Which it was now.

His heartbeat increased. His gaze zeroed in. Eye on the puck. Eye on the puck. Woletsky shot to Damon, who flicked it forward to Pavel, who struck it back to Macoretti. The L.A. players were good, their shots sharp and crisp.

Jake moved closer, getting in Beau's vision, and Beau barked at him to move away. Jake mustn't have heard him, for he stayed too near, maybe thinking he was doing Beau a favor. He wasn't. He cluttered things. Pavel shot at the goal, and Beau deflected it, but the puck didn't go to Johan as he'd hoped, instead bouncing off the wall to Woletsky. Woletsky shot, and Beau caught it in his right glove, holding on as the yappy forward got in his face.

Woletsky swore. Beau ignored it, waiting for the other man to move before himself moving to shift the puck behind the net to Johan.

Then Woletsky charged at Johan, stealing the puck from the Swede's stick and shrugging off Jake's frantic move as he shot at Beau. Beau's adrenaline soared as he caught the puck. Then caught the full force of L.A.'s goon as momentum drove him forward and propelled Beau backward, hitting his head and his back into the pipes as the world blurred and turned black.

CHAPTER 20

Maggie trembled as she followed Claudine into the hospital lobby. Her skin was clammy. She'd been here before. She'd sat in those same gray plastic chairs, hoping for an answer that had never come.

"It's going to be okay," Claudine assured her.

Non, it wasn't. The incident replayed through Maggie's mind like a horror film. Beau getting struck. Beau collapsing. Beau lying still.

The game had stopped as the horror of the spectators echoed the shrieking within Maggie. How badly was he injured? Claudine had rushed to find out while Maggie sat there, numb.

Eventually, someone had come to tell her he was going to the hospital and that he was conscious but couldn't feel his legs. Was he paralyzed?

Fear clutched her chest as she slumped on the seat, praying over and over again. *Lord, heal him. Lord, heal him.*

A team official entered, and Claudine moved to ask him for an update. "I've called his mother," he informed them.

Guilt squeezed. Something Maggie should have done.

"She's on her way." He cleared his throat. "He's awake, but the doctor wants to keep him calm."

The way he eyed Maggie when he said that made her bristle. What did he think she was going to do? Cartwheels in Beau's room? She pushed to unsteady feet. "I would like to see him."

He looked at her apologetically. "I'm afraid you're not on the list of approved visitors, Miss Joly."

She wasn't? "It's Mrs. Joly," she said, irritated.

Claudine shot her a surprised look.

"Mrs. Joly, I'm afraid the team protocols mean that unless you're on the list submitted at the season start, you're not considered an approved contact." He eyed her in a way that she supposed was meant to convey sympathy. "I'm very sorry, but I'm afraid you need to remain down here or go home."

Go home? That didn't sound very family-like.

"Who is on the contact list?" Claudine demanded. "Can I see him?"

"I'm afraid not, Mrs. Lemieux. Your husband is, so if Gabe arrives, you can find out from him." The man's phone rang, and he excused himself and walked away.

Maggie slumped in her chair. "I just want to know if he'll be okay."

If he wasn't, she wasn't sure if she could do this anymore. It was one thing to look on from a distance; it was another to watch the man she'd kissed and exchanged words of love with just last weekend collapse on the ice like he was dead. And she'd seen that before, when Alain had suffered his stroke and she'd frozen, not knowing what to do, before calling 911.

Ice traveled up her spine. She couldn't do this again. Couldn't do this. Couldn't do—

"I'll give Gabe a call," Claudine said, getting up and moving to the corner to talk.

Maggie peeked from behind her veil of hair. Claudine shook

her head and kicked her heeled boot into the floor. Oh non. Oh non. *Lord?*

"It's not good news, I'm afraid."

"Is he—?" She couldn't say the word.

"They don't know."

She blinked. "They don't know if he's alive?"

Claudine's face relaxed. "He's alive, he'll be okay. But apparently the doctors have said there's not any obvious cause."

"Apart from that idiot barging into him like that."

"Yeah, apparently that might've caused Beau's concussion, but they think there's more at play than that."

"What about his legs? What if he's paralyzed?"

"Hey." Claudine wrapped an arm around her. "Don't borrow trouble. It might be temporary, that's all."

It might be. Or it might be permanent. Or he might die. The hope that had buoyed her soul in recent weeks had fled, the world shrinking back into fear and pain. "I can't do this," Maggie whispered. "I can't do this again."

What would this mean for Beau's health? What might this accident mean for their future? Should she even be here? It wasn't like they'd known each other very long. Would his mother consider her insistence on staying strangely desperate? What should she do? *Lord?*

Another team official walked in, and Claudine hurried to speak to him. Maggie's eyes filled. God bless the woman for helping. The man glanced at Maggie, and she wiped her eyes and straightened, then tried to smile and look like she hadn't been about to cry.

"Paul, this is Maggie Joly. She's Beau's girlfriend and would like to see him."

His gaze, which had moments earlier looked sympathetic, suddenly sharpened. "Ms. Joly?"

She didn't have the heart to explain her name. "Have you any news?"

He frowned, and her heart sank. "I'm afraid our protocols mean we can't share such details with just anyone."

"But she's not just anyone," Claudine complained. "She's his girlfriend."

His expression blanked. "As I said, we cannot break protocols."

Claudine glanced at Maggie, then back to him, as if she couldn't believe what she was hearing either. "Come on, Paul. You always say we're a family—"

"Excuse me, Claudine. Ms. Joly." He moved away.

"What?"

Maggie shared Claudine's confusion. She didn't want to be conspiracy minded, but there seemed to be more to his refusal than mere protocol. "I don't understand."

"Neither do I," said Claudine. "I'm going to try Gabe again."

She called him again, then said he'd be down in a moment, so Maggie waited, praying as she clasped and unclasped her hands. When he finally appeared, Claudine rushed to hug him, and he kissed her before his gaze shifted to where Maggie still sat.

"How is he? What do you know?" she asked.

"He's suffered a concussion and is likely to be in the hospital for a few more days while the doctors try and find out what's gone wrong."

"Isn't it obvious? That Woletsky guy hurt him. He should be sent off for the season!"

Gabe patiently listened as she shared her opinion of the referees and Woletsky and the dangers of the sport while Claudine rubbed her back. "I know it looks bad, but chances are he'll be fine soon," he said gently.

"But he can't walk!"

"He's got movement in his lower legs now."

Maggie exhaled. Thank God. "Why didn't you say so?"

"I'm sorry." He glanced at Claudine and seemed to communicate a silent something to her before his gaze returned to Maggie. "I just saw Paul Forges, who mentioned you wanted to see Beau and that he recommended you go home. I think maybe he's right," Gabe said kindly.

"Beau doesn't want to see me?"

"I don't think he'd want you worrying."

Worrying? How would it be any easier to not worry at home than seated here? "Worrying isn't based on the location," she snapped.

"Claudine, do you mind helping Maggie get home? She probably shouldn't be driving if she's this stressed."

Maggie allowed herself to be helped up, her mind unable to process what had happened. No. She shouldn't be driving. And she shouldn't wait here. And she probably shouldn't have fallen for a hockey player whose risk of injury filled her with fear.

"SHE'S WHAT?" Beau blinked, his blurred vision clearing as he tried to focus on what Paul was saying.

"I'm sorry, but she couldn't stay. But the good news is your mom is on a flight as we speak, so we'll get her settled in a hotel so she can see you tomorrow morning. We put a high value on the importance of families here."

His head felt foggy still. Mom coming was great, but, "Maggie?"

"Who?"

"My girlfriend."

Paul's glance grew penetrating. "Am I correct in assuming this is the woman you met at the Gardens a few weeks ago?"

"Yeah."

He pursed his lips. Beau was tempted to ask, but a nurse came in. "I'm sorry, but Mr. Nash really needs his rest." She glanced at Beau. "The doctor said he'll be along to check on you shortly."

"I'd really prefer to stay until the doctor comes, if you don't mind," Paul said pleasantly.

"I do mind," the nurse said, her no-nonsense remark startling Paul and tugging a small smile from Beau.

He shifted on the bed, wincing as his back protested and his head swam again.

"Mr. Nash, you really should rest now." The nurse moved closer and adjusted his pillows. "I hope your visitor will leave and allow you to sleep."

"I'll be fine, Paul. You go. I'll see you tomorrow."

"The club wants to ensure you're okay."

"He will be," snapped the nurse, "once certain people leave."

Paul held up his hands and exited, and Beau released a sigh of relief. "Thanks," he murmured to the nurse. "I know he means well, but he's persistent."

"He is that," she said. "Now, close your eyes. The doctor will be in soon, then you can sleep."

Beau closed his eyes as images of the night replayed. The barreling charge of Woletsky. The way Beau had blacked out, only to waken with the rafters of the Bell Centre high above. Fear as he couldn't feel his legs. The noise and chaos as he was loaded into the ambulance. Sweet relief as pain meds lessened the aching tenderness of his back. Hurt as he wondered why Maggie hadn't come.

He exhaled slowly, deliberately relaxing his fingers and thanking God he could relax his toes as he fought the whirlpool of emotions. Anger. Fear. Frustration. Hope. That had been close. Woletsky was a thug, but these things happened, especially in the heat of play. He wouldn't mind an apology but knew that even if he didn't get one he'd need to forgive the guy —for Beau's own sake, anyway. Nothing good came from holding on to the past, and lining his heart with regrets and offence was a sure way to make it hard. He needed to forgive, even if he might not forget anytime soon. *Help me to forgive. Help me to let go.*

He stayed motionless for a few moments longer as the chaos within eased.

The wheeze of the door opening snapped his eyes open. The doctor. Accompanied by the team doctor and the team owner. Looked like Paul had managed to bend the hospital rules again.

"Beau, how are you feeling?" Tony asked.

How many more times would he have to answer this question? He pushed down the irritation. "My head and back hurt, but I can see now, so that's a plus."

"We hate that this has happened. We've got a protest in with the league about the leniency of Woletsky's penalty, and we hope to see justice soon."

"Stuff happens."

"Stuff that shouldn't," Tony said. "I just wanted to come by and see our star goalie and assure you we're doing all we can to help you and your family at this time."

"Is Maggie still downstairs?"

"Who's Maggie?"

"Girlfriend."

"I wouldn't know, but if she is then of course she should be here to see you," Tony said. "You want to call her?"

"Don't have a phone." It was likely with the rest of his stuff, still at the stadium.

"We'll sort that out soon," the team doctor said. "Let's hear what the latest is so this young man can get some rest."

The doctor explained about the battery of tests he'd conduct tomorrow on Beau's heart and brain. "Gonna check I still have one, huh?" Beau managed to say.

Neither doctor smiled, although Tony's mouth lifted half an inch.

"You need to be careful, Mr. Nash," the doctor cautioned.

"We don't want to tire you out, so I must insist you get some rest now."

"Happy to oblige," Beau said, tugging the thin blanket higher. "Thanks for coming, sir," he said to Tony. "I'll do my best to get back to it soon."

"That'll depend on what these guys say," he said, gesturing to the medical staff. "But I have full confidence that you'll be ready and playing for us as soon as possible."

Beau nodded, the movement spearing pain across his brain. He knew that timing would be up to God.

"I DON'T UNDERSTAND," Beau said. Morning sunshine streamed across his hospital bed as his mom sat in the seat nearby.

"She's likely working and unable to come."

Beau shifted higher against the pillows, careful to hide the wince in case he alarmed his mother. "Everything from yesterday is a blur. I don't know if it was the drugs I was on, but I was sure at some stage someone said she was downstairs. Then someone else said she'd gone home. But I would've thought—"

He bit off the rest of that comment. Yeah, he would've thought that Maggie cared enough to want to see him. Her kisses had suggested that. But her lack of appearance or even any text message beyond the simple PRAYING FOR YOU that she'd sent last night, suggested otherwise.

"She might well feel that she doesn't want to intrude," his mother said. "I don't think you should read anything into it. Not until you talk to her, at least."

He nodded, the action straining his neck, and he reached out to feel the little bump.

"Are you in pain?" his mother asked.

"Nope," he assured her. Honestly, this morning, after a reasonable sleep, he did feel almost better. Apart from some stiffness in his legs and back. And the tenderness on the lump on his head.

The worry creasing his mom's brow eased.

"The doc this morning said he wanted to speak to me about the tests they're going to do. My results from the team physicals suggested everything was fine, but they want to do some genetic testing to rule out other things. It got me thinking about Dad."

"Your father had a heart attack, and they could never find a cause."

Exactly why the medical staff here wanted to learn all they could.

"You've been feeling well, though?" his mother pressed. "You haven't had any heart palpitations or the like, have you?"

Apart from when Maggie smiled at him? "No."

"Then we'll just pray that they find a result soon," she assured him.

He nodded, his gaze drifting to his phone, which someone from the club had delivered earlier today. He'd really like his charger, as his phone had been crammed full of messages he'd been unable to respond to. Except for that one from Maggie, to which he'd offered a simple *Thanks*. How was he to explain his disappointment that she wasn't here? No. Mom might be right; she might have work and other commitments, other things more important than him. And that was okay. He was a big boy. But he'd still love to talk to her.

"You're thinking about Maggie again, aren't you?" his mom asked. "Call her."

Wow. What a momma's boy he was, a smile sneaking out as he obeyed.

But it rang and rang and there was no voice message to leave, so he hung up. Frowned. Then carefully typed out a message.

Good morning. Hope yours is better than mine anyway. Love to talk with you when you can. X

"So you decided to go after her," his mom said.

"We've had a couple of dates," he admitted.

"I like her," she offered.

He nodded. He knew that.

"And you may find that this is a blessing in disguise."

"Seriously?"

"Don't look at me like that," she admonished, her rebuke hitching his features back to neutral. "I wonder if perhaps this would give her reason to think."

"Think about what?"

"You. What a relationship with you would involve. The reality is that you actually need somebody who is more than just a Christian. You need someone who will understand and support you with your work. And part of that is understanding that injury is a risk you face each time you're on the ice. And given her history, you may find this is something that's going to be very challenging for her to come to terms with."

Tension lined his heart. "Wow. Did you mean to give me heart palpitations?" He'd tried to joke, but it sounded lame even to his ears.

"Pray. I'll pray. We'll all pray, that if this is something that's from God, then she'll be able to deal with it in her own time."

He nodded as his phone beeped another message. This one was from Dan.

Hey, are you up for a quick chat with the guys?

He checked his battery. If it's quick, he typed back. Battery almost dead.

Two minutes later, his phone vibrated with the incoming Zoom call, and he positioned it on his knees. "Hey."

The screens of Dan, Jai, Mike, Brent, Tim, and Ryan appeared as they greeted him with varying expressions of dismay and tease.

"Love the PJs," Jai teased.

Beau half smiled. "Hospital gowns are in this year."

"Your hair looks pretty," Ryan mocked.

Beau pulled his hair up. "They chopped half the back to get at the bump. So sad."

"It'll grow," said Mike.

"You'll get your Samson strength back in no time," Tim said with a none-too-subtle toss of his own curly mane, which drew laughter from the others.

"Feeling better?" Dan asked.

"A bit. They still don't know what caused it."

"I would've thought they could tell," Brent said. "Woletsky's a—"

"Keep it clean. Mom's here." Beau shifted the phone to show her, and she smiled as they called out a chorus of *heys* and *hellos*.

"Is he behaving, Mrs. Nash?" Ryan asked.

"He's fretting," she admitted.

"Mom," he protested as his friends laughed.

"Yeah, fretting about missing out on his winningest goalie streak." Jai laughed.

"Hey, I don't know if that's broken yet," Beau protested.

"'fraid so," Brent said. "Your backup broke it for you."

"Man. Does that even count?"

"What have the doctors said?" Mike asked.

"They still don't know. I've got some more tests to do this afternoon. They want to do an MRI, and they're exploring if there are any genetic indicators for what happened."

"I would've thought that obvious," Brent said. "When are they going to do something more about suspending Woletsky? After what happened to Grenier, I would've thought he'd get kicked out of the league."

Beau's lips pressed together as the guys shared their opinions, nearly all of which regarded Woletsky's behavior as somewhere between rodent-like and pond scum.

Apart from Mike. He sat silent, arms folded, chewing his lip.

"Mike?" Brent, Mike's best friend, asked. "I bet you have an opinion. TJ the tool broke your ribs, didn't he?"

Mike nodded. "And I played with him for a season before he left Calgary." He shrugged. "Yeah, he can be a bit of a meathead, but he's not all bad. He came to my wedding, man."

Brent's jaw tightened. "I still don't get why you did that."

Mike shrugged. "I just think he's maybe a little broken."

"He's the one doing all the breaking," Jai scoffed.

"I don't know his whole story, but I get the sense he's working on things. And he's human; we all make mistakes. I know he apologized when he busted my ribs."

"Has he apologized to you?" Brent demanded of Beau.

"Not that I've seen. But then, I've got a million messages I need to read through."

"They like you there," Dan said.

"Most seem to," Beau said. "What can I say? Must be my Southern charm."

"Sure isn't because of your tiny ego," Jai chirped to the laughter of the others.

"Harsh." Beau shook his head and glanced at his mom, who was listening with a big smile on her face. "See what I have to put up with, Ma? They're mean to me."

"It's a good thing you're such a brave boy," she teased.

This scored Beau another round of mockery and laughter before Mike spoke again. "Hey. I gotta go. But we'll be praying."

"Thanks."

"Just remember that it's nothing personal, so don't let it get inside."

Beau nodded, offering a salute as Mike, then Brent and Ryan signed off.

He didn't like to think of himself as someone who let the grime of life stain his heart. It was funny how his friends' words had stirred the dirt again. They might be Christians too, but nobody was perfect. Including Woletsky.

Beau shifted on his bed. "Guess we're gonna be praying for TJ, huh?"

"He needs it," Dan said flatly.

"We all do," Tim said.

"Yeah, but I'm not above hoping this means he gets the boot from L.A.," Jai said. "I'd be real happy not having to play him when I'm at San Jose."

"Hey, we don't want him playing here on the east coast," Dan protested.

"We'll just have to pray that wherever he goes, God can get to him good," Beau said.

And that God would protect Beau's heart from resentment. And that God would help Maggie's heart too.

CHAPTER 21

The afternoon had turned chilly, the clouded skies holding the promise of rain. But Maggie didn't move. The Japanese Garden possessed an autumn beauty where the maple trees' reflection in the water was calendar worthy. She sat on the seat and lifted the camera, searching through the viewfinder for the best angle. An effective photographic composition usually required one third sky, one third ground, and the middle positioned perfectly between. She had the elements composed—the waterfall and reflection of the trees and the lantern to the left held interest. She took a series of photos, then placed the camera on the wooden bench beside her, the swirling heaviness in the skies the perfect match for her insides.

What to do, what to do? She touched the camera but felt no inclination to pick it up. The camera was present for the illusion of toil—her attempt to look like she was working, even if she was only really working through her thoughts and emotions as her heart teetered back and forth. She'd barely slept last night, thinking about what had happened, wondering what Beau's injuries would mean. For him. For her. For Noah.

For it was one thing to sit in the stands and cheer on her

man and be swept up in emotion and the rainbow fairyland of his kisses. It was quite another to watch him be injured before her very eyes and suddenly realize that a relationship with him could never be just rainbows without clouds and rain. The reality check had shrunk her message to him into a simple PRAYING FOR YOU, which in hindsight had been too brief. She could've said that she loved him. She could've said that she cared. She should've said that she was scared for him—even if what she really meant was that she was scared for herself. The draw Beau had on her heart both tantalized and terrified.

Could she really let this relationship continue when it meant that Noah would steadily bond with a man who might be injured one day, who could—God forbid—die? She knew it sounded selfish. She knew it sounded weak. But the faith that had flared to life only four weeks ago now seemed a dim echo of that certainty. What to do, what to do…

Beau had tried to call earlier. She'd seen his call on her phone but, not knowing what to say, had left it unanswered. What could she say? *Your job, a life with you, scares me* was probably not the best thing to utter to someone in a hospital bed. She'd managed to escape Danielle's probing questions earlier by insisting today was the perfect day to get some more shots of the garden to post on social media. But now she was here, the questions refused to go away, and she would need to come up with a solution, because she couldn't keep avoiding him. That wasn't fair to anyone.

A bird high in the sky drew her gaze upward and reminded her to refocus on heaven.

"Lord? What do You say?"

She closed her eyes, appreciating the soft caress of the sun on her skin, and stilled her heart to listen.

A hush of breeze rolled past, carrying the faintest earthy trace of wood smoke and decomposing leaves. Autumn's signature scent, signifying the end of one season and the transition into another. But she sensed that this new season did not have to be one focused on death and decay.

Over and over, God had been talking to her about how she had closed her heart for so long. How she had grown crippled in her emotions and experiences, letting fear from the past have its way. Oui, it was understandable. But non, she did not want to hibernate with her grief and fears in that same way. Not anymore.

She knew now that faith was more than an intellectual exercise. Just as she had once believed in God but not really loved Him, now that she loved Him she *knew* it was time to trust Him with her future. For too long, she'd walked life through the prism of fear. It was time to change that. It was time to let the God she now knew loved her help her to overcome her fears.

"Lord, help me."

A memory flashed, something she'd read a day or two ago. That faith was like a muscle and needed to be exercised regularly. That learning to trust God would take time, little by little, as she deliberately pushed away the fear-conditioned thoughts of the past and dared believe God for the new. Her faith would develop and grow from puny and weak to resilient and strong. Just like Beau's workouts had strengthened his shoulders and legs to the man he was today.

More memories flashed. Tears pricked. Breath escaped. Once upon a time he would have been as small as Noah or Brandon. She imagined it had taken years of growth and training for Beau to be as strong as he was today, to develop into the kind and generous and brave man she knew. Her faith might be weak, but nourished properly and given time, her faith would grow too. With God's help, the fears would lessen and her future would gleam with hope again. It would take practice, stretching, growing, learning, and letting God have His way. A God-enriched future would allow her world to get bigger and her heart to expand too.

"Help me trust You."

Another moment passed and stilled her soul. She opened her eyes. Exhaled. The scene before her looked the same but somehow felt different, the urge to trust God digging resolve deeper.

Her phone buzzed. Unknown number. She picked it up. Was it the school? Noah had been complaining about a scratchy throat last night, so her mother had said, but this morning he'd felt okay. She answered it.

"Maggie?"

The Southern lilt sounded awfully like—

"This is Andrea Nash, Beau's mom. I hope you don't mind me calling you. I got your number from Beau. How are you?"

She bit her lip. "I'm okay, thank you. But how are you? How is Beau?"

"He's doing okay. I know he wants to talk to you."

"Is he there now?" she whispered, like he might overhear.

"He's talking with one of the team doctors."

"How is he feeling?"

"He's itching to get out of the hospital."

"Have…have they said how long he'll need to stay?"

"They're not sure. The doctors seem happy with his progress."

"That's a good sign, isn't it?"

"Yes." A beat. "Maggie, I wonder, seeing I'm in town and Beau is still stuck here, would it be possible to see you today? I'd really like to know how you're doing."

"Er, okay."

"I know it's a lot to ask, but would it be possible to meet at Beau's place? I'm staying there, and while I like the city, it's a lot larger than I feel comfortable dealing with on my own."

Maggie didn't want to. It felt like an intrusion into his space, especially if he wasn't there. But the memory of her prayer just minutes earlier took over her mouth. "Okay."

"You will? Oh, that's wonderful. Thank you. Or should I say merci?"

She was tempted to smile at the Beau-like comment. "I'm at work until five, so I can come then. Or after dinner. Whatever suits you best."

"You couldn't come for dinner?" Andrea pleaded.

"I have dinner plans with my mother and son already."

"Of course." A beat. "I would like to meet your mother."

Was that a hint? "She's rather set in her ways," Maggie explained.

"One day, then."

Perhaps.

"Oh, I'd better go. See you tonight, then?"

That would give Maggie time to shower and get changed, at least. "Oui. À ce soir."

"Thank you, Maggie. I look forward to seeing you then."

They said goodbye, and the call ended, leaving Maggie wondering what tonight would hold and just what Beau's mother had to say.

"Hello, Ms. Joly," the doorman said, his white teeth flashing as he let her in.

She smiled, feeling very self-conscious as she explained she was here to see Mrs. Nash.

"Yes, she told me. Terrible accident for poor Mr. Nash, wasn't it?"

"Oui c'est affreux," she agreed.

"We're all so glad he's on the mend."

Andrea must have told him that. Maggie nodded and gestured to the elevator. "I should go up."

"Of course. Good to see you again."

"You too." Her smile eased into genuine.

Thank God for friendly doormen, she thought as the

elevator rose. Thank God for obliging mothers. Thank God for a sleepy son, Noah having gone to bed without complaint or the need for more elephant stories. All of which had helped distract Maggie from wondering what was about to occur.

The door swooshed open, and she checked her reflection in the mirror opposite. The green top and black corduroy trousers were comfortable yet classier than jeans. And it didn't hurt a girl to arm herself with her favorite clothes when going into the unknown.

Her knock at the door was soon answered, and Andrea drew her in with a hug. Maggie obliged, her stiffness at the unexpected embrace fading as she tentatively wrapped her arms around her.

"It's so good to see you," Andrea said.

"And you."

Andrea gestured to the comfortable lounge in front of the glorious city view. "Can I get you a drink or anything?"

"Is this going to be the kind of conversation that needs a drink?" Maggie asked with a small smile.

"No! No, of course not. Truly, I just wanted to see how you are. Especially after that wonderful time in church. How have you been finding things in that regard?"

The tension lining Maggie's heart eased. "It's been good. Really good. I feel lighter, more free, and like my heart is opening up to others more."

Andrea nodded. "Beau sent me a picture that he took at a Thanksgiving event at your home."

Maggie relaxed against the cushions. "I never expected my mother to be open to hosting such a thing, but I felt this prompting to do it, and it went so much better than I could've hoped. Fatima, one of the ladies in our street, keeps thanking us every time she sees me."

"How wonderful."

"It was. And a real answer to prayer. Oh! And that Bible you sent me is so beautiful, thank you. I've found the notes you sent really helpful, so I wanted you to know that."

"I'm so pleased." Was that a tear in Andrea's eye? "Now, may I get you a drink?"

Maggie nodded. "Water is fine."

"You sure? Beau has some special organic apple juice. I don't mind trying that if you wish to."

"I don't know."

"I'm his mother, and if I say it's okay, then it's okay, okay?"

"Yes, ma'am," Maggie said, biting back a grin.

The chitchat helped her feel a little more at ease in this space —his space—that felt way too cold and sterile without him in it. She missed him. She wished she could see him. She should have swallowed her pride and gone to the hospital to see him instead of coming here.

She accepted her drink and waited for Andrea to grow comfortable before asking how Beau was.

Andrea eyed her over her glass. "From the tests they ran, the doctors think it could be something called a neurocardiogenic syncope episode."

Neurocardio… Maggie's chest froze. Non. Was this something related to a stroke? Her palms grew clammy, and she wiped them on her jeans. She couldn't face losing someone else. Not like what happened with Alain. "That…that means his brain and heart, doesn't it?"

Beau's mother nodded. "They're still trying to determine exactly what happened. It could've been the adrenaline of having that Woletsky boy coming at him, but they don't really know. He's going to have to undergo some more testing on his heart and blood, and I think they'll want to rule out further issues."

Further issues? Her faith felt so tremulous. But non. She'd trust God. *Lord, heal him.*

"Mom?"

Maggie's gaze snapped to the tall man behind Andrea. The tall man yawning, dressed in a T-shirt and sweats, with his hair—

"You cut your hair?"

Beau's gaze, which had shifted to Maggie and never left, turned rueful as he touched his cropped head. "Actually, it wasn't me. They cut it at the hospital, and it looked so bad I needed it cut off properly." He shoved a hand self-consciously through the shorter strands, his shirt riding up to show toned abs. "But seriously, Maggie? That's the first thing you say?"

"I…" Her mouth dried. Weary and dressed so casually, he looked oddly vulnerable and approachable and oh so good. "Hello."

"Bonsoir."

His smile shot straight into her heart. Forget the past. Forget the fear. She pushed to her feet and rushed to him, wrapping her arms around his torso and hugging him. "I'm so glad you're alive."

"Hey." He smoothed her hair. "I'm okay."

"Are you?" She lifted her face to his and searched his eyes. "Are you really? Your mother says it's something to do with your heart and brain." She sucked in a breath. "I don't want to be afraid, but after what happened with Alain and my father and your father, I—"

He tucked a strand of hair behind her ear, pressed a kiss to her brow, then leaned his chin on her crown. "Mom, you didn't tell her?"

"Tell me what?" Maggie murmured from the deliciously-scented cocoon of his arms.

"Oh. Perhaps you should." His mother rose. "I'm suddenly feeling rather weary. It's been a big day with all that travel, after all."

"Mom, you're not getting out of it that easy. Much as I appreciate it, why is Maggie here?"

"You said you wanted to see her. I love you, so I wanted to help."

"Moms," he muttered.

"You have to love them," his mother chided.

Maggie wriggled in his arms. "That's true."

The curve of his half smile broadened into amusement. "I do, do I?"

She nodded. *Especially this one,* she longed to say. "But you need to tell me about your heart. You *are* going to be okay?"

"Son, you need to tell her."

His gaze grew somber, and he drew Maggie to sit on the sofa.

"What is it? Beau, what is this neurocardio thing your mother mentioned?"

"A neurocardiogenic syncope episode." He threaded her fingers through his. "It's something I don't want getting out."

"What is it? Is it life-threatening?"

"It's embarrassing."

"What?"

His mother bent to give Maggie a quick hug. "Thank you for coming."

"You're going?"

"I suspect my son will be happy to explain things. And I really am rather tired, so I'm going to find my bed."

Maggie kissed her cheek and waited until she'd left, studying Beau, her eyebrows raised. "I don't understand."

"Mom was just trying to help," he said. "I think she was worried that you didn't want to see me last night, then she thought you had work today."

"I did have work, and I *really* wanted to see you last night. I waited for ages," she continued, "but they wouldn't let me up. Someone said something about team protocols and that I wasn't family. And I was so worried about you."

His brows gathered together. "Who wouldn't let you up? I spoke to Tony last night, and he said it was fine."

"Tony?"

"The club owner."

"You're on first name basis?"

"He likes me. Anyway, who was it said you couldn't see me?"

She tried to remember. "It was a shortish guy. I think Claudine called him Paul."

His lips pressed together. "That makes sense. Well, I'll be making sure your name goes on all the lists in case this happens again."

Fear trammeled her heart. "Is this likely to happen again?"

"That's the thing." He sighed heavily.

"Wait, I thought you said you were okay."

"I am, but—"

"But what? Beau, please tell me. Whatever it is, I can cope."

"You're sure?"

Non. She nodded anyway.

"Apparently the doctors think I have this condition where there's a miscommunication between the heart, the blood vessels in my lower extremities, and the brain."

She inhaled. "It sounds serious."

"It is." He studied her, the intensity there setting her heart on edge. "It's seriously embarrassing."

"What?"

He sighed. A beat passed. Another. "The doctors think I fainted."

She blinked. "What?"

"See why it's embarrassing? I can't let anyone know. I'll lose all credibility."

"You just fainted?" She inched back.

"Come on, Maggie. What would you do if you saw a truck like Woletsky trying to run you over? I thought I was tougher, but no."

"You fainted?" She gently smacked his arm. "So you're saying there's nothing wrong with your heart or your brain?"

"Well, actually, the condition is a little more serious than that."

"Why? Is this likely to happen again?"

"I don't know. They say the biggest risk is that I'll hurt myself if I fall." He waited a moment. "But that's the problem."

"What is?"

"I *have* fallen."

"When?"

He sighed. "A while ago now."

"Why didn't you say anything? Do the team doctors know? What happened?"

"I fell head over heels."

She paused. Blinked.

"I saw you, I got to know you, and now seeing you makes me weak at the knees."

Her head tilted as she struggled to hide the surge of emotion his words induced. "Is that so?"

"It is. My eyes see you and my brain tells my knees they can't stand, and as for my heart..." His voice grew raspy.

"What about your heart?" she whispered.

"My heart skips a beat. Skips more than one, actually. I get these kind of palpitations..." His head lowered, his breath sweet against her cheek.

"Is there a remedy for that?" she murmured, his skin electric against hers.

"Yes."

"What is it?"

"You." He bent down and pressed his forehead to hers. "Je t'aime, ma belle Maggie."

She tilted her head so their mouths were only a half-inch away. "Je t'aime, mon bel Beau."

"Really?"

"*Certainement.*"

And she demonstrated once more what those words actually meant.

❧

"Good to have you back, man," Johan said. He lowered his voice and nodded to where Tomas, the baseball-cap-wearing backup goalie, was adjusting his pads. "He tried, but he's not you."

One win in five games suggested that.

There was a round of other welcomes, which included poor Tomas, the netminder's greeting holding more than a hint of relief.

The guys shifted outside for practice, leaving Beau to concentrate on lacing his skates, glad for the momentary respite. The past twelve days had been filled with medical appointments, genetic, heart, and blood testing, and discussions with his doctors and team officials as they waited for his concussion symptoms to disappear before he could be medically cleared. Today was his first practice session with the team. Tomorrow would be his first game, followed by the team party for Halloween.

He smiled, adjusting his leg pads. The past days had held fun moments too. Opportunity to sleep in. A few days with his mom before she returned south. He'd shared meals with Gabe and Claudine and with Maggie, her mom, and her sweet son. He'd spent time with Noah, playing Lego and snakes and ladders, reading stories, and they'd decided to go see elephants, which got Beau wondering about taking Maggie and Noah along on his next visit home, where he hoped they could swing a visit to the North Carolina zoo. He'd done his best to charm Maggie's mother, which seemed to be working, as she'd even returned his last hug. But most of all, he'd loved spending time with Maggie, talking, laughing, attending church, practicing French, and kissing.

"You coming?" Kris asked, bursting Beau's happy bubble with a pop.

"In a minute." Beau strapped on his chest and elbow pads.

Kris grabbed his water bottle from his stall, his lack of greeting suggesting a lack of goodwill, which pierced any scruples of Beau's own.

"Maggie and I had dinner with Gabe and Claudine this week," he said conversationally, shrugging on his jersey. "They're a lot of fun."

Kris's face tensed.

"What?"

"Nothing," Kris muttered, moving past.

"Hey, did Gabe know about you and Claudine having dinner together?" Beau asked.

Kris stopped, looked at him quickly. "I don't know what you mean."

"Remember? That café where Maggie and I saw you? I don't know what you were doing together, but it didn't look right."

"It was just dinner," he muttered.

"Was it? With another man's wife?" Beau grabbed his blocker. "Imagine how cut Gabe would feel if he found out. Imagine how much the fans would hate a man if they thought he was trying to cut another man's grass. Especially one they like as much as Gabe."

"Who do you think you are?" Kris hissed.

Beau pushed to his feet and pulled on his glove. "I think I'm Gabe's friend. And that he's a stand-up guy. And that they're a great couple and I'd hate to see them hurt." He lifted an eyebrow.

Kris muttered a few swear words and stormed from the room just as the trainer came in. "What's up with him?"

"I think he's thinking about what loyalty to the team means."

He hoped. And he'd continue to pray that Kris would leave Claudine alone and that Claudine would find fulfilment in her marriage. He strapped on his helmet.

"Speaking of loyalty, there's a fan out here who wants to say hi."

"Great." Beau motioned to the ice. "They're happy without me?"

"Nobody is," the trainer said, grinning. "But they're practicing drills, so you've got some time."

"Good."

He loved meeting the fans and had been surprised at the love they'd shown him in recent days, with cards, messages, and crayoned pictures all willing him to get better soon. His lips twitched. He hoped they'd never learn it had been caused by a faint.

He moved out through the tunnel toward the sound of skates and sticks on ice, offering the equipment guys a wave as they gave him a thumbs-up. A clutch of Montreal jersey-clad people huddled in the stands near the bench. The trainer pointed to them, and Beau recognized little Jacques, dressed in Beau's jersey, wearing a Montreal toque. Beau lifted his mask.

"Hey, Jacques." His heart thudded with sorrow. From the yellowish cast to his skin, the kid was really sick. "You're out of the hospital, huh? That's great!"

The boy didn't speak, just stared at Beau with haunted eyes. A glance at his parents saw them wiping away tears as the man shook his head. No. Oh no. He'd been released because there was no getting better. This was it.

"He wanted to come and see you since you're his favorite player," Jacques's dad said. "And when we heard you'd be here…"

Beau swallowed, blinked back moisture, and leaned across the railing. "Come here, buddy." Beau held out his arms.

The boy bent down, and Beau wrapped him in a hug as shuddering tears soaked through his jersey. Beau held him, wishing his strength and courage would somehow permeate Jacques's thin body as Beau prayed that God would do a miracle and heal him and that Jacques and his parents would know God's hope and peace.

He grew vaguely aware of others around them and murmured for Jacques's ears only, "I'll be praying for you. God loves you." Saying anything more was too awkward right now.

Beau released him, blinking back emotion. "Want me to sign your jersey for you?"

Jacques nodded.

"Got a pen?"

Jacques's mother handed him a Sharpie and encouraged Jacques to turn around.

Beau signed his name on the white-stitched number forty-five and added *John 3:16.* Surely that would be enough to get them thinking.

"Would you sign his stick?" Jacques's mother asked.

"For sure." He'd do anything. So he signed the plastic toy stick Jacques held out, then added his scrawl to his own stick and passed it over. He'd get another.

"Thank you," Jacques's mother said. "Thank you so much."

"Hey, I think we need a photo, right?" Beau shifted and wrapped an arm around Jacques's shoulders, grinning at the camera with a lightness he didn't feel. Then a trainer offered to take another one with the parents too, which took a little longer. Finally, Beau shook their hands, promised them he'd be praying, then got on the ice.

Wow. His throat tight, he lifted a hand and skated to the net as some of his teammates chirped him about being tardy. But he didn't care. He was so blessed to live, to be healthy, to play this great game. Blessed to love and be loved. And to know that, unlike his rusty net minding skills, his future was always safe in God's capable hands.

CHAPTER 22

"*N*ow remember, it's going to be a little noisy, but it will be fun."

Noah clutched Maggie's hand more tightly, the giant ears and trunk on his elephant onesie flopping back and forth as he nodded.

She smiled at the attendant guarding the door and moved inside. The room was decorated in fake spiders and webs, ideal for a little boy who'd recently decided Spiderman was his hero because Beau had said Spidey was his.

"Shouldn't it be the Hulk?" Maggie had teased him.

"You're mean," Beau had said, tickling her. "Or did you mean to say Superman, because, you know, you think I'm super?"

Well, oui, tout à fait, he was. But she didn't need to tell him that every day.

"You know I think you're Wonder Woman, right?" he'd said.

Again, oui. His kisses and compliments certainly gave that impression.

The chatter in the room drew Maggie to a pause. Where to sit?

"Hey, Maggie," Krystle called. "Looking good!"

Maggie touched the cat ears she'd donned along with skinny leg black jeans and a tight black jumper. Black cat wasn't a look she'd usually go for, but she thought Beau might appreciate it.

"You're here!" Claudine called. "Oh my goodness. Who is this? Noah? Oh, you're so adorable! Come and sit by me."

Claudine patted the seat beside her, and Noah glanced at Maggie. She nodded, and they moved to join her.

"I like the cat suit, Mags. Beau will be all *raoww*." She swiped a hand through the air like claws.

"I like your fairy godmother look," Maggie returned. "You handing out wishes tonight?"

"Not tonight." She glanced at Noah, her face softening before her gaze returned to Maggie. "But I told Gabe I'm willing to try."

Maggie beamed. "I'm so happy. He loves you, Claudine. You won't regret it."

She nodded and touched her wedding ring. "I'm starting to see that." Her gaze fell to Noah. "Hey, Noah, would you like to come with me to see if there's something you'd like to eat? If that's okay with your maman."

"As long as it's not sugar laden, it's okay," Maggie said.

"Sugar laden? On Halloween? Come on." Claudine winked.

Maggie smiled and set her coat and bag down as she watched Claudine introduce Noah to a couple of other children here to watch their fathers. She'd make a good mother one day. Noah turned and looked at Maggie, and she gave him two thumbs up. He nodded, his shy smile peeking out before he turned and Claudine put a hot dog on a paper plate.

A deep sigh of contentment escaped. It had been a challenge to get back from work then get dressed and here on time for tonight's earlier game. Her mother had been distracted by the invitation from Mrs. Chang to play mahjong tonight. Apparently this had grown into an invitation for Fatima as well, and

Maggie was glad her mother was finally making efforts to connect beyond her front door.

Now Maggie was here for Beau's comeback game, and she couldn't help but be a little nervous for him. He'd said he was fine, but he hadn't played in two weeks, and she knew this game was important to him. Apparently the little boy he'd visited in the hospital several times was going to be a special guest and drop the puck, and after seeing Beau's emotion yesterday after training, she knew it would be extra challenging now.

Noah and Claudine came back, Noah's face smeared with ketchup, which meant finding wet wipes from his rucksack. By the time she looked up, the warm-ups had started.

"Look, it's Beau!" She pointed him out to Noah. "He's there in front of the net because he's the goalkeeper."

"He keeps the goal?"

She smiled. "He protects the net from the other team scoring goals. He keeps the goal safe."

She kept her eyes trained on Beau, and once again it was like he could sense her presence as he glanced up, lifted his mask, and grinned.

"Look, Beau is waving at us."

"Hi, Beau!" Noah waved wildly, which caused Claudine's drink to spill.

But Claudine only laughed. "Oh, he's precious." Her soft expression as she smiled at Noah made Maggie wonder if there might be another potential babysitter one day—someone keen to get some practice before her own came.

Maggie's attention shifted back to the ice, and Beau tapped his chest two times then pointed at them. Maggie laughed and blew him a kiss, which he pretended to catch before saluting and returning to his net and practice.

"Oh my gosh. I can't stand it. You guys are so sweet."

Maggie's cheeks heated, conscious she was the center of attention. "I'm just trying to encourage him," she said meekly.

"Mags, have you seen how much love that man is getting?"

"What do you mean?"

"You haven't seen it?" Claudine pulled out her phone. "It's everywhere on social media."

"I was working outside all day and haven't had a chance to look."

"Here." Claudine shoved her phone in front of Maggie. "Press play."

The Facebook post—posted by the official NHL account, no less—included hashtags of #hockeyhero and #hockey-fightscancer and included a video of Beau hugging a frail boy.

The emotion in the video, in what she remembered from Beau's tear-filled words yesterday, caught in her throat and blurred her eyes. He was such a good man. Such a big-hearted man. Doing his best to save hearts and goals. She loved him so much her skin might burst.

She wiped her cheeks and returned the phone to Claudine. "Thank you for showing me. I don't think he knows that's out there."

"He's going to," Claudine said with a smirk. "That video is going viral."

Oh. She didn't know how Beau would feel about that. "I heard the boy will be doing the puck drop."

"Yeah. When Gabe heard about it, he asked the big boss, and you know how Tony is always going on about family, so it was an instant yes."

"I'm glad. This will be a special memory for that poor family."

Claudine sobered. "I know that when Gabe heard, he was really touched."

"He's a good man," Maggie said.

"That he is." Claudine smiled. She glanced at Noah. "You ready for some hockey, Noah?"

He nodded, and Maggie ruffled his hair as she pushed to her feet. "Let's go, Habs!"

WHAT A GAME. Highs, lows, sweet moments and sad. Beau was exhausted. He quickly dried his hair—much quicker these days —slapped on a Montreal snapback, then moved out to the room where the media had gathered and took his seat beside Gabe and Tony behind the bank of microphones.

"Beau, you were a wall tonight. How do you feel?"

"It was great to win, especially in a shootout against Toronto." Shootouts weren't his favorite, requiring him to remember footage of how his opponent liked to shoot and do his best to psych them out. Poor Dan. He grinned. "It was a good game, and I hope the fans were entertained."

Talk about a good first game to bring Noah to. Plenty of shots on goals, extra time, then a shootout for the win.

"It seems there's a lot of love out there for you."

He'd kinda felt that, with the huge roar when he was introduced. Made him feel all mushy inside. "This is a great city that loves its hockey. I love it here and hope to stay for many years."

"Mr. Francois, any comment on that?"

"Beau's proven to be a tremendous asset to the club in his short time here already. His contract is certainly locked tight for the next few years, and we hope he'll be here for many more."

Beau unscrewed the sponsor's sports drink and chugged some electrolytes. Getting tired. And there was still a party to attend.

"And Beau, have you got any more word on your injury?"

Admit he'd fainted? Maybe one day he'd let the club admit to the real cause of his injury. But that day was not this one. "My concussion symptoms are gone, obviously, which is why I was cleared to play. My back and head feel fine, so I hope it stays that way."

"But less hair," one wit called.

"Yeah." He removed his baseball cap and shoved a hand through his trimmed hair. "I was a bit worried I'd be like Samson who lost his strength when his hair was cut, so it was good to see that wasn't the case."

They laughed, as he'd hoped, and the focus veered to Gabe. Then returned to him.

"Beau, can you tell us about the little boy in the puck drop?"

"That was Gabe's instigation. And Mr. Francois's."

"But that happened because of Beau's commitment to the hospital," Gabe countered, leaning back from the microphone. "Tell them."

Beau shrugged. He had no plan to big-note himself, but neither would he hide the truth. "Jacques is a young man I got to know on my first visit to the Children's Hospital here in Montreal. He's been a fan of hockey for quite some time, so it was great to meet him and the other kids there and do what I could to try and brighten their days."

"And the video of Jacques is trending."

Beau looked at the reporter blankly. The puck-drop video? "Good?"

"You know about the video, don't you?" another reporter asked.

"Um, feeling dumb here. What video?"

He propped his hand over his mouth as Gabe showed him a video of yesterday's hug on his phone. His heart churned. Man. That had been filmed? He blinked hard. Exhaled. "Wow. I didn't know."

"Have you got anything to say about that?"

His chest was jam-packed with emotion still. He released a long breath. "Just to say that Jacques and his family, and all the sick kids at the Children's Hospital, are very special people, and

I'm so glad for the privilege of being able to meet them and hopefully encourage them a little. I hope that you'll join me in praying for Jacques and his family and wishing them the very best at this time."

He tried to smile but couldn't quite make it and was really glad when Gabe leaned forward and shared about the Children's Foundation and reminded people of how they could donate and support sick kids.

When Gabe finished, Tony leaned forward and gestured to them. "These are the kind of men that our club is made of. Strong men, kind men, good men. Thanks for supporting the foundation and supporting our team. We'll see you next time."

The interview ended and they were released, and Gabe and Beau walked from the room. Beau felt like he'd been run over by a eighteen-wheeler truck. "Thanks for saving me in there."

"That was kind of intense," Gabe said.

Sure was. He really needed to pull himself together before entering the party tonight.

But before he could do so, he was called to one side, where he saw Jacques and his parents. "Hey. How's it going?" He offered Jacques a gentle fist bump, just as he had before he'd skated onto the ice earlier. "You did awesome," he said. "You dropped that puck like a boss."

"It was fun," Jacques murmured, his eyes aglow.

Beau's heart grew soft, and he swallowed new emotion. "Thanks for helping us win tonight. I couldn't have played so well if I didn't know you were cheering me on."

"Thanks for all you've done," Jacques's father said. "It's a night we'll never forget."

"Anything I can do," Beau said, meaning it. "Anything."

He slipped an arm around Jacques and posed for another photo. "You want to come to the party?" he asked Jacques's mom softly.

"Thanks again for the invitation, but I really think he's too tired, so we're going to go home."

"Sure." Beau's smile wavered. "Well, I'll be praying for you."

"Thank you," she murmured, her eyes bright with tears. "That means a lot."

He shook hands with Jacques's father, then high-fived Jacques once more and swallowed hard as he wondered if it would be the last time he saw him. At least this side of heaven.

He blinked hard and worked to shrug off the emotion. The way he was feeling, he needed a long shower to release his tears. He definitely didn't need to put on a party persona and go pretend he cared about Halloween.

But he got changed and entered the room, managing a few jokes and smiles, his heart only really easing when he saw Maggie and Noah.

He swooped them into a hug and held them very tight, just breathing in health and wholeness as a few tears finally escaped. He felt Maggie's arm tighten around him, even as Noah wriggled and squirmed. Finally he exhaled and rubbed his eyes. "Man."

"You're amazing," Maggie murmured, her gaze soft with compassion, like she knew all the battles he'd faced tonight. Not that he had anything to complain about. *God, be with Jacques.*

"I'm so glad you're here tonight," Beau said, kissing her cheek.

"Me too." She gazed up at him seriously. "You've done so well—how you played and with Jacques." Her eyes shimmered. "I don't think you could've done anything better."

He loved this woman. Loved her support. The way she believed in him, believed *with* him. He could do life with her forever.

Whoa. The emotion of the past day was really getting to him. He crouched to Noah. "Have you had fun today?"

Noah nodded shyly, his thumb in his mouth.

"Did you enjoy the game?"

"Oui."

Beau grinned. "I like your costume," he said, grabbing the onesie's elephant trunk and gently waving it about.

"I'm an elephant."

"You sure are." Beau straightened to see Maggie talking with Johan's wife. Things would work out with him and Maggie, he just knew it. "Hey, bud," he said to Noah. "Want to get some food?"

Beau was starving. He'd need to refuel soon, or else that fainting thing could get real.

He checked with Maggie, her smile of appreciation bolstering his heart as he took Noah to the table and helped him find some food. Around them, the room buzzed with music, laughter, and conversation as the team's players and families mingled with management, supporters, and sponsors. It was good to tune that out and focus on something as mundane as retrieving pieces of watermelon and oranges cut to look like teeth for a small boy, for which he was thanked so sweetly. If things progressed as he hoped, he'd love the chance to be this boy's daddy.

"Beau! Great game tonight." Maurice smiled, patting his back. "Good to see you back on track."

"Thanks." He nodded as Juliette drew near, a camera strapped around her neck.

"Do you mind if I get a photo?" she asked.

He glanced across at Maggie, unsure if she'd want her son captured in a photo for the world to see. She caught his gaze and he raised his eyebrows. She nodded, her smile drawing his.

"Sure."

Beau crouched down next to Noah, and after adjusting the elephant ears, took a moment to ham it up.

"You're a natural," Juliette said after a moment. "And the way you managed to promote the team through that poor little boy? I couldn't have done it better if I'd arranged it myself."

"I beg your pardon?" Beau straightened, looking down on the team's media person from his ten-inch advantage. Yeah, he wasn't above using his height when needed.

"The kid from the hospital? Poor boy. But nice to see you getting in some mentions of the Foundation."

"I didn't do it for you," Beau muttered. "Excuse me." He picked up Noah's hand and steered through the crowds to Maggie.

"You okay?" she asked him softly.

"Yep."

"You sure?"

He nodded, forcing his shoulders to relax. She didn't need to hear his concerns about Juliette. Maggie and Noah needed to enjoy the evening, the first of what he hoped would be many. When he could be part of their family, in this organization where family was celebrated.

Maggie's hand stroked Noah's hair, the onesie elephant hood having slid to his shoulders. She smiled up at Beau, then her face stiffened.

"Maggie?" Beau followed her gaze to where Paul stood. With an Asian guy. Who was pointing at her. Uh oh.

"Beau?" Claudine grinned up at him. "You don't mind if I steal Maggie and Noah away for a moment, do you?"

"Uh, no."

Maggie shot him a worried look, so he forced a smile. "I'll be there soon."

She nodded, and Claudine guided Maggie and Noah to another family.

"Beau? May I have a word?"

Paul stood shoulder to shoulder with Mr. Lee, the sponsor Beau had met weeks ago.

"You remember Andrew Lee, don't you?"

Beau nodded but didn't put out his hand. "I remember."

Paul shifted closer. "Perhaps your concussion means you forgot what I said before."

"About what in particular?" Beau asked, feigning innocence. He had a pretty good idea what the man would say but didn't want to make it easy on him.

Paul cleared his throat. "About making sure our sponsors are being taken care of." He cast a significant look at the man beside him.

"Yes." Beau caught Gabe's gaze, hitching his lips to one side before his gaze moved back to the men standing before him. He'd kill for a drink.

"I was surprised to see you talking to that woman before," Mr. Lee said.

"Which woman?" Beau asked.

"That woman." Mr. Lee jerked his chin toward where Maggie stood with Krystle and Claudine.

"Do you mean Claudine?" He could act dumb all day. It was amazing how many people thought tall people possessed only half a brain.

"No." Paul was looking irritated now. "The woman with the boy. Mrs. Joly."

"Maggie, do you mean?" He looked between them. "My girlfriend?"

The word took him by surprise. How inadequate it seemed. Maggie was far more than a mere girl, far more important than a mere friend. She was light, hope, strength. And his future. As that word locked into place within his soul, he straightened and eyed Paul.

"Perhaps you can tell me why you were so insistent she not come and visit me when I was in the hospital."

Paul bristled. "Is that what she told you? She was mistaken."

"I don't think so," Beau said as calmly as he could. "Claudine heard you too, and Gabe, apparently. Shall we ask them?"

"That won't be necessary."

"No, what is necessary," Beau continued, "is for you to explain why you're against Maggie."

Paul shook his head. Glanced at Mr. Lee, then back at Beau. "I'd hope I'd not have to spell this out, but you leave me no other choice. You know this organization takes a very low opinion of racism."

"As it should." Beau caught Maggie's worried gaze and smiled to reassure her, beckoning her near, then, when she hesitated, holding out his hand for her to take. He wrapped his arm around her waist, glad to see Noah was playing a computer game with another boy who looked to be his age. "And that's exactly why Maggie is a great asset to us here."

Mr. Lee's eyes flashed, his expression one of strong dislike as he glanced at Maggie.

"I'm sorry," Paul said, his own glance at Maggie looking anything but apologetic, "but how can you say that?"

"Easily." Beau took out his phone, scrolled through the camera reel, and pulled up a photo from a few weeks ago and showed them. "See this? Maggie single-handedly organized this Thanksgiving event for the multicultural members of her community. She cares about people, about family, don't you?" He gently squeezed her waist and couldn't help but notice again just how nicely snug her top was. How long would it be before they could leave?

"Of course," she murmured.

Judging from the redness in Paul's face, he was set to implode, something which was put on hold by the arrival of Tony, accompanied by Gabe and Claudine.

"Beau!" Tony clapped him on the back. "Is this your girlfriend you were telling me about?"

"Yes. Maggie, meet Tony Francois, the club's owner. Tony, this is Magdalena Joly."

Maggie shook Tony's proffered hand. "Pleased to meet you,

sir."

"And you." Tony glanced at Paul and Mr. Lee. "What's got you making Beau look so serious? He had a great game. Let him relax and enjoy the party."

"I'm afraid, sir, that there was an incident between Mr. Lee and Ms. Joly a while ago."

"I don't understand."

Paul sighed and drew them farther away from the rest of the party and prying ears.

"I really don't appreciate being dragged away like this," Tony complained.

"I'm sorry, sir," Paul said.

Huh. Paul called him sir, not Tony?

"You might recall a video a few weeks ago showing a woman telling off a man in the Botanical Gardens. It was Ms. Joly here, speaking to Mr. Lee, who is one of our chief sponsors."

"Mr. Lee?" Tony frowned. "I'm afraid I don't remember."

"She was very rude to my family and me—"

"No, I mean about your chief sponsorship."

"Well." Paul cleared his throat. "I mean a sponsor."

"You say Ms. Joly was rude to you?" Tony said, his eyebrows raised. "I don't understand why you think I should be hearing about this."

"Because Mr. Lee has threatened to withdraw his sponsorship if she remains here."

"He can't do that. We have contracts in place. That's absurd." Tony glanced at Beau, then Maggie, his face stern. "But it's also disappointing. We like to consider ourselves a family here, and we can't take such accusations lightly."

"Sir," Beau interposed. "I know you're a man who's not given to prejudice, so if you would be so good as to hear Maggie's side of this story, I'd appreciate it."

"If it doesn't take long. I have guests I need to talk to." His gaze shifted to Maggie, his eyebrows pushing up.

"Tell him," Beau encouraged her. "Tell them about the animal killed in your workplace."

"Animal?" Mr. Lee interrupted. "What animal? That was just a frog."

Maggie's chin lifted, and the gutsy woman Beau had first met reappeared holding fire in her stare. "That was one of the species we protect at the Botanical Gardens, and when your son killed it, my colleagues saw you cheer him on."

"See? It wasn't even me," Mr. Lee said. "He was just being a boy."

"And is that how you excuse yourself for spitting at me?" Maggie demanded.

"What?" Tony's wrinkled-nose glance at Mr. Lee held disgust.

"I don't think it's racist to object to such behavior. Do you, sir?" Maggie asked Tony.

Beau bit back a smile. He hoped he'd not encounter her fire directed his way.

Tony seemed a little nonplussed at her directness, turning to Mr. Lee. "Did you really spit at this young woman?"

"I...I..." Mr. Lee blinked and shot a panicked look at Paul, who wore his own look of dismay.

"Surely you can recall," Maggie murmured. "You missed the first time, so you tried again. Remember?"

"You never mentioned that," Paul murmured to Mr. Lee, who looked away.

"I don't know if being associated with that kind of behavior is really the kind of image we want to portray, is it?" Beau asked. "If you want someone who's an asset to the club—who cares about family, who cares about community, who wants to make a difference in the world—then you have her right here." He squeezed Maggie gently. "I've been blessed by having Maggie in my life, which is where she'll stay if I have anything to say about it."

Maurice moved into view, diverting attention from Tony's nod, Mr. Lee's anger, and Paul's sagging jowls. "Sorry to interrupt, but someone here just wanted to say hello to Mr. Nash again." He motioned to a large man who drew forward. "You remember Bill from the golf tournament?"

"Bill." Beau shook his hand, relieved at the change of focus. "Good to see you."

"Hey, I just wanted to come over and say how awesome it was to see you with that poor little boy. It got me thinking, and my wife and I want to make a donation to the Children's Foundation."

"A very handsome donation," Maurice said with a wink.

"That's very kind of you," said Beau.

"Oh no. It's very kind of you. The sort of thing the rest of us can't quite do, eh? Make a little boy's dreams come true?"

"I'm sure there'll be many grateful children," Beau said warmly.

"Oh, and Robert? Remember him? Your partner on that day? I saw him at a recent executive meeting. He's keen to know if he can get more involved in the sponsorship kind of way. Apparently his girls are keen to meet you."

"Sounds good," Beau said.

Tony nodded. "Maurice, I want you to set up a meeting for me and this Robert man." His gaze swung to Paul. "You and I will have another talk about the kind of people we want involved here." His look at Mr. Lee held contempt. He then turned to Beau, put out his hand. "I'm real glad we've got you as part of the team, and Maggie—I hope it's okay to call you Maggie?"

"Yes, sir," she murmured.

"It's Tony, my dear. I'm looking forward to getting to know you more. Hey, is your son the little elephant?"

She nodded.

"He's a cute kid. I remember when my kids were that age.

My son had the same kind of big brown eyes. So sweet. You'd never think of it to look at him today, working the stock exchange." Tony chuckled, drawing Beau's smile. "Look after them, Beau, okay?"

"Will do."

The group dispersed, leaving Beau and Maggie to exhale. "He's kind of intense," Maggie murmured.

"But good-hearted," Beau said.

"Absolutely." She wrapped her arms around his waist.

He closed his eyes and held her as the emotions of the day slowly ebbed away.

"Thank you for all your support there," she murmured against his chest.

"Hey, you know I'm all about defense, right?"

"My hero."

"Finally." Beau tugged her nearer, enjoying her softness. "You want to get out of here?"

"Soon. I'm enjoying the fact that Noah seems to have made a little friend."

"Kaspar's son. Maybe we can get together with them sometime."

"I'd like that." She leaned her cheek against his chest. "Do you really think everything with Mr. Lee will be okay?"

"As far as you're concerned, absolutely. As far as he's concerned, no."

"I didn't mean to cause a problem," she murmured.

"You didn't cause any problems," he stated. "But hey, I don't want to think about that. Not when I've got far more important things to say."

"Oh yes? Like what?"

"Like the fact you look amazing in this cat outfit." His hands slid up her sides, and he enjoyed the squirming wriggle she gave that said she savored this touch too. "Incroyable."

Her eyes sparkled.

"And the fact I'm so thankful for God bringing you into my life."

"I am too."

"I meant to ask, does Noah get his tree-climbing skills from you?"

"I don't know." She smiled. "Perhaps."

"I'm pretty sure he gets those gorgeous brown eyes from you," Beau murmured, drawing her nearer still. "How do you say 'I want you to kiss me' in French?"

"*Je veux que tu m'embrasses*," she whispered.

He pressed his lips to hers, savoring the softness, savoring her response. After a satisfying moment he pulled back.

"And how do you say 'I'm so glad you're in my life'?"

Her head tilted, her smile flashing. "*Je suis tellement contente que tu sois dans ma vie.*"

He echoed it as best he could, and she chuckled, like he'd mispronounced a few things. "You know what I mean."

"I do." She slid her hand down his cheek, and his skin tingled at her touch. "For I feel like that too. I used to live in such a small, scared world, but since meeting you, then meeting God, I feel so much braver, like I'm truly living again and becoming who I'm meant to be."

His heart grew soft, and he tucked a loose lock of dark hair behind her ear.

"I don't know if I would have found God without you, without your big heart and kindness. The world feels richer now, like anything is possible."

"All things are possible," he murmured. Like being a husband. And a father. To Noah, and several equally adorable kids. His heart clenched. *Please, God, one day.*

Maggie's lips lifted, and he took advantage of the invitation. Her kiss tasted of apples and cinnamon, inviting him to kiss her more deeply. They really needed to get going soon, but he was enjoying this moment—enjoying her enjoying him—so much.

Enjoying her words that had funneled strength to his heart. He might sometimes feel a little different compared to others here, but her words provided confirmation of that Bible verse from so long ago. The world of the generous only grew larger.

Around them, the party was quietening, and a quick peek revealed Noah was still happily playing with Kaspar's son. Contentment filled his chest. "Hey, Maggie?"

"Mmm?"

"What do you think about coming to visit my family in North Carolina for our Thanksgiving?"

"That sounds fun."

"What do you think Noah would say?"

"Oui?"

He laughed, and traced her cheeks with his thumbs. "Je t'aime, Maggie."

"Je t'aime, Beau."

At her smile, he bent to reclaim her lips with his, this kiss tender, soft, and sweeter than ice cream. He drew back. "Hey, Maggie?"

"Yes, Beau?"

"How do you say 'I want to have you in my life forever'?"

"Like this," she murmured.

And she pushed to her toes, and she kissed him.

The End.

Thank you for reading *Hearts and Goals,* the fourth book in my new contemporary romance series, which combines my love of ice hockey with appreciation for the cities that comprised the NHL's original six teams. This story is partly based on my visit to beautiful Montreal, and the wonderful Botanic Gardens there. My horticulturalist husband and I loved our visit to these amazing gardens, and I've got plenty of pictures on my website that you can check out at https://www.carolynmillerauthor.com/the-original-six-romance-series.

Please make sure you check out the other books in the Original Six hockey romance series, a sweet & swoony, slightly sporty Christian contemporary romance series.

The Breakup Project
Love on Ice
Checked Impressions
Hearts and Goals
Big Apple Atonement
Muskoka Blue

Reviews help other readers find new-to-them authors, so if you can spare a moment to write a quick review at Goodreads / your place of purchase, I'd be very grateful.

I'd love for you to check out my other books and to sign up for my newsletter at www.carolynmillerauthor.com where you can be the first to learn all my book and contest news, and discover more behind-the-book details and photos.

A huge thank you to the following people for their encouragement and eagle eyes: Sophie and Karen for their help with Quebecois French (any mistakes are mine!), Rebekah, Nancy, Brittany, Lisa, Bea & Becky - I appreciate you all so much! Big thanks to the ladies in my Facebook group, Carolyn's Books & Friends, for all your support in helping promote my books.

Please turn the page for a peek at *Big Apple Atonement*, the next in the Original Six hockey romance series.

BIG APPLE ATONEMENT

Chapter 1

October
Tarrytown, New York

He was, quite possibly, the ugliest man she had ever seen.

Margarita Anastacia Moritello stared at the muted television screen as the mid-game interview continued. Curly red-blonde hair fanned away from under the hockey helmet, Ronald McDonald with a mullet. His nose was skewed, with enough bump to suggest a visit to a plastic surgeon might be in order. Bushy eyebrows menaced over eyes so blue and cold they could be mistaken for a wintry Hudson River. But it was his beard, full and messy, like a lumberjack's, crawling over his face that drew most attention. She could barely see his mouth, but he was talking, and from what could be seen he was missing enough teeth she could almost drive her Volkswagen Beetle through them.

"A face only a mother could love, poor thing," Lacey Carruthers murmured from her chair near the big room's empty fireplace, sidling a look at her. "Don't you think, Emma?"

Emma—easier to say that Margarita Anastacia, and sounding less like a certain kind of drink—sipped her tea and nodded.

"Hard to believe women find hockey players like him attractive."

"Really?" Emma almost choked on her tea. "Why?"

"I don't know. Maybe it's the glamor, maybe it's the money. I can't see it myself, but then, I don't need to." Emma's best friend smiled, stood, and moved up the creaking stairs to conduct the night rounds of the children's rooms. Yes. Lacey Carruthers certainly didn't need to worry about the handsomeness of other men, not when she had her own handsome husband already.

"Do you think he's attractive?" Jacob Browne, Hopetoun's direct support worker asked Emma.

Hadn't she just made her opinion clear? "No," she said firmly. Anyone of TJ Woletsky's character, let alone his looks, would never appeal.

Jacob studied her a moment longer, until she found herself wishing for Lacey to return from upstairs. Not that there was anything wrong with Jacob. It was just he had never tickled her fancy the way guys like Beau Nash or Dan Walton did. Not that she needed a guy to be handsome or play pro hockey, but it didn't hurt. And the fact that both men were unapologetic about their Christian faith which translated into good works, like running camps for disadvantaged kids—she'd seen Dan's amazing pictures on Instagram—meant they'd forever be a cut above the men she encountered in real life. Apart from her dad and brother, and Tim Carruthers, of course. And a million miles above the man whose history of fights were now being shown on TV.

"All asleep," Lacey reported, re-entering the common room

and settling into the sofa next to Emma, cradling a cup of tea that smelled like peppermint. "They're still going on about Woletsky?" she said, studying the TV. "Poor guy."

"Poor?" Jacob snorted, pushing back his floppy blond hair. "How can you say that? Woletsky's just a highly paid goon."

"But don't you ever wonder why he acts that way?" Lacey continued. "Tim and I talked about this the other day. I know TJ's apologized for some of his hits before, like when he cracked Mike Vaughan's ribs a few years ago. I don't think he can be all bad."

Emma glanced behind her. "Don't let Leona hear you say that."

Lacey sighed. "She's still bitter, isn't she?"

"With every right," Emma said, her chest heating. "After what he did to Nick."

"Poor Nick." Lacey's face softened.

Nick Grenier, Leona Cherry's nephew, was the man truly deserving sympathy here. Emma's heart panged as it did every time she thought about him. She really should see him again soon.

A noise at the door stole their attention to where Mrs. Cherry wandered in, her weariness evident in her slumped shoulders and lumbering step. Emma immediately rose. "Would you like a cup of tea?"

"Oh, yes, Margarita, thank you, dear."

A glance at the TV showed the first intermission interview had—thankfully—cut to commentary for another game. Not New York's though. As the others enquired about her visit to Buffalo Emma hastened to make her boss's chamomile tea, her heart soft with compassion.

Mrs. Leona Cherry, Residence Manager of the Hopetoun Children's Home, had had a trying few years, caring for her terminally ill husband whose death last year seemed to have precipitated her own health battles, which had necessitated

Emma stepping into the management role a few times. Then Leona's sister, Helen, had suffered a fatal heart attack in January, which was followed by TJ Woletsky's mammoth hit on her nephew Nick earlier this month, a hit that had seen Nick's team Buffalo fined by the league for questioning why Woletsky was only assessed two minor penalties and a five thousand dollar fine for roughing, when all the commentators thought he deserved his fifth suspension at the very least. Hopefully Leona would feel too tired to insist on watching the rest of the game between Montreal and Woletsky's team, LA.

Emma handed the tea to Leona, who thanked her wearily. "You're an angel."

"Saint Margarita," murmured Jacob, which provoked an exchange of rolled eyes between Lacey and herself, as she moved to resume her seat.

A scream punctuated the night. Emma held up a hand. "I'm up, so I'll go."

She hurried from the spacious living room and up the stairs to the first floor where the girls' rooms were located. Whimpers came from behind a pale pink door. She flicked on the light and moved to the bed where a small figure gasped, eyes shut, cowering under the bedclothes.

Emma gently rubbed the small form's back. "Shh, it's okay, Nessa. You're safe."

Lord, please heal Nessa's nightmares. Let her experience Your peace and sweet sleep.

She continued whispering prayers, stroking the curly dark hair until the whimpers eased. Nessa had experienced too much horror for one so young. She needed all the love and security that Hopetoun could provide.

Thank God that Karinda, a recent arrival to the group home, still slept. Nobody needed another night of broken sleep. Emma yawned, glanced around the girls' bedroom once more, then carefully closed the door.

She re-entered the big room and settled back into her seat. "Nessa. Poor sweetheart."

"What are we going to do with her?" Mrs. Cherry sighed.

"Pray."

"Yes, yes, apart from that."

Emma slid a look at her boss. Why did she always sound like dealing with Nessa was a hardship? Hopetoun existed to help children needing additional support after traumatic experiences, providing a safe, nurturing, family-like environment in a group home while children waited to be matched to a foster family. Nessa had seen counsellors and psychiatrists, Emma had driven her to the doctor's just this afternoon. All of them said she would talk one day. The girl's trauma had meant finding an appropriate home with a foster family who could understand her complex needs was taking longer than anyone liked.

Mrs. Cherry offered an apologetic smile. "Sorry, Margarita. It's been a tough week."

Emma nodded. With the recent bout of chicken pox and the furnace threatening to give up the ghost, this past week had been tough on all the staff. The part-time staff and volunteers like Jacob and Lacey who came in each day had a slightly easier time of it—they at least could escape the insanity that sometimes overwhelmed Hopetoun. Emma picked up her tea—cold now—but took a defiant sip.

"I don't know how you can drink cold tea," Lacey teased.

"I think I'm too tired to care," she admitted.

"I can make you another one," Jacob offered eagerly.

"I'm fine, sit down. The game's about to start again," she said, waving at the screen.

The television flickered to show highlights of the other games being played tonight. Emma sat back and relaxed back against the tattered cushions of the old sofa. Friday night. Hockey night. If she couldn't be at a game—like tonight's, when New York were playing in Texas—then watching favorite players like Montreal goalie Beau Nash on TV was a nice way to escape the worries. And the loneliness. And the fear that here she was, thirty-one and not-been-kissed-in-ten-years, destined to spend the rest of her Friday nights with television and a cup of tea for company. Not that she minded. Too much.

Lacey's phone buzzed. "It's Tim."

Tim Carruthers, husband of her best friend Lacey, and New York's captain. "Tell him good luck tonight," Emma said.

Lacey grinned, texting back. "He doesn't need luck. He's playing so hot right now. But then, he is so hot, right?"

How to reply?

"That's nice, dear," Mrs. Cherry murmured.

Emma smothered a smile as coverage resumed of the second period of the Montreal-LA game. They'd switch over to the New York game soon, but any hockey was better than none. And if it meant a glimpse of Beau Nash, well, all the better.

The LA players streamed onto the ice, and already she could feel Leona's tension. It was there in her rigid shoulders, her fixed glare at the screen, as if she was gathering her hatred for the man who'd soon appear.

A hiss Leona escaped as TJ Woletsky skated back on the ice. Emma exchanged glances with Lacey. Maybe it was time to change the station.

"Nash is playing well," Jacob observed. "Hasn't dropped a game since his move to Montreal."

"He must like it there," Emma said, glad for the shift in focus.

"I think he does," Lacey said, casting Emma a glance. "Did I mention he might have a girlfriend?"

"What?"

"I don't think it's a secret. Or maybe it is. Tim told me a little while ago, and I may have forgotten to share."

"Oh well." Emma gave an exaggerated sigh. "There go my dreams, crumbling into dust."

"You don't seriously like a guy like him, do you?" Jacob scoffed.

"Why not? He's tall," like, really tall, "and is a Christian, and seems so sweet, and I *love* his accent—"

"Have you even met him?" he asked, one dark eyebrow raised.

Well, no. But "I've met a few hockey players over the years," thanks to her work here, "and I can tell who is a good one and who isn't," she insisted.

"Like him," Leona muttered, stabbing her manicured finger at the screen.

Woletsky skated toward the goal, shooting to Damon, who flicked it forward to Pavel who struck it back to Macoretti. LA's shots were quick and clean. Pavel shot at goal but Beau blocked it.

"Yes!" Emma clapped him on.

The puck slid back to Woletsky who took his turn shooting at the net, but Beau caught it in his right glove, holding on as Woletsky got into his face.

"Woletsky's such a jerk," Jacob muttered.

No argument from anyone here.

A swift glance at Leona's narrowed eyes and tight expression showed it was definitely time to change the channel. But before Emma could pick up the remote control, Woletsky had charged into the net, in a move that saw Beau stumble backward, his head striking the pipes before he slumped to the ground, ominously still.

Emma's heart hitched.

"Oh no!" Lacey cried.

Jacob swore softly, but for once Emma didn't reprimand him, her attention focused on Leona who was breathing deeply, her brow furrowed, her hands clenched. "Leona? Are you okay?"

"No. No, I'm not okay," Leona cried, shaking her head with

jerky movements. "How could they let him play again? This is exactly what happened with poor Nick!"

Well, not exactly. Nick had been slammed into the boards, not a net, in a hit that the NHL had said was legal. Not that anyone here liked to admit that.

They watched as medics surrounded Beau, and the camera moved to where the back-up goalie was limbering up.

"God, heal him," Lacey murmured.

"Amen." Emma watched as Beau was soon stretchered off, before quickly changing the channel for the New York game. She clutched Lacey's hand and gave a gentle squeeze. No wife wanted to see the reality of what could happen in a game like this. Not that anyone had ever died from playing hockey, not that she knew of, anyway. But injuries happened, and could be severe. Witness Nick's possibly career-ending hit a week ago.

But even on this station, as the commentators gave a pre-game summary of New York's game, there was already discussion of the Montreal-LA game, the hit on poor Beau replayed again.

"Woletsky at it again," the balding former NHL player said, shaking his head. "How long is it gonna take before LA gets rid of him?"

"He's a liability, that's for sure. I can't see any team wanting him after this," his greying co-anchor said. "Especially after what he did to poor Nick Grenier last week."

Leona inhaled sharply.

"That's right," the sports host said. "Grenier, and now Nash, who has always been known as one of the good guys in the game. I really can't see what Woletsky was hoping to achieve there."

"Apart from getting kicked out of the game?" his co-anchor said.

"Here's hoping," Jacob muttered.

"I can't wait to see what the league does with him this time," Lacey added.

But when the referee assessed the hit as requiring only a ten minute game misconduct, the employees of Hopetoun House were as stunned as the sports hosts.

"Are you kidding me?" Lacey shook her head. "No way is that fair."

"Montreal is not gonna be happy about this, I can assure you," the balding TV host said. "I think the league will be hearing from Tony Francois soon. Ten minutes for that kind of play?"

"Everyone knows you don't hit the goalie," his co-anchor said. "This is a big mistake from both Woletsky and the ref. Considering Woletsky's history, I would've expected a suspension at the very least. He's played for three teams in the last four years, and how many times has he been suspended now? Four? And for what many would consider lesser hits. I think there will be plenty of people asking where's the justice."

Jacob muttered a less-than-glowing opinion of the referee's intellect, while Leona pushed to her feet. "I can't stand this. I'm going to bed. I hate this game. I hate that man!" she cried, pointing at the television, where Woletsky sat in the penalty box, expressionless, mouth-guard handing free, as around him red-clad Montreal fans pounded their anger on the glass screens.

"Leona," Emma called, but her boss waved her away, instead heading to her bedroom on the first floor.

Lacey grabbed her hand and drew her back to the sofa. "Leave her. You know she'll only get further frustrated and upset the more sympathy she gets."

True. Emma sank back into her seat, her nerves as skittish as Mom's cat Twinky.

Hockey was amazing, the game so fast and requiring such

skill, but at moments like this she realized how brutal it could be, too.

She gripped Lacey's hand, wishing she could impart assurance that Tim would be safe tonight. But she could barely watch New York's attempts to thwart Dallas's aggression, her mind and heart spinning with thoughts and prayers for what she'd seen tonight. Prayers for healing for Beau and Nick, for protection for Tim, for peace for their loved ones. And—as the sports commentators had pointed out—prayers that there would finally be justice for the thug who skated for LA. Her skin crawled. Bile rose in her throat.

TJ Woletsky.

~

Los Angeles

"WOLETSKY, TAKE A SEAT."

TJ nodded to LA's coach and sat down across the desk from his arms-crossed coach and LA's general manager. Uh oh. He'd seen that look before. It never bode well. He slid a look at Phil Mowbray, his stony-faced agent, and braced himself.

The GM looked at him, his expression hard. "I've just had Montreal's GM chewing off my ear. They're not happy."

No. He didn't imagine they would be.

"That hit on Nash was the final straw. Especially following the fight earlier."

"Yeah, but he started it—"

"Enough!" TJ jumped as his coach slammed his fist on the desk, setting things rattling. "Sooner or later you've got to admit to your bad attitude and take some responsibility."

"But coach—"

"No. Don't sit there and try and make excuses. You've been

making excuses for as long as we've known you. We thought taking a chance on you would being energy to the team, but you've brought exactly the wrong kind of energy."

TJ had always thought his coach's motivational speeches with their emphasis on energy and dynamics a little too touchy-feely airy fairy mumbo jumbo, like his previous girlfriend's fixation with Feng Shui. He also figured now was not the time to share that opinion.

Phil cleared his throat. "You brought my client here to do what he normally does, which is to use his skills for enforcing clean play."

Thanks, Phil. TJ settled more comfortably in his chair. That was exactly right. He'd always hated injustice and deceit. Maybe that was why he'd hated his childhood.

"But the problem is that he's not been."

Huh? Offense at being talked about instead of talked to spiked into protest. "Excuse me, Coach, but I have been. The league hasn't found my actions illegal. You saw the penalty I got for Nash. Ten minutes, and I barely touched the guy," he complained.

"The problem is that nobody else saw it that way," the GM growled.

When the GM growled it was time to shut up.

"We knew we were taking a risk with you, with your reputation for hard hits. How many guys have you injured now? I seem to remember something about Mike Vaughan in Boston when you were playing for Florida."

"That was a clean hit, and Mike and I were friendly enough when we played together in Calgary. The guy invited me to his wedding, for Pete's sake."

Phil nodded. He'd been there, too.

Why Mike had invited TJ to his wedding, and Thanksgiving the following year, TJ barely knew. But Mike had always been generous that way. Someone he'd almost dare count as a friend, if he had to count anyone. "Just because I play hard doesn't mean I play dirty."

"That's not how the fans see it."

The fans. TJ swallowed further protest. Fans meant dollars which affected contracts. Like his. He folded his arms and glanced out the window, catching a glimpse of sparkling Pacific Ocean.

"I was really hoping this could be a turnaround," his coach said.

Well, yeah. TJ had kinda hoped that too. A new team, a fresh start, a chance to finally redeem himself, to prove the critics wrong—

"And there's still time," Phil said. "He's signed for this season."

"But ever since that hit on Grenier, we've had sponsors threatening to leave, and now, with Nash, too, let's just say people's patience has worn thin."

Wait. TJ's gaze swiveled back to the GM. This wasn't sounding good.

"You're a liability, TJ."

He clamped his mouth shut. Exactly what he'd known all his life. The problem child. Skating on thin ice forever. Booted from team to team, as if getting drafted in the first round all those years ago had been forgotten.

"We can't afford liabilities."

"Sir, Coach, I can do better, I will do better," he assured, sitting straighter in his seat. "But you gotta know that I'm just trying to do the job you brought me here for. You wanted toughness, I bring toughness."

"You bring complaints," the GM muttered.

TJ cast a look at Phil, who had crossed his arms and seemed to be scowling at the GM's fancy fish tank, as if little Nemo might be responsible for the GM's bad mood. Uh oh. Looked like he wasn't gonna get any more help from his agent.

"I'm sorry, sir. If it makes anyone feel better, I apologized to Nash." Via text, but hey. The dude wasn't about to answer a call. They never did.

"Did you speak to Grenier like we asked?" the GM said.

Oh. That. "When I tried he refused to pick up. I told you last time that I'd texted"—he hurried on, not liking the look the GM shot him—"and that I'd visit him next time I was on the east coast."

"So you haven't."

Well, er, "No," he owned.

The GM sighed. Ah, the sound of disappointment. TJ knew it well.

"I think you'd have to agree that whole incident was very unfortunate," Phil said. "TJ can't be blamed for what was essentially Grenier not properly watching the play. The league seemed to understand that, which is why he wasn't fined more."

Judging from the scowl being shot Phil's way, TJ didn't think his agent was helping any.

"Blaming the victim for what he didn't do is not what we do here. Not when we're talking about what *you* didn't do." Now the GM's scowl was being levelled TJ's way. "Woletsky, we're trading you."

"What?"

His question was echoed a second later by Phil. The tension ratcheted up more. Why hadn't Phil done more to save him? What kind of useless agent was he?

"For a seventh round pick."

TJ blinked. "Are you serious?" How insulting. Humiliation prickled his skin, made his gut clench. He gripped the chair's wooden arms to force himself to not escape.

"Where?" Phil asked.

"New York."

New York? Why would an Original Six team want him? Maybe he could swallow the indignity—

"Apparently their farm team thinks you'd be a fit."

"Hartford?" Phil asked.

TJ's general manager—well, his former general manager—nodded.

TJ coughed. He couldn't be serious. "This is a joke, right?"

"No joke," his coach said.

"I'm gonna go play in the AHL?" Talk about a demotion.

"If they'll have you."

What? There were questions about whether he'd even play in the minors?

He shot a panicked look at Phil who'd sunk his head in his hand, and knew there was no hope for him there.

No. He'd give anything to not go back to playing in hockey's minor league. Goodbye dream apartment with beach view. Goodbye great climate. Goodbye great life. Hello the dynamics of professional sports. He swallowed a stupid desire to laugh— maybe his coach had known something about energies and dynamics after all—and forced himself to shrug, then stand. Not for anything would he let them see how much this cut him. He'd play the flippant card until the end. "Okay."

Purchase your copy of Big Apple Atonement today!

ABOUT THE AUTHOR

Carolyn Miller lives in the beautiful Southern Highlands of New South Wales, Australia, with her husband and four children. A long-time lover of romance, especially that of Jane Austen, Georgette Heyer and LM Montgomery, Carolyn loves to write contemporary and historical romance that draws readers into fictional worlds that show the truth of God's grace in our lives.

To find out more about Carolyn's books, and to subscribe to her newsletter, please visit www.carolynmillerauthor.com

You can also connect with her at

<u>Regency Brides: Promise of Hope</u>

Winning Miss Winthrop

Miss Serena's Secret

The Making of Mrs Hale

<u>Regency Brides: Daughters of Aynsley</u>

A Hero for Miss Hatherleigh

Underestimating Miss Cecilia

Misleading Miss Verity

'Heaven and Nature Sing' from the Joy to the World Christmas
novella collection